# JASON ANSPACH

# THE WANTED

SEASON 3                    BOOK 1

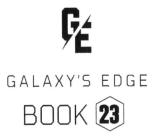

GALAXY'S EDGE

BOOK 23

ISBN: 979-8-88922-062-6
Library of Congress Control Number: 2024935200

Edited by David Gatewood

Published by WarGate Books

Cover Art: Marc Lee

Cover Design: M.S. Corley

Website: WarGatebooks.com

Newsletter (get a free short story): www.InTheLegion.com

# THE WANTED

# INTRODUCTION

Looking back, they called those turbulent times simply: *The Troubles*. A period of chaotic upheaval and destruction that sent the Republic reeling through successive crises, each growing more desperate as the galaxy spun out of control.

Exactly *when* The Troubles started... that was open to interpretation. After the Savage Wars were thought to have ended, said some. Others claimed that period of death and war began with the Republic's action on Psydon. Still others pointed to the Republic's forced migration of the zhee, or even the arrival of the Mid-Core Rebellion, culminating in victories against the Legion at Kublar and the genocidal atrocities extending as far as Rhysis Whan.

But no matter when they began, the galaxy-shaking events of the The Troubles were well remembered by those who suffered through them, and the scars of those upheavals would leave their indelible mark for years, and perhaps lifetimes, to come.

The brazen and open government corruption infesting the former capital planet of Utopion.

The arrival of the tyrant Goth Sullus, who briefly united opposition to the Republic before falling prey to the vanity of the title... *The Emperor.*

The Legion invoking Article Nineteen of the Republic Constitution, bringing an all-consuming flame to a simmering cold war that had long been stewing between the rulers and those forced to fight their needless wars.

The sudden unexpected attack by an alien race known as the Cybar. Relentless. Cruel. Inhuman in the extreme.

And finally, the long-planned return of a tribe of lost Savages, led by their messiah... the Golden King.

*The Troubles.* A quaint name for a horrific period in the galaxy's history. A period whose atrocities were superseded only by the terror of the Savage Wars that had come before. Almost no corner of the galaxy was spared a taste of terrible war, cutthroat intrigue... and remorseless death.

In the aftermath, this battered galaxy now longs for peace and stability. The Republic, now reformed, seeks to govern by rule of law. But no matter how sincere the reform, how earnest and well-meaning the ruler, some worlds refuse to place their destiny in the hands of others. Ever again.

Been there. Done that. Got burned along the way.

Because some things never change. Power summons would-be tyrants eager to seize it. Ancient vendettas cry out to be settled. Corruption worms its way through the souls of men too weak to resist it, or too wicked to try. And dead-eyed killers gather in all the usual star ports, awaiting the opportunity to do what they do best for the promise of a quick credit.

Through it all, the silent Legion waits for its cue to once more tread upon the stage and break their enemies through nothing more, and nothing less, than total violence of action capably applied. As though this time... things will be different.

Out on the edge, they say...

*Everyone's got a plan, until the Legion shows up.*

# PROLOGUE

**Planet Ulori**
**Mid-Core**
**Two Years Following the Death of the Golden King**

"I have orders to use my legionnaires to topple this government... if an agreement cannot be met. However, I do not wish to give those orders to my legionnaires. Not until I've spoken to you, Governor Teth Ala."

Sector Legion Commander Cody Aalberg settled back in his seat, watching the Ulori representatives sitting across the conference table look from one to the other. The Ulori were avian-like humanoids with high cheekbones and wispy, radiant feathers for hair. Their eyes ranged from black to the palest of blues. But despite their delicate appearance, in the last year and a half this species had proved itself quite capable of fighting, and

1

Sector Commander Aalberg knew that the silent looks among the aliens were confirming the consensus—that they were prepared to fight still more.

Governor Teth Ala blinked his large eyes, but said nothing.

"I want to assure you," the sector commander continued, "that my legionnaires are aware of the standoff between your people and the Republic government. They vehemently do *not* want to be given such orders by me."

The planet's governor was a firebrand who had led the once fervently loyal Republic world to secede. He tilted his head, flashing red and bright-green hair feathers. Ulori males were always more colorful than the females, whose feathers tended more toward the drab.

"Then we would request," he said, "that you, your legionnaires, and the entire Legion not follow such orders. Because we are prepared to fight you—our beloved *allies*—if we must. We will fight for our freedom."

Aalberg took the comments in stride. This was a diplomatic meeting, after all. Teth Ala was not making threats, just stating facts.

"The Republic has granted you your freedom *and* acknowledged Ulori's right to withdraw from the Republic," the sector commander said. These were also facts—though they both knew the situation was much more nuanced than that.

The Ulori governor tilted his head. "We will fight for a *full* freedom, then, yes? Not this *conditional* freedom meted out by a Republic we no longer belong to. Ulori has sent no senators to Utopion, and we reject the House of Reason—excuse me, *Liberty*—delegate 'offered' to us by the other planets in our sector of the galaxy. We will be the lords of our own nests. Tell me, does the Legion believe this is too much to ask?"

The sector commander liked the governor. Respected his vision and resolve. The man had extricated his planet from the Republic about as well as one could. There had been violence, yes, but it was contained and controlled, limited to military targets—mostly against zhee colonists who refused to leave the planet by the stated deadline, when the last of the colony ships slated to take them to worlds more accepting lifted off.

Aalberg looked at his Legion helmet, which sat on the table, its visor facing him. He did not want to don that bucket and wear it into battle against the Ulori.

"The past fifteen years have been... difficult," he said. "The Ulori have been strong allies to the Legion in the fight against the Mid-Core Rebellion, against the usurper Goth Sullus, and against the Savages. And the Republic has changed much over that time. The very fact that you were able to bloodlessly leave the Republic is proof of that. But your decisions impact not only yourselves but also Republic citizens living on Ulori, and the Senate and House of Liberty believe they are acting according to the interests of those citizens."

Teth Ala closed his eyes in acknowledgment of the truth of these claims. He held up his hand, slim but otherwise human, with a ridge of feathers leading from wrist to elbow. Three fingers were visible. "You have named three conflicts that have resulted in the deaths of many legionnaires and many Ulori. I will add another: the forced colonization of the zhee, who made no secret of their ideal of species dominance." He extended a fourth slender finger. "All four of these ills were brought to us by the Republic, and paid for by the very credits extorted from us through oppressive taxation while those on Utopion amassed an unfathomable wealth for themselves."

"Those people were removed by Article Nineteen."

"But the grip of those people on Utopion remains, even if your Article Nineteen wiped away the heads of state... for a time. Those in the House of Liberty will slowly be replaced by the very type of person *they* replaced. And, in some cases, not so slowly—your Article Nineteen did indeed remove corrupt delegates and senators, but some were happily voted right back in.

"Yet even were those corrupt heads kept at bay, the *spawn* of all that corruption—the systems, the 'independent' regulators, the controlling corporations—is alive and well, Legion Commander. And I will not allow that Republic to devour our people any longer. Republic citizens are welcome here, but the rot built by the House of Reason and its schemes... is not."

The sector commander sighed. "Investigations into the links between the House of Reason and its corporate interests are ongoing. Justice will be served."

The governor shook his head. "That the Republic is willing to send the Legion to force us to keep those corporations on our planet, tells me that little has changed in the galaxy. How long until we have a House of Reason once again? You have my respect and admiration, Legion Commander. But we will not bow to the Republic's demands of us ever again."

The sector commander forced a smile. "I take it that's a firm no?"

"As firm as your armor," confirmed the planetary governor. "But not without reason. A reason I appeal to you with in order to prevent the helpless slaughter of my people. There is a *reason* we asked the Legion to stay on Ulori when all other Republic forces left. The Legion is *not* a part of the Republic. And so I ask you, Sector Commander: Is the Legion willing to destroy us? Do those who once protected our small world from ruin, now see fit to ruin us themselves?"

The sector commander paused. This was the moment they had been building toward. It was time to lay his cards on the table.

"What I'm about to say," he began at last, "is not said on behalf of the Republic. I now speak solely for the Legion, and for myself. The answer to your question is this: We are not."

The legionnaire let the weight of that statement hang in the air. The relief on Governor Teth Alla's avian face was evident even as he waited for more to come. There would be conditions. Of course. Perhaps recriminations or regrets before a speech about following orders. The governor waited in silence.

"The Legion was founded by General Marks as an independent fighting force to defeat the Savages," Aalberg went on. "It quickly became a dominant force in the galaxy. *The* dominant force. Its Legion commander could easily have ruled as an emperor." He drummed his fingers on the conference table. "Instead, it yoked itself to the fledgling Republic, putting itself under that government's authority. The question the Legion is now considering is whether the Republic can still call itself a proper government at all, one that represents the galaxy in its entirety."

"It cannot," Teth Alla said.

"I'm aware of the Ulori position on the matter, Governor. The Legion will need to make its own decision. We have arranged for Legion Adjudicators to examine the Republic's role in the events that led to the current instability. If they deem that the Republic cannot be saved... then the Legion will protect Ulori. But if the Adjudicators find that the Republic is worthy of our continued support... then Ulori will stand in defiance of the Legion, with all the consequences that entails."

"And what happens until such time as your decision is made?"

"Nothing. So please, Governor, be patient."

# 01

**Planet Lorrian**
**The Core**
**Three Months Later**

Cohen Chhun set his bucket down next to the holodisplay inside the darkened mobile ops room. "I'm not sure I'll get used to the tongue toggles being gone."

The black-armored legionnaire sitting at the station paused his monitoring of observation bot feeds to turn and look at Chhun. "It took most of the older guys a good year to adjust—" The leej cut himself off. He'd just called a former Legion commander an "older guy." Not good. He recovered as quickly as he could in the best way he knew how: by changing the subject. "Both shooters are in position, Legion Commander."

Chhun smiled, hoping it would relieve some of the young soldier's awkward discomfort. "I'm no longer a Legion commander, Sergeant. But I'd still advise against that sort of honesty with any of the more, ahem, *seasoned* officers still serving in the Legion. Have the shooters put crawlers on windows five, seven, nine, and ten."

"Yes, Sir."

Chhun watched the holoscreen as the Legion shooters launched the tiny bots through a specialized barrel attachment on their N-18 sniper rifle platforms. Each shot gave only the tiniest puff of a heat signature and didn't so much as trip the overhead observation bots' audio receptors. A second holoscreen displayed the status of the crawlers, which had positioned themselves near the windows' sensors and now set to work slicing the security of each individual lock. Soon they were all green.

"We're in, Legion Commander," the young legionnaire said. He was the hunter team's comms sergeant. HT-26. Chhun had the Legion IDs down but was still learning the names.

He patted the man's shoulder pauldron. "Solid work, Sergeant. But seriously, cut the 'Legion Commander' thing. I was out of the Legion for two years before all this mess brought me back, and I'm only a civilian Adjudicator now. You can call me CA or whatever the rest of the hunter teams call their Adjudicators."

"I think Sergeant D'het would shoot me if I called you that. He's a traditionalist, Sir."

"Well, best listen to your team sergeant, then."

"Yes, sir, Legion Commander."

Chhun could hear the twinkle of humor in the young man's voice and realized that it was these interactions with his fellow leejes he missed, not the mission itself. He had been worried that, once back in the armor, he would feel a pull to leave En Shakar behind and return to a life of war. Ravi had said that wouldn't happen. That the life of war was behind him... for now.

*For now.*

Ravi had a way of being clear without making sense. Chhun had figured that much out during their time together on En Shakar as he sought to...

What? Decompress? Deconstruct everything that had happened? Find some meaning in all of it?

If it was meaning he was after, it still eluded him.

Ravi had assured him that his return to the Legion was part of the process. Part of the journey. Just like becoming a CA. It was knowing that he had something to do, but not yet seeing why.

As an Adjudicator, he was still feeling out his hunter team. This mission should be an easy one. The target was known. The intel secured by Chhun's agent, Elektra, was rock solid.

Yes, things still might go wrong. Things always went wrong.

But even Major Slade had agreed to let "the Adjudicator" take command of a small contingent of the hunter team to bring in their target for questioning. That freed up Slade and the rest of his team to work out how to bring in another target, one that was also supposed to go easily.

Chhun hoped the task at hand was the sort of *easy* that wouldn't result in his men being covered from head to toe in skinpacks like the last *easy* mission he'd sent them on.

"All right," he told the comms sergeant. "Have the shooters stay in position and start Team One toward Front Door. Let's get Team Two on the roof. Time to go to work."

"Yes, Legion Commander."

The eagerness in the comms sergeant's voice was unmistakable.

Orders were communicated. Team One, six legionnaires wearing civilian clothing, emerged from a ground-floor unit inside the twelve-story condominium—

the only unit they'd been able to secure on such short notice. They carried NK-4 blaster carbines, and kneepads and ablative armor bulged from beneath their clothing. The front door to their unit closed on the blare of a seamball game, and they moved to the stairwell and began the climb toward the top floor.

The Legion snipers on adjacent rooftops lay at the edges of their buildings, looking through windows from the scopes of their N-18s, their armor so black that they appeared almost shapeless to the observation bot looking down on them.

Chhun's mobile command center shook as the stealth shuttle lifted off on gentle, silent repulsors. Back toward the ramp, Team Two's six legionnaires were kitted out in armor and gear that would have made any of Chhun's kill teams drool with envy. They would be set down on the target roof and then... it would be all but over.

Hunter Team Ranger had proved itself nothing if not capable. They were some of the best legionnaires Chhun had ever seen, which was saying something given the man's experience within the Legion. Few had seen half as much as Chhun had seen, fewer still done all that he had done. These men were the best... and they were all working together on a single team for a distinct purpose: the will of the Adjudicator.

"Sir," the comms sergeant said to Chhun once his orders were relayed and the teams were in motion. "Before the shooting starts, may I ask you a personal question?"

Chhun gave a silent chuckle. "What is it, Sergeant?"

"What were you doing on En Shakar, sir?"

Chhun paused. How could he answer that question when he didn't know the answer himself? At least not the implied *why*. And even the explicit *what*—literally *what he was doing* while there—wouldn't make much sense to a young legionnaire. Not yet. The truth was he had spent his time on En Shakar restoring its gardens with Aeson Ford's old co-pilot, meditating, and thinking. Working his body as hard as any legionnaire, and his mind harder. Learning bit by bit who Ravi was and what had happened in the galaxy. What had happened *to* the galaxy.

It had been a dizzying experience. The time had passed in a flash, broken only by the arrival of a Legion stealth shuttle and a disembarking cadre of general officers seeking Chhun and asking for him to serve the Legion one more time.

The former Legion commander smiled and grabbed his bucket from the console. As he slid the helmet over his head, he answered, "Vacation, Sergeant." He moved to the hold to join Team Two.

The comms sergeant sat in his seat for a moment. "Vacation."

Then he got up, grabbed his N-4, and followed the Adjudicator. Command was now mobile.

The stealth shuttle landed with a whisper. Its quiet doors opened more slowly than a combat assault shuttle's, but the legionnaires waiting inside exploded outward with the same intensity they always did. Off first were the four legionnaires tasked with securing the rooftop. The snipers on adjacent buildings were on overwatch, but these leejes were ready all the same for anyone who might come up to take a look at whatever caused the gentle bump on the roof. Behind them, two more legionnaires pulled repulsor platforms, two to a man, four in total. Chhun and the comms sergeant exited last.

As the stealth shuttle lifted off again, Chhun assisted in setting up the repulsor platforms at the edge of the roof, just above the crawler-infected windows. Meanwhile the comms sergeant worked the situation in his bucket, using the Legion's latest and greatest combat AIs to sync up the three teams for their hit on the condominium's penthouse unit.

"Team One in position," HT-26 told Chhun, sending a holocam feed from Sergeant Király, HT-34. Whenever a mission called for any leejes to operate without armor, Király made sure he'd be one of those men. He seemed almost *eager* to shuck the armor. As though fighting with it on made things too easy.

Chhun checked the feed by fixing his gaze on the tiny visual in his HUD and *thinking* about it expanding. The bucket somehow read those brainwaves and did the rest. No tongue-toggles required.

Seeing that the feed had been received and expanded, the comms sergeant said, "You're a fast learner, Legion Commander."

"Open the windows," Chhun ordered.

An execute command went to the tiny bots, which in turn interfaced with the pre-sliced automatic windows and caused them to rise.

"Windows up," announced one of the snipers. Flower Child, the man called himself, if Chhun remembered correctly.

Two of the rooftop legionnaires pulling security hustled toward the repulsor platforms, activating them and then pushing them out over the edge of the roof, where they hovered twelve stories above the street. Both men stepped out onto the floating platforms and faced inward toward the building. Chhun and his comms sergeant then stepped onto the other two platforms, Chhun positioned right beside the lead breacher, a top-tier legionnaire who had been hand-picked by Legion Command to serve on this hunter team.

"Hunter Actual to Reaper One," Chhun said, pinging his sniper team leader. "Anyone inside notice the cold air yet? Over."

Reaper One was the legionnaire the others called Flower Child. "Someone's just getting up to check now, Hunter Actual. Now he's asking who opened the window. Request permission to engage, over."

"Confirm target is *not* irradiated." Even as Chhun asked, the sniper's visuals came into his HUD. The person at the window was a Kimbrin, and he lacked the telltale glow in his eyes that would indicate consumption of the tracing element the VIP targets had consumed for lunch that day.

"Confirmed not irradiated," the sniper replied.

Chhun looked to the legionnaires around him. They were ready to go. "Reaper One, you are cleared. Break. Team One, go."

The sniper took his shot, sending a bolt dialed down to low power directly into the center of the Kimbrin's chest. The blast punched its way into the chest cavity and burned itself out inside without passing through, effectively cooking the humanoid's heart and lungs. Serving as a Legion sniper was as much about knowing the bolt intensity as it was about precision aiming. Sniping was a science, and Chhun's hunter team consisted of shooters the likes of which he hadn't seen since Twenties.

A lifetime ago.

Team Two followed the sniper's shot by dropping their platforms down level with the open windows. They stepped onto the windowsills and ducked inside carefully.

Nothing was to be disturbed. At the same time, Team One activated a sliced and compromised door lock and pushed their way into the penthouse from the other side.

The targets inside scrambled in confusion. Those humans and Kimbrin who glowed were struck in the head with a single stun bolt. Those who did not were killed. Legionnaires tore through the room at unimaginable speed—a quickness Chhun had seen only from men like Wraith. None of the operators missed, and none on the receiving side of the hunter team's assault mustered a return shot.

The guns fell silent, and each room in the penthouse was reported as clear.

"Close the windows once this haze dissipates. Hide the platforms," Chhun told his comms sergeant.

The mission had gone off perfectly so far, no hiccups, everyone performing as though they'd been operating together for years. And, as had been the case when Chhun was a Dark Ops team leader, no one needed to be reminded of their duties. Bodies were moved, overturned chairs were picked up, the living space was set back as it was.

"One more," Sergeant Király announced as he pushed a well-dressed Kimbrin into the living room where they had put the stunned prisoners. "Found him hiding in a safe room."

Király was square-jawed and looked nineteen despite the naturally silver hair he kept swept back atop his head and shaved at the sides. He was tall, well-muscled, and carried that Legion confidence critical to being an operator. This was the first mission Chhun had seen the man work up close. He seemed too young to already be this good... unless he'd joined the Legion when he was ten. Yet he was absolutely a killer, and not the mindless sort. In some ways he reminded Chhun of Aeson Ford... but the comparison wasn't fully apt. Ford had an ironic, devil-may-care attitude that flourished once he was operating solo, whereas Király seemed to know only the mission. Nothing else interested him.

"Thank you, Sergeant," Chhun said. "Have your team assist Team Two with the dead."

"Yes, sir. They're already on it."

"Good. You stay with me, then. Let's talk to our VIP here." Chhun motioned for the Kimbrin to be brought to his feet.

"Yes, sir."

The Kimbrin looked like a typical galactic businessman. Well-dressed, well-groomed, and carrying an air of dignity as though he were a mere spectator to everything unfolding around him rather than a prisoner who had been ener-chained by a team of legionnaires before his security detail had so much as managed to get their fingers on triggers.

Chhun took the sleeve of the Kimbrin's jacket, lifted it up, and let it drop back down. "All that blood on your hands and yet your cuffs are white as snow. You've got some excellent cleaners, Shik Margram."

Once upon a time, Shik Margram had been one of the galaxy's most wanted men. He had been instrumental in founding the Mid-Core Rebellion, using his financial savvy to procure weapons and supplies for those sufficiently whipped up against the Republic to start a war.

Now he gave an amused smile that caused his facial spikes to shift along his jawline. "We both have blood on our hands, Legionnaire."

"Blood, yes, but I see a distinct difference in the number of credits that blood has bought us."

The Kimbrin shrugged. "It took a considerable sum to fund the Mid-Core Rebellion. *Someone* had to keep custody of those credits. One might think you'd be happy they are no longer being put toward the killing of legionnaires."

"I assure you," Chhun said, "I am." He motioned to a nearby table and chairs. "Sit."

The Kimbrin obeyed. "Then I fail to see what the problem is. The Republic declared amnesty for those in the Mid-Core Rebellion who agreed to forever lay down their arms. I have." Shik Margram looked up at Sergeant Király, standing beside the Kimbrin's chair. "Or has the Legion already gone back to shaking down Republic citizens for their credits?"

"The Legion isn't interested in you at all, Margram. We're interested in the bounty hunter who's set to arrive in..." Chhun looked to Király. "How long?"

The legionnaire sergeant didn't have to check his chrono. "Forty minutes, sir."

"Forty minutes," Chhun echoed. "So I'm gonna need you to sit. Right there."

"And do what?"

Chhun tossed a deck of holocards on the table. "How well do you play cabet?"

# 02

The bounty hunter Blackheart moved inside the target building, passing a unit that blared the local seamball game so loud that the hunter could pick up the announcers clearly even through the fully enclosed helmet. A group of sports-obsessed young men were staying in that flat. Blackheart hoped the game would keep them inside. It was time for the hit.

Things might soon get a little messy.

A months-long chase was nearly over. Blackheart had traced one of the principal founders of the MCR and his entourage to this location. These were men who enjoyed an obscene wealth of credits—now that those credits were no longer needed to fund a galactic army—and had leveraged that wealth to make themselves a hard, hidden target. The multi-unit luxury condominium they now harbored inside had the latest and greatest in security features, including the kinds of locks that only Legion Dark Ops had keys for—allegedly—and the armed guards were well trained and vetted for personal loyalty, true believers picked from the best the dying MCR had to offer back when the inevitable began to happen in a hurry and it became evident to all involved that if you couldn't win the galaxy, you could at least make yourself rich.

Blackheart knew something about wealth. It could buy comfort, yes. It could buy safety. But it also could buy opportunity for a bounty hunter who'd lived long enough in a business where few ever lived long enough to enjoy a retirement.

A bounty hunter who enjoyed the challenge of a difficult target like Shik Margram.

Margram had once been a young political firebrand, stoking the embers of galactic unrest into a full-fledged rebellion against Utopion and the Republic. Now he could fit in seamlessly among the very elites on Utopion he once railed against. He dressed well. Dressed his people well. Lived comfortably and ate even better. Like so many who were never born into extravagant wealth, Margram had acquired a taste for all the delicacies the galaxy had to offer. He knew exactly what to order, and what not to order, at the absurdly expensive restaurants most people never even walked past, let alone went inside.

The bounty hunter wondered whether the former MCR leader felt guilt about what he had become. About what he had made himself into. His transformation was ultimately a form of self-betrayal, wasn't it?

Would the man he once was even recognize the man he was now?

If a man can't live with himself, where *can* he live?

Because it was clear, from what the bounty hunter had learned, that Shik Margram still thought himself devoted to the cause. He gave to charities that, to some degree at least, aligned with all those old revolutionary attitudes he'd once championed with other Kimbrins and then humans, most of whom were now dead. Yes, he lived a life of opulence, but that was only out of necessity. Influence required the ability to adapt and blend in with the crowd you wished to influence. It wasn't that he *liked* the life of luxury. He just... *had* to live that way.

To prove all that to himself, to prove that Shik Margram hadn't forgotten where he came from, that he hadn't become soft, hadn't fattened himself, too much anyway, on Sprigg eggs—about the only Kimbrin food that had ever become respectable among the galaxy's elite—he had made a point of living like he did back when he was a poor and humble revolutionary.

Sometimes. Within reason.

Not with regard to his clothing, of course. Appearances being what they were. Nor his living quarters, repulsor sled, or any other possessions.

Not that.

But... he still made a point, once a week, to eat the humble dishes of his youth. In particular the steaming *rie-rah* they used to inhale out of little square-shaped boxes back on Kima. Once a week, every week, he and his entourage ate the old food. Drank the old drinks. To prove to themselves that although the galaxy had changed... *they* hadn't.

And that had been Blackheart's opening.

Infiltrating a state-of-the-art luxury condominium without the kind of booms that would alert the local police was almost impossible. Infiltrating a dirty, hole-in-the-wall Kimbrin restaurant across town?

Easy.

Blackheart had made the delivery last week. Outside the armor. Just a human making a few extra credits. People liked that—getting served by a humanoid. Drones are faster, and bots are cheaper, but most of the wealthy, for whom price isn't a consideration, feel good believing they're helping a fellow humanoid make a living. So the food shops still hired out a few biologics. Because the rich customers liked it.

Margram's people tested the food, of course. Margram had enemies. Hence the Bronze Guild bounty on his head.

Fine. Poison wasn't Blackheart's style.

But a low dose of an irradiating dye, untraceable and undetectable without a specialized optics package...

The bounty hunter wasn't averse to that.

And no poison-detecting agent on the market was going to find it. It could be detected with enough time, but no one was going to go through the trouble of breaking down every element and every chemical in every meal before anyone could take a bite. Even if you knew what all those long scientific words meant.

So they ate the home-cooked food. Margram and his top people. The only ones for whom rie-rah held any fond memories. Most humanoids, and even most Kimbrin for that matter, found it disgusting.

Now Blackheart could see them through the walls. They were gathered in the large entertainment room, all except one, who sat at the table near the kitchen. All the bounty hunter had to do was put blaster bolts into every glowing head and get out alive before the others could shoot back enough to make it hurt.

The bounty hunter rode the speedlift to the top floor. The doors opened with a ding, and Blackheart stepped off, datapad in hand. With a single press of a button on the pad, an explosion mushroomed in the distance. The building lights went out. A second button press caused a second explosion, smaller and closer, that took out the auxiliary generator.

Blackheart thumbed the datapad a third time, and the target unit's front door swung open—thanks to the strip of clear slice tape the hunter had deftly put in place when delivering the food.

The datapad stowed, Blackheart brought up a rifle and moved swiftly toward the door.

It was then that the realization came. The glowing targets weren't moving.

Blackheart didn't have a moment to consider the implications before a sudden warping hit the bounty hunter's HUD, followed by a new set of data showing more people inside the penthouse unit. Bodies that the bounty hunter's sonar hadn't detected. Someone had just sliced into the bounty hunter's bucket to share this data; they *wanted* Blackheart to see everything waiting inside that apartment.

And according to the overlay that had forced itself into the HUD, there were legionnaires mixed in with the targets.

Blackheart froze in place.

A digitized voice, synthetic grit, called from inside. "You're a tough woman to track down, Blackheart. The Legion would like a word."

Blackheart sighed inside her bucket. She knew the voice of a legionnaire when she heard one. And she knew the bad days a hunter could have when they had a "misunderstanding" with the kind of people who waited for you in dark rooms.

But she also knew that the kelhorn she was targeting had the kind of credits that could buy old Legion armor. At least the shiny stuff.

"Maybe you wanna tell me why the Legion and the founder of the MCR are spending time together first,"

Blackheart suggested, her voice masked by her bucket audio relays.

"Just holding on to him for you, bounty hunter," answered the legionnaire, now appearing in the doorway in front of her. "Talk to us, and he's yours."

"Maybe I'll let you keep him."

"Either way, we're having a chat. The question is whether you want to wear an isolation hood before it starts."

Blackheart turned to look over her shoulder. A pair of legionnaires had slipped behind her in the hallway, shadows within the shadows. Not surprising. But the fact that the two hadn't shot her in the back told her that these truly *were* Legion, and not former MCR wearing stolen armor.

"You Legion boys always find a way to get what you want," she said.

"Yes, ma'am."

"Well... you're about to get more than you expected. A timer started when I blew the lights to this place. Shik Margram has a quick reaction force just a few blocks over, and it won't be long until we all have some company that won't be terribly interested in letting us have a 'chat.'"

The moment she spoke, the lights abruptly came back on. Blackheart's bucket adjusted to keep her from being blinded by the sudden glare, and she spotted the mobile generator conduits spread out around the unit, patched into various power supplies. The legionnaires had thought of a lot of things... but not everything. She could see that by how they were moving now: hastily. The armor-clad operators who had beaten her to the MCR leader were scrambling to prepare for the arrival of his private contractors.

The legionnaire she'd been speaking with reached up and removed his helmet. As the bucket came off, she had to stop herself from stepping back in surprise. The face he revealed was one she recognized, but very much not one she was expecting.

"Time's short, Blackheart," said former Legion Commander Chhun. "But we knew that before we got here. Let's go."

# 03

Chhun led the bounty hunter inside and directly to Shik Margram, who still sat at the table with the holocards. Blackheart had a reputation for being tough. A bit of an ego, but that was common with bounty hunters. Those without confidence didn't survive long.

Chhun had a thorough history on this particular bounty hunter. Blackheart came from a Legion family, with a father who was now practically a legend. She knew very well what a trained legionnaire was capable of, let alone a room full of them—which meant she knew not to let things get kinetic. And when Sergeant Király requested the bounty hunter's weapons, compliance came quickly.

"Over there is your bounty," Chhun said. "I'm going to need two days of your time in exchange for our grabbing him for you."

"I could have grabbed him myself. What's there to discuss?" Blackheart said.

"The truth. So let's call it a deposition."

Blackheart looked to the Kimbrin, who had gathered up the deck to play a solo game. He was examining his cards against those laid out on the table, acting oblivious to everything around him.

"Did you drug this guy or something?" she asked.

"I am not drugged," Shik Margram replied. He turned to look at Chhun. "Only... aware. Your bringing this bounty hunter only confirms what we both know: the *Republic* has no interest in me."

"Maybe the Legion does," Chhun said. "Either way, we won't be here long enough for your people to get a chance to say hello." He motioned to Király. "Sergeant, time to go."

Chhun knew Shik Margram had security teams inside the building, already moving up the stairs. And the Legion snipers had spotted groups of military-aged men moving along the streets in their direction. None of this was surprising in the least; they had known fully what they were up against. Elektra's intel remained impervisteel-solid. Even so, the last thing Chhun wanted was for a full-scale blaster fight to open up in a residential neighborhood on a core world. Legion popularity was mixed at the moment, thanks to what was happening on Ulori—which was why Chhun was where he was now to begin with. They needed to get clear quickly, before things could overheat.

"Yes, sir," Király said. He motioned for the comms sergeant to recall the repulsor panels from roof to window.

Shik Margram crossed his arms. "I'm not going anywhere. You had better get me away from here soon, Legionnaires. Before my people come. They only get paid if I am alive and free."

"Well, *I* get paid either way," Blackheart said.

Before anyone could react, she issued a retractable vibro-blade from the armor protecting her forearm, then drove the blade repeatedly into Shik Margram's neck and shoulders until the Kimbrin was practically decapitated. The legionnaires grabbed her and pulled her away, but it was too late.

The job was done.

Margram's body fell to the floor with a thud, blood pooling beneath the man's chair.

"Job was a termination," Blackheart said to Chhun through the wall of Legion arms that now held her back. "I think you still have another room full of targets I marked for the same."

Chhun looked from the dead body to the bounty hunter. He wasn't sad to see an architect of chaos and destruction come to the same end that he had forced upon countless others through his support for the Mid-Core Rebellion. There were too many MCR atrocities to count, for regardless of whatever revolutionary spirit it had begun with, it had all too often behaved as nothing more than a well-armed power leveraged to settle long-standing blood feuds.

Yet Shik Margram's death did complicate things.

The communications sergeant was soon in everyone's HUDs with reports that Margram's mobilizing forces were now really moving. They had little time before someone with a blaster rifle would be in shooting range.

So much for in and out and easy.

"Time's expired," Chhun told his hunter team. "HT-26, call our ride out of here. Everyone on the roof for exfil." He walked up to Blackheart and pointed a finger at the bounty hunter's face. "And *you*. No more tricks. It's a professional courtesy that I'm not using your real name in front of everyone, but understand that I know who you are and where you keep your bases of operation. We didn't have time to wait for you to come back home, and while I'd prefer to talk with you about a certain past associate, I'll put in the work to track down your father and get the information from *him* if I need to. Are we clear on that?"

The bounty hunter's face was unknowable behind the enclosed armored helmet. "Clear."

Chhun relented and stepped back. "Get her on the roof."

The legionnaires escorted the bounty hunter to the windows, then stepped out with her onto a repulsor platform and rose toward the rooftop, Legion snipers watching through their scopes.

"What do you want us to do with the others, Legion Commander?" Sergeant Király asked.

Chhun looked at the blood pooled about the body. "Would've been a lot easier without this mess."

"Yes, sir."

"Keep them bound and locked in the room. Their QRF can let them out once they get here. I want all of us long gone by that time."

"Understood."

Király saw to Chhun's orders, and in short order the former Legion commander was stepping out of the window and onto the last remaining repulsor platform.

He reached the roof in time to see the Legion snipers moving silently toward the exfil on repulsor platforms that had been sent to them. The shuttle would be an easy target if it had to stop to grab the shooters from multiple rooftops, and Chhun would prefer for the shooters to not have to exfil on foot to the pre-coordinated landing zone where they could be extracted by a second bird, although that contingency was in place all the same. As long as no one with a blaster rifle noticed the platforms hovering high above the city streets against the twinkling backdrop of the night sky, things should be fine.

The shooters reached the roof without incident and hurried toward the waiting craft, carrying their kit while the legionnaires who had been covering their movement pulled the repulsor platforms behind them. Chhun slapped the men's shoulders as they hustled past him up the shuttle's ramp.

"Sir, you should get on board," Király advised.

Chhun smiled. "Last man," he said, and then stepped past the sergeant and up the ramp.

The shuttle was in the air seconds later, invisible to sensors and, as soon as it gained enough altitude, to the naked eye as well.

Chhun found Blackheart sitting in a crash seat, her posture almost painfully upright. She was motionless, as if in deep concentration. He sat down next to her.

"Hey," he began.

She held up a finger. "Wait one, Legionnaire."

Then...

"You got all your men out, right? Get on the L-comm and tell them to duck if not."

As Chhun opened his mouth to ask what the bounty hunter was talking about, the communications sergeant announced, "We got a drone coming in hot toward the target building."

Chhun watched a visual track of the device as it hovered outside the window of the room where the rest of the MCR captives had been secured. A sudden sustained *brrrrrt* sounded as the drone filled the room with chemically fired projectiles that punched through window and wall alike until the entirety of its ammunition was spent.

The drone hovered a moment more, then drifted quietly through the shattered window and into the smoking room, where it detonated.

"Okay," Blackheart said. "Job's done. You legionnaires aren't the only ones with useful buckets."

She took off her helmet and handed it to Chhun. Strands of short, dark hair clung to her face beneath a headband that kept most of it swept back and out of the way. Long hair and buckets rarely mixed well.

Chhun inspected the inside of the helmet. It looked as advanced as any Legion lid he'd ever seen. The woman had clearly spent a colossal number of credits on getting her kit right up to the bleeding edge of technology.

When he looked back up at Blackheart, she crossed her legs and smiled.

"So. What did you want to talk to me about?"

# 04

## Legion Destroyer *Scontam Washam*
## Somewhere in Core Space

The interview room that Chhun led Blackheart into didn't look anything like what the name usually implied. Instead of spartan seating under the glare of white, clinical lights, with holocams ensconced in the corners and a one-directional transparent viewing wall, this place was soft and inviting, more like a cozy parlor, and very out of place on a Legion destroyer.

He was careful to look her straight in the eyes. She had declined the offer of fatigues or PT clothing, so now wore only a tight-fitting synthprene undersuit of gray and red that had drawn the attention of the spacers she'd walked by—men and women alike—and would draw Chhun's attention as well if he didn't focus. The bounty hunter had been relieved of her weapons and armor, of course—a standard security measure made more important by the fact that her kit was more than just protection against blaster fire and augmented strength; it was a mobile command station, akin to Legion Dark Ops armor, that must have cost a fortune in credits and favors.

Blackheart moved about the room, examining the wooden bookshelves and the assorted physical books and small pieces of art. "This the captain's study?"

"No," Chhun said. "Something set up for this. Have a seat."

She sat in a New Britannian–style wing-backed chair, crossed her legs, steepled her fingers, and waited.

"Impressive armor," Chhun said.

"Expensive, too. I'll want it back when we're done here."

"And you'll get it. Untouched and unaltered," Chhun said. "Did Wraith get it for you?"

Blackheart gave a slight smile. "Is he in trouble?"

"No. And neither are you. Like I told you earlier, this is not a criminal procedure. The Legion is only gathering information. You could admit to me that you personally killed the Legion commander, and that information wouldn't go beyond myself and the other Adjudicators. Just like how the fact of your armor being loaded down with proprietary Legion systems won't result in you facing any consequences. Incidentally, that's why I thought Wraith might have gotten it for you."

"He thought very highly of you, Legion Commander Chhun."

Chhun nodded, somewhat surprised by the conciliatory tone. So far, the bounty hunter had been large on swagger and attitude. "Well, it's him I want to talk to you about. Specifically the period of time when your father was assigned to work with him while undercover for Dark Ops. You were also brought in to help him establish his identity as a bounty hunter. Should I call you Blackheart, or may I call you Zora?"

"Zora's fine. And if you want to know all that, why not ask him?"

"Because you're easier to find. Although, if you know where he is..."

"I don't. Not for a couple of years now. Which, trust me, is typical."

"Same. A lot of people sort of... disappeared after the Savages. I tried." Chhun leaned forward in his chair and rubbed his hands together. "I'd like to begin with day one. I've talked with Wraith about this before, but since he's chosen to disappear, I need an eyewitness to corroborate my secondhand account. I'm sure there are some things he left out as well, so—"

"Legion Commander," Zora interrupted.

"Cohen is fine. Or Chhun if you prefer."

"Well, I'm sure you know that my father was Legion, and while our relationship is hardly the best, I feel like I'd be doing him a disrespect if I were to sit with a former Legion commander and call him by his first name."

"It's fine," Chhun assured her. "I'm not operating as a Legion commander, or even a former one. Just a one-time legionnaire who's being asked to assist the Legion. Like your father has done on multiple occasions."

"Which leads into what I was about to ask." Zora stared at Chhun for a moment. "What is this? Is this about the thing on Ulori? It is, isn't it?"

Chhun thought about how to answer. It was no secret that the Legion and the Republic were currently at odds. The Republic wanted the Legion to force the Ulori's transition to planetary independence to be done only under its rules, citing agreements made when Ulori first became a Republic protectorate and then a full-fledged

Republic planet. The Ulori countered that those agreements were no longer valid, as the Republic government had systematically and intentionally undermined the trust of not only Ulori, but the entire galaxy, for its own benefit.

The sector commander sided with the Ulori—so naturally the House of Liberty wanted him removed. The full Legion commander, having already consulted with the other sector commanders, informed the Republic that more study was in order. This was why two Legion destroyers were now in orbit around Ulori, determined to protect the planet until the Legion had made its decision. It was why six Republic Naval vessels were in system—albeit keeping a healthy distance from orbit—as a show of the Republic's will to force the Ulori to honor their commitments.

It was also why men like Chhun had been tasked with becoming Legion Adjudicators.

Chhun didn't know who the other Adjudicators were, and they didn't know who he was, only that he was one of five. The decision of those five legionnaires had the potential to change the galaxy.

Whether the galaxy yet realized that was another question.

"I'll tell you," Chhun said, "but not until you've answered my questions and given the account of how Captain Ford, in his alias as Aeson Keel, became the bounty hunter Wraith. I know that sounds like I'm stringing you along, but I won't clint you when I say that the reason for me not being up front will be evident. You've helped the Legion considerably in the past, Zora. And so has your father. We need your help again."

Zora pressed her lips together and looked up at the sky before blowing out her breath. She leaned forward, and whatever decorum she'd been hanging on to for her father's sake was gone.

"Okay, soldier-boy. I'll give you the scoop. How much do you know?"

"Let's work under the assumption that I know nothing."

Zora barked out a laugh. "Because if you've been talking to Keel, you probably don't. Or whatever you think you do know is just some sket he made up."

She paused, as if deciding where to begin.

"You guys sent Keel out there to work undercover, infiltrate some crime rings, keep his ear to the ground," she said finally. "You know that much, even if you weren't behind it. And it worked, though maybe not in the way you boys were thinking. Because the smarter guys on the edge, and there's a lot of smart guys on the edge, you have to be if you want to stay alive, they could all tell he was Legion right off the bat—there's no hiding it. It's just that, no one figured a legionnaire would be undercover. That kind of spy stuff, when it happened at all, was Repub Navy intelligence. They always like to wear other people's clothes.

"But out there on the edge, being former Legion is quite an asset. It means you know how to kill. It's not uncommon for you former bucket boys—at least those who are, let's say, *morally neutral*—to use their Legion-taught skills to earn credits as bounty hunters, mercs, private security. Less common to be a smuggler, which was what Keel insisted he was. He had the *Six*, did some jobs. But to get deeper, it wasn't enough. The only way to get the intel he wanted was by agreeing to be part of a security team for some crime boss or another. All the while looking for clues about Goth Sullus—although no one even knew what a Goth Sullus was back then. We figured it was all MCR.

"Anyway, things go sideways, Keel does what he knows how to do, and suddenly he's personal security for a *very* repugnant and equally powerful crime boss. And this guy thinks, because of course he does: 'I got this fearless kelhorned former legionnaire, I should have him do a few terminations for me.'"

Zora looked Chhun in the eye. "Now, most times those kelhorns just want to kill each other. I'm not saying Keel helped them do it, but I'm not saying he didn't, either. He always fed me those vague answers like he does when he wants you to believe both things are true. Drives me crazy. Other times, though, those kelhorns in the shadows want *another* type of person killed. Someone standing in their way. You catch my wash here, Commander?"

Chhun gave a fractional nod. "Innocents."

"Got it in one. Obviously he's not gonna kill some karking businessperson's kid to send a message for his piece of twarg-dung boss. But the twarg-dung told him to, and Keel is in the boss's employ, after all. So you know what he does instead?"

Chhun didn't know. Ford hadn't mentioned any of this to him.

Zora leaned back in her seat. "He brings the entire criminal gang down. Kills the twarg-dung boss, kills the other security guys, makes a big mess of things, and then alerts his handler. He lets himself get picked up along with the rest of the kelhorns who haven't gotten a bolt to the head, maintains his cover, and ultimately he gets out of prison and off planet. The galaxy has one less predator in it than it did before.

"That particular story is one that I can confirm is true. There's probably a dozen similar stories I don't know about. Make it two dozen, this is Keel we're talking about. But the mission your Legion gave him wasn't to wipe out mob bosses, was it? It was to uncover the sort of conspiracy that nearly blew up the House of Reason and *did* blow up that destroyer over Kublar."

Chhun must have displayed some lingering pain over what had happened to Victory Company, because Zora dropped her head and quickly mumbled, "Sorry."

"It's fine. Continue, please."

"Long story short, Keel extricates himself from the 'security' business, goes back to smuggling. This time he specializes in really dangerous loads, hoping someone's gonna try and use him to transport the kind of weapons that nobody should have. But mostly he found himself hauling H8. He got picked up for it from time to time, always managed to get sprung from jail by his handler. It became a pattern. But Keel didn't know how to do it any differently.

"It wasn't until he got to Rakka that things changed. That's when he connected with this pirate named Lao Pak."

# 05

"You drink now!"

Aeson Ford looked up at the spindly pirate standing over his shoulder. The man's hands were filthy, dirt crusted deep beneath his fingernails, matted black hair swaying well down past his shoulders. He smiled to reveal a glittering grille of gold and silvene filmed over with a thin layer of whatever the man had last eaten.

"You drink now, Keel!" the pirate repeated in accented Standard. "Not fair to take time. Drink while brain cells still dying."

Ford wobbled slightly in his chair, the warmth of the room making him feel hot under his collar. Around him pressed a throng of pirates, spacers, and galactic riffraff of all types and species. Sitting across from him was a writhing Tennarian male, his tentacles listless and still gripping the various empty tumblers and shot glasses the alien had downed in this contest of livers and wills.

How many livers did a Tennar have again?

"Keel! Why you pretend you not hear Lao Pak? You stall! You stall to cheat! Drink now!"

*You're not Ford*, Ford reminded himself. *You're Keel now.*

He had been Keel for months. Had gotten used to the name even before deploying aboard a rickety, stale-smelling light freighter acquired for him by the Legion. Responded to it. Introduced himself by it. But in times like this, while plied with exotic liquors, many of which weren't fit for humans... or even most human*oid*s... Keel sometimes forgot.

And right now... forgetting could cost him his life.

"Jus' a sec, Lao Pak," he slurred. He began to swallow and blink his eyes, prompting the gallery of pirates to lean forward and issue forth a unified "Ooohhhh!" in anticipation of seeing this new smuggler pass out or surrender the contents of his stomach—both of which would result in him losing the contest.

But Keel held it in, and the pitch of the crowd's "Ooohhh" went from eager to disappointed.

He held up a finger to Lao Pak, missing the real man but lining up with the double-vision-induced version of him just fine. "Jus' a sec."

"No sec! You drink now!"

Keel picked up the shot glass before him. Whatever was inside was the color of blood with the consistency of syrup. A film was forming on the surface of the spirits, and a gnat was helplessly trapped in the sludge at the glass's rim.

The smuggler tilted his head back and emptied the contents into his mouth. Some of it at least. The rest dribbled onto his chin and down his neck. That was technically against the rules, but this deep into the game, it was enough for the two combatants to simply drink *some* of whatever was placed before them.

Keel moved to set the glass down but missed the table, dropping it instead onto the cantina's floor with a crash as the galley of pirates and criminals cheered. Credit chits were passed back and forth which each turn of the inebriated tide.

"See!" Lao Pak shouted to the crowd as he collected chits from those who had bet against Keel lasting this many rounds. "I tell you he go far. He too stupid to stop!"

Now it was the Tennar's turn. The orange-skinned alien made many fumbling attempts with his tentacles, bringing empty glasses to his human-like face and mouth and drinking the phantom contents before slamming them back onto the table as he rocked back and forth and side to side.

"He's... cheating," Keel said between burps, and pointed a crooked finger at his opponent. "Stalling."

"Drink now!" Lao Pak commanded. A fair referee.

The gathered pirates took up the words, repeating them like a battle cry. "Drink now! Drink now! Drink now!"

A burly dwahser, rotund with thick green-gray skin, wrapped its nasal trunk around the Tennar's shoulders comfortingly and then took hold of the tentacle that held the *full* glass of the stuff Keel had just partially finished. The dwahser held the tentacle in front of the Tennar's eyes until the alien smiled and nodded, holding the shot glass before him with a new focus.

"Cheating," Keel burped out, again pointing at his opponent for a wavering second before letting his hand drop back into his lap. "No... help."

"You drink now!" Lao Pak repeated.

With all eyes on the Tennar, Keel deftly injected his leg with a bloodstream neutralizer, which would scrub the effects of the alcohol and help his mind clear itself of the drunken haze that was forming. It was the third time he'd needed to inject the expensive shot. Either the Tennar really was cheating, or it had an otherworldly tolerance for the drink.

The Tennar threw back the shot, missing his mouth completely and dumping the contents of the glass into his eye and down the side of his face.

The drunken pirate crowd cheered.

"Cheating!" Keel yelled, nowhere near as forcefully as he wanted.

Lao Pak shook his head, his matted hair flinging about wildly. "He absorb through his skin. It count."

Keel opened his mouth to protest but was cut off by a loud gurgling and low-pitched moan coming from the alien seated across from him. Keel stood up instinctively, if unsteadily, and barely missed being splattered as the Tennar emptied the contents of his stomach—or stomachs, Keel wasn't sure—all over the table. In addition to the brown, soupy mix of alcohols spewed out by the squid-man were half-digested fish, some of which were still flopping about—alive.

Lao Pak hid his nose inside his leather duster. "Oh, that smell bad."

The rancid odor was like that of a cannery shut down and left to bake in the summer sun after being carpet-bombed with twarg fertilizer. More than a few pirates hurled up their own drinks in solidarity with the night's loser.

A beefy human with a long black beard and wearing furs around his thick torso grabbed Keel's wrist and hoisted it into the air, presenting the champion to the roars of the approving rogues' gallery.

Keel staggered, his arm raised, a lopsided smile on his face.

"And he was *cheating*," he said, pointing at the passed-out Tennar, the alien's tentacles now wriggling independently on the table amid the gasping feeder fish and filth.

A second later Keel saw what he'd hoped to see upon coming to this cantina. He pulled his Intec x6 blaster from its holster, sending up a collective gasp from those sober enough to see what was happening.

"Don't shoot him for cheating!" Lao Pak cried. "He my crew! He good in blaster fight!"

But Keel wasn't aiming for the Tennar. He abandoned his façade of stumbling drunkenness—only partially a façade; the neutralizer could only do so much—and leveled his blaster at a ridge-faced Kimbrin fast-walking away from the revelry. Keel had been watching the alien as often as he dared throughout the drinking contest, and now he took note of the case in the Kimbrin's hand. A case that he hadn't brought in with him.

The powerful blaster bolt dusted the Kimbrin, and soon the rough hands of the pirates were all grabbing hold of Keel, who allowed himself to be buffeted as he dropped his arms to his sides. "It's all right," he insisted.

It wasn't as though someone getting shot was a foreign experience for this crowd or this dive. They just weren't keen on being this new hotshot smuggler's next target.

"He owe you money?" said Lao Pak. "How much?"

Keel shook his head, resuming his pretense of being intoxicated. "No. Don't worry about it. 'S'all right."

And then it *wasn't* all right.

"Republic legionnaires! Everyone on your knees!"

A squad of elite troopers in shining, reflective armor flooded the cantina.

Keel screwed up his face in bewilderment. What was a squad of leejes doing here? Aside from policing up the place. They were on Rakka, a planet that definitely wasn't under martial law or in rebellion against the Republic, which was what usually resulted in the Legion being deployed.

"I can explain," Keel began, holding both hands up in the air, his blaster holstered. Their reason for being on-planet aside, legionnaires were battle-hardened killers. He wasn't about to give these guys a reason to KTF.

The legionnaires surged through the motley crowd, covering pockets of confused and wary pirates with N-4 blaster rifles.

"Knees!" demanded a legionnaire.

It took Keel a moment to realize the leej was talking to him. He began to comply. "I said I can explain—"

The legionnaire grabbed Keel's neck and forced him roughly to the ground, clasping ener-chains around his wrists behind his back.

"By order of the Republic, everyone here is under arrest for violation of local Republic Ordinance N.779.631-2: resisting a lawful representative of government."

"What the hell?" Keel said.

A group of pirates attempted to run out the door. The legionnaires cut them down with a stunningly wild volley of blaster fire that looked rushed, panicked, and unprofessional.

"What the hell," he said again, muttering to himself.

Lao Pak, who was ener-chained next to Keel, leaned over to speak quietly. "This bad for you, Keel. Hope you have credits like me."

That might be a problem. Keel had been bilked on his last job and was running light on credits. There were ways to get credits, of course. The Legion was supposed to keep him in supply in order to continue the mission. But he hadn't gone through the official channels in a while. Not after the less-than-enthusiastic payout he'd received last time.

Easier to take credits off the scumsacks he now associated with. One of them owed him already. Keel looked hard at Lao Pak, ready to collect.

"Aren't me and the Tennar supposed to get a share of bets from tonight?"

"No. I keep. You both cheaters."

"What the hell."

# 06

*Just go with the flow*, Keel told himself—which was just about all a would-be bounty hunter could do while being frog-marched to some backwater prison by a squad of legionnaires who looked as jittery with an N-4 as anyone he'd ever seen. The destination was a large holding cell inside the Rakka spaceport's primary government building. Keel waited in line as the legionnaires unshackled the prisoners and pushed them inside the containment room.

"What's with the police work, Leej?" Keel asked as his ener-chains were removed. He looked over the reflective armor for a squad emblem or unit decal that he might recognize. There were no markings whatsoever.

"Inside," the legionnaire commanded, his voice sounding almost mechanical through his helmet's external speakers. The command left no room for dispute.

"Just sayin', this is a long way from the front lines, is all."

Keel received a glancing blow to the jaw in reply and was then thrown inside the containment cell. The last man to enter, and he'd entered the hard way, crashing to the floor as dusty pirate boots and naked alien feet stepped back to avoid being crunched.

He pushed himself up onto his elbow and turned to face the legionnaire who'd just struck him. "What was that for?"

The legionnaire stayed silent, stepping back to activate the glowing blue containment field around the double-door-sized opening the night's captives had just been herded through. The other pirates and assembled riffraff called after the troopers, who marched away down the hall without so much as a sideways glance.

"Don't I at least get a comm call?" Keel shouted after them. "Sket."

He turned and saw the pirates claiming whatever comfortable corners and floor space they could, the cell's benches having already filled up. Several looked as though they had done this before. Surely they had.

Lao Pak stood nearby, waiting to get Keel's attention. "You new to this planet?"

"Of course I'm new," Keel snapped back, rubbing his jaw. The shiny new armor wasn't much when it came to stopping weapons fire, but it still hurt like a thoran club-stinger to get hit by someone wearing it. "You just met me this morning at the port when I came in, and I told you that then."

"I thought you lying when you say that." Lao Pak looked over at the Tennar that Keel had bested in the drinking contest. The alien was lying across a bench, sleeping it all off. "Like you lie about being drunk with him."

Keel went over to the Tennar, rolled him off the bench and onto the ground with a thud, and then sat down, crossing his arms. "You're supposed to get one free comm call."

Lao Pak took the newly open seat next to him, putting his boots on the snoring Tennar like a footstool. "They not care about comms. They care about can you pay credits. That's why I say you new here."

"Who's they?"

"The Legion."

"Why would they care?"

"You smuggler and you not know. That make you stupid. It like this lots of places. Legionnaires not fight wars, they fight to find you doing something so they can arrest you and take your credits. It smart. Not like you."

Being something of an expert on the subject, Keel waved his hand dismissively. "You don't know what you're talking about."

"Lao Pak not know what he talk about?" The pirate shook his head in dismay at the thought. "Lao Pak tell truth. Like to you, I say: You stupid. That true!"

Keel scowled.

"Lot of people say to you, 'Oh, you big strong guy. I like you because you so smart.' But... you stupid. You get us all caught. Why you shoot that Kimbrin?"

"He had it coming."

"That stupid thing to say. What he do? How much money he owe you?"

Keel shrugged. "So tell me another truth. How much does it cost to get out of here?"

"Couple thousand credits."

"Sket."

Lao Pak smiled. "It okay. They give you week, and then if you no pay, they just take your ship."

"Over my dead body."

"That too." Lao Pak rose from the bench and stepped over the Tennar, tugging on his Fu Manchu as though thinking. "I have idea. You sell ship to Lao Pak. I use money to bail you out."

Keel scoffed and looked up at the ceiling. There were fewer holocams than he expected.

"You think Lao Pak not honest?" the pirate asked, sounding genuinely wounded and putting his hand across his heart as though physically pained. "That hurt."

"I'm not that stupid," Keel said, getting up from his seat. "And I'm not gonna let you skink out of paying me my cut of the credits, either. You said winner takes twenty-five percent. That's enough to cover my bail."

"I say that? You sure?"

"Yeah, I'm sure," Keel said, raising his voice as he stepped closer to tower over the pirate.

A few of the other pirates looked over and began to pick themselves up from off the floor.

Lao Pak held out his hands as though lost. "So much chit-chat in that cantina. Hard to hear. Also, you drink too much. Make your memory bad. I say: You get *thrill of event*. Not twenty-five percent. You not hear good."

Keel squared up on Lao Pak, his powerful frame a stark contrast to the skinny pirate. "I hear fine."

"Leave the runt alone," growled one of the pirates.

Lao Pak whipped around, his ratty hair following, the beads and other trinkets braided or tangled within his hair clinking together. "Runt? I pirate prince. Your leader."

"That'll be the day," grumbled another pirate, the same bearded man who had hoisted Keel's hand in victory back at the cantina. "Seriously, though, spacer: he's with us and you're not. So back off."

"Not until I get what I'm owed," Keel said, turning to face what was now a trio of pirates cracking their knuckles and shuffling toward him. Lao Pak attempted to sneak away, but Keel grabbed him by the collar, holding him in place while keeping his eyes fixed on the other pirates.

The big, bearded pirate stopped and looked over his shoulders at his two friends—a green-skinned Alene and a red-faced human. They both nodded, then the dark-bearded pirate looked straight at Keel. "Looks to me like you're owed an ass-kicking, kelhorn. And we're gonna pay you extra."

With that, the trio of pirates rushed forward, arms cocked back, ready for a tussle. It was an amateurish approach to a fight that might work in a bar among other drunken spacers and criminals, but it was hardly suited for attacking a legionnaire, even if he was outside his armor and an untold number of parsecs from his kill team.

Keel spun Lao Pak in a circle, lifting the man from his feet and hurling the scrawny pirate into the oncoming trio. The smuggler threw himself into the mix right after, leading with a sharp elbow strike against the temple of the Alene and dropping the alien to the ground, out cold. He then centered himself and delivered a thrusting kick into the sternum of the red-faced man, who backpedaled, tripped over Lao Pak, and crashed into the electric blue haze of the containment field. The jolt from the field reacting to his touch caused the man to freeze in place and then fall face-first onto the floor, spasming.

A ringing alarm sounded in the corridor outside the holding cell. The noise stirred more of the pirates to their feet, but hardly all of them. Most of the lot was content to watch the entertainment rather than join in. Which was a good thing for Keel, who was now backing up as two new groups attempted to close in on him from either side.

"Call 'em off, Lao Pak!" Keel shouted. "Or so help me, I'll go straight for you next."

Lao Pak, tangled up on the floor with the bearded pirate, swallowed and then puffed out his chest. "You not reach me from there. You too slow, you—"

Keel was on top of Lao Pak in an instant, sprinting right through the closing ranks of pirates even as he held up his arms to ward off the buffeting blows that came for his face as he ran the gauntlet. He pounced on Lao Pak, pinning him to the ground beneath his knees.

A meaty hand belonging to the bearded pirate groped for Keel's face, but went limp when the smuggler drove his own fist into the man's face.

Keel grabbed Lao Pak by the shirt collar and cocked his fist for another shot. "End it! Or I end you!"

"They not listen to me! I pirate prince but not in charge!"

Whether that was true or not, Keel had to act. He sent a right cross down into Lao Pak's cheek, causing the man's head to rock violently to the side and sending a bloody stream of saliva—and at least one tooth—flying.

"Okay! Okay!" Lao Pak screamed, holding up his hands to ward off any more blows. "Stop or he kill me! He crazy!"

The pirates reluctantly slowed and then stopped altogether, watching to see what Keel would do next.

Breathing heavily but by no means winded, Keel stood, pulling the skinny pirate with him by the collar until the two were again standing face to face.

Lao Pak rubbed his jaw. "Why you hit so hard, huh?" He opened his mouth and let out a stream of blood as his tongue probed the gap Keel had created by knocking out his lateral incisor and canine. "Those teeth still good teeth! I chew with those!"

Keel squeezed Lao Pak's collar even tighter, twisting up some skin in the process and causing the man to yelp as he drew him close. "You got off easy. Now I want my cut—"

Lao Pak spat, sending a glob of pink spit onto Keel's shoes. He looked around. "Where teeth go? They silvene-plated. Worth money."

"My *cut*."

A boom sounded from the other side of the containment field, and all heads turned to see a group of blue-uniformed guards armed with concussive surge guns.

"Let him go," commanded a woman in a business suit that had probably been the height of fashion on Utopion a few years prior but had only now made its way out to this edge world planet. She stood out in stark contrast to the wall of blue-uniformed guards. Obviously police. If she was with them, she was probably a detective. Plus she had that look about her. Someone who took everything in. Constantly.

"Sure," Keel said. He made a show of brushing Lao Pak off, then released him. As he did so, he leaned in to the pirate and whispered, "My cut."

Lao Pak pushed Keel's hands away and straightened himself. "You so greedy. You knock out my teeth! We even!"

An electric ring sounded, and the containment door powered down. The detective looked around in confusion, then looked down after a buzz on her wrist chrono. She frowned. "Everybody out. Let's go. Congratulations. You made your bails."

Guards watched as the pirates shuffled their way through the open cell door. As if every party knew the drill. Every party except Keel. He stood there, watching them move, watching as guards came in to pick up and carry out the man who'd been zapped by the containment field.

At last Keel moved for the exit with the rest of the motley crew, only to be stopped by the business end of a riot stick, its electrical charge powered down, thankfully.

"Not so fast, buddy. No one bailed *you* out."

"You should have sold me your ship!" Lao Pak called, smiling at Keel to reveal the bloody gap in his teeth. "You reaaal stupid, Keel. More than normal stupid person!"

The guard pushed Keel back inside with the riot stick. Keel balled his fists and turned away, too angry to even look at Lao Pak. Two guards were still inside, trying to lift the heavy, lubricated, and unwieldy body of the unconscious Tennar.

A glint of metal caught Keel's eyes from beneath one of the benches. He walked over, bent down, and surreptitiously picked up two silvene-plated teeth. Hiding them in his palm, he turned back to the two guards struggling with the Tennar.

"Need a hand?" he said.

The men were panting from the effort.

"Sure," said one. "But no funny stuff."

Keel nodded and came over, lazily grabbing a tentacle with one hand and lifting it in the air.

"If you're gonna help, smart-ass, *help*."

Keel opened his other hand, revealing the precious metal. "One for each of you," he said, and then closed his palm into a fist. "*If* you get me a comm call."

Each silvene tooth was easily worth as much as one of their paychecks.

"How 'bout we just *take* those and don't break every bone in your body?" whispered one of the guards. "How's that for a deal?"

"No good," Keel said, as though he'd genuinely thought it over. "Has to be for the comm call. Otherwise I'll tell all your buddies what I found and you can split it up in your own time. But we both know it ain't going nearly far enough if that happens."

"Sket!" said the other guard, showing his hand. The smuggler had them.

"All right," the first said. "We'll get it for you. Just shut up about it."

Keel gave a lopsided grin. "Thanks." He sat down on a bench in the newly empty holding cell. "I'll wait."

# 07

After his comm call, Keel waited another long thirty-six hours, the lone man in the holding cell, before the detective who had released Lao Pak returned.

"Grab your stuff," she demanded.

Keel looked around at the empty room and held up his hands. "Yeah... pretty sure I got it all."

"Good. Let's go. Your bail's been met."

With a wry grin, Keel followed the detective to a processing room where he met with a bot whose sole programming seemed to be to tell him where to sign on a datapad.

"Exit's that way," the detective said, pointing at a clearly labeled door and then turning to leave.

"Do I at least get a ride back to the cantina, or...?"

The detective wheeled around on him. "You *shot* a man."

"A Kimbrin. And he had it coming."

"In the back."

"He could have turned around."

"Without provocation, according to the witnesses I interviewed."

"Well, they only witnessed that very brief moment of time. I assure you, there was plenty of provocation before that."

The detective squared herself and put her hands on her hips. "I don't know who your friends are, but I know you have no business being released. Still, you're free to go. So *go.*"

Then she turned and power-walked down the hall, her shoes clicking angrily with each step.

"So that's a no on the speeder?" Keel called after her.

She didn't reply, though he heard an old-fashioned door slam from somewhere around the corner.

Keel turned to the processing bot. "How 'bout it? You got a speeder coming for me?"

"You have no more forms to sign. Good day."

"Thanks, pal."

"You have no more forms to—"

"I got it." Keel moved to the exit, pushing the doors open as early morning light washed into the building. He could hear the bot saying "Good day" as the doors swung closed behind him.

"Guess I'm walking," he muttered, his breath puffing out in a vaporous cloud in the chill air.

"No. I'll drive."

Keel turned to the voice and cracked a smile. "Long time, Captain."

Ellek Owens didn't return the smile. The big, red-haired operator's face was a mask, his emotions perpetually hidden behind opaque sunglasses and a bushy beard. "Major."

"A *major*?" Keel raised his brows.

"What?" Owens demanded.

"Nothing. I'm sure being that far away from the ops won't bother you at all. Forget I said anything. I'll start over. Long time, *Major*."

"Not *that* long," Owens said. "And it's the third time I've had to get you out like this."

Keel shrugged. "Hazards of acting like a criminal is that people treat you like one. Did someone pick up the MCR I shot?"

"Yeah. We got him. Being interrogated now."

"By us or by Nether Ops?"

"Us. Don't trust Nether Ops unless it's Broxin."

"I don't much trust *her*, either."

Owens snorted. "Well, we have a history, she and I. So I do."

Keel gave him a look.

An eyebrow shot up from behind Owens's shades. "Not like that."

Keel, legionnaire-turned-smuggler for the greater good, made his best attempt at looking innocent. "I didn't say anything."

They walked a few blocks beyond the spaceport jail.

"Got anything new I should be looking out for?" Keel asked.

"Hopin' for somethin' more than what little we gave you to begin with?" Owens asked, not bothering to hide the smile that came to his face over the vague absurdity of Keel's mission.

But it was all they had. That and too many dead legionnaires.

This guy—these guys—whoever they were. They were ghosts.

Except there was no doubt they existed.

"There is one thing," Owens remembered. "Maybe it's related, maybe not. Worth keeping an eye open for."

"Shoot."

"The MCR have some kind of... recruiter. Out among the spacers, we think. There's someone out there doing the rah-rah *Republic bad, Legion worse* speech that's resonating well enough that private haulers have been contributing their freighters—and their crews—to the MCR. Turnin' those ships into gunboats, or just loadin' 'em up with det and trying to blow holes in Repub customs stations. Or civilian space stations. Or whoever those kelhorns have a blood feud with that needs to be settled today. The usual sket."

Keel nodded. "I'll keep my sensors scanning."

A speeder hovered down the street, kicking up dust and sending a few scraps of garbage swirling in its wake. Keel crossed the road behind it.

"This way to the *Six*, unless you're parked somewhere nearby. It's a walk."

"No. I got a sled." Owens motioned for Keel to follow him. "Down this way."

The sled was a study in the shade of black. Keel didn't think he could spot one thing that wasn't colored like the deepest corners of dead space. The only thing that set one black section of the sled apart from another was whether it shined like the windows or side panels or had that powder-coated darkness like a blaster.

"Hop in," Owens said, opening the back door with a subtle hiss of whisper-quiet gears.

Keel hopped in, assuming that Owens would play chauffeur. As the smuggler slid to the middle of the deep-seated bench, he immediately heard the click-clack of a surge shotgun from the front passenger seat. In an instant the business end of the weapon was aimed at Keel's head, with an old but not quite geriatric man aiming down its sights.

"Rule One," the old man growled. "Never climb into a speeder without your blaster drawn unless you know on your life it's empty."

Owens chuckled from outside. Keel's hand, already on his own blaster, relaxed. Evidently Keel's former fellow team member, currently his only link to the Legion Keel had once served in, knew this guy.

But Keel wasn't a fan of having a weapon pointed at his face. Ever.

He looked from the old man to the major, who had slipped into the driver's seat. "Who the hell is this fossil?"

"That," Owens said, looking back with a grin his beard couldn't hide, "is your new partner."

"Partner?" Keel sputtered, incredulity giving way to annoyance. "What do I need a partner for?"

"Dark Ops sent me to keep you out of trouble," the old man said. "Clearly you're needing it." The shotgun was still leveled at Keel's head.

"Trouble!" Keel grabbed hold of the muzzle and shoved it down. "You're gonna learn about trouble up close in a minute." He turned to Owens. "The kind of trouble I get into is unavoidable. We talked about this."

Major Owens sighed. "I know we did."

He nodded to the old man, who said, "I may have run a few ops playing the bad guy. They didn't pick *my* team up."

"Well, I don't *have* a team, old-timer. And the leejes I run into seem more interested in locking me up than joining me."

"The point of it is," Owens said, "you're a lone operator trying to figure out how to be something else. You've done what we've asked you to do as best you can, without much help from Dark Ops. When we went direct action, we lost a lot of what made leejes like Doc here able to do what you're trying to do now. But this can't keep happening, me having to show up and get you out."

"Sorry to be an inconvenience."

"You're not," Owens said firmly. "We owe you. We owe you better than this. But eventually, this keeps happening, someone is gonna catch on. Someone will recognize me or another leej we send in. A merc who shared time in the Legion. And then... all you've done is for nothin'."

Behind his shades, Owens's face was set. This was happening.

"I got my work cut out for me," the unceasingly grumpy old man gruffed. "You sure can find the absolute scumsacks of the galaxy, I'll give you that much. But the Legion don't need intel on what the prison food of Herbeer tastes like, damn it." He stowed the surge shotgun away. "They musta lowered the intelligence testing since I was in Dark Ops."

Keel decided to ignore that. Every vet since the dawn of time thought standards were lowering, an easy thought to think from the sidelines.

He turned back to Owens. "Really, Major, I don't want a partner. Especially one this far past his expiration date."

Owens gave a fractional shake of his head. "Not your call."

"Then why couldn't it at least be Chhun? Or better yet, Exo."

The old man up front laughed, so heartily that Keel was concerned a heart attack was coming. "You got *me*, kid. And you don't know how lucky you are for it."

"Kill Team Victory is busy, Aeson," Owens replied. "More so now than when you were leading it. Doc here knows a thing or two about going out into the cold. He was Dark Ops first and moved to Intel for a while before calling it a career."

Keel rolled his eyes. "When was this? Eighty years ago?" Then, to Doc: "How were the Savage Wars, Gramps? As bad as they say?"

"Wise-ass," Doc muttered.

Owens checked his chrono. "I got things to do. Doc's mission is to better get you in the position Dark Ops needs you to be in. That's working underground, gathering intel... not in jail. This is the way it is going forward. Do you understand me, Captain Ford?"

Reluctantly, Keel agreed. "Roger that. Sir."

"Good. Take care of yourselves. Keep reporting anything you think is worth us taking a look at." Owens opened the repulsor door. "We're gonna find out what's building up out there."

Keel pursed his lips and gave a singular nod. That's what it was all about. The entire reason he'd left a place where he'd felt supremely comfortable in exchange for... whatever this was. For every two-dealing kelhorn criminal he brushed up against or long, lonely night of perpetual darkness out among the stars in his freighter, all Keel had to do was remember seeing his fellow legionnaires—Twenties and Kags—laid out dead on that shuttle.

More of that was coming—had already come. The edge was a brutal, violent place, and that mayhem was drifting ever closer to the core worlds. You could taste war coming on the air. No longer just local planetary skirmishes. A big, *galactic* war. Like the Savage Wars.

A generational meat grinder.

It was coming. Keel was sure of it. Someone was out there. Preparing. Planning. Probing. Weakening a Republic already atrophied by its own selfish greed. What prestige that Republic now had, built on the shoulders of those who had fought hard to unite the galaxy under its banner, was rapidly being squandered by those who could think no further than how to keep their personal credits flowing.

So... yeah. Keel would go the distance to find out what was building out there. He wasn't even opposed to having someone else along for the ride.

So long as it wasn't the old man.

Perhaps Owens could stick around for a jump or two. Long enough for Keel to catch him up on everything that had happened since he'd left the Legion for squalid back alleys and cutthroat—in the most literal sense—business dealings.

"Any chance you can make the jump off-planet with us?" Keel asked. He had resigned himself to the fact that the old man would be with him. Disobeying orders... that wasn't going to happen. Keel was still too Legion to ignore the chain of command.

From the front seat, Doc said, "You heard him, jackass. He's busy."

"Take care. Both of you," was all Owens said. He closed the door on the two men. The operators.

Keel slumped in his seat and rubbed his forehead.

"Let's get moving, kid. Gotta make your ship and get off-world before that inspector back at the station lets her curiosity get the best of her." Doc chuckled. "She sure as sket wasn't happy you made bail—which is the same thing as having all charges dropped on this rock."

"So drive," Keel said, motioning for the old man to slide the modular steering column over to his side and get the sled moving.

Doc gave a crusty grin. "Nah. You drive. I got the shotgun, so I'm gonna ride shotgun."

"You been waitin' a while to make that joke, huh?"

"At my age, there's nothin' to do *but* wait, kid."

Keel opened his door and got back in up front. The speeder hummed to life and adjusted itself to its new driver's height and shape, doing its programmed best to make Keel comfortable.

He pulled out and moved toward the star port hangars where his ship awaited. "Do you have some meds we need to pick up before we jump off-world... partner?"

Doc leaned back all comfortable-like in his seat, his clear blue eyes looking dead ahead but no doubt seeing everything—passing repulsor traffic, human and alien pedestrians, the light overhead flow of air speeders and other starship traffic. "You got the smart-ass persona of a smuggler down to a tee, Captain Keel."

"Only when I'm not in the armor."

"Which is all the damn time, ain't it? Not being jocked up and ready to rock."

"Yeah."

"You miss it," Doc said.

"Yeah." Keel let the silence sit as they stopped at a traffic light. Then, as they pulled out again: "Back in the Legion... there was an expression. A compliment, really. 'Same guy in and out of the armor.'"

Doc grunted. "I know it. Means you were all business, whether in full battle rattle or not. That was you?"

"That's what people said about me. But... no. This 'smart-ass' side you're talking about, it was always there. Drove my father crazy. He was old... like you."

"So Captain Ford wasn't a smart-ass? I think I'd prefer him."

"Well, you've got me. I've found out the hard way a couple of times just how much 'Captain Ford' stands out. It's like the kelhorns can *smell* Legion. Which is fine for security jobs. But if you're trying to get inside an org *without* becoming a hit man... well, that complicates the boundaries of my mission."

Doc grunted. They rode past a few more intersections on the way to the docking bays. Quiet.

"Why'd you agree to do this?" Doc asked. Keel knew the old man meant the operation as a whole, not the latest irritation of taking on a former Dark Ops leej as a partner.

Keel acted as though he hadn't heard the question. But Doc just waited, staring at him from the passenger seat, surge shotgun stowed between the seat and the door.

"Because if I didn't," Keel finally said, "someone else—probably Chhun—would have. And he's a guy the Legion can't lose. Someone who really is the same in and out of the armor."

Doc processed that. "Well, contrary to what I said previous... it's gonna help you. Being a wise-ass."

Keel glanced at the man. "Not sure it has so far."

"Give it time." The old man adjusted himself in his seat. "This seat is murdering my lower back. So much for luxury. So. First thing: You got a crew for that ship of yours? The... *Six*, you call it?"

"*Indelible VI.* And no. Just me."

Doc nodded like he'd expected that. "Good. Rule One is: Crews complicate things. Work alone. Keeps things tighter."

"You just said Rule One was about getting into sleds with your blaster drawn."

"Code of laws, kid. There's more than one code, and each one has its own set of rules. Rule One for vehicle entry is what I told you. Rule One for captaining a ship... now you know that one, too." Then, muttering to himself: "Kid thought he could get me on a technicality."

Keel scoffed. "Can't wait to hear 'em all." This was going to be a long drive.

"Next thing: contacts. Who do you know—outside the Legion—who can feed you intel?"

Keel's list wasn't long. "A few of the low-level info brokers anyone can get. Then there's Lao Pak."

"Don't know him."

"Pirate."

"No," Doc growled. "Pirates can't be trusted. Rule One: No pirates."

"You gonna write all these down for me?" Keel said. "My hands are busy."

"Don't worry. I'll be around."

"Great."

They drove the rest of the way in silence until reaching the weather-stained and rundown municipal docking bays. The streets were caked with grit from freighters landing and taking off under repulsor power, shaking their cosmic dust to settle among scraps of fabric, paper, plasteen, and all the other industrial refuse that litters a port.

"Here we are," Keel announced. "Docking bay lucky thirteen."

"Park it by the maintenance entrance," Doc ordered. "The ones the bots use. Don't go by the main doors."

Keel punched the sled's dashboard. "Dark Ops have someone to burn it?"

"Yeah. Owens has a guy ready. After we dust off, it'll get 'stolen.'"

"Hang on." Keel put on the brakes.

"What is it? Why're we stopping?"

"Private crew door is open." Keel pointed to the humanoid-sized door positioned opposite the cargo door on the rounded hangar. Inside was a glimpse of his banged-up but reliable old Naseen-model light freighter, sitting right where he'd left her, softly illuminated by the emergency lighting.

"Leave it that way on purpose?" Doc asked.

"Negative." Keel popped the sled door open, saying over his shoulder, "Park the sled or leave it. I'm gonna check it out."

"Fine. I'll go park. Too visible to leave it here."

Hand on his Intec blaster, Keel headed for the hangar door, just barely catching Doc's grumpy, "Kid probably forgot to lock the damn thing," as the old man pulled the speeder away.

The cavernous docking bay hummed, machines working, power generators thrumming as a trio of dented and battered bots went about their automated tasks. Keel could see his ship, a bit of rust revealing her age, but otherwise looking the same as he'd left her.

Except for the armored figure standing in the shadows by the *Six*'s open ramp.

Keel slipped inside, triggering a cheery AI whose voice blared over the PA system to greet him. He hadn't expected that.

"Welcome to Port of Rakka docking bays. Please examine your ship carefully for tampering. Port of Rakka and the city of Rakka are not liable for any—"

"So much for surprise," Keel muttered as the stranger's helmeted gaze locked on him, blaster rifle pointed in the direction of the crew door.

The AI continued, "—damage, theft, or any other—"

"System override," the stranger called out, the voice passed through a vocal modulator, emotionless and dead.

The PA system went silent.

"This your ship?" the stranger asked.

Keel took the speaker for a bounty hunter, not tall but fully armored, pointing an old-school K-17 at him. Whoever it was had him in a space devoid of cover. If they were a halfway decent shot, not difficult at this range, they could likely drill Keel in the back before he reached the door.

But the old man was out there, parking the sled. All Keel had to do was stall long enough for the numbers to swing his way. And anyway, if this bounty hunter wanted to shoot him, they could have.

... unless they were waiting on a positive identification.

"Who the hell are you?" Keel answered, taking a step toward the armored figure.

The bounty hunter twitched the K-17. "That's far enough, jump jockey."

Keel waved two empty hands. "Easy. My blaster's still holstered. You're the one pointing a weapon at someone's chest. What're you afraid of?"

"Nothing. Certainly not you. But that doesn't mean I'm stupid." The bounty hunter seemed miffed. Keel had struck a nerve. He could use that.

Keel walked forward, as casually as his body would let him through the adrenaline that naturally came with having the business end of a blaster pointed at you.

"Stop. Now!"

Keel did, then looked around, wanting to get the bounty hunter in the habit of doing the same. It would take only a split-second distraction for Keel to even the odds. "I'm stopped. Relax. So... you just came by to say hello, or...?"

"There's a bounty, Captain Keel," the armored figure informed him.

Frowning, Keel said, "Wrong guy. Name's Masters."

"Cute. But try again. You match the visuals."

Keel shook his head, a small smile on his face as though this were a minor inconvenience or misunderstanding. "So what did I do? Allegedly."

"They don't include the what. Just the *how much*."

"Well, at least tell me it's a lotta credits. I've got an ego to keep inflated."

"No one cares about you, jump jockey. The job is for your ship, which evidently belongs to someone named—"

"Lemme guess: Lao Pak."

"You know him. Sounds like confirmation to me."

Keel shrugged. "Really wishing I didn't right about now, but yeah. I know him. He *thinks* I owe him my ship. I don't."

"With what he's offering, you shouldn't worry. No bounty hunter would bother with the time and effort to repo at that rate."

Chagrined, Keel said, "So why are you here, then? With a blaster rifle. Pointed at me."

He again looked about the docking bay, this time really wondering what was taking the old man so long. Probably a prostate issue.

"Maybe I was just in the neighborhood and needed something to do. Maybe I'm here to see your ship," the armored figure said, nodding at the *Six*. "See what exactly is so special about it that Lao Pak went through the trouble of a guild contract just to get his hands on it. Must be more than meets the eye, because with how this wreck looks, he'll lose credits trying to sell it."

"Well, it isn't much. But it's mine. That's not gonna change."

"And yet I'm the one aiming a rifle at your chest, Captain," the bounty hunter observed.

Keel quirked a smile. "Safety's on, so I'm not sweating any cruel intentions all that much."

The bounty hunter laughed. "That old trick? I'm insulted, Captain. Why don't you—"

Keel drew his blaster pistol, which emitted a high-pitched whine, announcing his own intentions. The bounty hunter froze.

"How's that for a trick?" Keel growled. "And just to be clear: this is a *heavily* modified Intec x6 I'm aiming at your forehead. It'll go clean through that helmet of yours and out the other side if you so much as flinch. Oh. And my safety's off."

# 08

Keel let the hardened look on his face brighten. "So! You've seen the ship. Worth dying for?"

Boots tramped up behind him along with the exerted breathing that had to be the old man. Finally Keel's backup had arrived. He just hoped Doc had brought his surger, along with all that advice he was carrying.

"Oba's balls, Keel!" Doc hollered. "Holster that sidearm."

"Sure, right after I shoot this kelhorn for trying to steal my ship."

Doc walked up and put a hand on the smuggler's shoulder. "This is a misunderstanding, and you're about to make things infinitely worse, kid. She's a friend. Of mine."

Keel shrugged off the hand, but out of concern for the failing mental health of his senior partner, he tried to explain the situation. "She drew on me, old man."

"Ain't how it looks from here," Doc growled. "That true, Zora?"

"I couldn't be sure who he was at first," the bounty hunter—apparently named Zora—protested. "He just walked right in like he owned the place. So of course I drew on him."

"I paid for the bay," Keel insisted. "It's my ship. So guess what? I kinda *do* own the place."

Exasperated, Zora fumed, "This spacer is cocky as sket, and it's gonna get him killed sooner rather than later."

"Not by you, sister," Keel replied.

Doc frowned. "You were supposed to wait outside, Zora. I spent way too much time out there lookin' for you. You were always bad about keeping in contact. It's unprofessional. I taught you better."

"Oh, you're one to talk about not keeping in contact," Zora shot back, lowering her rifle.

Not only did these two know each other, Keel realized, but there was a history. And not a particularly pleasant one judging by their tone of voice.

"I'm sorry," Doc said, and it sounded almost like he was pleading. "It's tough to make a comm connection when you're busy overthrowing anti-Republic warlords out along galaxy's edge. You know how it is."

Keel looked from the grumpy old leej to the K-17-bearing bounty hunter. This... was getting weird. "Wait. What is this?"

Both Zora and Doc ignored him. The bounty hunter walked right up to the old man. Keel followed her, not yet willing to lower his own weapon.

"Right," Zora said. "Long live the Republic forever." Even from within her bucket, she radiated sarcasm. "Who cares about the lesser things in life? Like family?"

"Oh, no," Keel said, and then began an encyclopedic stream of curses meant for Owens. *How could the leej do this to me?*

Doc flushed red. "Don't take the high and mighty with me, Zee. We've been over that. Put it behind us. You can't bring it up like an ace up your sleeve every time you get caught with your guard down. *Bad Dad* ain't an excuse for how you live your life."

"This old fossil is your father?" Keel said. "My condolences."

Slinging her rifle, Zora pulled off her helmet and dropped it with a thunk. Her dark eyes flashed, her elfin features exuding rage. "Caught with my guard down, Dad? Oh, that's rich. If I'd wanted to kill this loser, I'd've dropped him two steps into the bay. He's completely clueless."

Now Keel had to set the record straight. "And yet here I am with a blaster pointed at—whose head again? Oh, right. Yours, sweetheart."

"He's got a point there, Zora darlin'," Doc said, then glared at Keel. "And will you stop pointing that at my daughter, kid?"

"I'm about to point it at *you*, old man. What the hell's going on here? Did Owens give the okay for me to join the family? Grandma gonna show up next towing a SAB behind her repulsor-chair?"

Doc shrugged. "Owens is on board. More or less."

"Okay, fine," Zora huffed, continuing on a completely separate strain of the conversation. "Jump jockey's fast, sure. But only because I didn't drop him when he first walked in." She turned to Keel. "And just so you know, I could have."

Doc flushed. "Yeah. And you did a great job covering your six in whatever fantasy you're spinning right now, Zee. I could have dropped *you* before you even knew I was here. Sloppy. Real sloppy."

"'More or less'?" Keel interrupted, trying to pilot the ship of conversation back on course. "Either he authorized Tina Rechs here or he didn't."

Doc's eyes flashed at the nickname. Tyrus Rechs was the most notorious—and wanted—bounty hunter in the galaxy. He was rumored to be a former legionnaire who still had Legion connections, and it was known that the House of Reason and most non-Legion branches of the military wanted him dead. Only the bounty hunters' Bronze Guild and his own mythic skills kept Rechs alive.

The old man clarified his statement. "Owens said to get you where you needed to be. That's what I'm doing and... I need her help with that."

Keel squinted at the old man. "What happened to Rule One: No crew?"

"She's not so much crew as..." Doc sighed. "Well, she's not part of the crew."

"She's just coming along, then?" Keel said, one brow raised. "Staying aboard the *Six*? Staying in crew quarters. Eating, sleeping, and otherwise using up resources. But not crew."

"I'm right here, you know," Zora said.

"Thanks for the update, sweetheart." Keel didn't take his gaze from Doc. "Listen, old man. I took you on because I was *ordered* to. I'm not looking to hand out free rides to wannabe bounty hunters."

"Sweetheart?" Zora growled. "*Wannabe*? Oh, I am gonna..."

"Nah, kid," Doc said to Keel. "She's good. Real good."

"Damn right I am," Zora said proudly.

"Trained her myself since she was this high." Doc's knife hand swept below his hip.

"Breaks into the bay," Keel began, ticking a list off on his fingers, "disables security, leaves the door wide open, ends up with a blaster pointed at her head. Forgive me for being unimpressed, but your definition of 'real good' needs some refinement. I know a drunk Tennar who'd probably have done just about as well."

"Her skills ain't it. She's not a killer. She ain't like us."

"Hey!" Zora exclaimed.

Doc pressed on. "It's what she knows. *Who* she knows. She's connected in a way *you* need to be, kid. So don't piss her off or we'll be playing from behind. My girl agreed to give us a real leg up here. And we need that."

Keel was firm. "No. Absolutely not."

"Screw you, kelhorn," Zora said. "Like you're anything special."

"I'm special," Keel replied, shooting her a smile that could charm an Endurian right down to her royal pedicured toes.

Zora scoffed.

"Listen," Doc said. "This introduction didn't go the way I'd planned it. Let's all get aboard your ship, have a few beers, settle down... and talk. You got beer on board, right?"

Zora rolled her eyes. "Fine."

But Keel wasn't fine. "No, I'm good," he said. "Tell your daughter you'll see her the next Unity Day. She doesn't set foot on the *Six*. What is it about this family and pointing blasters at a guy's head first thing?"

"You're letting a bad first impression ruin things," Doc said patiently. "Rule One: Don't, uh, let the first impression, shut you... down."

"That one been around long, old man?"

"Hey, lay off him!" Zora took an angry step forward.

Keel shot her a look. "I'm sorry, didn't you have another docking bay to leave unsecure somewhere?"

"*I* didn't do that," Zora sputtered. "It was open!"

"It was open?" Doc said, meeting Keel's worried gaze and then refocusing on his daughter.

"Swear on Chappy's grave," she said. "I'm sorry. I swear it, yeah."

Keel's blaster was no longer aimed at Zora, but at the ready, searching the docking bay.

Doc smiled sadly. "That's the type of thing you wanna tell us up front, sweetie. Rule One—"

A muffled but shrill voice cut in. "Lao Pak Rule One: Stupid Captain Keel owe Lao Pak his ship."

Around them in the docking bay, the place seemed empty, but the generators, repulsor loaders, and stacks of empty pallets cast long shadows.

"I owe *you*?" Keel shot back, loudly. Wherever that lanky-haired space rat was hiding, Keel wanted him to hear. "We went over this. *You* owe *me*."

"You still talk about that old time? No, we good friends for that now. I keep credits, you knock out Lao Pak's teeth. Ha ha. Good friends. It water under bridge. This new thing you owe me for."

Perturbed, Keel said, "Why don't you come out where I can see you and we'll talk about this... new thing."

"Okay. Nothing to hide. We friends. You just owe your friend Lao Pak a ship."

It sounded as if the man was talking from inside a cargo container, and as Lao Pak revealed himself, it became evident why. The pirate had apparently accessed the hangar through an underground drainage channel, because now he crawled out of it accompanied by several familiar-looking members of his crew.

Speaking low, Doc said, "I count eight of 'em. Probably all packing blasters."

"Ya think?" Keel muttered back.

"Two more to the rear," Zora said, her voice low. "Aiming at us from the shadows."

"How 'bout those two you got hiding in the back?" Keel called out. "They gonna join the discussion, or just point their fourth-rate excuses for blaster rifles at us?"

Lao Pak's hands flew to his mouth. "They still back there?" He shook a bejeweled finger at the lurkers. "Don't be rude to Captain Keel. He not like it. He not smart but he have eyes. Come around and stand in front of Lao Pak."

Doc had his surger out and kept it trained on the self-declared pirate prince. He spoke quietly to Keel, his lips barely moving. "They're all out in the open now. Have your ship dust 'em."

"With what?" Keel answered. "It's a Naseen freighter. Its defenses are enough shields and hull plating to run away. Slowly."

"You didn't modify it?" Doc barked. "What the hell is wrong with you?"

Lao Pak clapped a hand to his ear. "What your grandfather yelling about, Keel? You go senile, old man?"

Keel ignored the pirate. "This isn't Nether Ops," he said to Doc. "Funds are kinda tight." Then he called out to the self-proclaimed pirate king. "Don't worry about him, Lao Pak. He hasn't had his medication yet today."

Doc chuckled. "That's funny, kid. Real—"

"You owe Lao Pak your ship," the pirate snapped, "because Lao Pak get Captain Keel out of prison. Now you pay like person who is thankful."

"The hell you did," Keel replied.

"How else you get free?"

"The DA. I charmed her."

Lao Pak and his pirates burst out laughing. The pirate king grabbed his side like it was fit to burst.

"What's so funny?" Keel asked, bewildered.

"You no charm DA. Your girlfriend, maybe *she* charm DA. But you?" He shook his finger again and laughed.

"Just for the record, I'm not his girlfriend," Zora declared. "I need that understood up front, just so no one dies thinking otherwise."

Keel looked over at her. "Seems a little excessive."

But Lao Pak found it all amusing.

"What? That crazy talk from crazy girlfriend, Captain Keel. No one die. I just take Keel's ship for getting him out of jail like good friends do. Scratch backs. Best friends!"

Gripping her K-17, Zora growled, "I am not—"

"You're not getting my ship, Lao Pak," Keel interrupted. "Not today. Not ever."

Lao Pak tapped his chin. "You know, Keel, I get real drunk after I get out of jail. I wake up, and you gone. Poof. No way you get out on your own. So... Lao Pak get you out. Only Lao Pak can't remember because Lao Pak drunk. See?" He laughed once, then glowered. "But Lao Pak... gets paid."

Keel glowered back. "Over my dead body."

Lao Pak threw up his hands. "Why everyone say that? It just dumb ship. Ugly, too! I do you favor, taking it off your hands. You should be embarrassed to fly it. It probably death trap."

"Careful, kid," Doc muttered. "Those two are creeping back into the shadows."

"I'll take them and lower the ramp," Keel whispered back. "You two cover until we all get on the ship." Then to Zora: "And remember to thumb off your safe, sweetheart."

"Oh, *shut* up," she hissed.

Keel eyed the waiting pirate prince. "I've thought about it and... no deal, Lao Pak. But I've got a counteroffer I think we can live with. Some of us, anyway."

Quick as lightning, he sent two blaster bolts, each hitting a pirate in the shadows. He silenced the screams with two more blasts.

The pirate king dove for cover and cried, "What? Keel! We friends now!"

In a sweaty panic, one thug cried, "Both snipers down, boss!"

The air was alive with blaster fire, red bolts slicing toward the pirates' cover with few coming back. A pirate's discipline was no match for a pair of legionnaires. The bounty hunter wasn't doing bad for herself either. Zora snatched up her helmet and threw it on while her father took careful, aimed shots at targets of opportunity.

"C'mon!" Keel shouted from the open ramp. "I'm raising the ramp with or without you, so run!"

The boarding ramp of the *Indelible VI* whined upward, and Doc and Zora broke from contact and hopped onto the rising plank. Doc took a knee at the base of the ramp, laying down covering fire. Zora did the same from just behind Keel, shooting into the narrowing gap as the ramp closed.

Keel turned and pushed her further inside the ship. "C'mon, lady, we're not outta this yet!"

# 09

Keel heaved a heavy sigh in the safety of the ship's lounge. He'd started the day in a backwater planetary jail, and somehow things had gotten *worse*. Blaster fire still shrieked outside, but outside was outside. At least for now. Around him, the *Indelible VI* hummed. Warm. As ready for an emergency takeoff as she would ever be.

"Ship!" the smuggler called out to the ether. "We're leaving."

An ebullient voice exclaimed through the ship comm, "Oh! Captain Keel! Welcome aboard. And... oh! You've brought visitors. Well, I am honored and delighted. *Delighted!*"

"Shut it, chatterbox. I said get the engines going!"

"Of course, Captain! Oh, we're flying again! In the starry host again! Up! Up! Up! Into the delirious burning blue and beyond! Of course, port regulations require a minimum ten-minute—"

"Forget the regs. Just get this bucket ready to fly. And no more talking!"

Keel ducked a tangle of hanging wires—probably a fire hazard—and moved toward the cockpit.

"Oh. I see," the AI said, somewhat disapprovingly. Then the thing's enthusiasm returned. "I understand! Of course. Mum's the word, Captain!"

Doc looked askance at a dusty wall speaker that served as the artificial intelligence's voice box. "What the hell is that?"

"Ship's AI is a little... unstable," Keel admitted. With no slicer on crew to tinker with the code, nor a boatload of credits to buy a new one that wasn't likely to take control of the ship and fly it into an impound lot, Keel was stuck with the AI he had.

"Oba's balls, Keel. This ship is a real piece of work. No anti-personnel guns, crazy AI. Please tell me you at least got the engines upgraded for evasion. They're gonna send interceptors after us if we blast off unauthorized."

"Hey, at least it has exterior cams," Zora said, stopping at a viewport. "They brought an anti-vehicle cannon. Setting up now. Got this covered in your plan, flyboy?"

"Time to go," Keel said, rushing down the corridor.

"Where you goin'?" Doc asked.

"Cockpit. Stay here!"

"Who the hell puts a cockpit *there*?"

Keel rushed down the corridor to the cockpit. The Naseen was a freighter, meant for hauling heavy cargo containers that didn't fit in its cargo hold. As a result, things weren't always where you expected them to be. The cockpit, for example, sat at the end of a looping, inclined corridor, raised above the ship so the pilot could see above the magnetically powered tines that jutted out from the ship to secure those once-standard freight containers that no one actually used anymore.

It was an old ship.

The cockpit doors hissed open, and Keel dropped into the pilot's seat. With a few flicks, he brought the control panel to life in an array of beeps and colors.

"Bay door's open," he muttered to himself, eyes darting up through his front viewport to verify that the overhead doors hadn't stopped opening halfway. Each bay led into a labyrinth-like tunnel system that collected ships before releasing them into atmosphere. The design kept traffic down, but more importantly it kept the seedy spacers who called Rakka a home port from taking off without paying their bay fees.

Keel hit the comm button, and the comm request light flashed blue.

"Rakka Port," some bored official yawned.

Keel leaned over the comm. "This is Captain Aeson Keel of freighter *Indelible VI*, requesting emergency departure clearance."

Outside, the cacophony of blaster fire hadn't quieted down. Sure, those dinky blasters couldn't breach his ship, but the chances of vaporizing a hose or cable—breaking something too expensive to fix—were high.

"No registry of your ship, Captain Keel," the port authority replied. "Advise docking bay number."

"Uh, Docking Bay 13."

Behind him, the cockpit doors hissed open. Doc dropped into a well-worn seat at Keel's side. The navigator's station.

"Parminthian leather. Nice," he said, patting it. Then, looking over the lights flashing on the control board, said, "You know how to work all this stuff?"

"Yeah. Don't touch anything. It's temperamental."

Keel had played around with the controls, had studied the manuals extensively prior to assuming control of the Legion-provided freighter, and yet he was still mystified at how the defunct Naseen corporation had thought flight controls should be laid out. Plus, there were several tactile switches and even a few *dials* that Keel hadn't seen in the diagrams and that neither he nor the AI knew the purpose of. Someone, once upon a time, had made some modifications. Probably some sort of insectoid-type humanoid who lacked the appendages to use the usual glass or holographic control screens.

"Legion can spring for you to learn how to fly," Doc said. "Can't spring for a ship worth flyin'."

"I already *knew* how to fly. Mostly. Hand me that datapad over there."

Doc got up. "Which one? This?"

"Yeah. Just gave the wrong registry and I don't remember the fake one I touched down with."

Doc heaved a disappointed sigh and sat in a chair in the second row usually meant for an engineer and surrounded by monitors that read out the health of the ship like a patient's chart in a hospital. "That's just... pathetic. Here."

Keel caught the tossed datapad, found what he was looking for, and pressed the outgoing comm.

"You know what? I gave you the ship's old registry," he told the port authority, an implied "oops" between pals. "Should be listed under *Musky Dowager*. My mistake."

"Stand by for confirmation, *Musky Dowager*."

Keel grinned in triumph.

"What the hell kinda ship name is that?" Doc said.

Keel frowned. "Who asked you?"

"I gotta ride in it, so I don't need to be asked. *Musky Dowager*. It's an embarrassment."

"My ship, my fake registries."

"Well *your ship* is gonna be in pieces if we don't dust off before those idiot pirates get their guns set up," Doc replied. "Check the cams."

A portside holocam showed the docking bay, where the pirates had left off their small arms blasting in favor of weapons assembly. Apparently every head was needed for this project, as all the thugs huddled around parts. Gesticulating wildly up at the *Six*, Lao Pak gave the back of the nearest pirate's head a smack.

How all those cutthroats put up with the little twerp was beyond Keel. But Lao Pak *was* more cunning than the rest. After all, he'd managed to set up an ambush that might have gone real badly for the smuggler and his new "friends" had they not taken so long to execute.

"They're gonna figure out that thing's on backwards before long," said Keel.

"Yup," Doc agreed. "Of course, if you had some burst turrets built into the belly..."

The comm chimed, and Keel pressed the button. "Go for Keel."

"Registry confirmed, *Musky Dowager*. We've got a bit of a jam going on. Liftoff authorization effective in ninety minutes."

"*Ninety minutes?*" Doc exclaimed. "Oba's ass, tell him we're in a hurry, Keel!"

The old leej might have been a couple decades past his expiration date, but he wasn't wrong. Leaning over the comm again, Keel said, "Ah, Rakka Port... any chance we can get a priority takeoff? We've got some... stuff. To do."

"Stand by."

The chime sounded again, and a message appeared on the feed. A lot of words, all official-like.

Doc's white brows met. "What's that?"

"From the port. Priority takeoff invoice," Keel replied, then read some more. "Twenty-six-hundred credits? The nine hells—"

Doc couldn't see the problem. "So? Pay it and get us out of here!"

"This ship came in empty, and other than you and little Miss Starshine back there, it's leaving empty. I don't have that kind of credits. Do you?"

"Yeah."

"So *you* pay it."

Why did Keel have to be the one coming up with the solutions all the time?

"It's not *my* ship," Doc argued.

The cockpit doors swished open.

"Why aren't we leaving?" Zora asked, hands on her hips.

Rolling his eyes, Keel said, "Sure. Join the party."

Zora took the seat right next to Keel.

"Somewhere *other* than the navigator's chair, please," he added, wondering why it even needed to be said.

"What? I'm a Class Four Navigator. Besides, you should be worrying more about your ship getting blown up by those pirates."

Keel scoffed. "They don't even know which way the barrel attaches."

Doc gripped the seat in front of him and pulled himself forward so that his head was between Keel and Zora. "In ninety minutes, they'll figure it out, kid!"

Zora looked confused. "What's this about ninety minutes?"

"It's nothing," Keel snapped. "I just need to sweet-talk the port so we can—"

Beneath them, the *Six* shuddered, and dust sifted down from the ceiling. Keel used his sleeve to wipe off the screen, muttering, "Looks like they figured out the assembly." He shot his guests a look. "Strap in!"

The ambient hum of the ship climbed to a high-pitched whine as the repulsors powered up and hefted the old girl's bulk into the air.

Doc clutched his armrests. "Whoa, whoa! Without clearance, you're gonna hit a dead end once you leave this bay. They keep those docking tunnels sealed."

"Not all of 'em, Gramps."

The ship trembled again. Undeterred by the fact their target was now moving, the pirates in the bay kept up their barrage. Keel winced at the deepening thuds.

"Shields are holding," Zora observed.

"Surprised this dumpster has any," her father said.

"Are you now?" Keel growled, lifting the ship up through the bay doors into the complex tunnel system. He spotted a glimmer of receding light coming from around one of the curves. Someone had just left that way.

"Hang on!"

He rammed the accelerator, and the ship careened forward. Heavy cannon fire sounded from behind, but it did no more than send a shower of sparks down on the empty bay and set off alarms that sent the pirates scurrying. The *Indelible VI* zoomed through the docking tunnel, its walls uncomfortably close, a deliberate design feature to prevent just these kinds of unsafe speeds.

"Tight squeeze..." Doc remarked, white-knuckling the armrests.

Keel took a cleansing breath. "I got it."

"Watch the sides!" Doc cried.

Keel's calm turned to annoyance. He hated backseat pilots. "Relax! It's not as tight as it looks. Let's try and find a way out."

The sliver of light he'd been chasing had darkened to a close, but there were more tunnels. More doors. They just needed some luck.

Luck that another ship *authorized* to be in the tunnels wasn't heading in their direction.

Clearly fighting the urge to put her hands on the controls, Zora studied the display. "Dead end straight ahead, jump jockey."

"I see it. Hang on." Keel gritted his teeth and raced the ship on ahead, straight into the dark.

"You gonna turn?" Doc asked.

"Eventually."

Proximity warnings blared, screaming their protests. Red alerts lit up the screens.

"We're about to run out of room real fast!" Zora cried.

"Turn around, kid!" Doc advised.

The ship kept hurtling forward, nearing the duracrete-solid end of the line.

"Hang on..." Keel said.

Then, just as the tunnel lightened, he yanked hard and juked the ship left, swinging the passengers hard against their seat straps as they burst into the light of day. The alarms ceased as they swept up toward blue sky, leaving the bustling Rakka spaceport below.

"Woohoo!" Keel crowed. "How's that for getting us out of there? No need to thank me."

Zora wasn't amused. "How... *exactly* did you know that door would be open? If it'd been closed, they'd've been scraping us off the impervisteel for weeks. No, forget scraping—they'd just paint over us, we'd be so flat."

"Oba's balls," Doc growled. "Major Owens didn't mention you were insane, kid."

Keel grinned. "Left that part out, huh? Well, the major didn't mention you had a hoodlum daughter you wanted to bring on as crew. Guess we're even."

Zora stuck up a finger. "Consultant. Not crew."

"Uh-huh."

*Ding.* A blue light lit up from an incoming comm.

Doc eyed it. "You gonna answer that?"

"Nope. That's just the port ordering us to surrender for an illegal takeoff. Best thing they've got are a couple of grounded Preyhunters on standby. We've already outrun them."

Reading her screen, Zora said, "Navicomputer says you can make the jump in four minutes."

"Already had a destination in mind?" Doc sounded surprised. Perhaps even impressed.

Keel gave him a sideways look. "You were Dark Ops, old man. You know how easy it is for your planned withdrawal strategy to evaporate in a Huskan's whisper. Or is all that too hazy to remember? Always have a backup, always have somewhere to go when everything turns pear-shaped."

Doc processed that. "So that little stunt back there... you knew the doors would open."

"Of course. It's a bluff. One ship goes up in a fireball and the port loses hours', maybe days' worth of traffic. Everyone's grounded. Cheaper to let someone run out on the fees."

"I'll give it to you, kid. That was pretty pro."

The *Six* soared above Rakka's atmosphere, the planet a spinning brown-and-blue ball beneath them, a garbage heap of packed earth, duracrete, and crime.

Keel was glad to leave it behind.

# 10

"So," Doc said as the *Indelible VI* made its final jump calculations, "are we ready to talk about what comes next? Because everything I've seen so far tells me you ain't ready for this job, Keel."

"Really? After that bit of flying?"

"Ain't talkin' about your skills. I mean your reputation. Some lowlife nobody pirates think they can just drop a bottom-rate bounty and take your ship? That means they think Aeson Keel is a sucker."

Keel grimaced. Cheap shot, but Gramps had a point.

"Yeah. And now they're dead. Some of 'em, anyway."

"Until the next time," Doc pointed out. "When maybe they get lucky. And a rep'll do more for you than a blaster ever can, if you know how to use it right."

"Not sure how rep fixes a problem like that when dealing with people who, by definition, are murderous criminals."

"It makes 'em scared, dammit! So afraid of you that they piss themselves just thinking about what would happen to them if they tried something. Rep does all the work before you even show up."

Keel was skeptical. "That easy, huh?"

"Didn't say it was easy. But it can be done."

"Like Tyrus Rechs," Zora chimed in, speaking the name Keel had teased her with back in the docking bay.

Grudgingly, Doc said, "Yeah. Like him."

"Capture or kill on sight," Keel replied, reciting long-standing orders from on high. There seemed as much myth as truth about the notorious bounty hunter.

"You think that punk Lao Pak would have taken potshots at the T-Rex?" Doc said. "Hell no! He'd've packed his bags and gone into hiding until he was sure that maniac had left the planet. Then he'd wait another two weeks to come out of whatever gurp's nest he calls a home. That's who *you* need to be, Keel. That's what all your skills can make you into... if you know how."

"I need to be Lao Pak?" Keel joked. He just couldn't take this seriously.

"Oba, take me now," Doc groaned.

Zora crossed her arms and looked at Keel. "You really are an idiot."

"I'm *kidding*. So I need to be Tyrus Rechs. Sure. I'll put in an application. Or is that why you brought Zora—to help me study for the big Bronze Guild test to become the next Tyrus Rechs?"

"What you'll put in is work," Doc said with a senior drill sergeant's gleam in his eye. "That's what you'll do. And we'll help. That's why Zora's here."

"We're going to turn you into a bounty hunter, Keel. Like me." Zora tossed her head. "Just not as good."

"Well, one can dream," Keel said.

Zora raised a delicate brow. "Do you not have an off switch?"

Doc growled, "Woulda flipped it if he did, girlie."

"Bounty hunter." Keel turned the idea over in his mind. "And this is what Owens wants?"

"He gave the okay, yeah," Doc replied. "You want this mission to succeed, you go down this road. You wanna sit in some jail cell while your kill team chases ghosts... drop us off wherever you're going. Honestly, I couldn't care less either way."

Zora rolled her eyes at Doc's words. "Listen, jump jockey—you don't realize just how much bounty hunters can keep their fingers on the pulse of the galaxy simply by reading the contracts that come in. Especially once you're good enough to get the jobs they won't offer to the rookies." A green light flashed on her screen. "Navs are set," she added. "We're on standby to jump."

Keel sighed. "All right. I'll give it a try. This mission... it's important. To me. To the Legion."

Zora clapped her hands over her mouth, then turned to her father. "He has principles after all!"

"Don't spread it around," Keel said. "I'm trying to become a new kind of lowlife. Make the jump."

With the press of a button from his definitely-not-crew co-pilot, the stars extended into elongated beams of light and the *Indelible VI* shifted into the humming swirl of hyperspace.

Doc settled into his seat and let out a lungful of air in a raspy exhalation. "Okay, so—"

"Here comes the AAR," Zora whispered to Keel.

"—After Action Report," Doc continued. "Keel, you fly the way a leej shoots, and I mean that as a compliment. Sustain that. But you gotta let us in on what's happenin', kid. If Zee lost trust and tried to take the controls, we'd all be carbon right now. And *you*..." Doc leaned forward in his seat to look at his daughter. "We already covered the need to fill us in—*first thing*—on any security breaches. Still can't believe you didn't say nothin'. But my big issue is you weren't where you were s'posed to be. One of you was likely to kill the other over a karking misunderstanding!"

"Wouldn't have been me," Keel said, drawing daggers from Zora.

"Yeah, every leej thinks he'll live forever until he don't." Doc folded his arms, letting them rest on top of a paunch that surely hadn't existed when he was a younger man.

"Okay, my turn," Keel said.

"You don't get a turn," Doc groused.

"I'll go then," Zora said.

"You either, girlie. If I want either of your opinions I'll ask for it. What we need to do now is work out the details of our plan so everyone is on the same page."

"I was gonna say not to be so cheery," Keel said, giving his own AAR despite the old man's stubbornness.

Zora laughed into her hand.

Doc leaned forward again. "You ain't seen me in a bad mood yet, funny guy. And you don't wanna. Here's the plan. We're making you a hunter. Givin' you a rep. Zora lined you up some jobs that shouldn't be too tough for a leej but will get your name out there in a hurry so long as you get 'em done."

"I'll get 'em done," Keel insisted.

"Damn right you will, or I wouldn't have agreed to be here in the first place." Doc sniffed and wiped a finger beneath his nose. "We gotta give you a name, too."

"What's wrong with Keel?" Keel asked.

Doc arched an eyebrow, a twinkle of mischief in his eye. "Where should I begin?"

Keel frowned. He'd stepped right into that one. "I mean, what's wrong with the name?"

"Nothin', so long as you build up a rep to match, but we ain't exactly got all the time in the universe to do that.

You're a nobody, kid. And everybody's gotta hear about a nobody the first time before they become a somebody. You follow?"

"Oddly enough," Keel said.

"Good. So it's this way. Put yourself in the mind of some lowlife bunk killer. You got a bounty on your head. Hunters have been comin' for those credits and you've left 'em all bleedin' out in the gutters across a half-dozen star systems. But there's this new guy out for you, and his name is..." Doc held out his hands as if envisioning the letters on a marquee, "... Aeson Keel." He paused. "Don't exactly make a guy piss his pants, do it?"

"No," Keel said. "That would be the old age if you're asking."

"I ain't asking," Doc snapped. "And you gotta think of something better than Keel. Something that makes the kelhorn say, 'Sket, what kind of a guy is behind a name like that?'"

Keel turned to Zora. "What's your bounty hunter name, sweetheart?"

"Oh no," she said. "You have my first name, and that's already more than I wanted."

"It's Blackheart or somethin' like that," Doc announced from the back seat, drawing a look of annoyance from Zora. "And that's a hell of a lot better than Keel. *Keel* sounds like you're talkin' through a plugged nose."

Keel drummed his fingers on the flight console. He'd had a nickname in the Legion, and he wondered if that wouldn't be exactly what the pair sharing his cockpit might be after. "Back in the Legion... they called me Wraith."

"Wraith." Doc savored the word in his mouth, then snapped his fingers. "Wraith. Yeah. Good. Zee?"

Zora nodded almost begrudgingly. "Yeah. I can't think of any hunter who goes by that name. Wraith could work."

Doc clapped his hands. "Okay. That's settled." He held out a data chit for Keel. "Dump us out of hyperspace somewhere and deliver us here. We got a meeting for your first job. Zee and I are gonna go get ourselves settled."

The old man and his daughter stood up together and shuffled between the seats to the cockpit exit.

"Wraith," Doc mumbled to himself. "Not bad, kid. Not bad."

Keel almost missed a step as he walked into the *Indelible VI*'s armory. He had been overseeing some final readouts in the cockpit while the others settled in. It hadn't occurred to him that "settling in" might include standing around only half-dressed in his armory.

"Oh—" he said. "Didn't know you were—why are you changing clothes in here? You have a bunk. At least use the fresher or something."

Zora grinned at his discomfort. "I'm not changing clothes," she said, and went back to laying out her kit. She stood in jump pants and a tight-fitting tank top that covered... well, barely enough. Or just too much, depending on your point of view. Her overshirt and armor were laid out across the table along with an assortment of weapons that covered every square inch of usable space.

"Oh. My mistake," Keel said. "I see someone with their clothes half off and usually—"

"This is an *armory*," Zora said, cutting his sarcastic apology short. "So I'm modifying my armor. Need it to hide beneath my clothes."

"And here I thought wearing the armor on the *outside* was a bounty hunter's thing. Also, not sure if you're aware of the basic universal law of physics, but if you put *those* clothes over *that* armor"—Keel pointed to both helpfully —"people are gonna notice."

"I'm not going to wear the armor you're pointing at," Zora patiently, and somewhat patronizingly, replied. "*That* armor is unique. Last thing I need is for the Bronze Guild to think I'm anywhere near this... training exercise to help you become what you're supposed to become."

"Why's that?" Keel asked.

"Because you aren't going Guild. Because you want the real down and dirty jobs the Republic would declare war on the Guild for. Because *I* still want to go back to the Guild in good standing, and because that doesn't happen if it gets out that I helped you become an independent hunter."

She picked up the overshirt and held it out by the shoulders so he could see the synth-armor lining. "I moved the interior plating from the hardware into this. Some protection is better than none at all."

Keel grunted. "Suppose so."

Zora pulled the ungainly shirt over her head, exposing a bit more of herself, if that was possible, in the process. She attempted to pull the armored overshirt down, but it hitched up on itself. "Ugh, my shirt's stuck back there. Little help?"

Keel moved behind her to give the fabric a few downward yanks.

"Thanks," Zora said, pulling at her sleeves to get the shirt just right. "How visible are the plates?"

"You're welcome. And I can still see them. Maybe if you wear a jacket or something."

She grunted and grabbed a leather spacer's jacket, much like Keel's, from a pile at her feet.

Keel crossed his arms and leaned against a container storing an aero-precision launcher and missiles. "So, what is this little contract you and your father have lined up for us?"

Zora pulled the jacket on with a snap. "Don't say that word."

Keel was confused. "Contract?"

"Father."

The confusion faded. "Huh. Seemed like a fairly accurate descriptor."

"And yet."

Keel eyed the woman standing in his armory. "Yeah. I get it. So what is this little contract you and *Doc* have lined up for us?"

Zora didn't look up as she continued checking over her equipment. "He wants to be the one to give you the details. But it's a non-Guild job, as you've gathered. Not sanctioned by the Republic. Which is rich, because the Republic has no end of non-Guild contracts it puts out. If you're on their goody-goody list." She picked up her K-17 and proceeded to disassemble it, beginning with the charge pack.

"How 'bout you? You on the goody-goody list?"

"Not for a loooong time." She picked up the barrel, eyed it, then started cleaning.

"Fair enough." Keel raised both eyebrows. "So... an illegal bounty. I thought the point of your old—uh, *the* old man helping me was to keep me *out* of prison."

"So don't get caught."

Keel quirked a grin. "Planning like that... you should've been a general."

Zora's quick hands moved to the barrel and vent chamber. She took a brush to both.

"In all," she said, "it's not the route I'd take if I were looking to make a name in the trade. The Bronze Guild provides protection and legitimacy that are worth something out on the edge. That's how Tyrus Rechs does what he does. But this path you're about to go on... it has its own advantages. Faster, for one. And it seems to me that speed is something both you and Doc are after."

Keel rubbed his chin. "Just how much did the old man tell you about—"

Zora scoffed. "Less than you'd think. Look, Keel—"

"You can call me Aeson."

"I like Keel better."

The smuggler shrugged. "Been called worse."

Zora clicked her rifle back together. "Point is, none of us are angels out here at galaxy's edge. I don't need to know what you're doing. Don't want to know. And don't you ask about me."

Keel could appreciate that. "Closet full of skeletons, huh? I guess you look the type."

Setting her weapon down, Zora shot him a pixie grin. "Oh, do I?"

Keel wondered where this was going. In his experience, female bounty hunters often behaved a lot like female emergency nurses. There was a certain... craziness. "Yeah... you do."

Zora's smile widened, catlike. "What? What's that look?"

"Where's the blaster pistol?" Keel asked.

"What?" Zora looked confused at the change of topics.

"Usually you'd strap your blaster rig outside your armor. You're going incognito... so where are you concealing it?"

Her smile came back. "Wouldn't you like to know?" she said, her eyebrows lifting. "It's on the table... waiting."

Just then the doors swished open and Doc walked in. He looked from his daughter to Keel and asked, "Waiting for what?"

"Waiting for... the meeting," Zora supplied.

Frowning, Doc said, "What meeting?"

"For the job," Keel said hurriedly. "Can't wait. Can not wait. Gonna go put on my armor."

"Oh, I see," Doc said quietly.

"Listen, Doc—"

"You ain't puttin' on no armor, boy."

Keel wasn't sure how much Zora's father had picked up on the unexpected—but not unwelcome—sexual tension in the room, so he eagerly jumped on the new topic and kept talking. It was a tactic that had gotten him out of many a touchy spot in the past.

"Wait. What? I thought I... uh, *Wraith* had a job lined up. Wraith is a bounty hunter. Bounty hunters wear armor."

"They do, and Wraith does. But Wraith ain't showin' up to this meeting. It's beneath him. Rule One: Wraith doesn't ever talk to anyone unless *Keel* makes it happen."

"So what, I'm Wraith's messenger boy? Is that it?"

"I think he's got it!" Zora exclaimed.

"Cute," Keel told her, then to Doc: "I figured Keel *was* Wraith, and everybody would know it. We're tryin' to make people believe I'm two different guys? Nobody's gonna think that's weird? That Wraith and Keel... I can't believe I'm talking about myself as two different people... that those two are working together, only no one ever sees them in the same place?"

"It ain't as weird as you're makin' it out, kid. The big hitters, you can't approach 'em direct. They all got layers. You want 'em, you make nice with the lower level."

"He's right," Zora put in. "How easy would it be for you to get directly on comm with, say, Delegate Kaar's office? It wouldn't. His handlers have handlers. Same with the crime lords and big-time smuggling rings. For most of us hunters, it's the Guild that filters out the cheapskates from those able to pay for the real deal. You're independent, and from what Doc says, we're all the support you've got, so we have to be creative here."

"And you're *sure* you know what you're doing?" Keel asked them both.

Doc coughed a laugh. "Ha ha, smart-ass. Be ready to put us in the moment we arrive in system. If this don't work, it's gonna be because of *you*."

# 11

New Southampton prided itself on being an up-and-coming segment of Starijia's most cosmopolitan metropolis. Durasteel-and-glass skyscrapers had rapidly replaced duracrete tenements, forcing the poorer residents of past generations to the city's fringes. Property values had soared higher than a yoontz nest for the lucky few who'd managed to hold on to their colony plots, earned long ago by the first to settle this planet. All of which had given architects ample budgets and contractors cushy margins—before the local regulators arrived to stick their fingers in the financial pie, anyway. But as for the common man on the street, life had only gotten worse. Many of the downtrodden wore scowling faces the same as Doc at the sight of more off-worlders coming to visit, further driving up the cost of... everything.

Doc was grumpy for a different reason. The sun beamed down hot today, scorching his bald head and making them all sweaty.

"This is the place," Keel said, looking up at the walled compound guarding an elegant villa. Balconies peered over the wall, far from the contamination of local foot traffic.

"And we're late," Doc gruffed.

"So? What're they gonna do, call the cops?" Keel said. "They're criminals asking us to do criminal things for them. They'll wait."

"It looks bad. Unprofessional."

"Looks bad for *Keel*. Wraith isn't late. And they want Wraith's help, not Keel's." The smuggler was starting to see that there were certain upsides to this new double life of his. He just needed to lean into them a little.

"Oba's nose," the old man sighed.

Zora cracked up. "He's got you there, Doc!"

"And you. Don't call me Doc. It's disrespectful. I'm your father."

Suddenly serious, Zora said, "You want me to call you 'Father' on a mission? Pretty sure that violates a 'Rule One' somewhere."

Doc rubbed perspiration off his bald pate. "Just sayin'... things don't have to be the way they've been."

"Hate to break up this family bonding," Keel said, "but that guard at the gate is giving us the stink eye."

A hulking, tawny wobanki, clad in a leather vest and trousers, was balefully glaring their way. The hairy catman looked hungry. Or suspicious. Probably a mixture of both.

"That's Leeke, our contact," Doc said. "And he's *probably* mad that we're late."

"So... does anyone understand wobanki?" Zora asked.

"Yeah," Keel replied. "But most are good enough at charades even if we didn't."

"All right. Here's the plan," Doc started, but Keel was already moving.

"I've got it," he said, then gave a big wave and called out, "Hey! Wobanki! Leeke! Tell your boss Aeson Keel is here."

Striding to keep up with him as he headed for the gate, Zora muttered, "Going for subtlety, I see."

"Dammit, kid," Doc whispered.

"You two gave me the part, now I'm going to play it," Keel subvocalized. "So keep up and pipe down."

The trio walked up to the wobanki, who looked much larger up close, and much angrier too. He growled like a ram-panther who had just had his tail pulled, revealing teeth as sharp as ice picks.

"Don't growl at me, hairball," Keel said. "And don't keep us standing outside." At this time of day, the sun blazed straight overhead, and the musk of an overheated wobanki smelled none too pleasant.

"*Tenga nachu o'bong Wraitharoo,*" Leeke growled.

"Yeah. He is," Keel replied. "And he sent me."

"*Ocho chappa.*"

"You the one paying for the job?"

"*No tabu janki.*" The wobanki still looked mad, but at least Keel had his attention.

"Exactly. And Wraith doesn't take meetings. We all got layers. So let's hurry up and get this deal done."

"*Tengu janki nobba,*" the wobanki said, and held out an empty paw.

"A finder's fee?" Keel exclaimed. "I found you on my own. You were standing right outside."

"*Tengu janki!*" Leeke yowled.

"What's he saying?" Zora asked.

"He wants some credits to let us in."

"One of those, huh?" Doc said, then pulled out his surge shotgun. He primed it—loudly—and the wobanki yelped in surprise.

"Put the gun down, Doc," Zora said.

The old man glared up at the cat through his sights. "You wanna get paid, wobanki?"

Keel shook his head. "Always with the shotgun."

Clearly distressed, Leeke held up his paws, claws retracted. "*Gabba cho bagga! Gabba cho bagga!*"

"Yeah, well you *found* trouble," Keel told him. No turning back now, and it never paid to show dissension in the ranks in a situation like this. "If you don't want the old man, who hasn't had his prune-mush this morning so... kind of grumpy... to dust you, you let us in. Now. And as payment... you get to live. Sound good?"

Purring, the wobanki quickly agreed, then clawed the security panel. With a creak, the black gates behind him parted to a small courtyard and stone stairs leading up to the front door.

"Thanks, buddy," Keel said. "Up the stairs inside?"

The wobanki nodded. "*Yip! Gabba cho bagga.*"

"Then don't do anything stupid. C'mon, let's go."

As Keel and his partners headed up the steps, Leeke yowled out behind them, "*No kawa blasteroos!*" as if he'd just now remembered to do his job.

"Think we'll keep 'em anyway, Leeke," Keel said over his shoulder as he led the way into air conditioning.

The villa was less a home and more an office building with colony-world taste—tiled floors, stucco wall embellishments, a tinkling fountain, and a single marble bench that said *rest a while, weary traveler, but not too long*. Waiting behind a desk was another guard. This one human, in uniform, and armed.

"Hold it right there. No blasters allowed in the building."

"Look at you," Doc growled at the man. "You're s'posed to be the last line of security before your boss and all you got on is that uniform? Pathetic."

The guard gave a confused look at the trio.

Keel made a calming motion at Doc and then addressed the guard. "Leeke said it was fine. But if your boss wants to lose her shot at getting Wraith to work for her, we can leave." He took a step back as if he was ready to do just that.

Faced with a dilemma and a quick decision, the guard said, "Okay. Head in."

The doors ahead of them slid open.

"Nice armor you got there, doorman," Doc said as they walked past, then, under his breath, muttered, "Amateur."

They passed a plaque that declared this the private office of Mina Croft, and behind a massive mahogany desk sat the woman herself, her hair perfectly, painfully coiffed. She set down her glasses.

"Ardo!" she called, evidently wanting the guard at the front desk. Then to the trio entering her office: "You'll have to excuse me. I'm expecting someone, and in any event blasters are not permitted on—"

"Sorry we're late," Keel said jovially. "The wobanki you have stationed outside... he's a talker."

Understanding dawned on Mina Croft's face. The guard entered the room and was just as quickly shooed back out. He closed the door behind him.

Croft studied the three humanoids in her office for some time as a chrono ticked unseen from some corner.

"Which one of you is the Wraith?" she finally asked.

Keel looked around as though expecting to see the bounty hunter, then turned back to Croft. "None of us. I'm Captain Aeson Keel, and this is my crew. Zora and, uh, Old Man."

"Wise-ass," Doc said under his breath. Then he turned on his own gentlemanly charm. "Ms. Croft, I'm Doc. We spoke about making arrangements for your... concern."

"I remember," Croft replied. "I also remember stating the need for the matter to be handled with care and discretion. Forgive me, but the three of you barging in, *armed*, doesn't seem fitting with that instruction."

"You're forgiven," Keel said. "Now. What do you need Wraith to do?"

"My *intention* was to tell Mr. Wraith that."

"He don't go by 'mister,' and *his* intention is for you to tell *me*. Then I tell him, and then I tell you what he tells me."

Ms. Croft gave an icy smile. "And Mr. Doc and your female companion. Zora, was it?"

"We're just here to make sure all the details are correct," Zora explained. "Wraith doesn't allow us to holo-record or keep written records, so, three memories are better than one."

The chrono ticked some more.

"I can see that there's little point in arguing," Ms. Croft said. "Oba knows how hard it's been to get anyone—anyone qualified, that is—to accept this job. Damned spineless Bronze Guild."

"Yeah, it's a real shame," Keel agreed.

"Ardo, please close the door and keep yourself on the other side," Ms. Croft said.

Keel turned and noticed that the door to the room wasn't closed all the way after all, but was slightly ajar.

The guard poked his head in. "Ma'am?"

"I'm sure I made myself clear, Ardo."

Chastised, the guard said, "Yes, ma'am," and left, pulling the old-fashioned door shut behind him. All the way this time.

Ms. Croft studied Keel severely. "You have heard, I imagine, of Cal Camp."

Zora nodded. "The monster of Mirshra."

The woman gave a cold nod. "The very same."

"You want us to get Cal Camp?" Keel asked. "The Guild, the Republic, and half a dozen other planets already have bounties on his head. He's a ghost."

"Not Cal Camp. But a protégé of his, as it were. A man named Adam Maven. Though he usually goes by some variation of that name."

"Never heard of the guy," Doc said, looking to his daughter for some context. "But Zora, you have?"

"Yeah. His name is out there. But he's considered untouchable. The Guild won't go anywhere near him."

Keel wasn't too sure how he felt about taking on a bounty even the Guild wouldn't touch.

"Rightly stated," Ms. Croft agreed. "The man has... powerful connections. He is protected. A wayward son with influential parents who can't come to grips with the monster their child has become. And so they choose to protect him, careless of the pain he has caused to those with the great misfortune of ever having met him."

"Like you," Keel guessed.

"Not me. My daughter," Ms. Croft said quietly.

"I'm sorry," Doc told her.

Keel glanced at the old man, who looked like he meant it.

"It was years ago." Croft struggled for a moment. "He was... the last person she ever met. And her last hours of life..." She squeezed her eyes shut, steeling herself against tears or weakness, probably both. "The bounty is one hundred and fifty thousand credits. You will deal alone with whatever fallout may follow; my name will *not* come out of any of your mouths. I will deny all knowledge of this arrangement, and do believe me when I say that I have the resources to shut you up."

"Just not enough resources to catch your daughter's killer," Keel observed, to which Zora kicked his ankle without any pretense of subtlety.

Ms. Croft pursed her lips tightly. "No. It seems there is always someone with *more* credits at their disposal. Justice can be bought. But... so can vengeance. On that I've placed my last hope."

"Well, your secret will be safe," Keel told her. "Wraith doesn't talk."

"I'm more concerned with his messengers. *You* certainly seem to do a lot of talking, Captain Keel."

Doc stepped forward. "He won't talk, either. All of us know what Wraith will do to us if we did."

Ms. Croft's sharp eyes weighed the trio. "We shall see."

"What would help us right now, ma'am," Doc said, "is to see whatever intelligence you might have on the target. Last known whereabouts. Anyone he might associate with."

"If he's with Cal Camp, he's not being found," Zora put in.

"He's not," Ms. Croft replied. "Of that my people are sure. The pair had a falling-out. He's relying on his family to protect him, rather than Camp's considerable abilities in covering their tracks. That's why it is urgent that your employer take this contract. I have no way of knowing when he'll disappear again."

Keel nodded. "Well, send us what you've got and then Wraith will give you the final word."

Ms. Croft looked surprised. "I was under the impression Wraith had *already* agreed to the job."

"Not the job, lady. Just the meeting. Be happy you didn't have to pay for that privilege."

"I see. Well." She smiled thinly. "Since I'm left with no alternative, I'll await his decision."

As they headed for the door, her clear voice rang out again.

"A moment. Should he accept, tell Wraith that I don't expect or desire that Mr. Maven be taken alive."

Keel turned back. "I'll tell him," he assured her.

Ms. Croft held his gaze. "And tell him to take his time."

"I'll tell him that, too."

# 12

Leaving the cool of the villa and stepping back out into the city heat was like walking into a starfighter's backblast. Instant regrets. Keel tugged open his collar to let out what heat he could, then waded into heavy sled traffic, considering hailing a lift back to the *Indelible VI*. It seemed the locals knew better than to walk at this time of day; the repulsor traffic was so thick it had hovered to a halt, idling nose-to-bumper in all the lanes he could see. Walking would be faster, but no one was foolish enough to be out in this heat.

"Maybe this was a bad idea," Doc grumbled.

Keel assumed the man didn't mean walking. "Why? I did what you asked, right? Don't tell me you're getting cold feet, old man."

"You did great. Better than I'd hoped, actually. Really played it up like you were only a smug, irreverent punk who knew no one was gonna challenge you because of who you're friends with. Must've been a real stretch for you."

"Thanks. Nice to hear I'm so appealing."

"Appealing? Heck no. But mark my words: you keep this up and you'll get the access you need."

"Now we just need Wraith to do his end," Keel said.

"That's the part I'm not so sure about."

"Why?" Zora asked. "I picked out this job specifically for what you wanted."

Doc stared straight ahead, but his voice was hot and agitated. "And it turned out to be a kelhorned *termination* contract!"

"So?"

"So Wraith is a bounty hunter," Doc said. "Not an assassin."

"Contracts and terminations go hand in hand," Zora said. "The best hunters do both."

Doc considered that. "I suppose you're—"

"Let's not kid ourselves," Zora continued. "We've all killed before. You were in Dark Ops, Dad. You've probably killed more than Keel and me combined."

Feeling the need to interject, Keel said, "Well, let's not get carried away..."

Doc frowned. "My own daughter. Killing people for credits."

"Again, pretty much what you did in Dark Ops, old man," she shot back, "just for a much smaller paycheck."

Doc placed a hand on his daughter's arm, stopping their progress. "That was different, Zee. You know it was."

"Anyway." Zora kept walking. "This job being a termination isn't the issue. Oba knows this twarg-sniffer deserves it. It's a job that *everyone* knows about but no one will take."

She'd brought up something that Keel had been thinking about. "You just mentioned the part I need some help with. Hired killers aren't exactly known for their clemency. Yet you're telling me *no one* will go after this kelhorned piece of sket?"

Zora shrugged. "No one who can do what needs doing. For one, Maven is dangerous in his own right. He's a killer, and while he favors young women as targets, you dig deep enough and you see that he's survived more than his share of the rough and tumble. Couple that with the protection he's getting from his family and the attendant retaliation that comes along with that... and he's all but untouchable."

"Who's his family?"

"Byrell Tooms."

Keel blinked. "Hold up. As in House of Reason Delegate Byrell Tooms?"

"How many Byrell Toomses do you think there are?" Zora replied. "Yes, that Byrell Tooms. Maven is his grandson. They're a very close family. Tooms refuses to even acknowledge the accusations. It's like they're living in their own reality."

"Sounds like a politician, all right. Okay. That gives me an idea of how to handle this."

The wheels were turning for Keel, but the old man decided to stick his cane into the cogs.

"Best way to handle this is to forget it," Doc said. "Right approach, wrong job. This'll get you thrown right back in prison, and this time nobody is gonna get you out. Zee, you said it yourself. He's got connections, which means Wraith gets hounded non-stop if he does this. A rep don't do you no good if you ain't got room to maneuver."

They walked in silence for a while, past idling hover vehicles sweltering in the heat, the crisp stench of burning ozone competing with the spicy street food and sweet pastries vendors sold, not that much of anyone outside. The sellers, shading themselves beneath awnings, didn't even bother to make the exertion of calling out to Keel and company as they walked by. The only movement was the green-tipped sparrens—an invasive species of bird—darting about looking for crumbs.

"What? No smart-ass comment?" Doc finally asked.

"Being followed," Keel muttered. He'd heard a regular tread behind them for the past block or two; now it was getting closer.

"You see who it was?" Zora asked quietly, with no break in her smile or stride. Keel had to give the woman credit— she knew enough not to immediately turn and look for herself. A sure way to tip off whoever was following that you knew about it.

"Only heard 'em," he said. "Unless we want to buy some meat-on-a-stick and risk taking a gander. Humanoid from the way they're walking."

The other two strained their ears.

"I don't hear anything except repulsors," Zora said.

"So maybe it's my imagination," Keel answered. "But I've been listening to it for a while now."

"Here's the plan," Doc said. "We turn into the alley up ahead. I pull my shotgun, we shoot the first thing with an angry look that turns the corner."

"Yeah," Keel said. "That plan doesn't sound like anything could possibly go wrong with it."

"I got trigger discipline," Doc protested.

"Keel is right," Zora said. "No back-alley ambushes. Not the kind of attention we need."

"Law of the jungle," the old man said. "I sure as sket taught you how the galaxy works. Cities ain't no different. In fact, they're *more* dangerous."

Zora remained unconvinced. "No. It's probably someone with Ms. Croft. Let's just go to the ship. Way less crowded—and watched—than here. And if they want to try something there... it won't go well for them."

Keel wiped beads of sweat from his brow. "I'd rather as few people as possible know where we're docked. I vote we turn the tables on 'em soon as we can, but how about let's don't kill anyone until we have to."

"It could be a mugger," Doc said hopefully. "One of them Hool gangbangers. KTF, Keel. You know that much."

Keel looked at the man. "What is wrong with you? You some kind of vigilante?"

"Yes," both Doc and his daughter put in at once.

"I got some issues with street punks," Doc explained tersely. "Don't wanna talk about it."

Keel took in a breath and wondered if Owens—and Dark Ops for that matter—was as familiar with the old man as it had first seemed. Then again, it wasn't like Keel himself was being sent out to walk the straight and narrow. And he knew well enough not to pry when a man made his boundaries clear.

"Fine by me," was all he said.

Zora nodded across the street. "That alley is as good a place as any if you really want to have it out before we reach the ship."

Keel gave a fractional nod and led the trio through the stalled traffic and across the street.

"You two get about halfway down," Zora said. "I'll hang back and get the drop." And with the passing growl of a municipal repulsor truck, moving quickly in its own reserved and automated lane, Zora was gone.

"Why not let me make the introductions when this kelhorn follows?" Doc asked as he and Keel turned into the alley, which in the day's heat radiated a sauna-like stink and humidity.

"Because I'm worried you'll kill them on accident," Keel said. "Or on purpose."

Doc scoffed, but they both knew it was true.

They tramped down the alley, stained and soured by decades of unidentified liquids and neglect. From somewhere, a leaky drainpipe dripped.

They waited.

The silence lengthened.

"So... what should we talk about while we wait to be jumped?" Keel asked.

"Wouldn't be getting jumped if you'd have done what I said, kid."

Keel scoffed. "Sure. Let's just murder everyone who looks shady. How in the nine hells did Owens think *you'd* keep *me* out of trouble? I have to keep *you* out of it." Suddenly his situation seemed unwarranted and unfair. "Hey. You're not related to Owens too, are you? Like, some crazy father-in-law he's unloading on me?"

"Nah. He just saw the difference between you and me."

Keel sighed. "I'll probably regret this, but fine. What's the difference... aside from the amount of wrinkles on our —"

"Difference between me and you, kid, is that I know how to use this." The old leej hoisted his surge shotgun with its pistol grip one-handed and pumped it. "*Without* getting tossed in the clink."

"Put that surger away or you'll scare off our tail."

"I don't wanna just scare him. I wanna—"

Something pounced around the corner. Leeke. His green eyes fastened on Keel, and he growled.

"*Kobba janki nobba. Keel-oo.*"

"Oh. Hey, Leeke," Keel said, flashing Doc a look as if to say, *See?* "Didn't hear you sneaking up. And I already told you: no finder's fee. That why you're following us?"

The wobanki's gleaming eyes narrowed, and his tail twitched. "*Tangu janki.*"

"Sure. The credits. Is that what your boss wants, or are you going independent?"

Two tawny ears flicked back. "*Abu matchka, Leeke.*"

Keel laughed. "You were insulted? Forget it. The old man insults everyone. He's a crusty old tyrannasquid that wouldn't know happiness if she came swimming by with pink skin and violet eyes. That doesn't make what you're doing smart. You're bordering on some serious trouble, wobanki."

"*Pokka mok mok?*" Leeke asked.

Keel shrugged. "Maybe she had to use the fresher. What's it to you?"

"Careful, kid," Doc muttered. "Looks like he's about to draw."

"Not yet he isn't," Keel whispered back. "But I'm wondering the same thing as the cat. Where *is* your daughter?"

"She knows what she's doing."

Keel hoped so.

"Listen, Leeke. If I make the old man apologize, are we good? Wraith is waiting. We got a schedule."

"I ain't apologiizn'," Doc growled.

Leeke sniffed then sneezed, as if ridding himself of an offensive smell. "*Tangu janki. Janki tobba doe,*" he said carefully.

Keel rolled his eyes. "Credits *are* nicer than an apology, but that ain't happening."

Leeke growled, baring his teeth, then crouched to pounce.

Behind him, a blaster whined.

"Okay. I've heard enough," Zora said, stepping out into the alley, her hand blaster aimed at the wobanki's head.

"This cat's all talk. And you're gonna tuck your tail and leave now or I'll send a blaster bolt through your skull."

Leeke growled, rumbling through his barrel chest.

"Ha!" Doc cried. "You heard her, kittycat. Thought you wobankis were apex predators. Couldn't hear a human sneak up on you, though, huh? And for the record, *I don't apologize.*"

Keel shook his head. "Sure. Goad him on."

"Head back to your boss, Leeke," Zora said calmly. "Break time's over. If we see you following us again... well, you won't survive our next meeting."

Not to be defeated so easily, Leeke hissed, "*Jawa kop, taggu. Keel-o.*"

"Regrets I can handle," Keel said. "We'll pass on your compliments to Wraith."

With one final growl, Leeke slunk out of the alley.

Zora powered down her blaster. "He's gone."

"Shoulda blasted him," Doc remarked.

Keel watched to make sure the catman didn't double back. "Something tells me we'll get another chance."

# 13

"Ackabar," Zora said. She sat in the co-pilot's seat, studying the viewscreen as they neared the immense planet. Swirling purple clouds danced a slow waltz across the atmosphere, sometimes obscuring the orange-and-green terrain below. "I suppose it makes sense he'd be hiding on a planet like this."

The deliberations, once safely aboard the *Indelible VI*, hadn't taken long. "Wraith" accepted the mission, Keel contacted Croft, and they were provided a dossier put together by some "*very* capable" detectives that was supposed to lead to their target. Ms. Croft had spared no expense in her crusade; Wraith, as she saw it, was the final piece to bringing her dreams of vengeance to a satisfying conclusion.

But they had to find the target first. Kill him second.

As with most things, it was easier said than done.

"You ever do any missions on Ackabar, Keel?" Doc asked.

"Negative."

"Place is an armpit. Smells like a Drusic's undercarriage."

"You sure got a way with words, old man," Keel replied.

"Don't I know it."

"It's about as dangerous as a Drusic, too," Zora added.

Keel had had his own fair share of run-ins with the powerful ape-like aliens. Oba had blessed the oversized gorilla-men—and women—with a bit too much testosterone. Made misunderstandings at cantinas frequent and messy.

"I'm gonna call in to Croft," Keel said. "Make sure nothing's changed since we made the jump here."

Ms. Croft's pensive but severe face sprang up on holo, as if she'd been biding her time just waiting for his comm. "Yes. I'm here."

"So are we," Keel said. "Just arrived over Ackabar. Wraith will infiltrate once we do some surveillance. If your spies have any updated intel, now's the time to share it."

"Nothing new to report. We still believe he's inside the compound."

"Copy that. We'll report back in once the mission is completed."

He reached for the blue-flashing comm.

"Captain Keel." Ms. Croft stayed his finger.

"Yeah?"

"Though it is difficult to find a willing operative, this is not the first time someone has gotten close to that... murderer. Yet he always finds a way out. And those hunting him... disappear." A flash of pain crossed her face. "Always."

"We'll be careful," Keel assured her.

"I have no doubt." The clouds cleared, and Ms. Croft settled back into her usual icy calm. "Don't let him get away. For my daughter's sake."

Sober, Keel replied, "Wraith... will get it done. Keel out."

The holo dissolved.

Turning in his co-pilot's chair, Zora studied Keel. "Was that... *compassion* I detected?"

"Maybe she'll pay us a bonus."

"Of course." She winked.

"Worth a shot. You got us a landing pad?"

Zora tapped at the navigator interface. "Yup. Easy place to dock, Ackabar. As long as you pay in advance, they don't want to know anything."

*Pay in advance* weren't Keel's favorite words, but they weren't unexpected.

"They don't even want a registry?" he asked.

"Nope."

The incoming-comm chime sounded.

"Yeah?" Keel asked.

"Ackabar Ground to private freighter. You are cleared to land at North Pad 16-E."

"Copy that, Ackabar Ground," Zora replied.

"Private freighter?" Keel asked her. "Where's the fun in that?" He was honestly disappointed. "I had a good false registry lined up and everything. *Blooming Baroness.*"

"Save it for next time, kid," Doc said. "We gotta reconnoiter Maven's position. Then... let's take this kelhorn out."

"Who's staying and who's going?" Zora asked, looking at them both. "Because this is Ackabar, and Keel's ship can't defend itself."

"Well, I *have* to go," Keel said. "Wraith would insist."

"I don't wanna play no ship-nanny," Doc grumped.

Zora drew herself up. "We're only here because of me. So. Odds-Evens?"

Doc eyed her. "What're you, twelve again?"

Zora quirked a smile. "Worried you're gonna lose, like you always did when I *was* twelve?"

"I *let* you win back then. Fine. You're on. Shoot on three."

"Oh, this is high-speed," Keel said. "This how your kill team decided who had to hump the extra SAB packs?"

Doc and Zora gave each other the stare-down.

"Three, two, one... go!"

"Still no sign of him inside the compound," Zora told Keel as she used a pair of EM binos to survey the mansion ensconced behind duracrete-and-plasteen walls. The binos were an essential tool for every bounty hunter's kit, using the infinitesimally small electromagnetic pulses of an atom to map out, with decent accuracy, a building's interior. If Zora couldn't see Maven from here, the man must be deep inside the building behind some expensive shielding. Or... he wasn't there at all.

"But you see the two Hools," Keel said.

The presence of the two Hool bodyguards—Ms. Croft had reported that they accompanied Maven everywhere— were the surest sign of hope that the principal was inside as well. But anyone who had kept themselves free of consequences this long had probably learned a few tricks along the way. The Hools could be decoys, standing around aimlessly and buying the real guards and their charge time to get off-planet.

"Yeah... wait. Hold up. I'm counting about a dozen other armed guards all coming up from a shielded sub-level or something, on top of the six I can already see. That's more than we expected. Someone tipped him off. Sket."

"Had a feeling." Keel's voice remained even, undaunted by the complication.

"The wobanki?" Zora suggested.

"He'd be my first guess, yeah."

"Well, if it is him, he certainly doesn't think much of us," Zora said, putting her binos away.

"What makes you say that?"

She gestured at the mansion. "They're still here, aren't they? If they thought a real threat was coming—a Tyrus Rechs–level threat—they'd be long gone. They think they can handle us." She bit her lip in thought and then tapped her wrist-comm. "I'll call it in."

While they waited for Doc to answer, Keel asked, "You knew you were gonna beat the old man at that game, didn't you?"

"He throws a one every time. Hasn't changed since I was a kid."

"And you've never mentioned it. You just let your old man keep on losing."

"Of course. That's how he raised me."

Keel gave a fractional nod. He was stuck with this duo and the intricacies of their father/daughter relationship, unless he wanted to disobey orders and jeopardize the entire mission. Which would end up with some other leej being plucked from the ranks to replace him, or worse, the entire operation being dropped outright as unfeasible. He wanted to avoid both scenarios. So... may as well get a better understanding of what made those on his team tick. He'd done much the same as a kill team leader, and before that a platoon leader in the regular Legion.

Doc's voice growled through Zora's comm. "You gotta get your AI fixed, Keel."

Keel smiled at the old man's whining. It was nice to hear someone else complain about that karked AI for a change. Misery does love company.

"You don't have to use it if you know what you're doing."

Doc grunted.

Zora got down to business. "They know we're coming. Any problems at the bay?"

"Just a couple of punks here and there. Don't think they're connected to what we're after. Now and then I lower the ramp to see if I can get 'em on board to blast 'em, but no takers."

Zora's face was unreadable.

"Tell me he's joking," Keel said.

"I ain't kiddin' and the galaxy wouldn't miss 'em," Doc insisted.

In the background on the *Six*, a cheerful voice said, "I'm detecting three more life signs entering the bay. Shall I lower the ramp again? Oh! I do so hope we get visitors!"

"You pickin' up any weaponry?" Doc asked the ship's AI.

"I *am*! They are heavily armed. Oh! The stories these biologics could tell. Shall I lower the ramp?"

"No. Better not. Sket, I think this may be real trouble. And since the *Six* doesn't have any defensive weapons..."

Keel cut the scolding short. "Zora'll head back to help. Keel out."

The bounty hunter gave him a look that could have burned ice. "Zora will head back?"

Keel shrugged. "Only one of us can grab Maven, because this job is Wraith's. He can't work with Blackheart and the Bronze Guild, remember? And since they know we're coming... it's time to move."

"You cannot seriously be thinking about storming this compound by yourself like this."

"Oh. Right." Keel snapped his fingers. "Forgot my helmet." He slipped on his Legion bucket. "How's this?" he said, his voice as sharp and soulless as a karambit knife.

"You look and sound like a legionnaire."

"Makes sense, since this is Dark Ops armor. Hurry up. We can't lose the ship, and it's a good bet Maven's team is the one that's there, sniffing us out."

But Zora, like so many of her profession, wasn't easily dissuaded.

"You can't expect to single-handedly infiltrate a compound with over a dozen armed guards, ray-shielded walls, and Oba knows what other security features. You don't even know for sure that Maven's on site!"

From his ruck, Keel pulled a few pieces of cold matte-black durasteel, and with a few twists and clicks, it was ready.

He held the weapon up for Zora's inspection. "I've got it handled. See?"

"A micro-buster? Do you have any idea how illegal those things are?"

"Yeah. And I also know it'll do the job."

"This is crazy. *You're* being crazy. You'll kill everyone inside that compound with that thing."

"Hopefully."

Exasperated, Zora said, "There's no credits if you can't *prove* you killed the target, Keel."

"Not Keel. *Wraith.*"

"Oh, for the love of—" She shook her head. "Fine. I'll go back to the ship and clear out Doc's visitors. But if you have any sense, you'll wait for me here. Don't make a move unless you see the target trying to escape... assuming he hasn't already."

"I'll take it under advisement."

Zora thrust a finger at Keel's bucket. "Don't be an ass. And don't do anything stupid."

She stomped off and leapt on one of the two repulsor bikes they'd taken from the *Six's* cargo hold. In a storm of dust and grit, she zoomed away.

Wraith keyed his comm. "Okay. She's gone."

"Thanks for doing that, kid," Doc growled through Wraith's bucket. "Zora... you know how she is. She wouldn't have been able to stay out of it. The girl's good, but she ain't leej-good. Not yet anyway. Woulda been a lot easier if I'd have just beaten her in the game. Don't know how she manages to win so often. Bad luck I guess."

"Must be it. How'd you get the AI to play along? You didn't teach that thing to lie, did you?"

"Nah. Just had it read back a text string on cue," the wily vet said. "Simple trick."

"Not bad, old man."

"I ain't just a pretty face, kid. Okay. TT-16 bot is online. I got eyes on your position. Tryin' not to get too close in case they got something to shoot the drone down. Don't want you blind."

"Affirmative. I've got the micro-buster. Looking to make as big a splash in the courtyard as possible—take as many of the guards out as I can—and still have an opening into the building."

It was a hastily assembled plan that had been undertaken between the two soldiers while Zora was readying herself in her bunk. It was also the kind of mission that no Dark Ops commander would ever greenlight, and yet the kind Keel had always secretly hoped to execute. This kelhorn Maven deserved what was coming to him, and since Keel had left the rulebook behind when he'd signed out of the Legion, he was now free to deliver it.

Or rather, Wraith was.

"Now, Wraith," Doc began, "this ain't exactly how we learned to assault a compound. For my own conscience... you sure you wanna go forward?"

"Unless you've procured a kill team to cover my back, this is the way, Doc."

"Okay. There's a pack of 'em smoking H8 or something out back. I'll paint it and send your way."

Keel had already seen that through his own HUD. The old legionnaire was one of those fail-safe kind of operators. Do it all twice. Don't trust that the guys see what you see. Keel didn't mind it.

Four heat signatures were clumped together on Wraith's HUD map of the compound, just outside a northwest-facing back door that overlooked a patio and manicured garden beyond. Keel doubted they were smoking H8—that was just elderly paranoia. But they were clearly part of a security team. All well-armed. Legitimate targets.

And since Wraith had to make an entry point somewhere, taking out four potential problems right up front seemed like a no-brainer.

He synced the micro-buster's primitive launch system with his helmet's HUD, aiming the missile skyward until it confirmed that it had adequate room to maneuver its way to the target Doc had painted. He got a lock, and pressed the trigger. With a *FWUNG*, the rocket launched through the air, streaking into the compound like an angry star and detonating, raining grit and rubble.

"Direct hit!" Doc cried in his ear. "Compound is breached. Assault! Go go go!"

Wraith dashed forward into the cloud of dust, making for the main gate manned by two guards. The guards shook off their initial confusion to protect their post, rifles raised and searching for targets, but in the chaos, Wraith had the advantage. He double-tapped them both before they even saw him coming. Upon reaching their corpses, Wraith activated the gate controls and swung the entryway open, not bothering to disable any holocams; anyone watching already knew something bad was upon them.

"Gate breached," he said calmly.

Doc was equally sober. "Keep moving."

"Entering compound."

"I see you. Nice and smooth. You gotta get to the hole you made. Go around the north-facing side to reach, but mind the windows."

N-4 rifle ready, Wraith flowed into the courtyard, using his tech and senses to scan for threats. His heart raced from the adrenaline rush, but he slowed his breathing—in through his nose, out through his mouth—as he made his way through the rubble-strewn space. Above him, the mansion's dark windows stared down balefully, and twisting black smoke poured out of the ones on the lower level. The missile must have blasted deep into the target Doc had painted, reducing the "H8 smokers" to sticky stains in the rubble. At a minimum they were neutralized; the old man would have told him otherwise.

*Krish!* Window glass broke overhead. Wraith snapped his head up toward the sound, spotted movement at the gaping hole, and fired off two shots. The would-be sniper fell back inside with a lung-deflating groan.

"E-KIA," Wraith announced. "No more windows between here and the back of the house."

He made it to the back door without further incident. The missile blast had carved out a gaping hole in the wall that had taken a lot of house with it. That hole was being watched by someone with a blaster rifle, as was a window farther down. Wraith got low, skirting the impact crater and strewn body parts of those who'd been on the patio, and used the settling smoke to get up close to the mansion while avoiding detection by the guards.

Doc continued to report visuals from the TT-16 observation bot. "You got two Ecs showing on thermal. Can't make an ID through the infrared. Advise you frag 'em."

"Can't." Wraith reached the patio door, which seemed a pointless obstacle given the wide hole in the side of the mansion just ten meters down. He tried the handle, and it proved to be unlocked anyway.

"Why the hell not? Not like we're takin' our boy alive—"

"Popper out."

Rifle hanging on its sling, Wraith pushed the door open with one hand and tossed his ear-popper with the other. In an explosion of sound and light, the thing burst, ruining the day of anyone inside not currently wearing a Legion-rated bucket.

Wraith came in to find two guards slumped on the floor, holding their ears and writhing in blind, deaf agony. He put them both out of their misery.

"Two E-KIAs," he reported. "One Hool, one human."

"Maven?"

"Negative. Moving."

"Bot can't see you in there, kid."

"Roger. See you on the other side."

Wraith moved through the smoky house, his boots crunching on debris; even beyond the immediate blast radius, the force of the impact had sent decorations and lighting fixtures tumbling to the floor. Despite its luxurious exterior, the mansion looked built for a long stay under hostile conditions. Purely utilitarian. Duracrete walls, spare hallway, reinforced blast doors. Wraith pied the corner of the first doorway to find disordered boxes and supplies littering the floor. A storage closet.

"Room One clear."

He continued down the dark, hazy hallway, checking doors, to a stairwell leading up at the end. The remaining lights flickered. Something popped overhead and sparks flew, tracing their way down through the gathered smoke like little strands of lightning.

A power overload.

"Hallway clear," Wraith announced, then moved forward.

As he reached the foot of the stairwell, he heard a voice from the next level. "... can't leave it, so hurry *up*! Sket!"

Demanding. Petulant. Panicked.

"I think that's him," Wraith whispered. "Maven."

Wraith did the math. He'd dropped two guards at the gate. Four came apart on the patio. Two more when he breached. One sniper in the window. That made nine, whereas Zora had counted nearly twenty. He could have a real problem waiting for him upstairs.

Doc recognized the threat as well. That was a lot of blasters for someone all on his own to handle. "Careful. Just shoot the bastard and get out of there."

In the distance came the faint cry of approaching sirens. Emergency crews inbound.

Wraith slowed as he neared the top of the steps, hugging the wall. He expected someone to be covering the stairwell; surely they had heard him make his entrance. But no one was there. This was a sloppiness very uncharacteristic of Ms. Croft's description of Maven.

The man's voice—surely it was him—sounded from the end of the hallway. "Oba! Hurry up, man. You Hools are slow as sket for what I'm paying you!"

"*Yong awah heesee*," hissed a Hool in its own tongue, its voice low and guttural.

Wraith didn't understand Hool and didn't bother to ask his bucket for a translation. Maven, however, did understand.

"Because if I leave this, it's all over. And I—oh sket."

Pretty Boy's manicured face froze in terror as Wraith appeared in the doorway. The giant reptilian Hool at Maven's side, its claws clutching a blaster, swung to face the threat, but two blaster bolts tore through his chest and he crumpled to the floor.

Wraith would have put two more bolts in Maven if he could have. But the "Maven" in the room was only a holographic projection.

Wraith spun around to see three more guards, all human, hustling down the hallway behind him and setting up to spring their trap. They must have imagined he was going to clear the room first rather than ducking back out, and seemed surprised to encounter their armored foe face to face.

A quick but decisive blaster fight ensued. Wraith dropped the three men with successive trigger pulls as two shots went wide of his head and a third glanced off his shoulder armor. That might hurt for a while.

Moving smoothly back down the hall, he reported the encounter to Doc. He needed to find Maven quickly—if he was even in the house. It was possible the holostream originated from somewhere offsite, but there was no question that Maven was watching. The man had been able to time his statements perfectly, even to register alarm at Wraith's entering the room.

"Gonna push the bot inside the compound," Doc said.

"Copy," said Wraith.

That was a risk, but one that both men knew they now had to take. If the bot was taken down by an automated anti-surveillance system or simply shot down by a guard, they would lose that helpful eye in the sky for when Wraith sought to slip out past the emergency responders, police, and any backup that might be headed his way. And considering Maven's connections and credits, the local government probably doubled as the criminal's quick reaction force.

Entering through the window where Wraith had shot the would-be sniper, the observation bot moved quickly but steadily along the second floor, checking every open door. As the machine made its checks, Wraith cleared his own rooms.

They were all empty.

"I'm gonna check the sub-level," he announced, feeling the pinch on time.

"Watch yourself," came Doc's reply. "I'll sweep the rest of the house."

Wraith hurried as fast as he dared down the stairs and then to a reinforced blast door that he'd marked on his HUD as the spot where most of the guards had emerged from during Zora's initial scan. The door was locked, and he had to apply a piece of slice tape and wait the thirty seconds for it to do the job of cracking the system.

The blast door slid aside with a hiss, revealing a darkened stairwell that an unlucky Hool was just at that moment hustling his way up. Wraith, ready from before the slicer tape beeped to announce success, sent a pair of bolts into the alien's head and chest, sending it crashing down the stairs, dead.

A stairway was no place to linger, so Wraith descended swiftly, then carefully stepped over the dead body at the bottom. The last thing he wanted was to brush up against the Hool's venomous quills and accidentally get a lethal dose of neurotoxin through a gap in his leg armor. Even dead, Hools can kill you.

The sub-level was nothing but a bunker. Chairs positioned around several tables studded with dice and cards revealed how many guards had been employed. There was a round hatch at the far end of the room—probably an underground escape tunnel.

"Doc," Wraith said over the comm. "Unless you've got something in the house, get that bot outside and look for a hole. Think I found an escape tunnel."

"On it."

Wraith moved to the escape portal. It required a biosignature, and naturally Wraith's didn't match. He had his slice kit, which might be able to spoof it, but that would take much more time than the easy cryptology solution he'd used on the door above.

But maybe the Hool could help.

It was a move of desperation, but not without some reasoning. If this Hool was one of the target's personal bodyguards, he would likely be keyed into whatever secure bioscans were in the building.

Wraith dragged the Hool corpse—again, very carefully—to the sensor. It read the Hool's biological data and granted access with a cheery ding.

That was the downside to this type of interface. It was secure against strangers, but only if you—and your biosignature—remained on the *other* side of the lock.

What the Hool had been hoping to do by coming up the stairs was beyond Wraith. Maybe stall for time. It should have stuck with its boss, but Wraith wasn't complaining. Hools were deadly, but not always all that intelligent.

There was, as expected, a tunnel on the other side of the door. Perfectly round and no doubt the exact same diameter as whatever drilling rig had carved it out. The floor had been leveled with the addition of metal grating, and the walls and ceiling were coated in duracrete, with recessed emergency lights dimly running its length.

It was the flooring that betrayed Maven. In the echoing passageway, Wraith could hear the distant footfalls of someone moving.

He took off on foot, sprinting to catch up.

Back in the Legion, the man called Ford had built a reputation for his speed. He could out-run and out-sprint every other legionnaire he'd ever served with. And the tunnel was long, which worked to his advantage; that gave him more than enough time to catch up.

He came around a wide, arcing corner, ready for another gunfight, and found a lone human, his face pale, sunken bags around his eyes, a pack on his shoulders. Not running. Just waiting.

Maven.

"Hands!" Wraith demanded, advancing violently.

Maven blanched further, staring wildly, hands shaking as he reached up. "Don't shoot me, man! No blasters, see?"

"On your knees. Down."

Maven complied. "Okay, man, okay. What're you, some kind of legionnaire?"

Wraith pulled the man's hands behind his back and locked on a pair of ener-chains.

Maven squirmed. "Ouch! Not so tight with those."

"Shut up," Wraith barked. Then, in his comm, he said, "Package secure."

"Secure?" Doc cried. "Kill the kelhorn!"

"Just bring the ship directly here once Zora arrives."

"She's here, and she's angry as a Taurax caught by the tail," Doc told him. "See you in five. Can't promise you'll live long after that."

From his knees, Maven sought to broker a deal. "Listen. Legionnaire, I can make it so you never have to work a day again in your life. More credits than you can imagine. Just... walk away. The credits'll be in your account before you get back to the house." He peered down the tunnel as if hoping his Hools were on the trail. But the tunnel was empty and quiet. No one was coming. "I... I don't care about any of the damage you've done. Or the guards. Just let me go."

"Not happening. What's in the bag?"

Maven frowned. "Clothes. You're making a mistake."

Wraith produced his Legion combat knife, eliciting a gasp from Maven, and cut the pack free. He made a show of opening it directly under the man's chin, just in case Maven wanted to announce any booby traps. Hearing no objection, Wraith picked through the bag until he found what he wanted—what he'd expected would be there.

"Don't—Hey, that's private property you're taking. I have rights!" Maven exclaimed.

"Not anymore. Up. Let's move!"

"I'm not going anywhere with you. I demand—"

His blaster thumbed all the way to its lowest charge intensity, Wraith shot Maven in the thigh.

Maven stared disbelievingly at the small, burning hole in his leg and screamed in pain as his brain and nerves all agreed on how to react.

"You're going wherever I say you're going," Wraith said, his voice digital grit from behind the legionnaire's helmet. "Only question is, how much do you want the trip to hurt?"

He hurried the man back the way they'd come, ignoring Maven's gasps and groans as he forced him to double-time it on his injured leg. When they got back to the bunker, Wraith had to support him—drag him really—up the stairs and into the house.

From overhead came the repulsor roar of a Naseen freighter, shaking the remaining windows and in some cases shattering them. Maven looked around in bewilderment.

"We're here, Wraith," Doc announced over the comm. "Get your ass outside and get in. And thank Oba for what passes for Ackabar police. They saw the dead guards and signs of a gunfight and then turned right around. I don't think these are the types who get paid to risk their lives."

"Let's go," Wraith told Maven, the target's shoulders firmly in the bounty hunter's grasp as he pushed him outside.

Wincing in pain as he hobbled along, Maven tried one more time. "You can still make this right!"

"I know," Wraith replied.

He would.

# 14

Gas hissed as the *Indelible VI*'s boarding ramp lowered, and Wraith tramped Maven aboard. Maven flinched and moaned with every dragging step.

Zora reached out to take hold of the captive. "Let me help you."

"I have him," Wraith said, and then tossed the man onto the ramp. Without free hands to soften the landing, Maven's chin hit the deck.

Wraith hit the ramp's activator and closed the ship up as Doc—or the AI—took on altitude.

Maven grimaced and rolled onto his back, his manacled arms between him and the deck. "Fine. You've got me. At least give me something for the pain."

"Not happening," Wraith said.

Zora sneered at the killer. "Oh, I got something for you." She kicked Maven's leg, her boot connecting firmly with where the man was shot.

Maven crumpled into a fetal position.

"Kelhorned scumsack," she muttered.

"Oh! A new visitor!" A cheery voice rang out through the ship speakers. "And injured! I'll power up the med bay!"

Humming a happy ditty, the *Six*'s AI went to work.

"You wanna turn that thing off now that you're here?" Zora said.

"I tried to explain to our friends that I can only be powered off by the captain himself, as an anti-theft measure," the AI exclaimed. "You see, after I was *stolen* from Captain Keel on Antares—"

"Mute," Wraith said. He'd forgotten to adjust the ship's operations to allow Doc and Zora more control. Something he would have to do if they were to keep working together. As it stood, not only could the annoying AI not be turned off by anyone but him, but it was programmed to not let the ship fly farther than twenty kilometers unless Keel was on board. All the more reason to allow them to disable it.

Still crumpled like a deflated Unity Day balloon, the criminal on the floor moaned.

"Why's he still alive?" Zora asked. "The job was a termination."

That woke Maven up. "No no no!" he said, panicked. "I can pay you more than whoever hired you. Much more. I can triple it. Quadruple it!"

"We'll see," Wraith answered.

"My grandfather, he's rich! He loves me. Please!"

Ignoring him, Wraith pointed to the decking. "See that seam on the fourth deck plate? Right in the middle?"

"This one?" Zora asked once she'd moved to it.

"Yeah. Press your foot down on the edge there and then pop it up."

She did, and a panel popped up and slid away.

"A smuggler's hold," Zora noted, impressed.

"In you go," Wraith said, and shoved Maven inside with the sole of his boot.

"No, wait—" Maven fell to the bottom of the hold with a thud. His demands started right up again. "Let me out! Let me—"

Zora slid the hold panel back in place with her own boot, muffling Maven's pleas.

"Can he hear us?" she asked.

"No." Wraith removed his helmet, and Keel took a breath of fresh, bucket-free air. His hair was wet with perspiration despite the climate controls Legion armor attempted to afford.

Zora, arms crossed, motioned her head toward where they now kept the prisoner. "Fill me in. Because this isn't what we discussed."

"Yeah," Keel admitted. "Sorry about that. There was—"

"Ooh! Captain Keel! There you are!" the AI exclaimed. "I didn't recognize you until you removed your helmet!"

"You saw me put it on, you idiot! And I said mute!" Keel snapped.

"Yes of course you did, but everyone loves a compliment, and you look *dashing*, Captain! Mister Doc is assisting me in the cockpit—he's such a *saucy* fellow!—and I'm off mute because Mister Doc *demands* that you," here the AI did an unconvincing impression of the old man, "'get your ass up here and explain yourself!' Message delivered!"

"Explain it to me first," Zora insisted. "Seeing as how you and Doc decided that going behind my back to plan this operation somehow wouldn't be a problem."

"Yeah. Sorry." Keel hated that word, and he had a feeling he'd have to say it more often with partners around. "Didn't want you to get mixed up."

"Yeah, Doc told me this was about protecting my standing with the Guild. I'm still angry you two left me out of it."

Keel smiled wryly. "You woulda gone in, huh?"

"I want that kelhorn to pay for what he's done. Yeah, I would have gone with you. Which is why I need you to answer my *real* question. Fill me in on why he's still breathing."

"Let's go see your—" Keel corrected himself. "The old man, and I'll explain."

"Explain it *now*, Keel. Without him. Turnabout is fair play and all that. I want to know."

Keel wasn't sure how much to tell her. How much she needed to know. How much he really trusted her.

Finally he shook his head. "Doc is right. It's not going to do any favors for your bounty hunting career if you get mixed up in any of this. Not gonna do anything good for Doc, either, for that matter. If this is gonna work... really work... I have to do some hard things. *Just* me. This... mission I'm on—I can't drag you or your father down as deep as I need to go."

"Why not?" Zora asked. It wasn't an accusation or a complaint. She just needed to know.

"Because I know how deep the bottom is. And it's not fair. To anyone. But someone had to go all the way down. That's me."

Zora stared at the smuggler, searching his face to see if he meant what he said. He did.

"Okay," she said. "Let me know how I can help anyway."

The *Indelible VI* hummed in flight as Keel sat in the armory cleaning his weapons. The table was full again, but this time with his kit—everything laid out in neat orderly rows. He had his Intec x6 blaster on his lap, and he was giving the barrel extra attention, to make sure all the carbon scoring vanished.

He'd told as much of his plan as he was willing to Doc and Zora. If they agreed with it—or even fully understood it —they didn't show one way or the other. But they did understand that Keel was adamant that they couldn't be involved in any way, shape, or form with what he had planned.

Since then, both had given him space.

Until now.

The armory doors hissed open and Doc walked through. "Always keep your blasters clean," he remarked.

"Yup. No trouble out of Ackabar?" They'd been in hyperspace for an hour now. Keel had left Doc and Zora to handle the exfiltration. Chances were slim that anyone had followed them, but not zero.

Doc grunted. "Place like that? No. No trouble. Some information brokers are probably trying to sell news, *if* they actually knew who was at that compound. Usually I'd say we need to let at least one of 'em in on things and have 'em start talkin' about Wraith. But I guess your way might work, too." He looked over Keel's kit, clearly something on his mind. Then settled his gaze back on Keel. "I'm not... I'm not sure this is the kind of heat you want. Holding that scumsack for ransom."

"I'm not holding him for ransom."

"So what are you doin'? Your debrief left out a few things."

"Just tryin' to keep you and Zora protected," Keel replied.

"We don't need protectin'. But we do need to know what's going on. Rule One: Never keep your partners in the dark."

Keel set the barrel down. "Like I said to Owens, I don't need a partner. You and Zora aren't even crew, remember? You're advisers. And in retrospect, I can admit you both came through with good advice." He gave the barrel one last look, then locked the Intec together and primed it. "There we go."

The doors swooshed open again, and this time Zora entered, datapad in hand. "What's this?" she said. "Another secret meeting?"

"Told you it wouldn't happen again," a repentant Doc said.

Zora gave a half-frown and held up the datapad. "I cracked the kelhorn's data chit like you asked."

Doc looked from Zora to Keel. "Feelin' a little left out here. What's all this?"

Keel arched an eyebrow, impressed. Zora had asked how she could help, and Keel had given her a job, but it wasn't something he figured she'd actually be able to *do*.

"I figured we'd have to hire on a code-slicer and wait the better part of a month to unlock that thing," he said.

"I know a few things about ciphering code keys," said Zora with a shrug.

Doc's eyes went wide. "You didn't torture the little bastard, did you?"

"No. Not that he doesn't deserve it. I've just got a few algos that work pretty well. Got lucky, really."

"Nice work either way," Keel told her. He looked to Doc. "If she'd have tortured him, we would've heard it. The hold isn't *entirely* soundproof."

Doc shook his head. "Fancy that being there to begin with. No PDCs or blaster turrets, but they took the time to hollow out a smuggler's hold."

"Well, being a smuggler was part of the original plan," Keel said. "So the secret hold was paid for."

"Just not the weapons package."

"Just not the weapons. But maybe after this job…"

"Job was to kill Maven," Doc pointed out.

"Who says I won't?"

"He absolutely deserves it," said Zora grimly. "That data chit is a record of all his... encounters. Real grisly stuff."

Doc looked askance. "You *watched* that twarg dung?"

"Of course not. Not that I couldn't stomach it, if that's what you're suggesting. I ran it through an AI that sifted and categorized. This datapad has it all, as promised, Keel. Organized into a nice clean list. But follow the holovid links at your own risk."

Keel took the datapad and tapped on the screen. Blue light flashed on his face as he scrolled through a wreckage of human lives.

"Wipe the AI," Doc told his daughter. "They can get weird from seeing too much of that garbage." Then to Keel: "So whatcha got on the datapad?"

"Murder. Rape. Torture. About what you'd expect from a guy like this. But that's not the gold mine. Here." He tapped the screen, then held up the pad. "Security detail info. This is what I was looking for."

Doc's eyes went wide as he read. "Holy hell. This links the punk's hired guns right to Delegate Tooms's payroll. Didn't think they'd be that obvious about it."

"Pretty easy to stay ahead of non-Guild hunters with that kind of backup," Zora noted. "Those prices aren't cheap."

"He overpaid," Keel said. "Okay. I gotta get back in the armor."

"Why's that?"

"This Wraith plan is going to work. But like I said earlier, it means crossing a line. I don't expect either of you to follow me. In fact, neither of you should. Can you hand me my bucket?"

"Sure," Doc said. "Catch."

Keel snagged the black helmet and put it on, his armor complete and his voice soulless as he said, "I'm gonna have a talk with Maven." Then before anyone could say another word, he left the armory and tramped down the corridor.

Zora rushed to catch up with him. "Hey!" She took two steps for his every stride. "No more vagueness here. What exactly do you mean, crossing a line?"

"This is well outside of Republic law."

"So was taking a non-Guild termination contract. Wait." She reached out and stopped him. "What do you really have planned?"

Keel stopped, fighting against his desire to just kill Maven and be done with it. Move on the way Doc and Zora had intended. But this was a chance he needed to take.

He removed his helmet again and looked Zora in the eyes. "I can do capture/kill missions. That's not an issue. It's everything that comes next. Zora, you ever feel like you're fastening a noose around your own neck?"

She studied him. "Yeah. I know that feeling."

"I have to remind myself of why I'm out here. Of what happened to guys like—to friends. I don't have time to build a rep, because we were out of time when all this first started."

"Well I hate to break this to you, Keel, but unless you're a serial killer, it can take years of doing hard jobs like this to get your name across the galaxy."

"Not if this works." He put his helmet back on. "I just gotta live with myself, is all," the Wraith now rasped as he resumed his stride down the corridor. "You should stay back with Doc in the armory. Plausible deniability."

Zora once more hastened to follow. "I'm a big girl. I set this job up, and I can see it to its finish."

"Suit yourself."

They stopped directly above the smuggler's hold, and Wraith pulled out a small orb that lit up blue with a squeeze. He released it, and it floated in the air before him.

"What's the holocam for?" Zora asked.

"Gonna call the delegate. Stay out of the shot."

Zora's face went pale. "You're going to do *what*?"

"Shh."

From his HUD, Wraith sent out the string of code that connected the comm across the galaxy, straight to the Republic's capital planet of Utopion. Above the hovering bot, the visage of a noble elderly statesman sprang into view.

"Adam! It's becoming more and more rare to hear from my favorite grandson. Tell me—" His face froze. "You're not Adam."

"No," the Wraith answered.

The delegate drew himself up. "A legionnaire. A Dark Ops legionnaire, judging by your armor. How did you get this comm key?"

"I'm not with the Legion."

"A deserter then." Delegate Tooms sneered. "I have no interest in helping a traitor to our Republic."

"I have your grandson."

"Do you?" Tooms replied, lacing those two words with doubt. "I'm sure I don't know what—"

Wraith pressed open the hidden panel and sent the holocam down into the dark. Likely waking up from a nap, Maven exclaimed, "Ach, I can't breathe! I can't breathe! Whoever's up there, let me out! I'll pay you one hundred thousand credits right now. Let me out!"

Wraith dropped down into the hold, drew his blaster, and primed it. "No."

His hands still bound behind him, the wilting sadist started to weep, shivering on the floor.

Beside the Wraith, the floating specter of Delegate Tooms's holo turned furious. "This is kidnapping!"

"A bounty."

"Damn it all. Show me the boy. In detail! How do I know it's really him?"

"Talk," Wraith ordered, and then sent the holocam floating down before Maven's face.

The serial killer lunged toward the holo as though it were a life preserver in a stormy sea. "It's me, Poppo! He blew up everything. Killed all the guards. He *shot* me!"

"We'll see," the delegate replied. He uttered a pass phrase. "Tangerra."

"Ustari," Maven answered. "Poppo, it's me!"

Delegate Tooms choked, "Oh, Adam. What have you allowed yourself to fall into?"

"You've got to get me out of here! Please! He won't listen!"

Wraith recalled the holocam, bringing it before himself, where it cast a soft blue glow inside the darkened smuggler's hold.

"I believe you," Tooms told Wraith. "You have him. I won't deny it. And now what would you have me do? Triple the bounty in exchange for his freedom? Fine. Done. Upon release at a destination of my choosing." Then he muttered to himself, "Damned criminal. Extortion."

"I don't break contracts," the Wraith replied.

Delegate Tooms clenched his jaw. "And yet you've contacted me. So just what is it you want, Mister..."

"Wraith."

"Wraith. How formal."

"Place a bounty on your grandson," Wraith replied. "One million credits."

"Let me guess: and then you'll collect and turn him in to me. Fine. I see your game. I'll notify the Bronze Guild momentarily."

"Not the Guild. Black Channel. Asking for me by name."

Tooms tapped his desk. "And how do I know you'll deliver him to me alive? I need to have him safely with me before I can do what you're asking of me. You do see the problem with your little scheme?"

"I wasn't finished. Because you're right. There is a problem."

Delegate Tooms leaned back in self-satisfaction and laughed smugly. "I *know* it's a problem, and it's one *you'll* need to determine the logistics of if you wish to be paid."

"No."

With a twitch of his wrist, Wraith put two blaster bolts into the back of Maven's head. The young man fell forward, his face smashing against the hold with a terrible *smack* as both Zora above and Tooms in the holo gasped.

Wraith turned to glare into the holo at the delegate.

Horrified, Delegate Tooms exclaimed, "What did you—! What! Oba's tears... you murdered him! You executed my —"

"I don't break contracts. His was a termination. The one you'll set up will be as well."

Tooms flushed red. "If you think for one minute that anything more will come from me except a blade in the dark—"

"I'm sending you a data packet. Evidence. Of your grandson's crimes. *You knew.*"

Delegate Tooms blinked once. Then said slowly, "If you think you can pin what he *allegedly* did on me—"

"You covered them up. Paid for him to have protection. To avoid scandal. To avoid justice. All recorded. By him. It's in the data burst you just received."

The color drained from Tooms's face. "I... he was sick. Needed help. I was keeping him *away* from trouble. Away, do you understand?"

"Your opponents in the Senate and House of Reason would also send a blade in the dark for this information, Delegate Tooms. Wouldn't they?"

Delegate Tooms glanced around as if that blade were nearby. "I... I..."

"You have one hour to set up the bounty. I will collect in two days. Fail me, and the galaxy—starting with those who want your seat in the House—will know your part in every stolen girl, every rape, every torturous murder your grandson committed under your knowing protection."

Tooms withered under Wraith's gaze, but not from guilt. His politician's knack for survival at all costs was now sniveling in self-interest. "How can I trust... How do I know that you won't—"

"I don't break contracts."

Wraith killed the feed and recalled his hovering bot.

Zora dropped down beside him, walked quietly over to the corpse, then turned to look at him. "Aeson..."

Above them, Doc came running down the corridor, then peered into the secret hold. "I heard blaster bolts," the old man said, winded. "What... Oh. You killed the kelhorn. Good."

Zora frowned. "Are you out of your mind, Keel?"

"Would've been easier if I was."

"What?" Doc said. "Good grouping. Didn't make the bastard suffer."

"Not that, Dad. He just blackmailed Delegate Tooms."

Doc's eyes bulged. "You did what? That wasn't part of the plan!" Then: "For how much?"

"A million credits," Wraith replied calmly.

"A million! You're telling me you just earned another seven figures on a job you were already hired to do?"

"If Tooms even pays," Zora put in, skeptical. "He's just as likely to put a bounty on your head now. What were you thinking?"

"He'll pay."

Zora rolled her eyes. "I'd love to know where you get your delusions from. And take that helmet off. You're creeping me out."

Wraith complied, and Keel looked apologetic. "I tried warning you."

"Vaguely!" She threw up her hands. "You didn't let me know the tough job you had was committing treason by blackmailing a House of Reason delegate! I thought you were just nervous about executing a target after you brought him in."

"Why would that make him nervous?" Doc wanted to know. "Punk deserved what he got!"

"I did what needed to be done in order to get where I needed to go," Keel said. "You want Wraith to be feared, want him to be known? Well, he's about to be notorious if what's in that data burst is true and Tooms knew about it."

"He did," Doc groused. "All those House of Reason bastards are crooked. All of 'em."

With the help of a stowed-away ladder, Keel and Zora climbed out of the hold and booted the panel shut behind them.

Doc dusted off his hands. "So what next? Because I figured we'd slowly ramp up to a rep. But you went ahead and hit the switch for a hyper-jump."

"There's a few loose ends," Keel told him. "And then I gotta figure something out about the armor. Tooms pegged me as a legionnaire right away. I didn't like it."

"'Course he pegged you," said Doc. "It's leej armor—what'd you expect? But with a million credits, we can do something about that."

"If he pays." Zora stuck to her guns.

"He'll pay," Keel replied, sticking with his own.

Doc shrugged. "Guess we'll see. Should I have the AI plot us a course back to see Ms. Croft?"

"No," Keel said. "I mean, don't wake up the AI. I hate that thing. I'll go get the nav computer working on the coordinates."

"I'll let Croft know we're comin'."

Keel stopped him. "Don't. Not yet."

"All right..." Doc said, looking puzzled, and followed Keel up to the cockpit.

Still standing in the corridor, Zora called out, "I'll just stay here and think about how you just made us both accessories to something I don't want any part of!"

"Sounds good!" Keel shouted back.

"I don't really mind all that much, sweetie," her dad replied. "Punk got what he had comin'!"

With a growl, Zora headed for the lounge, hoping to wipe out her frustration with a meal and maybe something stronger. Like Bendorian chocolate.

# 15

Keel's boots were kicked up on the cockpit control screens as he dug into a warmed-up ration pack, waiting. Finally the incoming comm light lit blue.

"Go for Captain Keel."

"Freighter *Loose Dutchman*," the port authority said, "you are paid up on docking fees and free to exit your ship. Enjoy Starijia."

"Copy. *Loose Dutchman* out."

Doc had already finished his own meal and was picking his old-man teeth. "Ain't so bad paying them fines when you know you've got credits coming in the account, huh?"

"Not bad at all. You think the Legion'll make me give up anything I've got left over once this op is over?"

Doc tossed the toothpick back into the ration pouch and sucked his teeth clean. "What do you think?"

"Yeah. That's what I was afraid of."

"Don't get caught up in thinking about credits. Makes good operators go bad. Besides, I got a plan to spend a whole lot of 'em to get your armor up to speed."

"Always felt up to speed before. The problem is the appearance, not the quality."

"That's part of it," Doc said. "But you don't wanna lose that look entirely. People are conditioned to show respect to leejes. Because we're badasses. We want you to look *enough* like a leej to make folks uncomfortable, but not so much that they assume a kill team is nearby. Fathom?"

"Yeah. So what's the plan?"

Doc grinned. "There's things out there that Owens and Darks Ops would love to have. Only they can't. House of Reason went cheap on 'em."

"Yeah. The new shiny armor they issued is... somethin' else."

"Tactical coffin is what it is."

Keel laughed. "That's about right. That's the House of Reason and Senate for you, though. Make it cheap and make sure you own a stake in the companies that get the contracts. Guys on the lines pay the price."

"Fortune and glory, kid. They make the fortune, we get the glory."

"Hmm," Keel said, inspecting the hunk of gray meat on his fork. "Never bought much of anything with all that Legion glory. What's the exchange rate on that?"

Doc gave a half-smile and shook his head. "'Course, it's only the junior delegates that make money like you're sayin'. The *really* rich ones, your Tooms and Kaar, they got a better way."

"What's that?" Keel asked, digging into his food again.

"They got shares of the companies that do the *research*. See, you eventually gotta deliver something when you're pumping out armor or weapons. Cuts into the bottom line. But research? That's always on the horizon. Milk a budget for a decade, sit on the results until the contract expires, and sell off whatever the taxpayers funded to the highest corporate bidder."

"Good gig if you can get it."

"You aren't doin' so bad yourself, kid." Doc gave his daughter a nod as she entered the cockpit. "A million credits..." he mused.

"Just because he set the bounty up doesn't mean he'll pay it," Zora said, feeling somewhat better after dining by herself in the galley. "He's not gonna pay it."

Keel stabbed the last meat hunk swimming in sauce at the bottom of the pouch. "He'll pay it, Zora."

"He's gonna end up stalling for time. Watch. Try to find out about Wraith."

"Let's see about that," Doc said. "Anything in the Guild for Wraith, Zee? A termination?"

"No. But I wouldn't expect to see one. We have damning evidence. He can't make a move that's so obvious. Plus, what's he gonna say: go kill the first legionnaire who turns his head when you shout 'Wraith'?"

Doc chuckled.

"He won't make any move," Keel said. "Trust me."

Zora narrowed her eyes. "I can't tell if this is wishful thinking or if you actually have a plan."

"He's got a plan," Doc replied. "He's just not sure if it's the right one."

"Wonderful. I'm oozing with confidence."

"Both Zora and I think that wobanki was tipping Maven and Delegate Tooms off," Keel said. "This time and all the times before. They were on the alert at the compound. Extra guards. Distractions set like the holo. Maven was moving out the moment we hit."

"So what're you gonna do about it?" Doc asked.

Keel tossed his trash away. "Wraith needs to show Tooms that he's got every angle covered. Keep the delegate seeing shadows. Keep him so afraid of what might happen that he follows through on actually paying the bounty."

"Told ya you shoulda blasted that kitty cat," Doc said. "But yeah, that's the next move. Let's get this finished up, kid."

That night they returned by invitation to Ms. Croft's residence. The elegant place of business it served as by day had been transformed into a gala by night. In the courtyard, hover globes twinkled in the trees like fairy lights, and in the great ballroom inside, a multitude of races, the wealthy and elite, were decked out in their evening finery. Serving tables lined the room, artfully laid out with culinary delights from half a dozen galaxies.

Bypassing the globs of fish eggs and pink Vikram smelt, Keel snagged a cooked sausage. He popped it in his mouth, feeling the skin snap, and juices from the oversized bit dribbled down his chin. Zora's look suggested that she didn't know whether to be disgusted or impressed at how well Keel was playing the part of a devil-may-care brash smuggler.

As the evening wore on, Tennarian servers came out with champagne trays in their tentacles and drifted through the crowd. Ms. Croft took a glass and chimed it with a spoon to catch the room's attention. The music stopped, and everyone looked her way.

"Thank you all for coming tonight. And thank you for supporting me, and working with me, for such a long time to achieve justice for my daughter Esha, as well as for the many other victims of Adam Maven. By now I suppose you've all already put two and two together, but it's my duty and privilege to make it official: the bounty hunter Wraith has delivered justice to Maven in a manner the

Republic long refused. Earlier today I received the biosignature confirming that this is so."

Here there was some applause, and the room buzzed with conversation.

"This is the culmination of years of hard work," Ms. Croft continued. "Many gave up. Many thought this day would never happen. But *we*, we faithful... we believed in something more. *We* believed in justice." She looked grandly around the room, a dramatic pause before continuing. "Today... justice has been served!"

The room broke into applause again, and while Ms. Croft continued her speech, Doc muttered, "You're a hero, Keel."

"Wraith, maybe," he said quietly. "I'm just the messenger."

"Either way, good riddance." Wearing a scintillating one-shouldered sheath dress, Zora downed her champagne glass like a Backblast whiskey shot.

"Captain Keel..." Ms. Croft's voice rang out. "Are you able to say a few words, seeing as how the man responsible isn't here?"

The audience turned and searched for the man Croft was looking at. A repulsor-powered bot hovered in Keel's direction and shone a spotlight on him.

"Uh..." Keel looked down at his champagne flute.

Zora took the glass and gave him a shove. "Get up there, man of the hour."

The audience politely clapped as he made his way to Ms. Croft's side.

"Ah. Well... I wasn't really... planning on saying anything." He cleared his throat. A room full of measuring looks waited for his next words. "I guess... I guess I just want you to all know... there was nothing valiant, noble, or admirable about Maven when the end came. He showed no remorse. No sorrow. And no spine or backbone. He was a coward in life, and he died the same. He was scared. Pathetic. He deserved every blaster bolt Wraith put into him."

The audience waited, some somber, some aghast.

Keel cleared his throat and continued. "He thought he could buy his way out. Again. Only he went up against a man who couldn't be bought. And now he's dead. And anyone else like him... anyone who puts aside what's right for what's convenient, Wraith has a message for them, too: You're next."

The room was dead silent.

"Hells yeah!" Doc shouted, clapping loudly, and the crowd awkwardly joined in. "Let 'im rot in the nine hells!"

Looking like she'd tasted something sour in her champagne, Ms. Croft pursed her lips. "Um, thank you, Captain Keel."

"Sure."

She lifted her glass. "Everyone! It's time to celebrate the life of my daughter, and the demise of her persecutor."

The synthstring music picked up again, signaling to the crowd that all was well at the party and in the galaxy. Balance had been restored. Right had prevailed.

Keel rejoined his friends. "How'd I do?"

Zora sipped Keel's champagne along with the rest of the glittering guests. "Not the best speech I ever heard, but you got your point across."

"You think?" Keel asked.

"Look." Zora tilted her glass toward a staff entrance, where a tall, broad-shouldered figure with a tawny tail walked by a table filled with empty champagne flutes. He hesitated, eyeing the delicate glasses—and the temptation proved too powerful for the wobanki. His paw dashed out, and in one swipe the tottering lot crashed to the floor.

In the ensuing distraction, the catman slipped out the door.

"There goes the wobanki," Doc said. "Callin' it a night early, huh?"

"Or callin' it time to get underground," Keel said.

"Only one way to find out, right?" said Zora.

Keel gave a quick nod. "Let's go."

# 16

It's never wise to stalk a wobanki in his home territory. His swiveling ears can detect the lightest footfalls, his keen nose can pick up a scent carried on the wind over a distance of kilometers, and his sharp eyes can catch colors in the dark. So any self-respecting wobanki will tell you, right before his razor claws slit your throat. But TT-16 observation bots, small and silent, are designed for stealth. So Keel let the bot do his legwork for him while he and the team followed in the relative comfort of a rented repulsor.

The flow of traffic at night was much better than during the day.

Leeke led them a few blocks away to where the grand residences gave way to faceless duracrete apartment complexes. Street vendors had shuttered their stalls and gone home. A sanitation bot did its final nightly sweep, but otherwise the street was vacant.

"Looks like kittycat went straight home," Doc said as they watched Leeke scan his way into a building. The TT-16 waited above him, then slipped inside before the doors whooshed shut.

Keel gave it a couple minutes, then asked, "He made it to his place yet, Doc?"

His face was lit up blue in the light of his datapad. "Just now entering his front door." He turned the pad to show Keel the apartment's position within the building.

Keel pulled the sled around to park beneath the wobanki's curtainless windows. "How about getting that bot back outside to keep an eye on him, Doc?"

Zora, who was watching the same feed from her own datapad, suggested Doc bring the bot down a few levels. "I can see a common balcony with the door propped open on floor ten."

"Yeah, I see it," Doc grunted.

He moved the drone back down the stairs and outside, almost scraping the doorframe, then zipped it out above the heads of a trio who were spending their evening sipping wine together on the balcony.

"Bringin' it around to the 'banki's window." The old man stared into his datapad, watching the feed provided him by the observation bot. "There you are. Kelhorn's bugging out. Gathering things up in a hurry. Making a mess. I think your speech got to him."

Keel frowned. He had intended to find out where the wobanki lived and then pay him a visit when the predator was asleep. That seemed like the sort of thing that would add an extra element of fear to those who crossed Wraith. But if Leeke was preparing to leave, he would do so alert. You needed every edge you could find if you were going to have a fight with a wobanki, and Keel's expected edge hadn't developed.

"Weapons?" he asked.

"It's a window, Keel. I can only see so much." Doc scratched his scruff. "But he's gotta be packing. *Assume* he's packing. Rule One: They're always packing."

"Okay. Time to get ready," Keel said. "You got my kit, old man?"

Doc broke from his vigil and tossed the smuggler a bulky bag. "I didn't forget nothin'."

Keel was pulling off his jacket. "Help me put it on then."

The two former leejes worked quickly to get Keel set, but when they were done, Zora eyed Keel skeptically. "That's it? That's all you're wearing to go in? Where's the rest of your armor?"

"It's enough," Wraith told her. "We can't just lug around the entire full battle rattle."

"Helmet. Torso. Shins. Forearms. It'll do," Doc said.

"Not if the wobanki gets in close, it won't."

"So I won't let him get in close," Wraith said.

"It's not like the kid's tryin' to kill the cat. Just make him think it."

"Actually I'm keeping my options open," Wraith said. "Gotta go. You two good?"

Zora lifted her datapad with the observation bot's display. "Holler if you get in over your head, jump jockey."

"I'm always ready," Doc said.

"KTF."

"Yeah, KTF, kid."

"Oh, would you hurry up?" Zora exclaimed. "Before he's out the door?"

"He's still packing," Doc grumbled.

"Just go!" Zora said.

Quick as a rhobat on the wing and nearly as silent, the Wraith ran out into the night, sprinting to the apartment complex. With one smooth leap, he hit the wall and began to climb. His setae gloves were equipped with millions of submicroscopic hairs that allowed him to cling to the vertical surface and make his way upward. One story down, fourteen more to go.

Doc tested the comm. "I've got eyes on you, how copy?"

"Copy. Climbing."

"Watching the window for surprises," Doc told him. "Out."

"He certainly is a fast runner," Zora remarked, keeping one eye on the catman packing his bags on her datapad and the other on the human doing a decent moktaar impression out her repulsor window.

"Kid's good, kid's good." Doc nodded, then said, "You could be a little nicer to him."

"Me? I'm nice."

"Just sayin'. He's done some... well, some high-speed stuff. He's not gonna lose the wobanki. Why'd you jump down his shirt like that?" He gave his daughter the side-eye. "Oh. *Ohhh!* I see. You got a thing for him."

She scoffed. "That's ridiculous."

"Not so much. Good-lookin' kid. They call legionnaires—and we both know he used to be Legion—they call 'em heartbreakers and life-takers for a reason."

This was getting painful. "Dad. Stop. We have... assignments."

Doc chuckled to himself. "It's just that... you can be a real ice queen, Zora. You know that."

"Gee. Thanks, Dad."

"That's your SOP," he went on. "Only when you like a fella, you get mean, too. Snippy. Kinda bossy. Like your mother."

"Wow, Dad. So charming. And no, I don't. I'm not any... meaner than I usually am. Which is not at all. I'm not mean."

Keel—Wraith—was now eight stories up, and Zora wondered if he'd ever get there. Leeke had one bag already packed and was dashing around his apartment throwing more things into a second bag. Any minute now he'd be done and long gone.

Doc wasn't fussed. "It's like when you were twelve. Remember that boy? The one with the black hair and the green eyes?"

"Dad. This is completely unprofessional."

"You had the biggest crush. I could tell. Anyone with two brain cells sparking could tell. But not that poor kid. You treated him like a doormat."

Rolling her eyes, Zora commed Wraith. "Be advised, target is moving from sleeping hab to the fresher."

"Copy that. Almost to the window."

"All I'm sayin'," Doc continued, "is guys are thick-headed. If a girl acts like she hates him, he'll think she hates him. If she acts like she likes him... well, poor sap won't know *what* to think, but at least you got a chance that he'll figure it out."

"Thanks, Dad, for the love advice," Zora deadpanned. "That's exactly how I thought tonight would go."

Out her window, Wraith was dangling from a window ledge thirteen stories above the parking lot. He gave himself a heave, then caught the top seam of the window and kept climbing. "I'm surprised you'd encourage me about *him*."

Doc shrugged. "Maybe he reminds me of myself."

Zora sighed. "Wave that red flag high."

"Cute."

Over the comm, Wraith said, "I'm at the window. No visuals. He still in the fresher?"

The observation bot drifted to the relevant window, and then back to where it could maintain the best viewpoint of the larger apartment.

"Confirmed," Zora replied. "Cat is in the litterbox."

"Okay. Doc... gimme an entry point."

"Comin' up," Doc said. He leaned out of the repulsor, lifted his blaster, and put one silenced shot square on Leeke's window, breaking the locking mechanism.

"Nice shot," Wraith said, then pushed the window open. "I'm moving inside. Zora?"

Her eyes were on the feed. "If he hears you, he's a good actor. He's going on like nothing."

Wraith slipped inside. "Gonna kill the lights and wait for him."

In the feed, the apartment went dark, but a ray of light streamed out from beneath the bathroom door. Then it too went black.

"He's coming out," Zora said.

The TT-16 switched to night-vis mode as the fresher door opened. Leeke stepped out and growled. The cat knew a hunt when he smelled one.

"*Chop ratta?*" he asked the darkness.

"He's going for the light switch," Zora said.

"I see him," Wraith replied. "I'll be right behind him."

Light flooded the apartment.

"Leeke," Wraith said.

The wobanki hurled himself round on Wraith in a flash, a cyclone of claws. One strike caught an unarmored part of Wraith's arm, causing him to cry out in pain over the comm.

"Keel!" Zora exclaimed. The combatants moved so fast it was difficult to follow, but she could see punches thrown, tables and furniture knocked over, drywall crumbling.

"I told you those creatures were dangerous," she said to Doc. "Keel is fighting the wobanki hand-to-hand. You need to get up there to help him!"

"No!" Wraith said, panting as he fought back against the wild catman. "It has to be Wraith alone."

"Not lettin' you get yourself killed by that thing, kid," Doc said, grabbing his shotgun.

"Can I just focus here?" Wraith cried.

"Your funeral," Doc grumbled, and then settled back to watch Zora's feed.

The wobanki hurled a table at Wraith, catching him in the chest. Winded, the bounty hunter managed to duck the catman's follow-up swing, then pushed up from the ground to land some kidney strikes on the furry creature, followed by one to the feline's chin.

Leeke shook it off, yowling, "*Cho bagga! Cho bagga!*" Then he let out a violent roar and hurled himself once more at Wraith, claws extended, this time catching him in the chest.

The armor saved Keel from being cut into pieces, but the force of the blow still drove some of the wind from his lungs.

"*Cho bagga! Cho—*"

Leeke's shrieks were cut off by several blows to the head. The wobanki growled in frustration, clawing wildly, but Wraith kept up the attack, grappling him and taking him down.

As he pounded away at his opponent, Zora cheered him on. "That's it! Bash his head in, Keel!"

"Holy hell..." Doc muttered, still peering over her shoulder at the feed.

Wraith threw a final punch, and the wobanki fell back, though still moaning, on the floor.

Wraith pushed himself up off the ground, panting. He primed his blaster and aimed it at the catman's face. "Not another move, Leeke. Or I pull the trigger."

Leeke yowled a cry fit to break a molly-cat's heart. "*Gabba... cho bagga. Gabba.*"

The alien was pleading for his life.

"You should kill him anyway, kid," Doc advised.

"You sold your employer out, Leeke," Wraith said. "Tipped off Maven and Tooms. Kept them a step ahead. Put my life in danger, and that of my crew. Tried to keep me from collecting my bounty."

Leeke cringed. "*Nehgoo rowa.*"

"Usually," Wraith said. "But I'm giving you a chance to buy back your life."

Leeke retracted his claws, and his ears went limp in a pathetic display. "*Pogga toppa. Pogga.*"

The Wraith pressed his blaster between the catman's eyes, gaining his full attention. "Tell everyone who matters —*everyone*—what I did to Maven... and what I did to you. If Captain Keel gets word through the underground that you're talking, you get to keep on living. If *not*... you'll spend the rest of your brief life waiting for a shot that you'll never hear coming. No more up close and personal because there'll be nothing left to say. Do we have a deal?"

"*Hatcha.*" Leeke nodded. *We have a deal.*

Back on the *Six*, Keel flinched as Zora applied a skinpack, certain it wasn't supposed to sting like that. He was sitting on the med bay table, bare-chested except for the other skinpacks already swathing cat-claw cuts, some of them folded and doubled to help with a couple of particularly deep lacerations. Zora hovered over him playing nurse, but Keel found her alleged medical training dubious.

She frowned at his wincing. "Stop that, you big baby. This can't be hurting you. There. Last skinpack's in place."

"Thanks," he said.

"You know, you should keep a med bot on board for things like this."

"Kind of figured I could put a skinpack on by myself."

"Sometimes you get scratched in a place you can't reach," Zora pointed out.

"Those wobanki claws didn't feel much like any *scratch* I know."

"I told you to wear the full armor."

"Yeah. You did," Keel admitted.

Zora's expression softened. "I'm glad you're all right."

"Thanks."

"And... I'm sorry if I've been... If I've been..." She trailed off, looking around the med bay as if the room held some answer Keel couldn't see.

"If you've been...?" Keel prompted.

She shook her head. "Just... sorry if I've been too... mean."

He turned his face up at her in confusion. "Mean?"

She glared at him. "You're making fun of me. Don't. Seriously, I'll knock you right out."

"Let's not kid ourselves."

Her glare intensified. "I will punch you right where I placed that skinpack."

He threw his hands up. "All right, all right, let's not get crazy. Although now you *are* just being mean."

Quick as a trap viper, Zora punched Keel straight on the wound, exactly where she'd promised.

"Ow!" he cried. "What the hell was that for?"

Now she was angry too. "I warned you! And you... you... antagonized me!"

"I didn't expect you'd actually do it!"

Zora tossed her head. "Sorry not sorry."

"I hate when people say that," Keel muttered.

Doc walked into the room looking bewildered. "What's all the racket in here?"

Keel hopped down from the table and pulled on his shirt. "Your *charming* daughter just decked me where that wobanki tried to cut me into ribbon steak."

Doc looked from Keel to Zora. "With no warning?"

"I warned him," Zora said, to which Keel gave his grudging assent.

"Yeah, well, cut it out and get up to the cockpit," Doc replied. "The senator came through."

"He paid?" Keel asked.

"A million credits. You're rich, kid."

"Congrats," Zora said, hardly sounding as though she meant it. "I think that's more than I've made in my entire career."

"Well, they mostly pay for talent, so—"

Zora threw another punch, this time into Keel's shoulder, which was still purple from the blaster bolt his armor had absorbed while capturing Maven.

"Ow! Again with the punching!"

"Oba's balls," Doc gruffed. "When you two are done flirting, there's more."

"We are *not* flirting," Zora said.

"Yeah, and I'm not old."

Keel muttered, "Girl packs a punch. Oba that hurts." Then to Doc: "What else?"

Doc cracked a smile. "That's what I wanted you to come up and see—you've got some new job offers. Black Channel stuff, mostly."

"For Wraith?"

"Uh-huh. Seems folks think if he can handle a million-dollar contract, he must be pretty good."

Zora had said that the two things that got a bounty hunter the most attention—and the most job offers—were pulling in a lot of credits and doing the jobs no one else could. Wraith had just managed both in one mission. There was much more that needed to be done, but Keel was feeling proud of himself. "I *am* pretty good," he said.

"Those skinpacks say otherwise."

Keel ignored the jab. "How many offers? And for how much?"

"Didn't open any of 'em. But don't expect to get another payout like you did with Tooms."

"So it worked," Zora said to her dad. "He's in. Unbelievable."

"Wasn't that the plan?" Keel asked.

"It was, but—I didn't think you'd be getting Black Channel contracts by name this fast. Keel, *I* don't get offered Black Channel contracts, and I've been doing this for a long time. And so help me, if you make *one more* snarky remark—"

"No, I think I learned my lesson," Keel said, gently rubbing his shoulder. "But more offers—this isn't a problem. We're just moving quickly."

"It *might* be a problem," Zora corrected. "You could get some attention you don't want with your name out there just out of the blue like that. This part of the galaxy is full of people looking to make a name for themselves by cutting down the next big thing. Gunfighters looking to land a security job with a Lizzaar—things like that. But if the goal was to be in the middle of the galaxy's seedy goings-on... well, you're there. So long as you keep delivering on your contracts."

"I'll deliver."

"Let's take a look at the jobs and figure out what the next step is," Doc said. "Also, we need to get Wraith set up with a secure account. Somethin' on the Sharon moon.

Anything else'll be traced. Rule One: Don't let anyone trace your credits."

"Fine," Keel said. "Just keep enough on hand so we can pay docking fees and bribes."

"There'll be enough of that left over." The old leej may have been wrinkled and grizzled, but he had a gleam in his eye like a kid let loose in a candy emporium. Thinking about some weapons depot somewhere, was Keel's guess.

"Left over?" Keel asked.

"You heard me, kid."

"I'm sorry, I missed the part where Major Owens made you my accountant."

Doc quirked an eyebrow. "It's your armor, kid. You look like a legionnaire out there. You said so yourself. Dark Ops don't need that, and the kind of people we wanna corner are exactly the type who'll run scared so long as you look like you vacation with the kind of guys they're doin' their worst to kill. But don't worry. I told you, I got this figured out."

Keel sized the former operator up. "You're gonna spend all my credits, aren't you?"

Doc shrugged. "Not... *all* of 'em."

Keel sighed. Funny what a lot of credits can do to a man. "Fine. I don't really care, as long as it finishes the mission."

"That's the spirit, kid."

Zora looked from her dad to Keel. "You boys can go shopping for clothes later. Besides, you're dangerously close to letting slip things you don't want me to know. Let's go check those contracts. Prioritize whatever might enhance the status of 'Wraith' and his lapdog, Aeson Keel." She turned on her heel and left.

Keel watched the door snap shut behind her. "Such a friendly daughter you've got there, Doc."

"Don't I know it, kid. She's a good girl, though. Deep down. She's—"

The door swished open, and Zora stuck her head back in. "You comin', Keel? Or am I picking the job for you?"

Keel gave a slow nod. He was about to dive into a world far vaster, far more corrupt than anything a synth-hauling smuggler was likely to get himself caught up in.

"Yeah," he said. "Be right there."

Zora—Blackheart—paused her account and tilted her head, examining Chhun. "He tell you about all of that?"

"Parts of it," Chhun said. "It's helpful to have your perspective of things. If I recall correctly, he *did* capture Cal Camp. Later, with Ravi."

Zora gave a slight smile. "He *terminated* Cal Camp. Yeah. That was big news among the hunters for a while. But by then... Wraith was almost as big a legend as Tyrus Rechs."

"When did Ravi come into the picture?" Chhun asked.

"Not for a while. I wasn't there for it, so you'd have to find Keel and ask him."

"I'll ask Ravi when I have the opportunity."

Zora raised her brows. "Or that."

"Let's see," Chhun said, checking over his datapad. "After that you—"

A distinctive comm chimed in the room.

Chhun rose at once. "Excuse me."

"What's that?" Zora asked. She sounded concerned, like it might mean bad news for her somehow.

"My team has zeroed in on another ghost we've been hunting. I'll need to monitor the operations. This will add time to your stay. I apologize. If you like, you can record your recollections using that holocam." Chhun pointed to the one in question. "This may take a while."

"That's not what you said before."

"I'm sorry. We have some private areas set up for those being interviewed. Quarters, galley, gym—"

"Shooting range?" Zora asked hopefully.

"I'll see what I can do. I have to go. There are legionnaires at the door who can escort you once you're ready."

"All right," Zora said, looking around at the room as though she might like to spend some time investigating the books on the shelves. "Most of what happened after that was small jobs anyway. Just building up the rep. But I can record those on the holo for you."

"Thank you." Chhun was already halfway out the door when he said it.

# 17

## Candalon V
## Present Day

"Don't like to be this close to them wobanki..." grunted Farnsmatt Two Gunz. He worked the stogie he'd been chewing as he studied the quality of the morning light out there on the salt flats.

Two Gunz spit into the dry sand and ran a weathered and scarred hand along the landing gear of the ship they were under, cool in the shadows before the heat of this stray world began to rise.

No one ever called him Farnsmatt.

That was an old family name and one he'd gone a long way to erase as a hardened mercenary killer turned legit—sometimes—bounty hunter. A long time ago when he was a young man getting older, Two Gunz finally went legits and picked up enough bad no-bet contracts for the Bronze Guild to certify him as licensed to bounty hunt.

That wild, young, and crazy slug-thrower kid he'd once been was all but gone now. And all that remained was an old man getting older who'd been through enough scraps to smell a bad time even when he couldn't see nothin' that said it was gonna break that way.

In time the cagey old killer came to be known simply as "Two Gunz," and anyone who wanted to lose their life real quick could do a data crawl over the webs and nets that revealed his long-ago-lost real name. And then speak it to his face.

Two Gunz because he carried two old-school slug throwers, weapons of quality and craft in an age of cheap throwaway blasters. Never mind the bloodstains. He wore an old Sandwaste wide brim for a hat, and it had only been shot through once by a blaster bolt that nearly killed the old bounty hunter. He had considered that lucky and left the gaping singe blast, stapling it up toward the top of the hat and cutting a rather rakish look for an old gunslinger.

"Yeah... you ain't gonna like it even more when we go in there for Ol' White Claw himself," growled the other man there in the blue shadows under the grounded ship. "Ain't gonna like it 't'all when we goes to collect on this here contract for the Guild. So... you wan' out, old man? Now's the time to get clear o' this contract before we start blastin'. 'Cause wobanki is crazy on any day you pick and twice on the day you didn't. Ain't gonna lie. Some of us gonna die on this one. Maybe even you."

Two Gunz worked that old half-bit cigar between impervisteel teeth that shined brightly in the morning desert air as the re-arm ship came from deep atmo with the dawn. It made ready to set down near the bounty hunter's ship way out in the Cantata Flats where the wind whistles mournful songs no one can forget.

Or so say those who've heard them. Sounded like regular wind to Two Gunz.

But then his hearing had never been the same since that time he'd been shot in the mouth in a long-ago firefight and all his original teeth had been shattered to pieces. Hence the impervisteel. And, maybe, hence the wind sounding like dry, desert wind.

And only that.

Engines whined in the descent as repulsors howled like drowned ghosts to arrest forward momentum and put down in the marked LZ to service and resupply the ship out here on the flats. A Margetti-Fundt Vampire-class frigate that had seen better days as an interdiction picket until the worst of the last hours of the Savage Wars. Now she was modded and ready for bounty work, with heavy weapons, boarding tractors, cloaking instruments on all spectrums, and holding cells rivaling most ultramax Repub re-education facilities.

She had a few other tricks too. In space and on mission she was a deadly foe that could easily deal with local and even Repub-level authorities as long as there weren't fighters or capital-class ships in the mix. On the ground, waiting for a re-arm... she was fat and lazy like most ships are. But the bounty hunters, a cabal of them, were always on hand and looking for any trouble about to go down when they were most vulnerable.

As they say in the Bronze Guild... *There are two types of hunters: old hunters and bold hunters. But there are no old, bold hunters.*

"Didn't say I wanted outta this one, MaCrease..." moaned old Two Gunz. He rubbed his flank where he'd been shot in the back once. "Jes' said I don't like i' this close to the wobanki. No one with half a brain would... Ask me how I lived so long."

And in that, Two Gunz was right. This close to wobanki space invited all kinds of raids from the big hunting cat clans, and few ever survived a wobanki blood raid.

MaCrease, the other man there with Two Gunz in the cool shadows under the belly of the frigate, bots preparing to receive cargo, beeping and chittering like they did... MaCrease who ran the five-man bounty hunter team that had picked up the contract on a wobanki pirate White Claw who operated out of the Crimson Flare sector of space just half a light year distant... MaCrease settled to cleaning his scatter blaster he ran as the re-arm freighter they'd called for made ready to land right next to their bounty-hunting ship. The beast of a resupply ship brought in the repulsors to full, spraying caustic salt and sand everywhere. Massive landing gear extended to support its ungainly bulk.

Those struts sank into the sand beneath the odd resupply freighter that was shaped more like an old sky blimp than the boxy and utilitarian junk haulers that normally served in this role. Not to mention the occasional fast pancakes that did the lighter cargo and contraband work.

"That's one ugly ship..." hissed Two Gunz quietly, working his foul old cigar over to the other side of his mouth. He smelled the engine draft as the jump turbines began to throttle down to idle.

He also felt the hair on the back of his neck tingle for a second.

"You ever work with this outfit before, MaCrease?"

"Nope. Called it in through the Bronze. Said we needed a top-off on munitions, blaster cores for the main gun, and as much PDC as they can deliver, 'cause word is Ol' White Claw lives for them scatterpack SSMs."

Two Gunz made a sound as though this satisfied his curiosity. But it didn't really. He was getting old and failed to notice when one of his hands felt for one of the finely made guns he was known for.

The re-arm freighter was down, and already the cargo doors were dropping along the sides. The main boarding ramp extended down into the white salt and cream sand drifts.

One of the bounty-hunting team's goofier bots, a stores-and-steward Pylonia model, gesticulated widely with its spidery arms and began directing the other bots to prepare to receive the cargo transfers. Some bots hummed melancholy ditties while others motivated via servo-whining tracks toward the re-arm ship.

"Dammit to hell..." screeched MaCrease a moment later when he saw the legionnaires coming down the main boarding ramp. And this wasn't in ceremonial fashion or standard-protocol tax-interdiction-and-collection site security. This was high-speed low-drag operators in slick tactical armor moving out from the boarding ramps and splitting off into teams, clearly assuming a combat posture.

Two Gunz swore and didn't spit out his smoking cigar as he drew his revolvers and began to fire while moving for cover.

He might have been old, but he wasn't slow or stupid. He'd decided as he pulled trigger and moved for the exit where there was none that this was gonna be a fight, and there wasn't any talk gonna come up front of this one.

Firing both Daltron Pythons, specialty revolvers he'd had fitted and tricked out a long time ago in one of the better night markets he'd ever found, Two Gunz found cover and weighed his options as the incoming blaster fire started... incoming.

A Lahurasian gunsmith had dialed the Pythons up, and they had a number of features that made them deadly accurate and ready to deal death at the drop of a hat.

The first team of legionnaires was already pushing forward, firing disabling shots into the perimeter defenses the crafty bounty hunter team had set up and neutralizing the aft PDCs—perimeter defense cannons—for the bounty hunter frigate tagged *Justifier*. The legionnaires' armor had already adapted to the environment, location, quality of light, and even background within the selected battle space, practically cloaking them against targeted and automated fire, as they oriented toward the danger areas the armor's AIs had identified for likely threats and violence. Visually, they looked like shadowy wraiths one had to concentrate on to distinguish from the surroundings and background. It wasn't invisibility-level stealth capability, more like pencil sketches of what a legionnaire carrying death and coming at you would look like. Their images shifted crazily as though they were life-like drawings constantly updating with each movement.

A second team of legionnaires had covered behind the forward landing gear of the re-arm vessel and within seconds had the squad automatic blaster up and suppressing the two perimeter security bots the bounty hunters had been maintaining in the shadows beneath the hulking Vampire-class frigate *Justifier*. Other bots got hit in intersecting fields of fire and exploded in showers of sparks or careened off into the sands beyond the two ships, spilling oily smoke and trailing flames as they ululated and beeped internal damage reports.

Two Gunz swore at his good luck running out and started dumping old-school, no-joke lead at the nearest legionnaire. The fast-moving and compact target leading the combat wedge of the assaulters took one round right in the chest armor.

Two Gunz's shots were accurate, always had been, and the legionnaire got hammered by two revolvers doling out five-hundred-caliber rounds in titanic blasts out there on the quiet salt flats as all hell continued to break loose. The kinetic force of the shots spun the legionnaire around. Two

Gunz's accuracy allowed him to land another five-hundred-caliber round right in the man's back.

The gunfighter erupted in wild laughter. He shouted, "That'll learn ya, boy," and then got tapped in the head by one of the Legion snipers.

The old bounty hunter's skull exploded. Brain matter turned to red mist drifting on the heat drafts coming off the re-arm freighter's engines. His body flopped down and leaked out onto the thirsty salt and sand behind the landing gear of his own frigate.

The legionnaire that Two Gunz had hit went down too, but only to his knees. The trooper on his right pivoted away from the rear observation canopy in the back of the *Justifier*. A co-ax perimeter defense gun on the ship was just spinning up into action, as the trooper grabbed the armor's drag handle on the hit legionnaire, yanking him for cover behind the *Justifier*'s rear main landing gear.

One of the blaster-struck bots ran past the engaged legionnaires, on fire and shrieking about the re-arm delivery protocols being utterly disregarded.

Meanwhile MaCrease ran for the Vampire freighter's boarding ramp. He had some idea of what they could do to repel the assault and perhaps buy some time for a hot dust-off.

The cabal would go on.

"I'll get the boys in action... Gunz!" he shouted.

The fighting had happened so fast, the blaster fire going from nothing to immediate and intense in a heartbeat, that MaCrease had no idea that Two Gunz had already been domed by one of the Legion snipers.

Still, he had plans and solutions, and he was working the game of wily survival every bounty hunter must when needs require.

MaCrease had walked away from more battles than most had. It was well known that he'd shot down his fair share of Legion boys during the Troubles, which was how most in these sectors referred to the Galactic Civil War and the turbulent times that had followed. But the truth was, the ones he'd killed had never been Legion. They were typically hullbusters or RA.

He'd never let fact ruin a good fiction.

Bots were all gone and Legion blaster fire now concentrated on the under-hull defenses that had spun up on the *Justifier*. The Legion sniper pulling bottom-side security from his position stood instead of covering, like he was some kind of old-school frontier gunfighter himself instead of one the best snipers the Legion had ever seen. He raised his slick matte-gray N-18, sighted, exhaled the merest graveyard whisper, and dialed in the running MaCrease. Targeting data and intel on this op confirmed the figure as the ringleader of the bounty hunter crew of the *Justifier*.

The sniper pulled the trigger and drilled the man... not center mass.

Too easy.

But right in the head.

At a dead run.

That is not an easy shot no matter what the streams and comic holos say.

MaCrease, now headless, continued to stumble and died at the foot of the boarding ramp of his cherished vessel.

Perimeter defense fire exploded around the sniper, who seemed heedless of the streaking sizzling death.

"Always a show-off, Heckler?" grunted one of the legionnaires over the L-comm. It was the support team leader directing fire for the SAB currently suppressing the bounty hunters' automatic defenses with short doses of high-volume fire.

The op order had specifically called for no headshots. There'd even been a line item specifically for the target that had just been terminated. Heckler had done it anyway.

"It vas nothing, HT-02..." the sniper said.

Heckler's own hunter team identifier was HT-19. The man was a native of the Bavar March. A series of worlds once colonized long ago by mercenaries rumored to be from Earth itself. A region of it called Germany, specifically. He spoke a heavily accented Standard as a result.

"Center mass ist for ze amateurs, Shredder. A shot like zat is vhat separates ze sniper from ze... der mere... *enthusiast*. Like Flower Child ist. If one expects more of onezelf... zen one delivers more."

By that time the *Justifier* was dropping a variety of illegally modified bots the bounty hunter crew had picked up from all across the galaxy's edge in their long and acquisition-laden travels. Many was the time the bounty hunters had needed ground security and extra troops to get some contract done, or just to get paid by the client intent on cheating them out of what they were owed. The bots were deployed from the various ramps meant for crew and passengers out into the salt and sand to respond to the immediate threat of a ventral boarding action against the ship.

Three surviving bounty hunters aboard the ship were still in play. The captain of the *Justifier* had ordered a cold start on reactors three and four to prep the ship for emergency takeoff. The bots would be left behind; their sole job now was to slow the legionnaires down long enough to allow an escape. The boarding ramps began to rise, including the main one where MaCrease had been shot, and as it drew itself upward it carried along the limp headless body of the bounty hunter and crushed it as it sealed itself against the hull, leaving the legs somehow dangling by a gory thread on the outside of the vessel.

Sand and salt turned to furies as the ship powered her mains and prepared to bolt.

# 18

Major Slade, commander of the legionnaires currently striking the *Justifier*, keyed his L-comm to the pilot of the *Tomahawk*, a Legion assault corvette modified for stealth and insertion. *Tomahawk* was also rated for short but heavy combat, which was within the operations mandate for this special assignment that the newly formed Hunter Team Ranger had been assembled for.

"Strike team going topside, Tomahawk Flight. Stand by for ECM strike."

The crew of the *Tomahawk* was always referred to as "Tomahawk" followed by the specific duty section as outlined in the signal and command section of the operations mandate.

Tomahawk Flight was a former Repub Navy captain who now flew for the new Legion after its post–Article Nineteen restructuring. He'd been designated to fly this mission to support the team's capture of the bounty hunter ship.

He acknowledged the active ECM strike with generators powered up. "Disengaging active camo now.

Standing by to support with deck guns while making breach, Ranger Actual."

He got a two-click acknowledgment from the team leader of the four-legionnaire striker force taking the topside lift to the upper surface of the assault corvette.

Captain Adwers from the flight deck of the *Tomahawk* gave a terse, "Disengaging active cloak now. Firing ECM generators..."

Then... "Cleared to board enemy vessel, Ranger."

From the perspective of the crew of the *Justifier*, which was currently being hammered by Legion fire from the ground, and had just been electronically shotgunned by a powerful signal burst that had savaged many of its internal and defensive systems, the re-arm freighter that had landed to the rear just suddenly shimmered, fading out of existence. The image of the bulbous cargo hauler, a late-era Urstogon deep-space repair vessel most pilots and scouts called "the Fat Man," disappeared... and reappeared as something else. Once the ECM jammers and holo-camo had fully shut down, it was clear to those aboard the *Justifier* that the vessel aft of them was not a Fat Man deep-space repair vessel at all, but rather a mean and chopped-down Hammerhead corvette that had been refitted as an assault ship. Matte-gray with no designation or insignia, the assault corvette reeked of covert operations that tended toward extreme violence of action and no traces left. A powerful twin-barrel ion gun had been added aft near the lean and mean Mark IX jump engines, and the main forward landing gear increased bow angle giving the vessel an almost combative sneer that challenged anyone, even a battleship, to a good old-fashioned scrap.

As the lift carrying the four legionnaires in heavy jump armor reached the upper hull of the assault corvette, a hatch irised open to the burning blue skies and the swirling salt and sand. At once a fusillade of turrets opened fire from the *Tomahawk* and raked the *Justifier*, shutting down a number of defense systems that had been active to protect the ship from dorsal boarding actions, and suddenly ship-to-ship combat erupted savagely right there on the salt flats.

The legionnaires now on top of the *Tomahawk*, a striker team kitted and trained just for these types of actions, prepared to make their move, while down below, in the shadows beneath both ships, the Legion assault and support team continued to destroy the makeshift war bots.

The machines hadn't been a surprise to the hunter team. Intel had said the bounty hunters would deploy if ground combat ensued and things looked bleak for the tangos. Elektra, the intel collection and assessment specialist who moved ahead of the team on occasion, was good to her word. The bounty hunters were indeed playing their hole card, because things didn't just look bleak, they looked downright stark and awful.

Every trick, prayer, and desperate *just-might-work* would be employed now. Until the inevitable.

Gun Boy drones deployed out from under *Justifier*'s various drop-down defense hatches, which had once held missile racks back in the day when missile combat was all the rage in some of the micro wars between the upstart colonial empires during those lulls between explosive Savage invasions. Gun Boys, an early, unrefined precursor to the Legion's own terrifying war bots, were dwarfish automatons, each carrying a sub blaster and a battle belt full of fraggers and bangers, and had been acquired at an expense the bounty hunters had thought hefty but worth its weight in synth. They'd purchased seven racks, each rack containing twenty Gun Boys, to defend them in bad situations like a compromised LZ.

Those Gun Boys were now suddenly everywhere, shooting at everything that moved and attempting to take down the Legion ground assault teams with one wounded near the *Justifier*'s rear main landing gear. Gun Boys were known for battery-pack-dumping with wild abandon on anything that moved and never mind the incoming because they were just bots. Once deployed, the battlefield was unsafe for friend, foe, and bystander alike.

The legionnaires immediately re-tasked their blaster fire to clear these obstacles just as had been outlined in the op order.

The ASL, assistant team leader, for the assaulters was calling for medical support for the downed legionnaire, Team Leader SSG Harm. His armor's medical diagnostics were malfunctioning, and he was gasping and couldn't breathe. Tension pneumothorax was coding across the combat management screens.

The Legion medic, overwatched by another legionnaire carrying a breaching scattergun and a chopped-down N-4, raced for the downed legionnaire behind the *Justifier*'s main even as the fire from the Gun Boys reached a cacophonic insanity.

HT-34, Sergeant Király, had dragged SSG Harm out of the way so the armor could begin medical treatment without him being under direct fire. SSG Harm had at first gotten to his knees, seemingly intent on standing up, and had then fallen over. His armor was sending bad signals, and Király, returning fire one-handed with his N-4, had hard-jacked himself into his team leader's armor and gotten the priority medical code indicating the impending tension pneumothorax.

The impact from a five-hundred-caliber round had shattered something and caused the lung of the wounded legionnaire to swell and push on his heart. Normally the onboard medical suite in the armor would decompress the swelling with a needle insertion, but somehow that feature had been destroyed by the impact of the round.

If direct action wasn't taken immediately, Harm would die.

Medic and security raced for the landing gear and the downed legionnaire out there on the sand and blowing salt. Király moved aside, and the medic hard-jacked in in his place. The Legion medic decided on a course of action in seconds as the security legionnaire assigned to him opened fire with the breaching blaster on Gun Boys pushing danger close on the stand near the landing gear.

"Harm's coding... goin' direct!" shouted the medic, who had been a Repub Navy warrant physician's assistant with advanced medical training before going Legion during Article Nineteen when the Legion absorbed the loyal ships, marines, and featherheads and became something more than just legionnaires.

They sometimes called the medic by his old Repub Navy rank: Chief. Sometimes Demp. Most times Doc, like all the other medics.

Mad Dog had said of the Medic, "He got your back come hell or deep space."

And if Mad Dog said it was so... then it was so as far as any leej was concerned. Mad Dog was already legend if even half the stories were true. And as one of the team said, "He ain't even dead yet."

"Get 'er done, Doc," muttered Mad Dog, slam-firing blaster shots at incoming killer bots relentlessly swarming for the legionnaires. The maniacal little killer bots gaggle-chirped, issued targeting directions to one another in their robot voices, then went offline as they got wrecked straight-up point-blank. "Ain't no one gonna get close enough to spit, Demp," he added.

"Copy, HT-68... cracking his plate now..." drawled the medic as he dragged out "the jaws," a tool made specifically for getting into the armor when there wasn't time to take it apart piece by piece. "Oh boy, oh boy... we got us a situation, Hunter Team Ranger. Dealer's choice..." continued the medic as he studied the diagnostics and what his years of training and expertise were showing him. "You jokers would attempt to relieve pressure on the affected lung by doing a needle D, if ya had to... right into the second intercostal space. Second and third rib, amirite, fam? Feel me, Legion boys? Bad move. This guy's oatmeal all up in there. We gotta go through the fourth and fif'... Gotta punch the anterior axillary site for this stick 'cause this is consistent with an upper chest injury as mid clavicular line would be compromised. Nicely done, Demp. Get yo'self a prize outta the prize draw'!"

The SAB gunner in support of the assaulters saw the fresh push from the Gun Boys and opened fire after swapping in a new heavy charge pack while the medic made ready to do what he was gonna do. Under fire.

"Get some," grunted the gunner and drew a bright line of heavy blaster fire across two racks of deployed Gun Boys surging for the rear main and the legionnaires firing from there.

The medic cracked the armor, shucked the needle-ator from off his battle belt, and cried, "Here goes nothin'. Sorry, buddy..."

Then jabbed the lung between the fourth and fifth ribs to stop the tension pneumothorax from taking Harm's life.

Whoever was on board and running the ground defense systems for the *Justifier* now realized the brilliance of the legionnaires' attack plan as it all came together. In the maelstrom of dying Gun Boys being torn apart in intersecting blaster fire, it suddenly became clear that this was the distraction, and the real boarding assault was coming from another direction.

A surprise attack. Then a smash.

Whoever oversaw defenses aboard the *Justifier*, whether the captain or one of the remaining bounty hunters, tried to dump the sandcasters, defensive systems used in space to chaff incoming SSMs, hoping to shut down the battle on the ground so they could recall the Gun Boys to the ship to respond to the breach in progress along the top side of the hull.

Whoever it was, they saw what was happening, and why all was lost now...

... and always had been.

The Legion assault ship, while holographically skinned as a Fat Man in a usage of holo-camo technology none of the hunters had ever seen done so well, had set down close to the vessel they were purportedly there to re-arm. That was too close for the Gun Boys to use their frags, as the defense paradigms coded into these bots prevented the Gun Boys from using fragmentary devices within fifty meters of their own ship to avoid damage to the hull.

The Gun Boys had been made ineffective as assaulters. Reduced to moving targets that could only fire back with underpowered sub blasters.

The Legion had developed a kill box outside that left little to chance. Even a chance aided by the deployment of the sandblasters. Two of the fearsome soldiers fired from the rear main. Two other legionnaires had shifted off to the left to cover behind a cargo module the bounty hunters had offloaded as a form of payment for the re-arm services they were expecting instead of the surprise

Legion assault corvette that was now shooting their frigate to pieces. Add in the SAB gunner with sniper support and a few other nasty surprises, and the seven racks of Gun Boys streaming in to clear the underside of the *Justifier* of enemies were being murdered with mechanical patience and excessive violence by the legionnaires.

Legionnaires who'd attacked, and then somehow... amazingly set up an ambush at the same time. Which was quite a trick.

Meanwhile, the Legion striker team, led by Major Slade, Ranger Actual, egressed from the top of the *Tomahawk*, activated the jump jets on their armor, and rocketed in a sudden terrific bound that had them on top of the shot-to-hell *Justifier* three and a half seconds later.

They landed on an upper freighter hull that had been devastated by the fusillade of ship-to-ship fire; it now looked like the surface of some moon that had seen heavy combat back in the Troubles and was now little more than a blackened and scorched chunk of rock orbiting through a debris field of torn-apart capital ships.

The first two legionnaires down on the hull, Major Slade and his comms sergeant, immediately took up security positions as the team sniper moved into overwatch, scanning for any deployables along the hull. The master breacher moved in, planted the charges, and pulled back from the hatch they'd selected for entry. Selected due to the fact that it was on the same deck as the flight bridge and would give them total control of the ship within the two minutes it would take them to reach that compartment and eliminate all resistance along the way.

Elektra's intel had been rock solid.

"Good to go," said the master breacher over the L-comm as the charge that would breach the hull was set and ready to go. The breacher was from Legion Special

Munitions Section, D Group as it was known, and all called him Wizard, but officially he was known as Master Sergeant Roosenlooper, HT-09.

Major Slade, down on one knee and scanning the forward hull, merely whispered, "Do it, Oh-Nine."

With no delay and total calm like a schoolteacher quietly working through the syllabus in some learning hall, not a war zone of ship-to-ship fire across hulls, Wizard went live with his magic.

"Affirmative, Actual... execute, execute, execute."

Then the shaped demo blew straight through the reinforced hatch inward, clean and crisp like a breaching torch, killing one of the bounty hunters just below.

Her name was Cafidia Vex. She had just been headed topside to inspect the damage the ship's AI had been screaming on and on about. She'd thought to deliver some sniper support from there as well, as that was her specialty. She'd built a solid career in the Guild for terminations with the Antarez fifty-watt anti-materiel sniper engagement rifle she ran.

The detonated charge pulped her and her combat armor with overpressure at the gas giant level. The Antarez anti-materiel clattered off down the passage, its tens-of-thousands-of-credits x-ray holographic imaging scope ruined as the optics were shattered into tens of thousands of pieces.

Cafidia herself was a mess of flesh and ruined armor, and it was hard to tell where the once beautiful yet cruel woman ended and her armor began.

In expert and efficient fashion the Legion striker team entered the ship, boots treading through the goo that was now the renowned bounty hunter terminator, killed three more crew members farther along the passage, moved to the bridge, precisely shot down one of the bounty hunters who'd been managing the defenses from there, and also gut-shot the captain of the *Justifier* who'd tried to return fire with a holdout he carried.

The captain was still alive despite the blast from Flower Child, who'd been running the SDM, squad designated marksman, version of the N-18. Shorter barrel. Vented Hex System suppressor. Thumb-dial power-usage snapshot trigger. Perfectly vengeful for boarding actions and CQB in tight quarters. It had left a giant seared hole in the captain's stomach and the man screamed in pain as the legionnaires secured and sliced the bridge.

The N-18 is a ruiner of men. Flower Child used the chopped N-18 Alpha Six variant developed for fun and games by Dark Operations. Variable power allowed the sniper to move forward into a CQB support role when close-quarters combat in tight spaces was demanded. Using the notoriously heavy-grade sniper system up close and drilling a man would cause all sorts of secondary injuries. The captain was alive, but he wouldn't be for long.

For now, though, the tango was wanted alive. According to the op order the captain was to survive initial contact so that security protocols could be bypassed via biometrics. His dead body could be used to do the same, but only if they acted before the bio-signals faded.

They had to move quickly either way. Access was needed within five minutes of landing.

Two minutes from breach.

Seven racks of Gun Boys lay shattered out there in the shade underneath the frigate resting in the vast emptiness of the salt flats.

The other bounty hunters were dead.

Now it was time for the ship's computers to give up their secrets to the legionnaires. That's what the operators had come for.

The captain was dragged to the biometric scanner near the main computer by Major Slade, who said little and worked fast as reports across the L-comm were handled by the team sergeant, HT-02 to Slade's HT-01. Sergeant First Class D'het. Shredder. The captain authenticated and was dropped unceremoniously to the deck of the bridge of the *Justifier*.

No loss.

Elektra's intel had said he was a bad one.

Even the bounty hunters he worked with didn't know he'd once run with a pirate outfit that had left no survivors on the pleasure liners they'd preyed upon near the Emerald Worlds where the rich, young, and beautiful had gone to have their on-the-rails adventures and then got a little more than they bargained for along the way.

The Guild hunters didn't know he'd once been called Throat Cutter.

But Elektra knew.

And she made sure the legionnaires knew too.

Ten minutes later the legionnaires had the trail of HVT Blowtorch, as the op order identified Master Sergeant Bombassa, formerly of the Legion, and the *Tomahawk* was gears up and heading for low atmo and jump as the assault corvette screamed skyward.

On aft visual, Captain Adwers, from the bridge, flying the exfil as the *Tomahawk* shuddered and bucked through upper atmo, watched as the *Justifier* detonated in every direction along the vast and empty waste that was the Cantata Salt Flats.

The sand and salt would take what it would take, and the pieces that remained would be a mystery no one would ever understand.

And the Legion hunter team was a little further along the trail it pursued.

# 19

## Assault Corvette *Tomahawk*
## Inbound on Hang Kong Station

The Legion assault corvette *Tomahawk* hurtled through the howling dark wastes of hyperspace, pushing the mains and bearing toward Hang Kong Station in the Surrari Cluster.

Time was crucial, and there was little to spare.

The sensitive intel yield from the *Justifier's* sliced main computers had been profitable, granting the Legion hunter team a brief glance into the Bronze Guild's encrypted outstanding contracts.

A non-Guild member looking at those contracts—even if a member of the Republic, even if a legionnaire—was against the law. The fruit of an agreement between a guild so powerful it had once harbored the infamous Tyrus Rechs and a galaxy-spanning government that did not desire war with a vast, well-armed cadre of bounty hunters.

Usually, information on those contracts had to be bought. Usually, the seller was terminated—after a contract was placed on their own head.

Slicing that information? No. Near impossible, even by the best of code-slicer standards.

But the hunter-killer algos the Legion team ran hadn't just been state of the art... they were unheard of, light years beyond the tip of current commercial development.

And even with that advantage, the Legion had had only five minutes to find what they needed before the Guild's powerful encryption cycles destroyed everything and started afresh, rolling the quantum dice for the next signals, locations, and updates.

The man the hunter team was after was a former Dark Ops legionnaire. A warrior just like them, or he had been. The target had played a critical role in recent galactic events, thunderclaps that had lit the galaxy on fire and almost destroyed galactic civilization as it was known in the process.

For just a brief moment, the seekers in armor had gotten a glimpse of where the target was heading, and who he was blasting for.

HVT Blowtorch. First Sergeant Bombassa. Now a bounty hunter pulling down contracts for the Guild. It was this former legionnaire that Hunter Team Ranger now followed along a desperate trail across the stars, shattered worlds, and even now into some of the lowest of dens of iniquity the galaxy had to offer.

Amidships on deck three of the *Tomahawk*, the commander and team leader of the hunters conducted a final AAR of the events that had taken place on the wind-blasted salt flats of the world they'd just left.

Just the commander and his team sergeant.

Ranger Actual and Shredder. Major Slade and Sergeant First Class D'het.

"Heckler's gonna be a problem, sir," grunted Sergeant D'het, working dip and drinking cold kaff at the same time as he watched the captured holofeed update the sand table they'd run for the op.

The teams moved once again to their assault positions, letting go with the outgoing blaster fire and cleverly moving to assemble a kill box, knowing the Gun Boys would be used to defend the ship expertly in short order.

Sergeant Harm was hit. Comms traffic appeared in holotext. Sound off. They'd heard it all before. Everyone on the team was pure pipe hitter. No one got excited even though the assault team leader got tapped hard.

Even the Navy medic kept it together.

Solid. No complaints.

And yet here they were, exploring the cracks and looking for the fractures. Yeah, it was mission, but if things continued going where they were... going... then what had just happened would feel like just practice.

Major Slade looked tired and rubbed his jaw as he studied the recorded feeds on the virtual sand table. The assaulters and support team creating the feint. SAB fire going high dosage. The striker team boarding the enemy vessel for a straight-up savage right cross that gave the hunter team access to the information they needed to follow Blowtorch's trail.

No easy feat. CQB inside a ship. Hullbuster work. The team had run that on the shoot deck and had it cold. Nothing to critique with the striker team. Wizard was on point with his demo, but then... why wouldn't he be? He was the Wizard.

Everyone in the Legion knew who he was.

Then Flower Child did the captain exactly as indicated in the order, and they got the bioscan and then access to the slice.

The slicers ran amok inside the system for a few seconds with a comm line through jump space posing as the bounty hunter frigate updating its mission via Guild contracts. This had been the chokepoint, and there was no amount of time on the shoot deck that could overcome a bad slice and a total lockdown on Guild servers. Add in that the Bronze Guild was fanatical to the point of religious about maintaining their encryption of contracts and the identities of their bounty hunters, and this could have gone all kinds of wrong.

There was always another Guild hunter nearby. They were everywhere.

But the slice was good. The mission moved to the next phase.

HVT location.

They now knew First Sergeant Bombassa's ship: the *Antari Shark*, a small yet heavy-duty scout tender modified and upgraded. Rumored to carry a couple of very powerful surprises when pressed. The *Shark* was now inbound on Hang Kong Station to capture and deliver one of the most notorious hit men in the employ of one of the most violent tongs operating out of that particular space station.

Now the hunter team had a window to connect with the former legionnaire and convince him, whether he liked it or not, to submit to an interview with the Adjudicator.

Answer some delicate, but needed, questions.

That was a tomorrow problem. The Adjudicator's problem. Major Slade and the team just needed to arrange the meeting. That's all.

The sand table reset to the beginning of the op planetside, and froze.

Major Slade ignored the assessment regarding one of his snipers. It was valid. *No headshots* had been made clear. But Slade knew why it had happened anyway.

Everyone on this team was an alpha. They were, and this was not cliché... the best of the best the Legion had to offer at the current time. And then some.

Hell. One of them was actually a quad.

Sergeant Király. Legionnaire. Dark Operations OT graduate. Hullbuster Commando School. Naval Repub Special Teams course.

There were very few quads in Legion history. Less than ten.

All you needed to do was complete the absolute hardest and most extreme courses the militaries of the galactic civilization had to offer. And have a reason why that should happen.

Sergeant Király's reason was above the commander's security clearance.

And maybe... that was what Slade was looking for as he ran the AAR longer than was needed. Looking for the faults. Looking for the fractures.

Looking for something...

When Major Slade had tried to decrypt the redacted portions of Király's file, entering his own high-security code authentication for clearance and access—which should have granted him total admittance; hell, he had access to all of Mad Dog Shriver's records, and that guy had been up some really dark alleys the Repub wanted to pretend didn't happen—but this time with Sergeant Király the screen on his battle board had merely flashed...

*Not Cleared for this level of Information.*

There wasn't even an admin note advising the major to seek clearance from higher up. If he really wanted to know. A helpful tip that would flash in ominous red and stark white. A warning, really. Turn back or invite unwanted scrutiny. Some things you are not meant to know. Don't make someone have to come have a conversation with you about that... and your career.

No-go. Don't even try.

Just live with the rock star you got, Major.

Király. Sergeant Király was quiet. Kept to himself. Focused on the mission with a laser-like intensity that even the best of the best could have used to improve their game. He was pure operator, and if there was anything else to him, a personality even... it had yet to be detected.

Slade had worked with the best. The frighteningly good. Most had this same trait. Major Slade had played a vague imitation of them to get the mission done and lead the hulkas that they were, in battle and on ops. But Slade knew he wasn't one. The major was wily, yes. He was no Király. Slade would play every angle to get the mission done. Hitters like Sergeant Király saw only one way.

They blast their way to daylight. They're killers in the way most men never will be.

And usually no one knew it unless you'd met one of their kind before. Or had been on the teams in Dark Ops that weren't even Dark Ops and had no designation. Teams that didn't exist and didn't get talked about.

Teams with flashing red and stark white warnings. *Danger.* Turn back, and live.

Sergeant Király quietly fit in with the newly formed unit known as Hunter Team Ranger, even though he was, being a quad, clearly on a level most couldn't even appreciate. He fit in so well that none of the other alphas even suspected he was a quad.

On the surface, Király was just another one of the alphas. All of whom had gone to all twenty-eight of the best schools the Legion had to offer. Courses completed over the length of their careers orbiting around Dark Ops. CVs that had recommended them to the hiring pool for the team. Five hundred possibles across the Legion had formed that pool... and the vast majority were passed over when it came to selecting the hunter teams.

In the one percent of the one percent... this was something that couldn't even be measured.

And then there was Király.

*You got dealt an ace on that one*, Slade told himself. *Take it and don't ask questions.*

But he did ask questions. Or at least... he thought them.

Sergeant Király was a rising star in Dark Ops and beyond. But what was the beyond? It certainly wasn't Nether. So what was it? And why was he *here*, now, on a team hunting down a ghost?

Hard to say.

All they were doing was the bidding of their assigned Adjudicator. A former Legion commander, a legend in his own time who was following a trail that only he knew. On a mission only he had the full brief of.

Nothing strange there.

*Ha. Yes there is. It's all strange. This is where it gets weird, and dark.*

Here be monsters.

As General Combs had told Slade when giving him the assignment, the hunter team, a new concept for the Legion, "You're hunting dogs, Major Slade. You go. You hunt. You seek. You find. And then you kill if you have to. But you get what, or who, the Legion Adjudicator wants, and you do what he wants done. Do you understand, Major?"

They were meeting aboard the *Fury*. The brand-new Legion state-of-the-art cruiser just out of the shipyards at Jamari.

"I do..." began Major Slade slowly in the heavy silence, not with hesitation, just choosing his words wisely because things were dangerous and you'd have to be stupid not to feel that. And Major Slade was far from stupid. This was the edge of Dark Operations.

Here, everything, every word... it was all selection. Even now. It was always selection at this level.

And this was big.

"And I don't, sir."

For a moment the general said nothing and... more importantly... gave nothing away. Then...

"What don't you understand, Mark?" the general asked, leaning forward and going informal inside the secure briefing room aboard the *Fury*.

"What is... an Adjudicator? And why does it need... hunting dogs? Sir?"

The general smiled, and it wasn't really a smile. It was just something the powerful and quiet Legion general learned to do to look human, not the stone-cold operator he'd been for most of his career.

A warrior.

A killer.

A warlord.

Now, as a *general*... he occasionally needed to deal with civs and politicians. Occasionally he needed to smile so they could... feel safe. He had in fact been told to do so by a now-retired mentor in Dark Operations command.

Had those civs and politicians only known how many lives that man had ended, personally, and by command in defense of the Republic, they would have soiled themselves right in front of him.

He was not tortured by what he had done, and he slept well at night. When he slept.

But the smile he'd been suggested he perform, it never matched the hooded and unblinking eyes that ran the numbers of killing everyone in the room no matter where or when the room was.

Those ice-blue eyes... those were all murder cold and nothing but. Even the general's wife shuddered sometimes when she accidentally forgot that he was her husband and not some dangerous stranger on a grav-tram. Or at their new little granddaughter's second birthday party.

The general was one of those, thought Slade. Just like Sergeant Király.

Where do they come from, he wondered sometimes in the night when he smoked and stared at the ceiling. Slade didn't sleep well. And when he did, he usually slept sitting up, sidearm in hand. Watching the door with one eye.

Even on the *Fury*.

Even on the *Tomahawk*.

The general took a long slow breath in the secure briefing chamber.

"We need to find out... what happened... Mark."

Major Slade said nothing. He was being... given a glimpse.

"Before the Legion goes forward after... the Troubles..." the general continued, "we need to know exactly what happened. Who the players were. And are all the threats... eliminated. Even now. The Adjudicator is... one of us. A legionnaire. His identity will remain undisclosed until you and your team meet him personally."

Slade processed this and then... took a chance.

"Why, sir?"

The general snorted what might have been a small sour laugh, or the warning of a tyrannasquid about to charge.

"The role of Adjudicators is to find out how to go forward. What the shape of the galaxy looks like."

Major Slade pressed his luck. Hell... he'd never make Field Grade, so why not, he thought. Why not.

"Sir, this sounds like some... some kind of... inquisitor. Something out of the dark histories. Savage empire stuff.

Old Earth history. Torture and questioning. All this because of Ulori?"

The general said nothing for a long moment, indicating he did not disagree with his major. Just merely murder-stared through his upstart questioner.

Then he cleared his throat.

"It's not that, Mark. This isn't show me the man and I'll show you the crime. This is... the truth. And nothing else but. Much of the work will be accomplished without the need of your team. But... the Adjudicator will go wherever this trail takes him, and nothing will stop him. That's you. That's where you and your team come in. Your part, Major. Nothing will stop this mission."

Pause.

"Even at the cost of your lives."

Long pause.

Then...

"I know you, Mark. I know your record. That's why you were selected to lead this team."

The heavy silence of the secure briefing room was so substantial and thick it was like a thing that could be reached out and touched.

The general looked off into nothingness and the gray twilight at the edge of the room.

"Ours, Major, is not to know why someone must die. Only that they must. Your time in Special Missions Section was clear on that point, and there is not one line item in the record that indicates you did not... fulfill these needs of the Republic. And you know about *my* time there."

The general looked around as though there were some invisible audience in the room who might be listening to what he had to say next that could not be overheard.

"But this time... I'll tell you why, Mark, because it's that important to us. And not just to the Legion, but all of us, every one of us who are... brothers in the Legion and the peoples we ride watch over. And yes, I mean that great stinking mass of alien and human civilization out there that we stand on the wall for, come storm or mass wave assault. It's all depending on what the Adjudicators find, Mark. This... *this* is how we go forward this time. A reformed Republic with the Legion maintaining the right to flip the red queen whenever we don't like the corruption and betrayal that will inevitably come from the scum who call themselves our elites and our betters—the politicians —or... a new way.

"And remember, every legionnaire knows to forget nothing. But there are other orders General Marks himself gave us. And one of those is don't ever lie to another legionnaire. You can lie to whoever else you want, but the Legion depends on the truth to get the job done. The truth has always been our greatest weapon, and that fancy armor we strap on and go out and get killed in when we're doing the stacking... that's nothing compared to the truth. So this time, before we ever let the tyrants take control ever again, or become ones ourselves in the process, we are going to find out the truth of what really happened. Come hell or high grav. We are gonna know this time.

"That's the Adjudicators' role, Major. You... your role is to protect your Adjudicator, even though he's every bit the warfighter we are. Even though his armor has considerable upgrades and... hell, might as well call them powers. Dark Science Lab stuff that will blow your mind. Probably lifted from the Savages. Legion is still sitting tight on that vault discovered on Kima. That doesn't matter. He's a life taker and a heartbreaker. But he needs a... call it a praetorian guard, Major. And *you* need to find those he needs to question, because you're going to find that not everyone wants to answer his questions. Not everyone wants the truth."

# 20

"Heckler's gonna be a problem, sir," said the senior team NCO once again in the quiet of the briefing room aboard the *Tomahawk*.

The rest of the team was busy training, eating, sleeping, at gear prep... or in the med bay.

"I know," muttered Slade, hearing it this time and knowing he needed to answer the question despite his ruminations and dire calculations.

"I get it, sir," continued D'het. "Straight outta the snipers and asserting dominance on a new team. He's found Flower Child to test his edge against. It'll resolve, but maybe not the way he likes it. Something about Child and the way he shoots... it's intuitive to the needs of the mission. But with Harm hit bad now and no replacements on this assignment... Sir, all I'm saying is it could have just as easily been Heckler who took a round. Then we're down a sniper rolling on another hit that's now less than eighteen hours..."

The team sergeant looked toward the current mission clock indicating exit from jump over Hang Kong Station.

"... thirty-six minutes and change, sir. We need the snipers in place and able to move as blockers as we go in to corral the HVT. We got four. If we'd lost Heckler, we'd be way under the power curve needed to corral Blowtorch and arrange a meeting with—"

"Understood," Slade said, cutting D'het off before he could finish the sentence.

The major didn't even like mentioning the title of the one they were there to protect... and hunt on behalf of. *Adjudicator.* Seemed wrong. Seemed surreal.

Seemed like something that shouldn't be in an age as modern as this one, never mind the Troubles.

They'd only met the Adjudicator a few times. As a team. He was personable. Capable. Legion Commander Cohen Chhun. Something of a celebrity owing to Article Nineteen. Maker of the modern Legion. A man who seemed destined to have his name alongside those of General Marks and Rex in the grand scheme, and spoken of in quiet reverence by those in Dark Ops.

He seemed out of character for the role the Legion now demanded of him.

He had remained on the host destroyer, the *Scontan Washam*, for this op. But it was clear he was right there in every mission. Sometimes in person, as was the case in the capture of the bounty hunter Blackheart, but more often inside his legionnaires' buckets. Always watching what went down. There had yet to be a prompt. But the major found himself, at times, waiting to hear one when the incoming fire was starting to exceed the outgoing.

Battle management. That's all. That's what officers do. Besides the shooting and the killing.

Yes, the Adjudicator was one of them. But it didn't feel like it to Slade, though he could never say it to anyone.

And that, too, is the fun of being an officer.

It was getting worse by the day.

Eighteen hours, thirty-four minutes to go and they'd make insertion at Hang Kong. Elektra would be on the ground within six hours to run down the players and give them a target to get *all involved* on.

They'd develop a plan, stalk the site... wait for First Sergeant Bombassa to show. Then they'd capture him.

But it wouldn't be that simple.

Legion Intel had already tried to get ahold of the man, thinking he would be one of the easier to interview. Certainly one of the more critical. He had been integral to so much that had occurred inside the Legion. He'd even been a member of Kill Team Victory, and no other Dark Ops team was so highly regarded in its history. But the former legionnaire had, not so politely... *declined* the interview.

The squad responsible used up a month's worth of skinpacks to recover from that little sket cluster.

Now it was Hunter Team Ranger's turn.

The operations the major was used to, Dark Operations to be specific, took months of planning to execute. But for this op, they didn't have months. They didn't have days. This, what they were in now, this was... *fly by the seat of your pants and keep rolling on locations and hits.*

This was direct-action gangsta stuff. Which is what most of Dark Ops had become leading into Article Nineteen. Kill teams and all the clown games that came with. But Major Slade had managed, not without effort, to stay in a unit that was more... traditional. More Kel Turner than Ellek Owens.

Slade was a legionnaire first, and a Legion officer next, a real one. His men, those under his charge, were his concern. He was determined that they survive and go make more legionnaires. Forget dying to get it done.

Command always got way over-serious with that stuff. Slade was interested in whatever it took for everyone to make it *and* accomplish the mission. Every unit had come to respect him for that. Every legionnaire remembered an officer who didn't shirk point or going in first on a breach.

If it was rough...

If it was dangerous...

*Why not you*, he'd always told himself and then pushed through the legionnaires toward the danger area.

To Major Slade, a great mission was when everyone made it back to the rear, behind the walls, and the enemy never even knew it had happened.

If you had to get wily about getting it done, then so be it.

Now, going into a smuggling capital run by the Komo-tang Tongs, an old criminal organization that traced their ancestry back as far as Earth—the swarm of archaeologists on Kima might have something to say about that now that the truth was out—and running down a legionnaire who had a real appetite for destruction, a giant who'd followed in the footsteps of General Rex—Tyrus Rechs—and joined the Bronze Guild...

*This*, thought Slade, *this right here is a great way to get somebody killed.*

If not... everyone.

But the question was Heckler and the games snipers played.

"He's just asserting dominance, Sergeant," Slade told Sergeant D'het. "That's how snipers are. They're the best of the best at distance engagement, and it has to be proved among them for it to be known and accepted. Once I make him section leader, he'll dial it back. I've seen it before."

Sergeant D'het cleared his throat and spit dip into a cup he was using. Dip was his thing. But every scout in Legion

Division Recon, the highest of the highest in the line units, took their stim that way. No smoke on the stalk.

"So why not get it done now, sir? Make him the section leader. We need everyone locked down hard going into this next hit. We'll have two hours tops to dev a mission plan and insert. So why not right now? Respectfully. Sir."

There was no real respect. It was just pro forma with the team sergeant. D'het was a pro. He was still feeling out Slade. He never would have made it into Dark Ops, thought the major. He was too line. But he was a great recon team sergeant. Best scout in the One-Three-One. So...

"That's my call, Sergeant," said the major.

Silence.

"A-firm, sir."

And yeah, Major Slade knew exactly what it meant when an enlisted soldier used *A-firm* exactly that way.

But he let it pass. The team sergeant was right, ultimately. But the timing was wrong. Slade couldn't articulate the why... but not yet. Now was not the time for a section leader. Let them compete. Let the snipers cook. Force them to push the envelope on their skills because...

And this was a hard reality for the team, but it was one Slade saw and no one else wanted to admit was true. But it was.

Because...

The snipers were the only support. There was no division arty. No dropships, buzz ships, or battle tanks. No orbital strikes.

This team would be going into very tense situations filled with killers of every stripe and kind. See Hang Kong Station for an outstanding list of wanted criminals that easily outmatched any of the worlds in the old Republic that was...

And then whatever location and hit would be next.

The Adjudicator would decide.

*You realize that,* the officer told himself. *He will drive the mission.*

Slade pushed that thought away. It felt like live electricity wild and dangerous, and he didn't like it.

The snipers, up and above the action, out there and ready to put bolts on target, were the only support the assaulters had when they had to go in. The only way out of some of these blind alleys they'd find. Very dark ones at that. It would only be a sniper like Heckler, or even Flower Child. Men dialed up and ready to get their kill on for the high score to see who was best.

The team would need that level of shooting. So...

So let 'em cook. Let's see what happens next.

Time to get D'het off this.

*He's a scout. He smells what I smell, and he wants to investigate. But... we can't. We just do.*

"Assessment of the rest of the team, Sergeant. Yours. We'll wrap it and wait for the transmission from our agent on the ground. Then... we make a plan, and we execute."

Sergeant D'het nodded, spat some more dip into his cup, and picked up his battle board. The tension was clear. But so was the resignation that the answer given was the only answer forthcoming.

The commander had spoken.

One of the reasons the recon sergeant had been selected as team sergeant was he had an excellent record for washing leejes who couldn't cut it in scouts, which was saying something. And the scouts he ran were the best, and ended up going on to leadership positions in other units.

So D'het had a good idea how to address the major's request, and right now that was what Slade needed—an assessment of his men, his legionnaires. Of who was right, and who wasn't.

Something the holovid sand table wasn't showing them.

"Start with the assaulters, sir," said D'het. "Strikers we've covered, and they're good. Sergeant Harm as team leader is going to recover, but I wouldn't run him on the next mission even though he's gonna tell you he's good to go, sir. Never mind that he's coughing up blood. Getting hit by old-school, hard-caliber, caveman weapons... that ain't no joke, sir. He will say he's good to go, and he executed on the objective. But he should have been more cognizant of cover going in. Blaster fire is one thing for a legionnaire. Armor can handle, but it still ain't pleasant, sir. Old-school lead is kinetic, and that bad guy was using hand cannons that tested our armor. He dead now."

Slade nodded at the assessment.

"Sergeant Király fell right into the role of team leader and led the ambush once Harm was down. Effected intersecting fire just like we'd run on the shoot deck. As usual... five stars, sir."

Silence. Big silence. The recon sergeant team leader smelled something and was waiting to see if the major would get uncomfortable and volunteer info.

Slade had been in Dark Ops long enough to just remain silent. On top of which... he knew as little about Király as D'het did. Though both of them knew something was off. Not *bad*. But...

There wasn't a word that described it.

Sergeant Király was... something. Extraordinary. Destined. The best, perhaps. And when alpha pipe hitters started checking themselves because they'd met some dude they couldn't compete with...

It felt... dangerous.

D'het had not seen Sergeant Király's heavily redacted file. Yet it was clear he had formed the same questions as Slade.

Like... who was this guy?

And why send in someone like him? Was Command expecting everyone gets smoked and this guy keeps on mission? Or was it just because the hunter teams were supposed to be the best, and therefore Király *must* be included?

The major said nothing. He knew nothing. That was the truth. *He knew nothing.* And in the business of what they did, the edge just beyond Dark Operations where there were no more fancy unit patches, special berets, and cool-guy designations...

Blank spaces in a guy's file spoke volumes.

Sergeant Király's secured file screamed.

"Solid," grunted Slade to get D'het off the trail they both smelled. "If Harm says he's good to go, we run with him. We need everyone."

D'het made a face unseen because he lowered his head and dropped some dip into his cup again.

Again, the major knew. *A-firm. Sir.*

"Sergeant Wasto's armor recorded the highest amount of accurate fire on the Gun Boys," said D'het, continuing with the assessment. "The assaulters are all shooters, so that's pretty good shooting. I ran an authenticate on his charge packs, and he was totally within the economy of fire parameters. So add that to the accuracy he demonstrated, and I'm glad we have him on the three position for the assaulters."

That's a plus going into these situations, thought Major Slade. Outnumbered and outgunned it was easy to get low on charge packs. Or so that had been Slade's experience in real life.

And it wasn't fun.

"If we start going black on packs, you draw from him first for redistribution, Sergeant," said the captain tersely and reached forward to make a note on his battle board that this would be SOP.

Standard operating procedure.

"That's the plan, sir." The recon sergeant team leader was way ahead of him.

Slade almost smiled at that. It was good to see his team sergeant was on the same sheet of music. And he was. Confirmed. Slade had almost allowed himself a rare smile and made sure the team sergeant didn't see it.

Truth was, he was pleased with D'het as a pull for team sergeant. Very pleased. Even if the man was suspicious of him. Slade had read D'het's file. That one hadn't been redacted. The sergeant had had some... *experiences*... with the old points. So the mistrust was to be expected. Anything less would be a flaw in judgment.

Moving on...

"McCoy in the SDM role for the assaulters picked up the strays and did his job out there, sir. Solid execution. I still have... questions about him. You and I have both read his records jacket. Kicked out of Legion armor for fighting and insubordination, repeatedly, suddenly some sniper section leader takes pity on him and gives him a shot, and he's got this undiscovered talent no one knew about with the N-18. Add in he went to Subsurface School with the navy demo teams... I get it. But he still feels dangerous, sir. To me. Half the time I feel like he's gonna swing on me even when he's smiling. He's got some demons, sir. I've seen it before, and nine times out of ten it ain't worth the cost of having that guy on your six. When in doubt... kick 'em out. Sir."

*That's how you picked up the tag* Shredder, *ain't it, Sergeant?* Major Slade thought.

"But I'm just the sar'nt, and I'm just assessing a team member, sir. Your call. You've heard this from me before."

Slade had.

He knew the sniper section leader who'd... *salvaged* McCoy. Legendary shooter close to retirement. They'd used him for a difficult hit in Dark Ops. Had a habit of finding stray dogs and then finding something inside them that kept them in the Legion. Dark Ops didn't need rescuers though, and so they didn't work more with him even though he was one of the best with the N-18.

Slade had respected the man nonetheless.

He also knew McCoy's file.

Orphan. Or might as well have been. Youth detention centers. Homeless on the Outer Worlds. *Stray dog* wasn't even half the story. Guy had been fighting his whole life and didn't know anything else. That sniper section sergeant had managed to give him some tools to hide it from everyone... but it was still there.

And the Legion was pretty certain there was stuff they didn't know about McCoy.

Sergeant McCoy made it on the hunter team because he was highly capable, a shooter in the top five percentile, a brawler who had yet to be beaten in combatives... add in the Repub Navy large hull demo skills—Wet Sox stuff—and the fact that at the Battle of Surimoon he'd not given up when over eighty-five percent of his platoon had been killed by Black Fleet shock troopers...

He'd just gone from body to body salvaging charge packs and holding the line in the face of more than overwhelming odds.

Add in too that somehow the point captain who'd gotten them all into that die-in-position battle had managed to get himself killed hiding in the command bunker and refusing to come out even as the line was collapsing.

The Legion had questions about that too, and all the questions seemed to revolve around McCoy.

Slade knew a survivor when he saw one. And the likable and handsome McCoy, who never showed his real side to anyone unless they wanted to fight... was one. There was no doubt about that.

Hunter Team Ranger needed survivors. There might have been a lot of questions about McCoy, and he was probably going to punch someone eventually... but he'd never leave them behind. He'd never walk away from a fight they'd gotten themselves into.

Or one the Adjudicator had gotten them into.

"Sergeant Shriver... what can I say, sir," continued D'het. "That's a lucky get for us, sir."

Slade agreed wholeheartedly with that and said nothing. Mad Dog was a DO legend.

"The medic..."

Sergeant D'het sighed tiredly.

*You'd like to punch him right in the face, wouldn't you, Sergeant D'het,* Major Slade didn't say. *And not just because he's Navy.*

"Talks too much, sir."

Typical recon sergeant remark.

"But he saved Harm's life right there on the field when the armor malfunctioned. Incoming and all. We would have handled it had we gotten him back to the ship... but..."

*We're going places where there might not be a ship to get back to, Sergeant,* thought Slade and didn't say that either.

"So, the assaulters were good to go on this one, and other than my rec... which you aren't gonna take, sir... they are functioning at the level we need them to. Sir. And I see no problems at this time."

*Good for you*, thought Slade. *You challenged my call. That is exactly what I need in a team sergeant.*

"What about your team? Sergeant."

Sergeant D'het, as they were currently organized, could run the assaulters from the support section with the gun. When he wasn't attached to Slade's hip.

"Solid, sir. I got after Heckler and... well, we're going to let him... *cook*, sir. As per your direction."

Slade had the feeling Heckler was going to get some kind of *counseling* nonetheless from the team sergeant. Performing an action inconsistent with the op order was a no-go in the Legion line units. One that would get you walking papers in the more elite units.

But Heckler was, in Slade's judgment, the best shooter he'd ever seen. Period. He was cold, and proud about it. It defined him. The major could see that coming in real handy when the incoming was so hot and heavy that a sniper suddenly eliminating enough bad guys for them to break through, slither, or pull back, might save lives. Or the mission.

Heckler was the kind of guy who took overwhelming impossible odds as some kind of personal challenge to demonstrate his superiority. Yeah, he'd run the sniper section, but the other snipers—Flower Child, McCoy, and Walking Fist—they needed to not just see, but *know* how good, and how solid and cold, and cruel, Heckler was.

He was the level they would measure themselves by.

And the snipers would support by fire, all of them. No matter what furnace they found themselves in.

Heckler.

The whole team knew about Expeditionary Ridge. During the Troubles, Heckler had been part of the Dark Ops team that got sent in as rescue team.

The MCR was trying to flip a world called Nomiu. Local species of humanoid amphibians. Fish people skilled at little more than mass wave attacks but augmented by lots of MCR military-grade equipment. The Repub Naval outpost got nearly overrun and called for an evac when things looked bleak. Three days later the destroyer *Reconciliation*, a useless House of Repub tin can, got torpedoed making orbital insertion by an MCR hunter-killer operating dark and quiet in low atmo.

The Dark Ops team jumped from the burning hangar and inserted orbitally via high-altitude low-opening gear. Bad insert way off the mark and deep behind enemy lines. They humped three days through a world of stinking fens and sucking marshes to relieve the lone listening outpost on a ridgeline made of dead coral.

Everyone got a medal.

Heckler recorded over four hundred confirmed kills and at three different times terminated the MCR war leaders inserted among the fish people making their mass wave attacks out of the muddy shallows of that rotten and stinking world, thus stalling the impending attacks that would have caused the loss of the station and the execution of all its personnel.

Two weeks later, everyone was pulled out and the frigate doing the extract saturated the local enemy attack force numbering at ten thousand with an orbital bombardment so heavy it seemed as though the planet would crack and thermal fissures would destroy much of that continent. But the House of Reason never let the hammer hit that hard. Banned weapons, their own special rules of war... this wasn't the Savage Wars, after all. No, those would come later. At the tail end of the Troubles. Or maybe that was just part of the beginning of the Troubles.

History would tell.

Point was, the post-tech fish people were still trying to climb out of the early Bronze Age history they'd been pounded back into.

*That'll learn 'em*, thought Slade, and wondered where he'd heard that recently.

Personality quirks could be overlooked. Heckler was a killer. Team Ranger needed killers.

Slade didn't know where they were going, or where this investigation would take them... but he knew that much. He knew there was a lot of death coming.

That was clear whether anyone liked it or not.

All killers would be accepted.

And maybe... just maybe they'd all survive the Adjudicator's mysterious investigation into a past most of the galaxy just wanted to forget, but was unable to move on from.

"What about your gunner?" Slade asked his sergeant.

D'het nodded, acknowledging what was unspoken and known between the both of them about the SAB gunner in the support team.

"Death Machine, sir. Yeah, other guys already know his tag from the line units. So of course it followed him here and there's already bad blood with some. Plus, there's that Order of the Centurion he's authorized to wear... and doesn't."

*Death Machine*, thought Slade. Hell of a name to hang on a guy.

"I will say it again, sir. For the record," said D'het. "That man went in with the Ninth against the *Invincible*. They took the hangar bay and got promptly overrun by enemy legionnaires. Guys that, for the most part... were once us.

Forget that Dark Legion, Black Fleet stuff. They killed two hundred and thirty-six legionnaires and ten got pulled out by a hot evac. HT-71, then-Corporal Buck Santaviellgo, went back in, not to rescue anyone, but to settle up. Pay them back for what they'd done, and he straight-up killed three companies' worth of the enemy, beating the door gunner on the evac shuttle senseless, disconnecting his mounted heavy SAB, and then... going back in. He rescues a point officer who got overrun and pretended to be dead lying among a pile of... our own... and that *officer* puts Santaviellgo in for the medal and he gets it.

"Sir, people got hard feelings about that, and I won't even get started about what my old platoon sergeant used to say about OOTC winners tryin' to live up to the hero everyone thinks they are. But that ain't why he went back in there lookin' for our guys to rescue. Facts are facts, sir, and they don't care about your propaganda. He went in there, into a burning enemy battleship, to kill as many of the enemy as he could, and he didn't care if he died doing so. I've asked him. He admitted it straight up and then blew me a kiss. He's arrogant and probably homicidal. He's a narcissist and he thinks it's all about him, sir. He will get people killed trying to make everyone believe he actually is the hero that that medal says he is. Sir."

D'het was staring right at Major Slade, challenging him to disagree one iota. Dip stuck in his cheek. Hard-as-nails recon sar'nt on full display for his commander.

"I said to him, sir, I said, 'Tell me, Santaviellgo... you didn't just go in there to get anyone out, didja?' And he looks at me with that wad of stim-dip he keeps in his cheek like he's a holo star and says... 'Nah. Went in there, Team Sergeant, to kill those bastards that ate up my brothers. Won't clint you, Sar'nt. And when you're dead, 'cause you will be before I go, then I'll do the same for you.'"

D'het paused.

"Sir, he's crazy. He's got a death wish. That's what they really call him down in the line units. I made calls when he came up in the pool for the team, just doing my homework. *Death Wish*, sir. That's what they really call him."

Slade knew.

"But here's the thing, here's the thing I don't know, and you know us scouts, knowin's the thing for us... Is it a death wish, or does he just like the killing a little too much. Do you wanna know what I think, sir? Do you really want to know what I think?"

For a long moment the two men just stared at each other.

Then: "I do, Team Sergeant."

Rank used.

Reminding... who was who. And what was what.

D'het seemed to hear that, and it didn't check him in the least.

He lowered his voice because it had gotten pretty high there, crescendoed.

"I think he's a psychopath, sir. Somehow he's avoided all the grading and testing. But that bad day, a real bad day in fact, on a burning enemy battleship... it revealed him. Who he truly is. He was always there. A killer. But that real bad day... it gave birth to him. And now, ask any legionnaire... he's a murder-star. And..."

The sergeant stopped.

"And, Team Sergeant?" asked Slade in the silence that followed.

"And... sir. I can see that being a problem we might not need when things go real bad for us. We don't need a hero making it about them, instead of the mission."

Slade nodded. Nodded and knew his team sergeant was dead right.

But...

"Sergeant... Santaviellgo is a killer. He may in fact get a thrill out of it. There is every chance you are one hundred percent right about that, that he is indeed some kind of monster. But, Sergeant... he's *our* monster. And all this might lead to some real dark places where there are *real* monsters still left alive. So my call is it's probably a good idea to take our own monster with us. But all your concerns are... valid. Team Sergeant."

And from there they discussed the striker team and a few other notes, and then tersely, and awkwardly, ended the meeting.

Fourteen hours later the first burst transmission came in from Elektra on the ground at Hang Kong Station.

It wasn't good.

The odds were bad. Real bad.

A plan was made anyway.

And from the ether over the holo sand table they studied, the quiet yet strong voice of the Adjudicator, always watching, ordered a go on the operation to take Blowtorch on-station.

"Make it happen, Legionnaires. We need this man. No fail."

# 21

Things didn't go according to plan.

"They never do," muttered Sergeant Santaviellgo through a mouth full of dip. "But I got somethin' for that..." Then the Death Machine began to lay hate from the dialed-up squad automatic blaster he ran as tangos appeared across all quadrants of the capture site. Outgoing blaster fire cut down the first team of Hang Kong hardboys in snow-eel-skin blazers and rain-slick trenches pushing into the district where the *Antari Shark* had just gone down.

It was accurate. Frenetic. And utterly devastating as the veteran gunner worked them over, shooting up the auto-bus they'd arrived on even as advert holos and lasers spelled out the "Loosest Slots!" and "Spice Garlic Noodle Number One Best."

Roughly translated.

A holographic party girl appeared and winked seductively from the display at the noodle bar near the crash site on level five of the station's main deck.

The sky was practically weeping rain and mist from the condenser's mains in the massive dome above.

"Support in position, clear to move on the wreckage, Actual," alerted Sergeant D'het over the L-comm as the incoming hardboys got handled by violent outgoing fire. Extreme and excessive violence was how someone else might have written it up.

Support was down a crucial asset as all snipers were now useless on the buildings above the target landing pad a few blocks over. That was where the capture of Blowtorch was supposed to have gone down. Instead of the crash site where it would happen now. The snipers were repositioning via the striker assault jump-jet packs—some good tech that had finally gotten out of R&D and had been used by the legionnaires who held Kima against the Savage invasion—but two more minutes were required before they would be in position to cover the wreckage site. The *Antari Shark*, the old scout tender converted into the battle-hardened mercenary light freighter, had become just that—a wreck. It had slammed into and then exploded all across the central data comms pylon within this district of the vast disc-station that was Hang Kong.

Hang Kong Station had once been a generational colony ship with a living biosphere habitat capable via massive anti-grav engines of remaining in the skies for decades over a selected world. Now it held a stationary orbit just beyond the main belt inside the Jao Sing Tao system. Part of the Sinasian cluster, although the station expressed a strong desire to be independent of those worlds.

One of the downed ship's jutting shark-nosed jump nacelles had been torn off and was probably the primary cause of the explosion on impact with the data comms pylon that had subsequently blacked out an entire district in the station. The other main nacelle was still alive but with coursing ropes of fire as the energy igniters destabilized and would soon fail to contain the power within the powerful star-spanning engine. Every legionnaire on the hunter team was made aware via HUD of the imminent catastrophic detonation and advised to move to a safe distance of at least two hundred meters, though five was best practice. The message blinked annoyingly in a lower corner of the heads-up display, as did thermal targeting for the Hang Kong hardboys moving in and beginning to return fire on the support position and the assaulters getting ready to breach the flaming wreck.

Overhead, a giant ghostly blue fish creature with a humanoid face giggled and slurped on fire garlic noodles in holo, thrumming on and on about how "super spectacular tasty they are indeed, handsome gambler."

The L-comm translated this until the legionnaires shut it down and concentrated on the battle they found themselves in now.

"Moving in to rescue the HVT," alerted Ranger Actual, Major Slade, now in command of the assaulters since the snipers were now making limited rocket jumps from building to building.

Theirs was a tough job: put eyes on the crash site as well as support by fire against the still-massing Komo-tang foot soldiers moving in from all points of the station to find the HVT and confirm he was indeed dead.

The first sergeant, it seemed, was rich with enemies.

"Probably fired that surface-to-air that took out yer boy there in the burning hunk o' metal that was once a ship," noted the medic, stacked behind the legionnaires and trying to get into the hull even as the fires spread across its twisted and cracked length.

Major Slade, who was working a breaching tool to get in, thought the same thing as he heard the doc opine on how, exactly, things went pear-shaped.

Except... something the major couldn't put his finger on bothered him even as he hammered at a hull plate just to get it bent back enough for them to get into the *Shark*.

That data comms pylon had been a lucky break for anyone looking to take out the station's power grid and security systems in the local district.

That bothered Ranger Actual. The luck factor.

But he didn't have time for that. He had incoming. Two elements now under fire. No sniper support. And the HVT that had to be acquired for the Adjudicator.

Bombassa was either dead now, burnt alive, and that needed to be confirmed...

Or he was somewhere else.

Jumped out?

Egressed the wreckage before they got there?

Never there in the first place?

Whatever had happened, the action was now here. The tongs were en route and engaged with his people. And the Komo-tang hitter... he caught a lucky break. The bounty hunter coming for him had crashed his ship and now all hell was breaking loose.

There'd be no paid contract at thirty minutes plus after midnight on Hang Kong Station.

"HT-26!" shouted the major as he put his back and armor into forcing the breaching tool to command the hull plate to bend just enough to give them entry. "Advise Tomahawk Actual we are under fire and confirming the HVT status. Tell them to prepare to defend the LZ. Guns hot!"

The tongs must have known the bounty hunter was coming. They'd shot down that ship, and now their foot soldiers, gamblers, pimps, assassins, and thieves were on their devices and letting their bosses know there were undisclosed legionnaires on station and about some business they weren't aware of.

In other words... they were gonna be mad. The tongs would try to make an example of them as a warning to the Legion and anyone else who thought they could come and play in the Komo-tang Tongs' playground.

In other words... consequences.

Just like the HVT found out. No one messes with the Komo-tang and tries to collect on a bounty like this hunter from the Guild calling himself Cobra had tried to.

Cobra. Blowtorch. The HVT.

Sergeant Bombassa.

Because even if you were a feared bounty hunter like this *Cobra* was gaining a rep for being, especially after having collected on a bad contract on a wobanki slaver called Red Scourge despite the odds and the death-defying numbers involved, the tongs of Hang Kong were gonna make sure the message was sent that you didn't try to collect on even the *least* of them.

Much less one of their best hitters.

Justin Wang. Rhymes with Song.

Or, as the criminal underworld knew him... Mr. Gone Wrong for You.

Elektra's intel on station with only four hours wasn't just solid... it was solid gold. Better than expected from the mysterious Deep Section Dark Ops operator. Deep Section was the civilian arm of the intel services, and only the commander and the Adjudicator of Hunter Team Ranger had ever met Elektra in real-time.

On station with the clock burning down, Elektra had moved about quickly and run down a landing platform booking for a freighter that matched the shape and tonnage of the *Antari Shark*, but with different idents. Inbound just after midnight local. Secondary and tertiary intel collection and development recommended that Blowtorch was going in there on that landing pad with his ship. It was easy, and it was quick access to the gambling den of one Justin Wang, the Komo-tang hitter. The den was basically Wang's personal fortress under the protection of the local big boss in this district on station at Hang Kong.

Elektra assessed that the *Antari Shark* would set down near midnight station time and that shortly thereafter the HVT the hunter team had come for would attempt to capture Wang.

This was not a termination. This was a capture contract. So it made sense Blowtorch would use this nearby platform, as he would most likely be fighting some kind of running battle back to the ship with a capture in hand.

No easy task. Best, then, to make the extraction easy under the circumstances.

Hang Kong Station was huge and seemed at first glance to be nothing more than one giant hab disc. But in reality it was a collection of warrens and neighborhoods under the upper dome with a weather system mimicking a permanent planetary effect of constant rain, which was somehow a design feature the old colonists had wanted in their ship.

And it was vast. In size it rivaled any city on the core worlds, and those who came out this far near the edge to find "their hang" on it were surprised at just how giant and extensive the station was.

The "Upper Sky" under the dome of the station was a main deck crawling with clustering skyscrapers lit up in neon and flashing ancient languages advertising everything from the best party girls to the highest odds to the best noodles from the MegaMan Corporation. "Enjoy and Prosper Much!"

Roughly translated.

Giant holos appeared everywhere and along each block, or exploded in light displays along the faces of the scrapers, images that gyrated and undulated as sexy-voiced women on booming broadcasters sold products to inbound ships coming into dock through the central iris or any one of the twelve smaller entry apertures under the main dome.

Most of those lesser and more discreet ports were owned by the tongs and charged their own private tariffs.

Below the Upper Sky inbound traffic came the intercity lumbering repulsor sleds and speeding grav vehicles. Even at this time of night the "Near Sky" throughout and around the scrapers was clustered with headlights, navigation lights, and the occasional flashing light of some emergency or enforcement vehicle on its way to yet another murder scene never to be investigated.

Ever.

It was that kind of place. Corruption was an art form on Hang Kong.

The gambling den where Justin Wang laired was located near the cyber-enhancement district, really yet another twisting maze of quaint and cozy noodle bars and state-of-the-art black market code slicers dealing in hard synth and working on legitimate and often illegitimate tech for the big movers and shakers back in the core worlds.

A lot could be done here that couldn't be done there.

But all of that was background.

The legionnaires had hustled through the rain and mist, threading warrens in CQB fashion as they moved toward the wreck of the *Antari Shark* with Tomahawk Flight and Navigation updating the scene of the wreck from onboard drone control.

Old women cutting meat eyed them suspiciously but said nothing as they moved into their modular dwellings and activated the auto-shutters.

Old men smoked and watched the night, seeing nothing and thinking of distant worlds they'd once dreamed dreams of.

It was quiet here in the warrens, and the mist and rain was a kind of white noise against the holographic cluster and blare of the bleating adverts.

And as it was said...

"Nothing ever goes according to plan."

The ship was down. The HVT wasn't in hand. And his status, dead or alive in the crash, needed to be confirmed.

Slade didn't need the Adjudicator, who was no doubt listening to the whole cluster gone wrong, to tell him what was required of him and the team.

Both the support and assault elements of Hunter Team Ranger had been stacked and ready in maintenance corridors that gave way onto the platform that HVT Blowtorch had booked.

The capture site that was now karked.

Industrial bots, maintenance, and security had been seen to with silenced and suppressed blasts from the assault team working as recon and cleaning the way into the capture site. Once Tube Four was cleared, support in the trailing element moved from the rally point Ranger Actual had left them at and went to their ready position in Tube Two.

Stacked and back in the shadows, beside a dead Kirin-88 security bot-dog shot to pieces lying in the pristine darkness within the tube, was the support element consisting of Sergeant D'het running the team, Sergeant Santaviellgo on the SAB, and Sergeant Morgan Cobb, a squared-away line legionnaire who'd gone through Dark

Ops OT school before being selected for the Executive Protection Unit. Cobb had done his time there close to the capital with outstanding reviews and was now acting in the security role for the assault team, glad to be away from "the politicians," as he'd quietly made it known, and enigmatically happy to be back to doing something useful. "Back at the tip," as he put it. Master Sergeant Roosenlooper, HT-09, aka the Wizard, a legend at what he did who'd worked in the highest of hardcore elite units, was there with the assault and hanging back in the dark with a tac-pack most certainly loaded with explosives of all kinds should the need to use them arise.

The Wizard blew things up. Creatively. That was all that was needed of him, and only on two occasions, ever, real deep in it and with team leaders dead, had he ever taken control and run a unit just to get it off the X.

With Heckler re-tasked along with the other snipers, Flower Child, Walking Fist, and McCoy, to the rooftops on overwatch over the selected LZ, that was the extent of the support team. They waited in Tube Two with just seconds to the HVT setting down on the landing pad and ready to be captured by the assaulters who'd sweep out and take the ship from Maintenance Tube Four, where several bots had been on standby ready and waiting to service the ship.

They heard the ship's engines spooling down for approach to landing, then the shriek and explosion...

The plan had been for the ship to be down on the deck, landing gears and all, engines spinning down and venting gases, when the assault team rushed the ship, disabled, then breached for capture. Support was there to handle any on-station response that got interested in stuff that didn't concern them.

Blowtorch would be incapacitated via stunner and then transported back to the *Tomahawk,* which currently ran a holo-projected camo of a large pleasure yacht out of the Beta-Jakkal Star Quarto—four pleasure worlds from which several "adventure lines" operated. Support would cover the backtrail as both teams took a new, shorter route through the station's venting tubes, large passageways just below the surface of the deck that would take them right back to the disguised *Tomahawk's* berth.

Only two legionnaires were flight qualified. Mad Dog and Király. They would get Bombassa's ship gears up and headed for exit from the station. Then both ships would make a short jump to a rendezvous with the *Scontam Washum* above the fourth moon of Gassimeo X in a nearby sector, a quiet forest moon, for the interrogation and debrief.

Then the HVT would be released.

Or so it was assumed, though this was ominously missing as a line item in the op order. A fact that was noted by Death Machine during the brief, but not remarked upon by the command team.

With updates from Tomahawk Flight and Tomahawk Tracking from the sensor deck, which was currently passive-sliced into the station, all was going according to plan with forty-five seconds to landing gear down on the surrounded landing pad.

That was when a surface-to-air missile lanced up from the Shinobi Gardens and Falls, a park installation just a few sections away from the target district within the station. In a now "slow and fat" configuration with no power to engines for maneuver at speed other than docking, and no ability to jump inside a space station, the *Shark* took the missile amidships near aft cargo. The missile didn't explode and instead tore straight through the souped-up twin-engine scout tender.

Control and maunder must have been lost to some extent as the ship crossed right over the landing pad several hundred meters up, trailing flames and debris, and then fifteen seconds later it slammed down into the central data comm pylon, narrowly missing three small skyscrapers that the pilot, probably Blowtorch himself, had fought for the ship to avoid before impact.

Legionnaires swore over the L-comm.

The ship hit so hard that the station shuddered and power went out across this whole section.

The L-comm did not.

Warning sirens and emergency horns wailed forlornly in the distance as backup and emergency power came on. Somehow, the insane cartoon holo-adverts and laser displays continued unhindered and recommended "All Night Dancing and Love Most Satisfying" at the Crimson Palace and "All U Can Consume" at the Raw Noodle Fish Supreme Palace. But Tomahawk Comm was advising that all in-station comm was down and all local networks were offline as everything went to hell.

That, at least, was good for the teams out there and in the wind now that the mission was pear-shaped, thought Slade as he scrapped the capture and moved to Plan B, bringing up the drone feeds that were still active in his HUD.

But... the mission *was* pear-shaped.

In any other unit, they'd pull out and do it some other time. If ever.

The Adjudicator said nothing. He had proven to be more... "hands off" than Slade had expected. Though why he'd expected anything else from an enlisted leej who went Dark Ops and assumed command of the Legion during the Article Nineteen crisis, Slade couldn't say. Maybe he was thinking of how *he*—Ranger Actual—would have acted had they asked *him* to be an Adjudicator.

It wasn't Slade who was asked, though.

Still, the major knew that his Adjudicator was listening. He was paying attention, if not actively directing the operation.

"Copy, Tomahawk Flight," said Slade, falling into command tones and getting a plan he'd barely formed articulated.

They'd go after the HVT for one push.

If they couldn't confirm his status, or get him alive, then they'd get out.

And even as he thought that, it felt like a bad plan that any Officer Command School would have no-go'd him for.

But that silence on the net.

The Adjudicator had not told them to wave off. Did Slade expect him to? Or did he merely *want* him to?

*Get out of your own head*, he told himself. *Focus.*

They were still on.

"I need nav on the crash site. Support... form on the landing pad. Combat recon posture and we push on the crash site to confirm HVT status. Let's roll."

That was all eight minutes ago.

Now, with eyes on the crash and the assaulters moving on the flaming wreckage of the *Antari Shark*'s flaming hull, the first of the Komo-tangs' hardboys were on scene using small auto-buses to arrive and conduct their own investigation that probably amounted to pulling Bombassa from the wreckage. That or double-tapping him right there... or snatch him until interrogator time in one of the Big Bosses' palace dungeons on station.

The hardboys came out, narrow eyes and cruel faces looking demonic in the hellish flames coming from the hull and internals of the downed bounty hunter vessel. Their snow eel-skin suits shining as flashy trick blasters came out and they chattered angrily to themselves. Each had the tats curling out from under tailored shirt cuffs or writhing up from the jackets. And the tears along one eye denoting the tong-approved murders.

Their haircuts were easily five hundred cred.

The first of them spotted the shadowy legionnaires in armor moving on the breached hull, and then opened fire.

Death Machine responded in kind and began to kill them with savage doses of triple power off the SAB.

But more were coming in now and there was no sign of Blowtorch on board.

# 22

Under fire, with assault and support having established a perimeter by outgoing fire, the direness of the situation had just gotten infinitely worse.

There was no sign of the HVT on the ship.

He wasn't there and maybe he'd never been.

More and more Hang Kong hardboys were showing up, and an out-of-control and very one-sided firefight with a lot of local dead was starting to get seriously out of hand.

There was no way guys in high-cred suits with fancy blasters were going to be any match for two squads plus of legionnaires on any day that ended in "y."

And yet here they were blasting away and acting like they might do something.

"D'het..." said the major, dropping out of tactical ident. He was firing from the cover of the ship. Still inside a ship's hull that was recently on fire. Black smoke billowed out wherever it could. HT-34, Sergeant Király, had tossed in an inferno-quencher and popped the onboard fire-suppression bottles and systems when they'd reached the flight deck. Now the imminent explosion of the number two engine was contained, and the fires were out.

But they were surrounded and only holding back the locals with heavy amounts of lethal violence.

The initial intent in the capture of the HVT had been to make it seem as though the Legion was never actually there. That was impossible now, and there would definitely be ramifications.

But that was a tomorrow problem, Major Slade thought to himself. And... someone else's problem. Ain't no point here.

Get everyone out alive.

Get the target.

"D'het... break contact. Have your team use the primary fade outlined in the initial op. Assaulters are going over the side three klicks station-east of our position. There's a support walkway down there and we should be able to reach the ship through the maintenance catacombs. RT *Tomahawk* and gears up. We're outta here before they throw the whole station at us."

"Copy, Actual," replied D'het. The blare of the SAB hard and heavy over the comm. "We're getting pushed from the main street now. We'll throw bangers and fade into the tubes on five."

Slade switched over to Tomahawk Flight, but really he was talking to the Adjudicator, who still remained silent.

Why hadn't he called this off yet? It was clear that the mission, as conceived, was no longer tenable.

To Slade the Adjudicator's silence was a message, one the former Legion commander was making crysteel clear: they'd failed.

Ominous. Silence.

The mission was not complete.

But... it was completely pear-shaped. Beyond a doubt. There was no way they were...

"*Break break break!*" It was Tomahawk Sensors. "Ranger Actual, we have some kind of fight in progress at our HVT's primary oh-bee-jay..."

The primary OBJ was the original location for the capture. Wang's gambling den.

Major Slade swore as he saw it all coming together now.

Over the HUD he watched all contacts. Saw his support team pulling back in teams, firing and fading in the tubes even as the hardboys pressed them and died for their troubles.

There was no way...

*No way...*

... to still pull this off.

As if to confirm his suspicions, Tomahawk Sensors was back in his ear.

"Ranger Actual... we are tracking an inbound freighter, last-minute station entry on full burn with a station intercept for our HVT's primary. It's flashing *Antari Shark* idents."

The major swore again.

*Cobra.*

He'd strangled the district with a distraction freighter, some cheap lookalike he'd autopilot-smashed into the data comm pylon to cause confusion, and now he was going to put himself right in over the target, fast-rope in while it hovered, and get his contract... fangs out.

Brilliant and deceptive.

And there was nothing Slade could do about it.

In fact, there every chance, if he and his legionnaires didn't fade right now, that some of them were going to get killed as more and more of the station hardboys showed up to get it on in a real fight with real live legionnaires. The station had heavier weapons that could yet come out to play, and that could be a problem if this didn't end quick.

The major updated his team.

"All elements, Blowtorch pulled a fast one. He's going for the primary now. We chased a fake. Pull back to the *Tomahawk* and prepare to depart station. Tomahawk Flight, stand by to algo-strike station controls so we can leave whether they want us to or not."

Then HT-34 spoke up in the L-comm. His voice was neither emotional nor overly calm. It was nothing but gravel and truth.

"Actual... we still got a shot. Let me go native and enter the HVT's primary loc. I will get him out and meet the *Tomahawk* on the roof for extraction."

Incoming blaster fire smacked off the wrecked and ruined hull of the fake *Antari Shark*. The plan was destroyed. The opportunity missed. And now... here was a chance.

*I will get him out.*

A ridiculous, impossible, stupid chance to get a legionnaire killed in order to not fail a former Legion commander who might just as well be the new version of the point officer with what he was asking the team to do.

Nah, thought Slade. Not this time. Not...

The operation was pear-shaped. And here was the super-secret soldier, the mystery man, the quiet guy with all the skills, the unbelievable quad card he'd been dealt for this force... asking to shuck his armor, "going native" as the legionnaires called it, and then walk right into a full-on firefight, alone, to get hands on the ex-legionnaire stone-cold-killer bounty hunter who'd just outsmarted them.

Alone.

He'd been one of the guys, Slade recalled, who had shucked armor for the op to get that other bounty hunter. The mission prior to the mission.

"Negative, Three-Four... it's all bad. We're pulling—"

The L-comm went silent dead.

All comm with the rest of the unit was cut. Like some great mysterious and invisible hand had just come down and isolated the major from everyone he was trying to get out of a very bad situation gone totally six shades of wrong.

Snipers.

Assaulters.

Support.

And a starship crew that was probably dropping bricks.

D'het would have said this was just the Adjudicator overriding the L-comm so his orders could get to everyone. But Slade knew better. Slade saw the ghosts in the darkness.

Then a voice came over the net. "Zero to Oh-One."

The Adjudicator.

"Pull back," the voice said. "Send Three-Four in."

# 23

"No way," Mad Dog Shriver said as he watched Sergeant Király stripping off his armor. The veteran operator switched up the sub blaster he'd been securing the perimeter with as the slight medic danced from one boot to the other near the two hard-as-nails legionnaires. The major had just returned with utility pants and work boots, acquired via a smash-and-grab of a working man's store near the site. The store's holo proclaimed an offering of the finest in "Lucky Joe Clothing for Prosperity and Handsome Times on the Job Site!"

Roughly translated.

"No way he's going in alone. Sir," said Shriver like it was some kind of fact that could not be refuted. Then he pulled off his bucket. "I'm goin' with."

Where Sergeant Király was handsome in a rock-hard way, Mad Dog Shriver would never be accused of such. He had fine hair combed over to cover the time he'd been slashed in the scalp, thin lips, and a sneer made worse by another scar from a battle injury in some past conflict.

But there was this: in all the Legion, Mad Dog Shriver was known for having been there, and having definitely done that.

And he was known for doing it his way.

And then getting it done.

The major would have given him a look, but he was wearing his bucket. And things were pear-shaped. And though he was in charge, it was clear that it was the Adjudicator driving the mission. Which, to Mad Dog Shriver, was good. Because Király was right. This op wasn't dead and it wasn't lost.

You just had to go and get it.

For the moment incoming had subsided, and support was in the tubes and on the fade back to the *Tomahawk*.

"We need to disappear, Sergeant. You're on point," ordered Slade, trying to get some kind of authority asserted despite the situation. "I'll go with him and stay in armor... in case we need that firepower to get him out."

Shriver was tall. And... resolute. More of his armor was coming off even as the major told him what was what going forward. He peeled off his assault pack and pulled out fatigue pants and shoes from deep down inside.

"Always ready to go native, sir. I am going with. Legion don't go alone, sir. This is my jam."

*Might as well have added "A-firm,"* thought Slade.

The intent was the same.

Slade took a deep breath. Shriver was a solid choice. Shriver was known for going native.

"A-firm, Sar'nt," said the commander, using the enlisted man's way of talking. Two can play the disrespect game.

Truth was... he had nothing but respect for Mad Dog Shriver. Guy had once been listed KIA for six months. He came back with a body count. Getting him for the team was almost as good as getting dealt the quad.

"Go in. Grab him. Meet the *Tomahawk* on the roof. It's that simple, Three-Four. We'll sling-link you off the roof."

Then he looked at Shriver.

"Six-Eight."

HT-68.

Both men nodded.

Slade was still in command.

Shriver went off into the bodies the legionnaires had stacked, and grabbed two trench coats. Both were ruined, but they'd do the job. He was already issuing orders to Sergeant Király on how they were going to do this.

"We do this low-key. Take my scatter blaster. Keep it under the rain slicker and get the sling around your shoulder so yer ready to go, kid. Shoot, move, and communicate. We'll do the entrance and work our way to Blowtorch's target. Read me?"

*Kid.*

Sergeant Király nodded and said nothing and did as he was told because that's exactly what he was already going to do.

"Gimme your sidearm, sir," ordered Mad Dog of the commander. Then he stuffed it into one of the pockets of Sergeant Király's wet trench.

"We got two each now. I always carry two. Each got a primary. You guys hump our gear, and we'll meet you on the roof for the sling-out. Let's do this, Leejes."

His voice was hollow and cold and deep and like some contract killer who knew his business and was in a hurry to be about it.

Then the two men were trotting off in the rain and the mist, consumed by the ethereal holos and chanting ads promising a better tomorrow. Just two lucky working joes out after a night of beer and noodle bar fun, heading home before the rain got worse as the station descended into chaos and madness and tongs came out looking to get their kill on.

# 24

Mad Dog Shriver talked, low and angry, all the way to the place where Justin Wang had holed himself up at the coming of Cobra.

*Bombassa.*

Like he was angry about a fight. And that was Mad Dog's way. He took everything personally. Sergeant Király guessed that was what made him dangerous. What made him a killer.

Mad Dog was definitely the kinda guy you didn't want as an enemy.

But Shriver was always business. Going over how they'd do this, how they'd do that once they were inside, and then...

"This is gonna be like those mean old fights from the galactic frontier days, kid. Like that hard caliber the old man back on the salt flats was carrying. Ain't gonna be pretty. Ain't gonna be nice. Nothin' about that. Shoot everything until we get to our boy, then we're gonna ask nice for him to come with us, 'cause the way I see it that's the least we can do for an old leej like us, right, kid?"

He coughed. The bar was in sight now. They were making their approach.

Three guys out front immediately reacted in a hostile manner as they emerged from the obscuring mist and drooling rain.

An ad for "Super Dogs and Noodle Beauty Perfection!" barked hungrily as a giant cartoon dog ran around with holographic noodles, dragging them all over the rain-slick street.

"Didn't like it the other way, kid," muttered Mad Dog. "Wouldn't want it that way for me when they come lookin' for me someday. When I disappear... they ain't never gonna find me."

Mad Dog was walking fast just before the desperate fight began.

Sergeant Király instinctively matched his pace.

The three hardboys with nice hair turned, reaching for the fancy blasters that made them so tough and dangerous. No idea they were dealing with real danger this late night turned to dark early morning in little more than a rainy alley.

The patter of rain was all that was left in the sudden abrupt ending of the silly ad.

Then the firing began.

From under the trench Mad Dog yanked his cut-down N-4 rifle savagely, and then expertly shot them down with an economy of fire and nothing but cold violence, his twisted sneer of a face briefly illuminated by the pulses. Some weird smile formed there as he did them all and did them quickly.

Out of the door came the first responders to contact and blaster fire outside.

Sergeant Király had the scatter blaster up and out and wrecked four then five as he slam-fired mini charge packs of blasts at them. The last to get hit turning away as he came out and firing a blaster shot into the night of the station. Then flopping over into a puddle as the rain beat at his lifeless body.

Blood mixed with the rain.

They entered the gambling palace and the next phase of the assault. Hardboys came out of the walls and corridors, already firing at the intruders. Five gangsters turned to ten, then twelve.

Using cover and moving, the legionnaires worked their way across the room, blasting, kicking, and even punching hardboys when they got too close. Shattered bodies with smoking blaster wounds lay all across the room by the time the two killers, brothers from another mother in the art of murder, made the grand staircase leading upward.

"Everyone getting hole-punched tonight," muttered Mad Dog and checked the stairs for more killers waiting to die.

The scatter blaster was empty and Sergeant Király threw it aside with little regard as he drew both sidearms. Mad Dog Shriver chanced a peek up into the cavernous hall that reigned above the grand and gaudy gold-and-jade staircase adorned with curling dragons, climbing higher and higher toward the gambling rooms and card tables up there where Wang reigned supreme.

A man screamed and came down hard on the stairs, his neck breaking with a pulpy *crack* from the fall. Twisted, he lay sightless and staring upward.

More blaster fire sounded up there.

Then an explosion.

Shriver nodded and then moved up the staircase, finding more ruined bodies.

The main fight was three levels up past the card rooms and tables where scared and frightened gamblers lay under tables or sprawled dead where they'd been shot down. Mad Dog and Király were two levels up, entering a wide and gaudy hall filled wall to wall with a tacky and seizure-inducing assortment of flashing, blinking, chirping electronic gambling devices, including what looked like a few old-school holo-slots, when a pair of hardboys came running down the aisle between machines. Shriver popped from cover and blew them both apart with a fusillade of furious bolts from his blaster rifle.

He ejected the charge pack and slapped in a new one he pulled from a trench pocket, nodding toward the direction the hardboys had come from. From above, a psychotic exchange of whining blaster fire erupted across the next level.

"Probably an advance team sent down the back stairs to clear the way," Mad Dog said. "Blowtorch's target has gotten pinned, and he wants out. Let's go that way and meet 'em."

Thirty seconds later Justin Wang and his entourage ran into the two leej killers slithering through the garish electronic chaos, and a short yet ultra-violent blaster fight erupted in which there were more losers than winners.

No quarter was given.

None was expected.

The entourage, with Wang carrying an automatic blaster in the center, scattered to jade columns for cover as Shriver opened fire on them all.

Wang wasn't carrying a SAB, but he might as well have been. He opened fire and generated an impressive amount of destruction as he tried to ruin his way out of the death trap he now found himself in. His light automatic blaster rifle was definitely premium-grade stuff, and both legionnaires had to dive for cover or get torn to shreds.

No words were exchanged as both legionnaires went wide, working their way through the machines and shooting down Wang's guards as the two men closed on him from different directions while the cornered man desperately changed charge packs.

Sergeant Király moved low and quickly, working like a greased snake through the aisles and landing blaster shots in the covering men who had no idea that cover and concealment were two different things.

One popped on Király to the right, and the sergeant raised one blaster while firing another into a punk ready to use a sub blaster on him. The bolt went straight through the man's skull who'd just appeared to his right and then as the punk broke cover, Sergeant Király drilled him with both guns, shooting the hardboy several times before he made it to the floor and changed shape forever.

He was even a little on fire.

Wang was falling back, spraying the room and his own men with as much fire as he could dump at the two killers coming for him from two new directions.

Mad Dog shot three more hardboy killers begging for their lives and spitting curses, emptied on another, and let the blaster rifle dangle on its sling as he pulled both pistols faster than anyone could have thought possible and started shooting down the last of Justin Wang's guards.

Wang had drawn a bead on Sergeant Király, who was high-crawling, rolling, and shooting down the covering guards in front of him.

Sergeant Király came up not ten feet from Wang, who smiled wickedly and dragged the high-cyclic bolt-spitting automatic blaster right at him...

Blaster fire slammed into the ornate dragon sculptures around Sergeant Király and then Shriver drilled Wang twice from off to his left.

First bolt in the chest...

Wang's auto blaster went low.

Second went into the man's skull which exploded in every direction sending blood and brain matter over a gaming machine featuring wide-eyed and overly sexualized unicorns as the gangster fell backward and then crashed to the floor.

The criminal's death brought with it a silence that transcended the games' trilling cacophony.

From the stairwell beyond, a woman, dark-skinned and giant, wearing high-cred armor that had been hit several times, limped toward the dead man, ignoring the killers who had slain him.

The moaning of the wounded and the sobbing of the cowardly could be heard drifting down the stairs behind her.

The whine of the blasters, still primed to fire again, faded.

The building began to vibrate as the repulsors of the *Tomahawk* went into full *hold and hover* just above the structure.

The woman in armor limped toward the prone body of Justin Wang.

She stared at him for a long moment.

Then fired a bolt from her heavy blaster into him.

The body jumped, but the gangster didn't care anymore.

"You dead, Justin. You dead now," she muttered, almost to herself.

Sergeant Király and Shriver approached her from different angles. Slowly even as the building thrummed and hovered from the starship just above.

Mad Dog ready to blast her.

Sergeant Király lowering his blaster.

A tear ran down the woman's carbon-stained face. But she didn't cry.

It was Shriver who spoke first.

"You know Sergeant Bombassa. Lady."

His voice cruel and hard. A man who'd never know pity.

She looked up at the operator, and her eyes were as dead as all the dead in the room.

She said nothing.

"Come on, girl... time's out and we gotta blow. You know where he is," continued Mad Dog. Still on mission. "He dead up there somewhere? You partners?"

She stared at Shriver but still said nothing.

Like she was never going to say anything.

Ever again.

Then she nodded.

"He dead. But... somewhere else. Not here. Three months ago."

She turned back to stare at the mess of gangsters on the ground amid all the chaos and carnage.

Sergeant Király walked toward her. His voice was soft and low. A whisper.

"Come on," he said to Bombassa's woman. "We got a ride outta here. Time to go."

She mumbled something like, "Ain't finished yet."

But she allowed them to lead her toward the roof.

The crew chiefs on the cargo deck of the *Tomahawk* had the slings ready to haul them up.

And a few minutes later, despite interceptor fire, the *Tomahawk* departed the station and made hyperspace.

Gone in an instant.

Gone... like it was never there.

# 25

**Legion Destroyer *Scontan Washam*
Hyperspace**

Chhun was already in the interrogation room when Zora arrived. The lead his hunter team had followed on Candalon V was a good one. The team had performed well. A few hiccups, but nothing that Major Slade—or more likely Sergeant D'het—couldn't iron out for next time.

He'd heard the rumors among the officers running the teams. How the Adjudicators were all-watching and all-seeing. As though the judgment the Legion asked them to render was on how well the team was run, instead of what the team was meant to recover.

Officers.

Major Slade was one. A good one, but an officer all the same. It was all he'd ever been. He couldn't help but think like one. Couldn't imagine his Adjudicator doing anything less than eyeing those beneath him with a full sensor sweep, because that's what a man like Slade did to his own men.

Chhun, a mustang, had approached things... differently. Had it not been for Dark Ops, had he been surrounded by points in a Legion line unit following Kublar, well, he knew his story would have turned out differently. His Legion career would not have been anywhere as long.

*Maybe you would have followed Exo*, Chhun thought to himself.

And what would have happened then?

Had Hunter Team Ranger brought Chhun's old friend in, perhaps the two of them could have pursued that line of thinking together. But it was clear that Bombassa wanted to be done with the Legion. Chhun could understand that— because he'd wanted to be done with the Legion too. After all that had happened, from Kublar to Kima, a time already being referred to as "The Troubles," Chhun had wanted to just disappear for a while.

So he had. Until the Legion needed him again.

But all the reasons Chhun had left to make sense of everything, all the death and carnage, the loss of friend after friend as the galaxy spiraled and seemed only to demand more death with each new victory... those questions were still with him.

Those questions were with a lot of the guys. Nearly every legionnaire that Chhun called a friend had... disappeared.

Ford, the *Indelible VI*, and his crew were gone almost as soon as the dust settled on Kima.

Chhun later heard a rumor that Ford and Leenah married, but that came from Masters, who never answered how he'd come by it. Which most likely meant he'd made it up. The kid was still Legion—for now. But Chhun detected the itch. He wouldn't be for much longer.

Bombassa was out of the Legion within two months of Kima. He'd had enough. Cheated death too many times. At least while wearing Legion armor. His becoming a Bronze Guild hunter was unexpected, considering.

Bear was still in. Dark Ops needed him.

Ravi said that one day all the warriors who'd fought to destroy the Golden King and the Dark Ones would join Chhun on En Shakar. That seemed... unlikely.

Chhun now realized that he'd been looking for a reason to leave the isolated world himself. The Legion had come with just such a chance.

*Maybe*, he'd thought, when the Legion commander and the old generals had come to talk with him about what had happened on Ulori, and what the Legion would do about it, *maybe if I see this through, see how it all happened, it'll help.*

Ravi seemed to offer another way to help. But his way was esoteric and mysterious. Fixed on a larger picture and attuned to a galaxy so big that Chhun was afraid to look at its face.

Whereas the Legion... the Republic... even the Troubles... these were familiar. These didn't require Chhun to stand side by side with one of the Ancients and know the galaxy afresh. With the Legion, the galaxy might change, but at least Chhun himself could remain the same.

And with Ravi... with Ravi there would be no coming back. Ravi signified the death of the old Chhun.

The Legion commander wasn't ready to die.

Not yet.

Not until he'd done the work of Adjudicator. One last mission for the Legion.

The door chimed and Zora stepped inside, her legionnaire escorts snapping to parade rest as they took their post outside. The bounty hunter leveled Chhun a look.

"We're running up against that time window you promised I could be out of here by. The Legion gonna pay me for any jobs I miss?"

Chhun gave a noncommittal smile. "I looked over some of the recordings you made. I appreciate the thoroughness."

Zora took a seat across from the former Legion commander. "I may as well have just recorded the whole thing."

"Why didn't you?"

She paused to consider her words. "Because... because I started to think about everything that happened. And what happened after we parted ways, and then got back together with Arkaddy Nilo. And Jack."

There was something to the way she said that name. Jack.

"I only have a passing familiarity with him. He was the Navy intel officer?"

She nodded.

"What happened to him?"

"I don't know. We were ambushed, he moved to keep Nilo and me safe. I think he's dead. Aeson said there hadn't been any sign of him when he and Ravi came for us. Is this... does the Legion need answers about that, too?"

Chhun saw a vulnerability that seemed like it shouldn't exist in the woman.

"Nothing that we need to go over right now," Chhun said. "But if you would record the facts you know about him for us... there are some connections we're still trying to make involving him and Nether Ops."

He hoped Zora would be spared the pain of revisiting whatever emotions she may have once had for Jack. Still had, if he was reading her correctly.

Bombassa could help with that background as well. He had once infiltrated Nilo's Black Leaf private military contracting agency for Dark Ops, and could very well have something on Jack they could follow beyond the Dark Ops records—although it was information about certain missing officers from the Black Fleet that Chhun *most* hoped his friend would be able to provide.

There remained much to uncover and document.

All the more reason to find Bombassa and keep things moving.

And they *would* find him.

Despite what the bounty hunter Team Ranger had recovered on Hang Kong Station said, Chhun didn't believe his friend was dead. Bombassa hadn't survived a hostile upbringing on a deadly world, a Legion frontline unit operated by an inept point, the Black Fleet's invasion of Tarrago, and all that followed suit just to get dusted by the kind of scumsacks Kill Team Victory rolled over and ate for breakfast three times a week.

Chhun's immediate thought was that the woman was lying to buy Bombassa more time. What she didn't know was that was unnecessary; he'd get that time whether she bought it or not. The hunter needed a chance to recover, and Major Slade needed a chance to regain control of his troops. It was a tough assignment, that many egos. When the best come together and see about proving they belong.

They'd break the woman's story down in interrogation, and then they'd get back on the trail.

For now, though, Zora had a different account to give.

"Most of what you covered spanned a few months where the three of you—Ford, your father, and yourself—worked to get contracts for Wraith. Were you together the entire time?"

"No. I took a few leaves to work as Blackheart. Keel and my father had built a solid rapport, but Keel and I were still getting to know one another. I rejoined right before he found that MCR ring responsible for stealing ships for the fleet."

Chhun nodded. That had been the closest Ford had come to finding Goth Sullus, though they didn't know it at the time. Or even know that Sullus was who they were looking for. Major Owens was working from the belief that a cabal inside the Mid-Core Rebellion had been responsible for Kublar, and thus the focus for Keel and Doc —once they'd built up Wraith's rep—was to work with, infiltrate, or smash MCR cells in hopes that Dark Ops might just turn over the rock they were looking for.

For a time—the time that Zora had already covered in her recordings—Ford didn't turn over any useful rocks at all. Just the usual independent terrorist cells, the smugglers, the thieves, the crime lords who had gotten a little too good at getting ahold of Repub military weapons and equipment. But the job in question... the big one that Zora was about to give her account of...

That one was an almost.

If Kill Team Victory had been closer. If they had arrived first.

*Almost.*

What might have happened then? They would have found Goth Sullus before his fleet was finished. There would have been no time for the Mandarins in the House of Reason to cover themselves for their slip.

The points would have been purged from the Legion.

Article Nineteen would have been declared.

Countless good leejes, men like Exo, wouldn't have had to fight their own brothers in a galactic civil war.

Almost.

"You ready, Legion Commander?" Zora asked. "Or should I go back to the shooting range?"

Chhun looked up. "Which legionnaire let you use the range?"

Zora gave a coy smile. "I'll never tell."

"Fine. Tell me about the job that led you to the MCR starship smuggling ring."

"All right." Zora nodded. "Let's talk about the big one."

# BEFORE.
# BEFORE IT WAS TOO LATE.

Wraith pushed his way through a downtown street market not unlike a thousand others bustling across the edge. One Jaberwotha vendor leaned out of his stall, red fruit in hand, singing as he switched from his native tongue to Standard, *"Hoo-sha! Hoo-sha!* Tarpples, tarpples! One credit. Only one!"

The neighboring vendor—sharp golden eyes catching sight of Wraith—pushed a clawed, reptilian hand out as the bounty hunter passed by. "Hunter! Bounty hunter! I have what you need. Weapons. *Legion* weapons. If you have credits..."

"Not interested," Wraith replied. He still wore his old Legion bucket, but his Dark Ops armor had been set aside for a custom-made set that dripped of pure black menace bristling with weapons. Apparently not strongly enough.

Over the comms, Doc said, "What're they tryin' to sell a guy like you, looking like death walking the streets?"

"Gestori was trying to hawk some Legion weapons. Night market," Wraith said, pushing on through the crowd and keeping his eyes and HUD alerts keyed for threats.

"Well slow down and see what they got, kid. Rule One: Buy the good stuff before someone else does."

"I marked it for a possible lead. Something to report to Major Owens. Could be tied to the MCR."

"You know if the MCR was involved they'd keep whatever's there for themselves, kid. He's more likely trying to pass off some surplus all the way back from Psydon on you. Not that you'll know unless you go back and check."

"I'll pass. You spent plenty already on armor and weapons, old man. Between that and your medication, we're practically broke."

Doc scoffed. "Near half a million credits left and you call that broke."

"That's an aggressive way to round the numbers, Gramps."

"Okay, so it's half of a half million credits. Still a lot. And your armor and your ship are better for it."

Wraith hoped the old man didn't strain a muscle patting himself on the back over that.

"You wanna know what this really is?" Doc went on.

Zora joined the chat. "What what really is?"

"You're back," Doc said. "Target still in place?"

"Right where he should be," Zora replied. "Big dwahser. Can't miss him, Wraith. Three more blocks up, filling a couple tables by himself at a kaff stand."

"Acknowledged," Wraith said, and continued pushing his way through the crowd as comm discipline broke down entirely on the other end.

Doc had been with him for months, and by now felt almost like a partner. A grumpy, overly critical partner, but someone Keel could rely on. Zora he'd seen less frequently, as she drifted in and out of the operation, taking on jobs as Blackheart to preserve her own cover. She'd proven herself during that time, but Keel wasn't sure where the two of them stood.

There was no denying that, *professionally*, the two of them gelled, despite their rocky beginning. It was the *personal* that had him confused. Occasionally Zora would act like she was interested in being... more. More than just part of the mission or crew. But any hints that were dropped were just as quickly followed up with a meanness that left Keel frustrated. He'd sworn off pursuing the matter any further; Doc surely wouldn't approve anyway.

Yet sparks kept flying when he least expected it. Usually when they were alone and just being themselves.

"So what's the situation?" Zora pressed.

"Uh... nothin'," her dad answered. "Operational secret."

"Oh, please. Between the two of you, I think I have a good idea of what's going on with your little secret mission."

"Oh, yeah, girlie? Go on and take a guess. Let's find out."

Zora sighed, as if spelling out the obvious was tiresome. "You and Keel are Legion or working a contract for the Legion. The Legion wants you to look for... something."

Doc laughed. "Yeah. You got us pegged, all right."

She wasn't wrong, though. To be fair, neither Keel nor Doc actually knew what the "something" he was looking for was, either. Only that it was impending, military in nature, and poised to cause trouble for the Legion and the Republic.

Eventually.

Up ahead was the targeted kaff stand, faux silvene tables out front and a trembling chair barely holding up under the girth of a gigantic dwahser, his ears flapping happily as his trunk brought a frothy cup to his mouth.

"Approaching the target," Wraith informed his crew.

"Careful, kid," Doc said in his ear. "Can't let it see you."

"Seeing me is part of the plan," Wraith said, stopping right in front of the dwahser. He pointed at the ground. "Is that your credit chit?"

The metal chair groaned as the big alien stooped to look. Something golden gleamed on the ground, and the thing's enormous trunk delicately plucked it up.

"*Urah poosh uhr*," he said in a deep voice, inclining his head politely.

"Don't mention it," Wraith replied and continued on his way. "Transponder planted," he told Doc.

"Nice. Reverse pickpocket," Zora said. "Where'd you learn that little trick?"

"We call it a put-pocket. Learned it in another life—it was the favorite of a joker in my old unit."

"Good, clean signal from the transponder," Doc said. "Exfil is two blocks north. Nice work, kid."

"Green sled with black windows?" Wraith said, spotting one up ahead, waiting.

"That's us," Doc said. "Got visuals on you now."

"Coming in."

Moments later, the sled hummed softly as Zora weaved it through traffic and onto the *Indelible VI*'s docking berth.

Wraith leaned back in his seat. "Signal still strong?"

Doc gave a nod. "Yeah. Doesn't look like the target found it because it's moving. I doubt anything as big as a dwahser could mimic your work and plant it on someone else."

"I tried to tuck it as deep into the fat folds as I could."

"And it didn't feel that?" Zora asked.

Wraith shrugged. "They don't feel much through that hide of theirs. Had a few scraps with them in the past. Big MCR supporters."

"So, not the sensitive types," Zora replied, and when Wraith didn't laugh, said, "You know, these windows aren't see-through. You can take your bucket off."

"Not until we're aboard the *Six*. Not worth the risk."

"Kid's right," Doc said. "Anyone who saw Wraith leave in this sled—not sayin' you were followed, kid—needs to see Wraith get out, too."

Doc's wrist-comm lit up with an incoming call.

"What's that?" Zora asked.

"Someone's trying to get ahold of Keel," Doc said. "Using the Black Channel freq set up for this job you just finished."

"Think they were watching?" Zora asked. The timing was... interesting.

"If so, why pay twenty thousand credits to have someone place a transponder on a target you already know the location of?" Wraith said.

"Either way, they'll be expectin' to talk to Keel," Doc said. "Which means they'll have to wait."

They entered the *Indelible VI*'s lounge to the sound of the AI's too-jovial greeting. "Welcome back, welcome back, welcome back! It's been *lonely* without you all."

Keel pulled his bucket off. "Shut up, AI."

"We were gone twenty minutes, you needy jumble of bad code," Doc growled.

Though the crew had grown accustomed to one another, none had developed a fondness for the grating artificial intelligence.

"Oh, I *know* that, Mister Doc," the AI exclaimed. "Trust me, my chronometers were counting down from the second the ramp closed. But *I* think feeling that sense of separation, especially in so brief a time, highlights the grand bond we all have, don't you? Now! What are my orders? Fire up the engines? Begin astronavigation? If you grant me clearance, I can warm up those new weapons systems—"

"Mute," Zora said.

"Thank you," Keel grunted.

"Honestly, I don't know why either of you even engages with that thing. It only encourages it," Zora remarked, collapsing on the couch and stretching out enough to send Doc and Keel looking for other places to take a load off.

Keel chose to sit atop a holo-enabled card table. "Engaging it wasn't quite the problem it is now until your old man had those belly turrets installed. Now the damn thing comes online every time the boarding ramp drops. Something got crossed up."

"Credits well spent regardless," Doc said. "You saw what those guns did to those mercs who wanted a piece back on Marat. You just need a good code slicer to fix up the AI, that's all." The old man rubbed his hands together, and Keel could smell credits burning already.

"Yeah, and how much'll that cost?"

"Won't be cheap if you want it done right. But that's only because you gotta pay someone enough so they don't leave a back door for themselves to get in later. I know a couple guys. Just gotta wait for the contracts to go through. Like I said, won't be cheap."

That was Keel's signal to get back to work. He hoisted himself back to his feet. "I'll go get the comm lit up."

Zora practically jumped up to follow. "I'll come with you."

The pair walked down the corridor to the cockpit. The door swooshed open and they dropped into their seats. Keel pulled up their latest contract and sent an outgoing comm request.

While they waited for their contact to pick up, Zora said, "Any idea who it is?"

"No. Contract only named the target." A green light lit up on their screen. "We got visuals connecting. Let's look pretty for the holocam."

A Pellekanese pirate, his face thin and sharp-featured, his jet-black hair braided and bedecked with gems and silvene rings, crowed a laugh.

Lao Pak.

"Captain *Keel*? What? Lao Pak's good friend! This a small galaxy!"

Keel shook his head. "Not this guy," he muttered. Then to Lao Pak: "How did you—"

"Oh, Lao Pak hire Wraith for job he just finish. You know Wraith? What, you take his calls? You his secretary?" Lao Pak laughed some more.

"We work together, yeah."

The pirate leaned forward. "He the one who spring you from jail? Not Lao Pak?"

"Right again. And I wasn't going to ask how you got the comm channel. I was going to ask how you survived."

Lao Pak looked hurt. "I thought you miss on purpose! You mean you were trying to kill Lao Pak? What? You must be really bad shot, Keel. I thought you let me live because we friends. Kill the other guys, that okay. Gunfighters cheap. I can't believe you try to kill Lao Pak. I not forget this."

"You tried to jump me and steal my ship," Keel protested.

Lao Pak waved that off. "That in past. So long time ago I forget."

Keel looked at Zora. She shook her head. He returned to the holo.

"What do you want, Lao Pak?" Keel asked, ready to end the transmission, but also aware that if the pirate had paid the credits for Wraith, personal grudges needed to be set aside.

"You still with girlfriend?" the pirate asked, ignoring Keel's attempt to keep things moving. "She prettier in this light."

Zora furrowed her brows, but there was no mistaking the reddening of her cheeks. "I am *not* his—"

The cockpit door hissed open behind them, and Doc stepped into view.

"You still run with bald old man, too?" Lao Pak said.

"Who's asking?" Doc gruffed.

"Lao Pak," Zora supplied. "The pirate who tried to steal the *Six* back on Rakka."

Doc rubbed his scruffy chin. "I thought we killed that little worm."

Aghast, Lao Pak placed a hand over his bejeweled cravat. "I not worm... I pirate king. And now that Wraith do first job, I hire him for second job. Where is he?"

"Doesn't work like that, Lao Pak," Keel said as the holographic pirate searched the cockpit. "You want Wraith's help, you gotta go through me."

That pulled the man up short.

"Go through *you*? But you stupid. Why he use someone stupid? He good."

"Goodbye, Lao Pak."

"No no no!" the pirate protested, waving his hands. "Wait! I need Wraith. I work with Captain Keel, okay? He not stupid. He smart, okay? *So* smart. *Everybody* admire him. Say he so smart all the time! This big job. Big. So big."

"Sorry, Lao Pak. Wraith doesn't work for pirates. Knowingly, anyway," Doc said, reaching for the comm button.

"It good money! It—"

Keel reveled in the silence a moment, then said, "If you were trying to kill the transmission, old man, you pressed the wrong button. All you did was shut off the audio and visual connections. The link is still there."

"I know. Comms ain't changed that much since I was your age, wise guy. Anyway, I don't think you should write the kelhorn off just yet."

"What happened to not working with pirates?" Keel asked.

Doc shrugged. "What, you got a rule against it or somethin'?"

Keel pointed an accusatory finger at the old man. "No, but you do. Remember? Rule One. No pirates. You said it."

Doc made a face as though he'd never heard this before in his life. "Nah."

Unable to tell if this was dementia settling in or the old man's way of walking back what he'd said before, Keel turned to consult the man's daughter. "Zora, is there a history of mind-bind in your family? Feeser's Disease?"

Zora ignored him. "That *does* sound like something you'd say, Doc."

"Don't call me Doc, honey."

"Don't call me honey, *Dad*."

"Fine, *Zora*."

The two stared at each other with all the intensity of competitors in a galactic-class skittra match, both seeking to check the other's move.

"I'm putting Lao Pak back on," Keel said, then muttered, "Not like it was *my* rule..."

He re-established audio and video. Unsurprisingly, Lao Pak was still waiting.

"All right, Lao Pak. Let's hear it. I think Wraith is willing to hear you out since you and I are 'old friends.'"

Lao Pak primly studied the tiny diamonds on his long fingernails. "I knew that happen when I say *credits*. Only... there not any credits."

Keel sighed. "Goodbye."

"Up front! No credits *up front*! I spend last credits just getting Wraith to take last job. You know how many Black Channel contracts I write and cancel before Wraith finally take one?"

"That was you? All those cheap jobs?"

Offended, Lao Pak said, "Twenty thousand credits not cheap!"

"It is for Wraith. You got lucky he was already in-system for another job."

"He lucky when I pay twenty thousand credits for him to put tracker on dumb, slow alien," Lao Pak insisted. "Now he get lucky again. No credits up front... but lots of credits on back end."

"Explain, pirate boy," Doc said.

"That take too long. I busy. I send you details in writing. Keel, someone can read them to you, and then you tell Wraith. Then he tell me, 'Okay, Lao Pak, that good idea, I do it,' and then at end, we all get paid."

Keel highly doubted it but decided to play along. For curiosity's sake.

"All right. Send it over."

Lao Pak reached a flashy finger forward. "Transmitting now."

*Boom.* The explosion was distant, but they felt it rumbling through their boots, into their bones.

"What the hell was that?" Doc growled.

"Oh!" Lao Pak exclaimed. "Oh, I press wrong button. Blow up dwahser's ship."

"You *what*?" Zora's hand instinctively went to her blaster.

"It okay," the pirate assured her. "He was on board. That was close one though!"

"Don't think that's what she meant, bucko," Doc drawled.

"Oh. It still okay. He mutiny," Lao Pak explained. "Steal one of Lao Pak's freighters and some of Lao Pak's crew. Just the stupid ones. But stupid crew take credits with them, same as smart crew."

Keel ran his fingers through his hair, not quite believing what had just happened and yet somehow feeling no surprise. With what he'd seen of Lao Pak it seemed... fitting.

"You had Wraith place a transponder just so you could blow up the target? Why not just put in a termination contract with the Bronze Guild?"

Zora nodded in agreement. "Would've cost you half of what you paid if it meant knocking off a pirate mutineer."

Lao Pak winked at her like he was about to share a secret. "But that not make me repeat customer for Wraith. Also... termination just kill him. That no good. He double-cross Lao Pak! But... if I blow up ship, I kill stupid crew, too. How cheap that, Keel girlfriend? Hmm?"

Doc gave an old-man growl. "So for kicks, you blew up a stolen ship, the mutinous captain, and whatever crew he picked up."

"Not to mention anyone working in the docking bay," Zora added.

Lao Pak shrugged. "Yeah, that part too bad. If I have trouble sleep tonight, I say, that docking bay only have bots working for it. Then I sleep good. Also, I meant to wait until he take off. Press wrong button by mistake; not Lao Pak fault!" The pirate seemed to accept what fate had delivered, and then forgot the whole ordeal. "Okay. I send you details for Wraith. Glad we best friends again, Captain Keel. This work good. I feel it."

The transmission ended.

"Unreal," Keel muttered at the blank screen.

"That's why you don't work with pirates, kid," Doc said. "Rule One."

"Don't even start to tell me—"

"He's trying to get under your skin, Keel," Zora interrupted.

Keel settled back in his seat. "Yeah. Yeah... I knew that."

Doc just laughed, then reached for the controls as they received a data packet. He pushed a burst to his datapad, scanned through it, and grunted.

"Are Lao Pak's 'written instructions' in complete sentences?" Zora asked. "Even worth reading at all?"

Still reading, Doc said, "I'd say so. Yeah."

"So what's the job?" Keel asked.

"Ain't finished reading it yet, kid. But if I was you, I'd hurry up and get back in the armor."

# 26

It was just the two of them that evening, sitting in an outdoor café on a bustling street corner near the LaKalb Spaceport. Music played through the open glass doors. They sat close, not making eye contact, pretending to enjoy their kaff. Keel raised his cup to his lips just as the air filled with the vibrating hum and boom of a landing craft. The steaming kaff trembled, rippling in his mug. When the air stilled, he took a sip.

"This is nice, huh?" he said.

Zora's eyes darted from left to right suspiciously. "What? Sitting on a backwater planet, sipping kaff in a dirty café while starliners land in the distance? Oh yeah. Lovely."

"I meant mostly the kaff." Keel's was pretty good. Black, hot, unadulterated. Strong.

Zora frowned at her over-milked blend. "It's okay."

Keel sat back, still holding his drink. "You're a hard one to please, aren't you?"

"I have standards. That shouldn't be written off as hard."

"Hey, *I* have standards," Keel protested. "And I've had enough burnt cups of kaff in my life to be thankful when one halfway decent one shows up in front of me. Even if half of it vibrates out of the mug whenever a star hauler sets down."

Zora let slip a laugh. She looked up and then panned her head to take in her surroundings. "Seriously. Who in their right mind would authorize a café to do business this close to the star port?"

"About the only thing on Marat that makes any kind of sense is the Republic spaceport on the other side of that mountain range to your left," Keel said with a nod. "Spent a long time there when I was... anyway, spent some time there. Everything else is a free-for-all among the humans, Kellochs, and whatever other species are trying to scratch out a living here."

Zora nodded like she was updating her mental database. "You know, you can say it around me."

"Say what?"

"Legion. I know you were, or possibly still are, in the Legion. Always have known."

Keel waved that off.

Zora leaned forward. "It's Doc who's the giveaway right from the start. He wouldn't be helping you if you *weren't* Legion. It's in his blood. All he knows. All he ever truly loved."

The conversation was drifting uncomfortably close to family and feelings. *Zora's* family and feelings. Keel took a loud sip of his drink. "Hey... we can talk about something else."

"Oh, I'm not feeling sorry for myself. Just stating a fact." Zora shrugged it off. "So you were here while in the Legion. And please don't insult my intelligence with another wink and denial."

Keel decided to own it. "Did a rotation here, yeah."

"What company?"

"Can't tell you that. Classified."

"By who?"

"Classified."

Zora raised a brow. "So you'd have to kill me if you told me? *Try* to kill me?"

"That's classified, too."

Zora laughed, and Keel's wrist-chrono lit up.

"Go for Keel," he said, taking the call through the micro-comm in his ear.

"Just saw the target enter atmo," Doc said. "I'll have the ship come down in two hours. Should be enough time for you to get visuals."

Keel kept his kaff hand very still as another freighter touched down, rumbling the ground, their chairs, table, and him.

"Yep. Sounds good."

"Sounds good? What the hell kind of comm protocol is —oh, that's right. You didn't want to wear the armor for surveillance like I said, so now you gotta hide everything you say. Moron."

"Okay, well, I'm on a date, Gramps. I'll call you tonight after you've taken your pills."

"A date?" Doc grumped. "What the hell are you talking about? Don't pull that Gramps crap on me either, kid, or I'll —"

"Yeah. Okay. Yeah. Bye. Okay. Gotta go. Bye." Keel tapped his wrist.

Zora raised an eyebrow. "Oh, so this is a date now?"

"It's meant to *look* like a date to anyone watching us. Which is why I didn't gear up like your old man wanted. Gotta be inconspicuous. *Obviously*, this isn't a date—"

"It isn't."

"—because you're not the only one with standards, you know."

Zora smiled in rueful appreciation of the joke she'd just walked right into. "You kelhorned—"

"Ah-ah-ah! Put your fist down. No hitting on the first date. I was only joking. My standards are much lower than you."

Zora gaped for a reply, then settled for, "That's the worst compliment I've ever heard."

Keel went back to sipping his kaff. "I meant it more as an insult to myself."

Zora laughed despite herself. "What did Doc have to say?"

"Running late but says he should be coming down soon."

"Keel. You don't need to speak in code. No one else is around, and if anyone *was* trying to listen, they'd never hear us over all the ships coming down."

"No sense getting sloppy. If bad luck doesn't get you killed, that will."

The approaching roar of another large freighter rumbled the café so hard that the windows behind them practically rattled out of their frames.

Lao Pak's job was the sort of intra-pirate family squabble Wraith usually wouldn't have bothered with. Lao Pak had been angling on seizing a shipment of weapons on behalf of an undisclosed arms broker. An informant inside a defense company had tipped the broker to a large shipment intended to outfit a small, edge-world planetary police force. Idents and schematics for the transport ship —a heavily armored Krusanne corvette—were supplied to the broker, who then passed them to Lao Pak. Lao Pak and his crew were to steal the weapons, pass them to the broker, and earn a percentage of the weapons sales. As a bonus, he could keep the Krusanne corvette for himself.

*That* got him excited.

The trouble came when a sizeable portion of Lao Pak's pirate crew—the entirety of the Hools, several humans, three Kimbrins, seven Doros and a pair of Tennar; Lao Pak had catalogued all of the "traitors"—decided to take the job for themselves. They stole the mammoth Grendel-class freighter Lao Pak had intended to use for the transport of the weapons—a large, first-rate hauler that he was extremely proud of—and set out to raid the corvette themselves.

Lao Pak had called them that—*traitors*—never mind that he himself had relied mostly on double-crosses to scheme his way to his current standing among the Pellekanese pirates. Among pirates, fairness was never a consideration—just whether you could get away with it. The mutinous elements of his fledgling pirate empire *had*.

Gotten away with it, that is.

So far. Wraith was hired to change that.

The contract was surprisingly generous. Wraith's job was to wait for Lao Pak's crew when they landed in the seedy starport where Keel and Zora now reconnoitered... then terminate the crew. That was non-negotiable. Lao Pak needed to look strong on the other side of this.

A pirate who could hire the rising star among the circle of hired guns, contract killers, and mercenaries that bounty hunters orbited would set himself above the others.

Lao Pak was ambitious.

Once the crew was terminated, Wraith could take ten percent of the cargo for himself. Everything else, especially the Grendel-class, stayed with Lao Pak. In addition, Wraith would receive a payment of ninety thousand credits.

Which of course meant the cargo was worth far more. But there were rules. Lao Pak knew the ship and its location.

For Wraith and the Legion, it was the weapons angle that made the job worth looking into. A planetary police force on galaxy's edge might not have tremendous numbers, but certainly enough to keep the MCR's war machine going for a little longer. Of even greater interest to Keel was the identity of this weapons dealer—and the informant who'd tipped off the initial shipping, giving the pirates an opportunity to hijack the ship.

Keel had already found that once someone breaks bad for credits, they don't stop. It's never enough money. They'll never get caught.

And when they are... they'll tell you they'd never done anything like that before. Which is probably true. Or was true when they started.

*I've never done anything like this before. I can't believe I was so stupid.*

And the Dark Ops leej sitting across from the guy will say, *I believe you, but it doesn't matter. Hope you like Herbeer.*

You let the guy cry for a bit as he thinks about the life he's about to lose. A good life that had only gotten better since those credits started to come in. You let him blubber and sniff his nose.

Then...

*But maybe you can avoid Herbeer. Maybe you can help us—the good guys—find the bad guys who* do *do this kind of thing. All the time.*

And you go from there. Maybe all the way up to the cabal of MCR fanatics who blew up a Legion destroyer, fomented a civil war on Kublar, and worked with the zhee to nearly crash an explosives-laden corvette into Utopion.

Then it's over.

Back to the kill teams.

*Back to your old life*, thought Keel.

Thought Ford.

First, though, Wraith had to do his job. Which would be messy. The kind of thing Keel and Zora needed to verify before the blasters came in and the dying began.

Zora lifted a hand to search the skies. "That looks like our bird," she shouted over the thunderous backblast. "Grendel-class hauler. Formerly owned by Lao Pak."

"That's it," Keel shouted back in confirmation. "Surprised they weren't dumb enough to just fly the Krusanne corvette here directly. Just gotta wait for the crew to come out."

"Shouldn't be hard to miss. They're putting down practically right next to us."

"What?" Keel shouted.

"I said—"

The hauler landed in the next-door star port, its shrieking repulsors cycling down to a whine, and the vibrations rattling the patio ceased.

Keel shook the ringing out of his ears. "How are the owners of this place not deaf?"

Zora grimaced. "Who says they aren't? I asked for that spish roll ten minutes ago. Still hasn't come."

"Lazy doesn't mean deaf," Keel told her, then shouted back through the open café door, "Hey! How about that roll and some more kaff?"

"Oh, that's endearing." Zora fluttered her eyelashes. "Or are you just wanting people to *think* you're that guy—the jerk in the restaurant."

"It's not being a jerk if they really *are* terrible at their jobs. And anyway," he checked the time on his wrist-chrono, "we gotta kill at least a little more time before the crew cycles down and leaves the ship. Might as well get what we paid for while we're at it."

The owners of the café powered up a dull-looking servitor bot that used a uni-wheel to drive through the tables. Another customer had stopped in, and the slothful owners—a pair of female Kimbrin who seemed more interested in the blaring holoscreen behind the counter than their customers—evidently needed the bot's help to handle "the rush." The upside was the spish roll was delivered with a full carafe of kaff so that Keel could just help himself and leave the owners alone. He topped his drink off and did the same for Zora after dumping out half of her milky slop on the duracrete sidewalk where the tables were gathered.

"You're making a mess," Zora protested when Keel returned her mug along with a much darker shade of kaff inside it.

"Look around," Keel said, waving his hand as an invitation. "That's the closest these streets have been to a cleaning since the last monsoon season."

She took a drink. "Much better."

Keel gave a knowing nod. "You're braver than me. I'd never have my kaff any way besides black. You've got no idea what kind of oily beast they squeezed milk from on a backwater like this."

Zora's face soured. She put her cup down.

It was a while longer before they caught sight of the crew walking down the street. They wore the typical garb of spacers—workmen's boots and thick pants or jumpsuits, sturdy jackets to keep the cold of deep space flight at bay. They were all pulling repulsor crates behind them.

Keel frowned. "How many humans did Lao Pak say jumped?"

"Four," Zora said quietly, tearing a fibrous thread from her roll and popping it into her mouth.

There were ten now. Humans.

"Maybe they picked up some new hands," Keel suggested, but it didn't sit right.

"And the rest are back at the ship."

"Only one way to find out," Keel agreed. He picked up her free hand and rubbed it with his thumb. Just another boyfriend on a date with his girl. "Here they come. Try not to look too interested or they'll think you're coming on to them. You know how spacers are after a long haul."

"Ha ha," Zora said, and let her face light up like he was hilarious. "I know what I'm doing, Keel. You've got the view coming, I'll have the view going."

Keel winked. "Feel free to stare at me in wondered awe, like a girl usually does when she's on a date with me."

Widening her brown elfin eyes, Zora gave him an adoring stare. Keel leaned forward. For a moment, their eyes locked together and a sense of warmth fell over both, but it quickly faded as Keel looked intently right over Zora's shoulder.

*The mission*, he reminded himself.

Keel was just about to take another casual sip of his drink when Zora fumbled hers and splashed it all over the table and him. Keel got up, and Zora exclaimed her apologies while helping him wipe down as best she could with table napkins. Meanwhile the passing crew chuckled and moved on.

"So much for being inconspicuous," Keel said, dropping back into his seat and watching them go.

Zora gave a small smile. "That's what you think. We looked like a couple whose date just got memorable. That's the kind of moment that reinforces what you already think. Those pirates, if they remember anything about us at all besides what my backside looked like, are only gonna remember the spill. Not our faces if they catch us looking around their docking bay."

"That... does make a little sense," Keel admitted.

"*You* think you don't want people to *notice*," Zora continued. "But mainly, you don't want to give people a reason to study your face. They can notice all they want, but we're wired not to care unless we give them a reason."

"A bounty hunter and a philosopher, huh?"

"My father taught me that lesson a long time ago. Guess what he calls it?"

"Rule One?"

"Bingo. C'mon... let's go take a look at their ship. See how much Wraith is going to be up against on that Grendel hauler."

# 27

"Welcome to LaKalb Spaceport, Marat's largest independently run star port," an emotionless voice intoned as they walked up to the target's docking bay. "All docking fees must be paid within one hour of landing or ships will be subject to seizure. *Urururur muwawl me'vuru t'tra Marattatra urka ka meryu...*" the message continued, repeating itself in the local language.

"This way," Keel said, indicating an open bay door.

"Why would they leave the door open?" Zora said, casually walking beside him as they threaded their way past loaded repulsors, busy bots, and kit-wielding mechanics.

"Most pirates aren't all that smart to begin with. The ones that decide following Hools is a good idea..." Keel made a face.

"Doc still on his way down?" Zora asked.

"Yeah. Waiting to get a landing clearance. Wants us to wait until we can get our armor."

"But here we are."

"Here we are." They'd stopped by the wide-open bay doors. "Better to get a peek before those crew members come back. This kind of thing is always easiest with fewer eyes around. Ready?"

"Ready."

They headed through, just two spacers strolling into the docking area where the monstrous Grendel-class hauler loomed. Keel had never seen such an ugly example of the craft. Swamp-brown and rust-stained, a blocky metal bulk. But what that class of freighters lacked in aesthetic beauty it made up for in raw power. Grendel-class engines were capable of hauling six times the tonnage of most merchant freighters.

Still, Lao Pak hadn't put many credits toward maintaining this one.

Keel knife-handed towards the shadows behind some power cells, and they took cover.

"That's a giveaway, you know," Zora said once they were out of sight.

"What?" Keel asked.

"The knife hand. Screams military."

"Huh." Keel had been working to make his life in the Legion less obvious to the outside observer. It wasn't easy.

Zora pointed toward the underbelly of the ship. "Looks like the doors to the bay aren't the only thing left open."

Keel frowned. Cargo *and* crew doors unsecured.

"You'd think they'd at least post a guard," Zora whispered. "I don't see anyone."

Keel nodded. "Let's take a look. But be careful... they surely left *someone* behind."

Zora cocked an eyebrow. "Hey. Actual bounty hunter here—I know the drill. When Doc gets down here, we can have him launch a TT-16 and get us eyes inside this hunk of scrap."

Keel wasn't interested in waiting on Doc, and besides, the docking bay was empty enough to risk him taking a closer look. "I'm gonna go look inside for myself. You stay here."

"You're not serious," Zora hissed.

He gave her a half-smile. "Maybe they're all passed out drunk. Won't even have to bother Wraith at all. Keel can handle that."

The smuggler moved from cover and swiftly approached the ramp, careful to look down to avoid his face being detected in the docking bay or shipboard holocams. He kept his Intec x6 loose in the holster on his thigh, ready for a quick draw but not wanting to look like he planned on violence from the get-go in case someone on board was watching the holocams. Pirates might welcome a thief into their crew if he talked well enough. But a murderer... well, that was different. At least when it was them the killer had come to murder.

From the moment Keel stepped inside the ship's cavernous cargo hold, he recognized trouble. On the walls were signs of a recent firefight. Scorch marks from blaster bolts and what looked like bloodstains on the deck. *Hool* blood, which was poisonous and didn't come off easily, though it looked like someone had tried. A single large, sealed shipping container sat alone in the center of the space.

"Something's wrong here, Zora," he called into his comm.

She didn't answer.

Fearing that his backup was discovered and captured before she could call in a warning, Keel pulled his blaster pistol and carefully moved back toward the cargo ramp that led out of the freighter.

Zora remained hidden where he'd left her; she was watching the ramp, and gave a wave upon seeing Keel.

The smuggler tried his comm again.

"Yeah, solid copy," Zora answered.

"There's some kind of jamming going on inside," Keel said, lingering at the ramp. "Comm was dead."

"Any crew or cargo?"

"Cargo, yes. No crew, but I saw signs of a fight. Maybe Lao Pak's pirates got to double-crossing one another early. I'm gonna go back in and check the rest of the ship."

"That ship's *huge*," Zora protested. "It'll take you forever. Wait for Doc to land and we can come back in our armor."

Keel shook his head. "No. Something's off. First, the crew we saw had too many humans, and now we find that they left this place unguarded and wide open. The ship hasn't even stopped ticking from its cooldown. I need to see about it now while we have the opportunity."

"Okay, I'll come with—"

"Stay there," Keel said before she could finish her sentence. "If someone's coming, I need you to let me know. Activate the fire alarm. That should be loud enough for me to hear inside, so long as I leave all the blast doors open while I go."

Zora frowned. She clearly didn't like the arrangements, but time was wasting. "Okay. Hurry."

Keel had been looking over his shoulder as they spoke. The cargo hold remained abandoned. He had just turned to go when Zora called out a warning.

"Some kind of repulsor truck is coming through the bay doors over there." She pointed.

Keel looked, but the bulk of the ship blocked his view. "Probably coming for the freight," he said. "Get outside and move into a position where you can watch it go. Try to get the old man to look for it from above."

"What about you?"

"I'm going to try and see if I can catch a ride out on this container."

The sound of the repulsor truck pulling into the docking bay covered Keel's footsteps as he receded into the cargo hold. The comm was dead again, but the hastily put-together plan was clear enough. He hoped.

He moved cautiously just in case some of the crew might be somewhere nearby. They weren't. That only seemed to support the growing suspicion the smuggler harbored that the crew that Lao Pak wanted dead... *was* dead. He would need to check that. Catch up to the humans who'd left the docking bay. But for now... he wanted to know who was coming to get this freight and where it was going.

Because if this was another Lao Pak double-cross...

Wraith wouldn't be as forgiving as Keel had been.

Keel only had to ride the top of the cargo container—the automated repulsor truck slowly moving him down the spaceport's rundown access lanes—for a few minutes before Doc had an observation bot in the air to track the freight's destination. Keel jumped off as the repulsor truck slowly took a corner, and then found his way to Zora, who had been following on foot and was now catching her breath a few blocks back.

"Feels like something we're going to need that armor for," she said as Keel jogged up to her.

"Yeah. Let's go see where Doc landed."

They cut through a few alleys until they reached the medium-sized docking bays reserved for ships the size of the *Indelible VI*, which took considerably less room than a Grendel-class freighter.

Keel and Zora dashed aboard the *Indelible VI* the moment the ramp dropped, then ran straight to the armory. Doc walked in to find them both pulling on their armor as fast as they could. Boots, synthweave, chest plates, pauldrons, gauntlets, the works.

"You wanna tell me why the two of you are putting on armor so fast you'd think I caught you together in bed?"

"Not funny," Zora said, locking her pauldrons in place.

"Sorta funny," Keel amended.

"Ship came in like Lao Pak said it would," Zora told her dad, tightening an ammo belt around her waist. "Only his pirate crew was gone except for a few humans who left it unguarded."

"Uh-huh. And where did they go?" Doc asked.

"Dunno. We went to see how well the defenses were set up for when Wraith came back. Keel figured doing it while there were fewer eyes watching was worth the risk. Turns out there were *no* eyes watching. Nobody was there."

Doc looked incredulous. "No one? You checked the whole karkin' ship?"

Keel shook his head. "No. Hangar was empty. Ship was wide open. Hold only had one shipping container in it—that's what the truck you're tracking took." He paused. "You *are* still tracking that truck, right?"

Doc waved away the concern and held up a datapad. "Yeah, yeah, I got it. Still moving. Skipped a couple of exits to the city proper, so my gut is it's going to another bay. Probably a cargo transfer."

"That's where I want to be, then." Keel primed his blaster.

"Maybe the little twerp was lying to you," Doc cut in. "Fake you out to try to take the *Six* again, only it was off-planet. Rule One, remember?"

Zora set down the blaster she was checking. She looked to Keel, wanting to gauge what he thought of that being the case.

"Could be," Keel admitted. "We can try and call him and grill him about it—he's not smart enough to avoid telling us the truth—but I still want to see what that cargo is before it gets off-planet again."

"Or maybe something else entirely is going on," Zora said. "Only way to know is to investigate."

"All right, yeah," Doc said. "Weapons smuggling is the kind of thing your, uh, boss is gonna wanna hear about, kid."

Keel gave a curt nod as he rummaged through sliding drawers built into the wall that contained everything from charge packs to blaster parts. Finally he gave up looking and turned to the old man. "The trackers. Where'd you put them, old-timer?"

Doc pointed to a higher shelf on an adjoining wall. "Over there. Didn't make no sense to have 'em next to the firing coils and barrel refractors. It ain't a gun part."

Keel walked to their new location, retrieved one of the expensive tracking devices, inspected it, and then held it up for Doc to see. "It makes sense to me, and this is *my* ship, so that's all that matters. Stop moving things around."

"Leave an old man to rot inside the ship, you get what you get," Doc grumbled. "But, since you're gettin' armored up, you expect a fight? I can help with that. What did these kelhorns look like?"

"Not much," Zora said, slipping her blaster in its holster. "And no, you can't help with that. This is an observation mission, not a fight. No one is going to know we're there—we're just going in prepared. You know you approve."

Doc went over to his daughter and gave her armor a few little pulls, checking it was secure. "You want backup or not?"

"Goal is to get in and out unseen," Keel said. "That's not gonna happen when a crazy old man shows up with his shotgun and starts sending rounds. But the Grendel, there's something going on there, too. Why don't you head over and see what you see while I try and get a look at this cargo. Or at least get close enough to put a tracker on the ship that's hauling it."

"I can do that." Doc looked to his daughter. "You comin' with me or goin' with this kelhorn, Zee?"

Zora gave her dad a little smile. "See you when we get back."

The *Indelible VI*'s ramp lowered with a thud, and the two bounty hunters ran off, leaving Doc behind to shout after them.

"Yeah, yeah. Don't count on me being around to open the ramp for you two! Not gonna wait up all night."

The TT-16 observation bot monitored the cargo container as it was transported to another docking bay, just as Doc had predicted. Keel and Zora took a hired repulsor most of the way, and then walked in their armor the rest. The locals gave them a wide berth; two mercenaries or bounty hunters patrolling a star port might just mean that some crew or cargo required specialized security... or it could mean a blaster fight was impending. Most didn't want to linger too near, just in case it was the latter.

This time, unlike on their previous outing, Wraith and Zora found the docking bay sealed up—but a quick slice of the rudimentary security system granted them access through a side maintenance hatch. They found a Galaxy-class hauler waiting inside, the cargo already being loaded, piece by piece, from the large container they had tracked. Despite the designation, the Galaxy-class was a much smaller ship than the Grendel. But both were far too large to be filled by the meager contents of the container.

"This place looks busy," Zora said to Keel through the comm in her bucket. "Lot more crew around. Not to mention all those bots."

Loading bots trundled like ants up and down the Galaxy-class hauler's ramp, working steadily. Each either carried a case or worked with a partner to haul up a crate. If any of the content was military, it had been repackaged; nothing was in the sorts of shipping containers Keel had seen during his time in the Legion.

"I'm gonna go in close and see if I can open up one of those before a bot transports it," Keel said, nodding in the direction of the cargo.

"Okaaay... and how are you going to do that without getting caught? Exactly?"

The situation changed before Keel could answer. A bald man with a long white beard walked swiftly down the cargo ramp, looking with displeasure at the loading bot that rolled his way, bearing another container. He wore a brown leather bomber jacket over a spacer's jumpsuit, and gave a whistle that pierced the busy hum of the docking bay.

The half-dozen members of his crew who were seeing to final checks and preparations around the ship all raised their heads at the sound. The crew were all human, but none looked to be the same as the crew of the Grendel-class. They quickly finished their tasks and then hurried up the ramp into the freighter, each one nodding at their captain as they went by.

This freighter was poised to take off. Only the loading of cargo remained, and the bots would have that work finished soon.

Wraith's inspection window was closing.

With each passing greeting of, "Cap'n," the captain merely nodded back at his crew. It was clear his mind was fixed on the cargo. He looked at an oncoming bot with displeasure, then stomped toward it, forcing the machine to stop in its tracks.

"Hurry it up, huh? You bots are taking forever. I've never seen loaders this slow."

After an unintelligible whistle in Signica, the machine addressed the captain in a mechanical-sounding Standard. "I am sorry, Captain Zaragoza. This cargo is marked as volatile. We are operating inside our programmed restraints for dealing with such shipments."

"Volatile?" the captain said, as if this was news to him, just as it was to Keel and Zora, who waited behind the cover of an old, rusted jump-ring that some big hauler had discarded in a corner and no one else had bothered to move to the scrap yards. The audio enhancers inside their buckets allowed for easy eavesdropping without them having to expose themselves.

"Yes, sir," the bot said. "Care is required in loading. Our programming will not allow movement at a faster rate."

The captain checked his datapad. "Burst me whatever manifest you're going by."

"I cannot fulfill your request, sir. It is beyond my parameters as a loading unit."

Scowling, the captain trekked off toward the bay's central control terminal, no doubt to get a readout of exactly what the bots were doing. Or at least what they *thought* they were doing. He pulled a comm cylinder from his pocket as he moved. "Clayton. Get that kelhorn to finish loading up the blind jump co-ords and get his ass out here. We need to talk about this cargo. Now."

"Aye, sir," the comm chirped back.

Wraith nodded to Zora. "He's distracted. Now's the time."

"This place is still buzzing," she replied, unheard except by Keel as the pair communicated via comm. "I count... ten, no twelve bots loading cargo."

"They're loading bots, not sentries. They won't care unless you try and stop them from pushing their repulsor pallets. We'll check whatever's still inside the container. C'mon."

Quiet as shadows, the bounty hunters slipped into the traffic of bots pushing softly humming repulsor pallets toward the cargo container being emptied near the loading ramp. Zora took the lead, with Keel spaced out a couple of machines behind.

With a quick look to make sure "Clayton and the kelhorn" didn't come down the ramp at the worst possible time, the pair moved past the loading bots and into the shadowy recesses of the container. There were only two pallets left, one of which had been down-stacked to just a couple of crates.

In the darkness, Wraith went to the short pallet and unsheathed his vibro-blade.

"Watch my back while I break open the seal."

"Okay, but hurry it up. More bots are on their way."

Keel slipped the knife into the tamper seal of the top crate and pulled it along the crease. Soon he had the crate open, revealing rows of matte-black weapons.

"Ho-ly sket..." Zora said, sounding just like her dad. "Are those..."

"N-6 rifles, yeah. Repackaged, but looks like the genuine article. These shouldn't be here."

"So Lao Pak wasn't lying."

"At least not about this crate."

Wraith pinged Doc.

"Go for I-Six Actual."

"Cargo confirmed," Wraith said. "Lao Pak actually tipped us to a legit weapons smuggling ring. I'm almost having trouble believing it."

"So take down the crew," Doc advised. "I'll alert Owens so he can send someone to ask questions once we're gone."

"I don't think this crew are the ones who—"

A loading bot trundled right up to Wraith and reached out its spider-arms to take the pallet. "Excuse me," was all it said before it snapped the crate shut and pushed the entire pallet away.

"What's going on?" Doc asked.

"Lousy bot just took the crate I'd opened before I could drop in the tracker," Wraith groused. It was his own fault. He should have done that first. The excitement over coming across something with the potential to be big had overcome his professionalism.

In fact, much of his new life was threatening to overtake his Legion professionalism. He would need to be more careful.

He cut open a crate on the second pallet. "Charge packs." This time Wraith immediately pulled the tracker from his side pouch, green light on. "Okay, Doc, I placed the tracker inside. Can you verify signal?"

"I'm gettin' nothin'. You sure it's active?"

"Affirmative. It's active."

"Then why am I gettin' nothin'? You gotta make sure you see the green light."

"I *see* the green light, old man. It's active."

"And I'm tellin' you it ain't. Just take down the crew, kid. You probably won't even have to pull a trigger between the two of you."

"I don't think the crew is in on this," Zora said, finishing what Keel had started to say earlier.

"Who gives a space rat's ass about that?"

Another bot arrived and reached out its spider-arms with the same robotic "Excuse me" before carrying away the pallet and the crate.

Keel barely pulled the tracker away in time. Something was going on. The crates, or perhaps the proximity to the ship, was jamming it. Keel had spent too many credits for the tracker to simply be nonfunctional.

Zora, still watching the bay from the opening of the cargo container, alerted Wraith that two men had just come down the ramp and were approaching Captain Zaragoza.

"All right, let's get out of here in case they come to check if the bots got it all yet," Wraith said. "I wanna hear what they're talking about anyway. Doc, you got any signal yet?"

"Use a backup, kid. I got nothing."

Wraith pulled out his backup tracker and activated it. "How about now?"

"Still nothing."

Wraith led Zora outside. They slithered to new cover in the shadows of the docking bay.

"*Now* I got a ping," Doc said.

Wraith had suspected as much. "Something in those crates is jamming the signal. I don't have time to dig in and find—" He cut himself short as the three men at the foot of the ramp began to shout and argue.

"...then why mark it volatile?" Captain Zaragoza bellowed.

"I already told you!" said one of the other men, the only one not dressed in a spacer's jumpsuit. This must be the "kelhorn" Zaragoza had wanted to see. "This cargo is sensitive equipment for comm relay stations. Our 3PL got jumpy that we were being tracked and ordered we cross-dock and do a blind jump on a new, registered freighter with Grade 4 safety ratings. That's you."

"Show me the cargo, then," Zaragoza demanded. "I want to see it. Prove it to me."

The kelhorn shook his head. "Absolutely not. These units are sealed. Those seals get broken, *none* of us get paid. If you can't do this, Captain, then kindly unload the cargo now so I can find someone who'll live up to their word. I don't see what the problem is to begin with. You're rated to ship volatile three-dot-eights, right?"

"That's not the point," Zaragoza began.

Wraith hurried back and placed a tracker on the final crate—just in case the jamming might be disabled later, though he seriously doubted it. He managed the job just before the last of the loading bots took the crate and trundled up the ramp. That was the last of it; the cargo was all loaded.

The third man, Clayton, put a hand to his ear, probably trying to better hear a micro-comm he had implanted there. "Captain," he said. "Altman says the *Peninsula* is ready for takeoff."

The captain nodded in acknowledgment and then pointed at Kelhorn. "Listen. This is a legitimate operation. Not some quick-cred smuggler outfit. I ain't haulin' no boosted goods, and that's what all this smells like to me. Now if we need to wait until your 3PL can get me some better paperwork, we can wait, but—"

"But nothing," Kelhorn interrupted. "Immediate takeoff upon loading of cargo. That was in the deal *you* signed. They pre-paid your emergency clearance—you gonna pay the fee for breaking contract? Because I sure as the nine hells ain't!"

Keel frowned. He'd been around enough spacers to know that if you were spooked by a cargo before launch, you unloaded it no matter what the penalty fee might be. Hell, he'd known spacers who'd dumped suspect cargo directly out of the airlocks. Smuggling wasn't for everyone.

The captain seemed to be of the same mind, resolute in his unwillingness to take off with the cargo.

Kelhorn, seeing he was getting nowhere, checked a datapad from his pocket and then shoved the device back in his pants. "Fine. You do what you like. I'm leaving."

"But the cargo—" the captain began.

"Work it out yourself!" Kelhorn called over his shoulder as he power-walked toward the bay's crew exit. "I'm dusting off."

"Doc," Wraith called over the comm, "you got eyes on us?"

"I got the bot watching that Grendel hauler you told me to check out. No crew, but a team of cleaners showed up— the industrial kind. This boat is getting a scrub-down. You want me to bring the bot across the port to your loc?"

Wraith was developing a bad feeling, but he couldn't quite piece together what was happening. "Yeah, better do that. Sounds like one of the guys in this bay is the captain of the Grendel-class. Didn't look pirate, though. Hands were too clean."

"I didn't see him in Lao Pak's dossier," Zora added.

Something was *definitely* off about all of this. Wraith thought about asking Zora to follow the kelhorn, but he was still trying to figure out a way to track the cargo that was now fully loaded in the Galaxy-class *Peninsula*.

"Still no reading on the tracker?" he asked, just to confirm.

"Negative," Doc replied.

The air instantly heated with the roar of gigantic repulsors firing as the Galaxy-class freighter warmed for takeoff.

Wraith looked around, bewildered by the abruptness of it all. "That was sudden."

Captain Zaragoza and his first mate seemed equally confused. The mate went to his comm to find out what was going on, and a moment later his eyes went wide. He shouted something to the captain that couldn't be heard above the rushing *whoosh* of the repulsors.

"You're lettin' 'em get away, aren't you?" Doc asked.

The cargo ramp was slowly rising. The captain and his mate rode it up for a brief second and then turned to hurry inside the freighter.

"Sket, we're gonna lose the trail!" Zora said. "Place another tracker on the ship's hull."

"Only brought two," Wraith said, kicking himself for not bringing a backup for his backup; he had never needed three before, though. These were supposed to be the best that credits could buy.

"What spooked those two, I wonder?" Zora asked, her voice a murmur in the comm.

Wraith looked around. He saw the answer approaching with clomping boots in shiny Legion armor. But there was something... off about the legionnaires. The kit looked ill-fitted and the buckets bobbed and rattled as the troopers ran—a sure sign that they weren't sized correctly.

If these were legionnaires, they were the sort he'd run into on Ackabar. Tax collectors. Armored thugs working for a point or local magistrate and using the Legion's rep to shake people down.

Wraith had half a mind to stick around and dust the lot of them.

He might get answers from the Legion impostors... although he'd have to keep a couple alive and get them to the *Six*, and do it all before any local support could arrive to assist. Meanwhile the biggest lead he had, the biggest lead he'd had since he became Wraith—the weapons—would vanish.

That cargo... that was the real deal.

Wherever it went, the Wraith needed to follow. And there was only one way he could think of to do that now.

"Trouble," he said, pointing out the approaching legionnaires to Zora. They were still a block or so away, but double-timing their way toward the *Peninsula*'s docking bay. "Get back to Doc and have him watch those leejes."

"What about that other captain?" she asked, and then added for what felt like the hundredth time today, "and what are you going to do?"

"Find out where this cargo is going." He took off toward the ship.

"Alone?" Zora called after him and then cursed like a deckhand.

Wraith arrived at the still-rising ramp in two seconds; the ramp was already above his head, but the black-armored Wraith leapt, grasped the edge, and swung himself up onto it.

"Wait for me, jump jockey!" Zora exclaimed from behind him.

Over the comms, Doc cried, "What the hell's goin' on?"

Wraith had already gotten himself inside the empty cargo hangar and had just looked around to verify there was no waiting loadmaster he'd need to take care of when Zora banged against the top of the ramp. She pulled herself up to the waist so that half of her was in the ship and half was still outside.

The ramp came perilously close to slicing her in half had Wraith not leapt over to take her arms and pull her inside. They crashed together onto the deck, her on top of him, their armor making a loud clatter.

Wraith rolled Zora off of himself and then put himself close to one of the larger crates, which was magnetically fixed to the floor to avoid being jostled across the otherwise empty hold during takeoff. Beneath them, the deck rumbled as the repulsors increased their slow thrust.

The loadmaster was nowhere to be seen. He was probably already stationed in preparation for liftoff, given the hasty departure. Even with repulsors, a ship this large was choppy while navigating atmosphere, and the crew would be strapped in to avoid injury. That was good at least, though Wraith couldn't help but think that someone had to be watching him and Zora on holocams.

The sound of whacks against the ramp and hull signaled that the legionnaires had gotten close enough to send small-arms fire at the ship. That was yet another sign that the shiny-armored troopers didn't know what they were doing; the N-4 rifles they were carrying would do nothing to the thick hull of a Galaxy-class freighter. It was a waste of charge packs.

Doc was still trying to get a sense of what was happening. "Answer me, dammit. Gimme a sitrep!"

Zora was still catching her breath, probably from the realization of how close her impulse to follow Wraith had gotten her to being cut into two pieces.

It was Wraith who replied. "On board the ship. Only way to keep from losing it."

"Oba's balls, Keel! What in the hell—"

The comm transmission went dead.

"Doc," Wraith said. "Doc, how copy?"

There was no answer.

"Doc, how copy?" Wraith tried again.

The freighter began to shake from turbulence as it followed a slow thrust path toward atmospheric departure.

"Zora," Wraith said, "I got zero comms with the *Six*. You try."

If she heard, she didn't acknowledge. The *Peninsula* took on altitude and began to shake so violently that Wraith felt as though his internal organs were being rearranged. He and Zora held on to the pallet straps to keep from bouncing across the hold and into the walls as they rode out the tremors while the freighter escaped from Marat's planetary gravity.

"Why can't it ever be easy?" Keel asked himself.

# 28

The ship settled into the familiar hum of hyperdrive, and Zora pulled off her bucket. She gestured for Keel to remove his own. He did so. It was dark in the hold without his bucket providing infrared vision. Almost a total blackout except for a few running lights near the exits.

"My comms aren't working," she whispered. "Not even with you."

"Same here. There's some serious jamming in place. Feels like more than what's in the cargo, blocking the trackers. I lost contact with Doc in mid-sentence."

"You think the whole ship is jammed?"

Keel shrugged. "Maybe. The fact that we aren't hearing alarms or facing down angry, armed crew members has me thinking that maybe this freighter isn't the one doing the jamming."

"That doesn't make any sense. Unless one of these crates is the source of the jamming. But that doesn't make sense, either."

"Well, something's doing it, and it's doing a good job. Too bad we don't all have L-comm. I bet we'd be fine."

"So what's the plan?" Zora asked.

"Haven't gotten that far yet," Keel answered.

"You had us jump onto a ship with no communication and no plan for what to do once we arrive at whatever destination we're headed for?"

The accusatory hiss in Zora's whispered voice made Keel's hackles rise.

"I told *you* to stay with Doc. *I* can handle myself in a situation like this. If you don't like it, then next time: listen."

"Forgive me for hoping you had something in mind beyond winging it as you go."

"I wasn't just winging it as I go. More like... *tactically* winging it as I go. And right now, we need to move out of this cargo hold to a hiding spot. An armed crew shows up along the catwalks up there and we're going to have a fine time trying to avoid getting shot. Though I don't think this crew has any idea what's going on with this cargo."

"But you *do* think that they might shoot us. Wonderful."

"What would you do?" Keel asked, and then forced himself to get calm. He really wished he'd been the only one to make it inside the freighter. But then again, even if the "legionnaires" closing in on them were fakes, they *were* armed. Zora might have been in just as much trouble had she stayed put.

"Look," he said. "I'm trying to stay optimistic here. You'd rather lie here behind crates of stolen weapons waiting for someone to find us? In a dark cargo hold? With me?"

Zora grimaced. "When you put it that way—let's go."

They moved toward the basic emergency lighting then followed it to the main exit from the hold. Wraith inspected the access pad.

"What I expected," he said.

"What?"

"Crew code required to open the hold door. It's not *locked*, but it'll alert the crew if someone unauthorized opens it. Some pirates still try to steal a ship this way."

"By hiding themselves in the cargo?"

"Worked for us, didn't it?"

"Except we're not stealing the ship."

Keel shrugged. "Never know. The day's still young. C'mon."

He led her to the back of the hold, looked around, then pointed up at a ceiling grate. "If I give you a boost, can you pull that ventilation cover down?"

Zora had to slip on her bucket to see the grate he meant. She took it off again and nodded.

"Ventilation shafts, really? That's your plan? A bit cliché, don't you think?"

Keel shrugged. "Big ship, big vents. Relatively. It'll still be a squeeze. Don't ask me how I know."

"I already know how you know, Mr. Legion."

Zora's feet went from Keel's hands to his shoulders, and she removed the grate and handed it down. He hoisted her up into the shaft, and she let down a synth-cord she kept in her kit to help him up after.

When he was inside, she asked which way. Wraith pointed in her direction.

"Guess that means I'm first," she said, staring into the pitch-black shaft. "Don't you dare stare at my butt the whole trip."

"Wouldn't dream of it," Keel said. "Not the *whole* trip, anyway."

The two belly-crawled forward.

"Bit of a tight squeeze," Zora said.

"It'll open up once we're out of the cargo hold and into the living habs," Keel said, familiar with the layout.

Zora grunted. "How far is that?"

"Not far. You're not afraid of tight spaces, are you?"

"More afraid of how unable to defend ourselves we'd be if someone found us."

Zora continued her crawl. "You certainly know a fair amount about these Galaxy freighters. I don't remember my father ever mentioning being inserted from something like this."

Keel laughed at the thought. "No insertions, but I may have rescued a few hostages from them in a former life."

That impressed Zora. Keel could tell by the way she said, "'May have'—but you can neither confirm nor deny, is that it?"

"You guessed right. Okay." He lowered his voice. "We're right up near the galley. Things'll open up there. Move quietly. Crew always seem to get hungry after taking off, plus that's the place that passes for a meeting room on a ship like this, and it's pretty clear these guys all have something to meet over, given how things went with the kelhorn just now."

Zora slithered forward and saw dim light up ahead. Then they heard voices drifting down the shaft. Agitated voices. Keel was right: the galley was close and the crew was there. The scent of something meaty drifted up through the venting. As Keel and Zora slithered closer, they could make out words.

"... dump it and be done with it!" someone yelled.

"Because we *won't* be done with it!" Captain Zaragoza shot back. "I been over why we took off more than once, and I'm not gonna repeat it again. It hasn't changed. Now fall in, or I'll dump *you*, Altman. And you know I will, so don't test me. Not today."

A short silence followed, during which Altman presumably stood down. Then the captain spoke again.

"What's the status on the AI?"

It was Clayton's voice that answered. "They did a real number on it—we can't get access to any of the ship's systems. Gasser's on his way to the hold to see if—"

A massive *BOOM* sounded from the galley, followed by a terrific rush of air so powerful that it sucked Keel and Zora toward the ventilation grate. Zora had to brace herself against the sides of the shaft, Keel slammed into her, and they clung to whatever they could grab—which was mostly one another—as the shaft bucked and trembled.

It was immediately obvious what had happened, though not why or how. An explosion of some sort had opened the galley to the vacuum of space, and that breach wasn't being sealed by the automated systems. The ship's pressurized atmosphere was now rushing through the ventilation system and out the grand opening.

And then, just as suddenly as it began, the chaos ended with a heavy metal *clang*. The alarms—which Keel hadn't even noticed until now—quieted except for a persistent, low-toned, *bip-bip-bip-bip-bip-bip-bip-bip...*

"What just happened?" Zora asked, sounding as though her heart raced inside her chest.

Keel pushed himself off her. The sudden spike in adrenaline had his mind surging, but he managed to speak calmly. "Hull breach."

The voices of the crew were gone.

"I don't hear anything down there," Zora said.

"My guess is they're done talking," Keel replied. "On top of which, they've all gone outside." He paused to listen. "I don't hear any other explosions... ship's not under attack. These Galaxy-class freighters have a large viewport in the galley—something for the crew to look out from that's not holographic. Maybe it lost its integrity, and the ship was just slow to activate the emergency blast shield. Ship doesn't look poorly maintained though."

Zora seemed to be picturing the crew, frozen in terror, drifting forever in space. "That's... that's not how I want to go out," she murmured.

"Them either, I bet," Keel said. "Your suit got mag boots?"

"Of course."

Keel inched himself backwards, putting some space between the pair, vibro-knife in hand. "Watch your feet."

With a few quick slices, he soon had a man-sized hole cut through the venting. The metal clanged down on the galley floor, a drop of some four meters. The room had already repressurized and, sure enough, where the viewport should be, a heavy emergency blast shield had now dropped into place.

Keel looked at Zora, who watched him over her shoulder. "Turn on those mags once you drop down to the galley. Just to be safe. I'll go first."

He dropped down with a thud, then stepped aside for Zora to follow. Once they'd magnetically locked their boots to the floor, they scanned the now-empty galley. Or started to. At that moment the lights flicked out. All was inky dark.

"System reboot beginning," a melodious voice said from overhead. It was the ship's AI, and it sounded feminine and light. "This wi—" the voice deepened, becoming masculine, "—illll-l-l-l take several minutes."

"That... normal?" Zora asked, and she flicked on her ultrabeam, sweeping it around the galley. Bare tables, empty counters, dark hallways.

"No," Keel replied, his expression grim and harsh in the beam's light. Nothing he'd seen on this ship was normal. "Can your kit be sealed for vacuum?"

"Negative."

"Okay. Put your helmet on anyway, then let's move out of the galley and toward the bridge. We should be able to talk freely over external speakers now that the crew is gone."

"You don't think the breach was an accident," Zora said. It wasn't a question.

"I have my suspicions. Don't think it makes much sense to hang out in one of the ship's most vulnerable spots in case it happens again, either way. Why test our mag boots' hold if we don't have to?"

That made sense to Zora. "Which way to the bridge?"

"Follow me. It's a big ship, so be ready for a walk. Keep an eye open for any crew that wasn't gathered in the meeting. I heard them mention someone named Gasser before all hell broke loose."

As they headed down the corridor, each step dragged and thudded, their mag-activated boots clamping to the metal decking.

"I hate walking with mags on," Zora said, feeling like she was wading through some swamp. Her calves and thighs were starting to feel the effort and the impaired movement made her feel vulnerable. She hated all of it.

"Beats floating in the cold," was all Keel said, and she had to admit he was right.

They tramped along. The vessel appeared to be abandoned—all hands lost. There was no sound beyond their own footsteps and mechanized voices. "Does it feel warm in here to you?" Zora asked.

The ship was dark and as she swept her ultrabeam around, lighting the path, checking for any threats. The shadows seemed to press in on them. Everything felt heavy and suffocating. Sweat prickled the nape of her neck and beaded on her scalp.

"It's just your imagination," Keel said. "Big empty ship like this... probably just your nerves getting to you."

"My nerves are fine. I tried Doc again. Still no luck with the hypercomms. You?"

"Yeah, tried. Same. We're still being jammed by... whatever." Keel paused a beat and added, "Oh, and Zora, there's nothing wrong with admitting you're freaked out."

The bounty hunter growled, "Honestly, sometimes it's hard not to shoot you in the back."

Far down the corridor, something banged. The sound echoed down the long walkway and continued on past the pair, toward the bridge.

"That came from the direction of the cargo hold," Zora quietly said.

"Kill your beam," Keel instructed. "We'll use the darkness as long as we can—ship shouldn't finish its reboot for a couple more minutes, best I remember."

Those mission briefs had been a long time ago.

"Which way now?" Zora asked.

"Let's go see what made the noise. Back toward the hold."

If they were going for stealth, relying on mag boots wasn't going to do them any favors, so they turned those off too. The walk along the decking was much faster, their footsteps soft and light. As they neared the cargo hold, they found the blast doors open. They heard a box scrape along the decking, tools clattering in some bin.

Someone was in there, fumbling about in the dark.

Wraith peered through the doorway. Through the blended spectrum of his bucket's night-vis he could see a man rummaging through tools in a container—one big blog of heat in an otherwise lifeless room.

"C'mon. Where is it?" the man muttered, oblivious to the fact that he was being watched. There was something desperate in the man's movements, frantic, like a space rat who knew it was trapped.

Wraith made sure Zora was watching him, then motioned that the two of them would enter the room and approach the man from either side. He wanted to see if this man might assist him in getting through the ship. Given that the rest of the crew having been spaced, the odds were good that the man would have to do as Wraith requested.

"Charged ultrabeams to be placed in every work chest," the man grumbled to himself as he searched. "Captain's memorandum 86-C. But is there an ultrabeam in here? Noooo. Of course not."

Wraith had drawn closer when the emergency lights flooded back on and the ship's AI announced, "Reboot complete. Reactivating emergency lighting and life support systems."

The AI's voice sounded clean and feminine again. Gone were the glitches and hitching speech that had occurred prior to reboot.

The man caught sight of the black-armored bounty hunter and shrieked.

"Easy," Wraith told him, but the man only shouted an alarm.

"Pirates!"

The man snatched something big, metal, and heavy out of his tool chest and waved it at Wraith, shouting, "Stay back!"

Wraith held out his hands, trying not to present any more of a threat than his armor did automatically. "Put the torque-driver down. We're not pirates."

"W-we?" the man stammered, and then looked about wildly.

Behind him, Zora primed her blaster. "Yes, *we*. Now put it down so I don't have to waste the blaster bolt."

Convinced by the logic of this, the man dropped what he was holding. The tool clattered back into the bin. He lifted his empty hands. "Okay, okay, okay. Don't shoot. Don't shoot."

"Not planning on it," Wraith replied. "Got some questions I want answered though."

"Yeah... I mean... okay. Just... I got questions, too. What'd you do with the others?"

Wraith and Zora exchanged a look.

"You didn't hear it?" Zora asked.

"Hear what?" the man replied. "I've been in here trying to locate whatever's causing havoc on our systems. Clayton figured it's something hidden in the cargo. Then the lights go out, door opens on its own, and I'm trying to find an ultrabeam when you two show up. Where's Clayton?"

"Everyone in the galley was vented," Wraith said. "Clayton, your captain, uh..."

"Altman," Zora supplied.

"Yeah, Altman. Maybe others. The viewport failed."

The man looked at Wraith in horror. "Wh-what?"

"The ship took its time locking things back down," Zora added. "Then the lights went off and it announced a system restart."

The man nodded, his mouth still hanging open. He'd probably heard the same thing they had from the AI's speakers in the cargo hold.

"What's your name?" Wraith asked.

The question seemed to shake the spacer loose from whatever was racing through his head. "G-Gasser. Gasser."

Wraith nodded. "Is there more crew on board?"

"They were..." he began. A faraway look on his face. "They were all in the galley. All of them."

Zora kept the blaster level on the spacer's head. "I need you to be straight with us, Gasser. Who are you hauling these weapons for?"

Keel frowned inside his armor. He didn't think this crew was the smuggling kind, and wasn't sure why Zora would play things so aggressively. But the question had been asked and Gasser was already answering.

"W-weapons? What—we're hauling weapons? Volatile, Clayton told me it's volatile, but... I mean, it's a blind shipment. Double blind. We have no idea what we're hauling and the previous drayage captain had to upload the jump calc coordinates in our system so we..."

Recognition seemed to fall over the man's face.

"If you're having system troubles," Wraith said, "I think your first mate had the right idea to be suspect of the cargo."

Gasser's brows knitted together. "But that's... that's not... they were a legitimate outfit. All the creds lined up. Captain Zaragoza... that's not his style. To smuggle illegal cargo or to let someone without the proper clearances upload a blind nav-jump. We're a legit operation. Look— see? *I'm* not even armed." Hands still in the air, he quickly turned around.

"Re-initializing shipboard scanners and defense," the ship's AI announced, its voice now deep and masculine.

Now Gasser looked really confused. "D-Denise?" he asked the air.

"Does 'Denise' usually change its voice like that?" Zora wanted to know.

Gasser shook his head. "No. Never. It's been actin' strange since we took off. Everything has."

Wraith took a step forward. "We need to get to the cockpit. Come with us."

Having a crew member along would help Wraith with the simple pass codes that would otherwise require slicing. He had only so much slicing algo and tapes in his kit.

"Hold on," Gasser said. "Just... slow down. Who are you? How did you get on board? No. No, I'm not going anywhere with you. You're the pirates who sabotaged us. Who killed —"

"We didn't do that," Wraith told him. "If we were behind all this, why would we have so many questions? We're bounty hunters. The guy who did this, that's who we want to find."

Gasser still looked uncertain. "I don't know..."

"We're also the ones with the blasters," Zora reminded him.

Before Gasser could respond to this inescapable logic, the AI's speakers blared. "Scanners online. Three unauthorized lifeforms detected."

Now the poor crewman was plain bewildered. "There are three of you?"

Wraith looked up as if the AI were floating just above them all, then back to Gasser. "Pretty sure the AI is counting you among us. And I think I know what's going on here."

"Maybe you can fill me in," Zora snapped.

"We'll talk as we move."

Wraith stepped to the cargo hold's exit, his weapons ready as he scanned for potential hostiles. Zora did the same. Just because the crew had been vented didn't mean there were no threats. Gasser hovered close, apparently having decided his best move was to trust himself to the protection of the two bounty hunters after all.

Wraith started down the long hall toward the cockpit. "The MCR have been 'recruiting' private freighters into their fleet," he said. "Refitting them to serve as poorly plated ships of war. But I'm starting to think the Mids haven't actually bothered convincing any crews to join them. I think they just kill them and take the ships for themselves."

"That is very astute of you," the ship's AI boomed. "It's a particularly easy maneuver on ships such as this one. Did you know that these Galaxy-class freighters can jettison their viewports to allow the crew to escape in the event of an atmospheric crash? They call it a 'safety feature.' I call it a serious design flaw. All a hostile AI has to do is tell the system that the vessel is in atmospheric and not vacuum flight. It's not even a challenge. I do hope that terminating the three of you will be somewhat more entertaining."

Gasser paled. "D-Denise?"

Wraith didn't break stride. "That ain't Denise, kid."

# 29

As the trio moved toward the bridge, the ever-present hum of hyperdrive took on a menacing buzz, like mummy-bees swarming in the walls. A moment later, the blast doors ahead of them snapped shut, cutting off their route.

"AI's closing all the doors," Keel said. "C'mon, we'll have to go the long way."

They turned back and ran toward an open door that led into a side corridor. That door snapped shut too, but this time right before their noses; Wraith only barely snatched Gasser back before his flailing hand could get caught in the closing metal.

Gasser shook himself, trembling and staring at the hand he nearly lost. "Sket! Sket sket sket! That woulda crushed me if you hadn't pulled me back..."

"I think that was the plan," Wraith said grimly.

A dire voice filled the corridor. "Indeed it was. One plan of many."

"Gonna be tough to get anywhere if we can't use any doors. Back through the vents?" Zora suggested.

The AI chuckled. "Oh, please do. An *excellent* idea."

"On second thought..."

"I can untether the doors from AI control," Gasser said. He ran back to the main door blocking the corridor. "Help me get this panel off." He started prying at the seam.

"Stand clear," Wraith said, and struck the panel with the butt of his rifle. Two whacks, and it clattered to the floor.

"I was gonna say help me find a multi-driver, but that works. Gimme a sec." He pulled a device from his pocket and started pulling some wires and connecting others. Tiny sparks flew and smoke wisped.

"Time is wasting," the AI said ominously.

From the direction of the cargo hold came a loud, hollow clang.

"What was that?" Zora asked.

"Whatever it was, it ain't good news," Wraith said.

"I better take a look," Zora said.

"Don't go through any doors."

Left behind with the spacer, Wraith asked, "How much longer, Gasser?" Every second given an AI was a chance for it to make thousands of actions, some minute and others consequential.

"Almost done..." the man said, focused on pinching a tiny wire into place.

"We're definitely not gonna have time to do this with every door," Wraith groused.

"We won't need to. Once I remove AI control, every door should open as normal, using local sensors."

Zora's voice came floating down the hallway. "Wraith...? Wraith!"

"What?" he shouted back.

"You'd better come see this!"

Wraith turned to Gasser. "Don't open the door until I'm back." He sprinted off down the corridor.

He found Zora standing by the door to the cargo hold, looking through a viewing port. He came up beside her and followed her gaze.

On the other side of the duraglass stood a machine with a seven-foot-tall durasteel skeleton, red eyes gleaming, wrists decked with blasters, and a rocket launcher on its back.

"Oh, no," Wraith said.

"What? You know what that is?"

"Yeah. That's a KRS-model war bot."

"From the Savage Wars?" Zora said, incredulous.

"Uh-huh."

Wraith grabbed Zora's arm and began to back away, then threw them both to the deck as the door opened, presumably controlled by the AI. A rocket came streaming out of the opening a second later, exploded against the bulkhead, and sent an overpressure that might have blown out their eardrums had their helmets not been on.

"You okay?" Wraith asked as he pushed himself off Zora.

"Yeah," she coughed. "I think so."

They could hear the war bot's heavy metallic footsteps getting closer.

"Then let's get out of here before that thing fires another rocket."

Wraith hauled Zora to her feet, and they ran back to Gasser through a cloud of black smoke that the ventilation system was struggling to suck away from the corridor.

"I've got the door open!" Gasser cried as they arrived. "The AI no longer has control."

"That's great, kid. Now run."

Wraith was on the man's heels as they dashed through to the now-open door and continued their run toward the bridge. Footsteps continued to clang behind them, and red eyes pierced the smoky hallway.

Gasser looked back as they ran. "What the hell is *that*?"

"Trouble," Wraith told him. He spotted another hatch up ahead. "Can you seal one of these blast doors behind us, so that bot can't get through?"

"I think. I... yes, I can fuse the drive system."

"Do it."

The door opened as they approached, and they sprinted through. The spacer removed the access panel and immediately went to work; he was clearly panicked, but his hands held steady.

"Seal it!" Zora shouted at the crewman.

"I'm trying!"

Wraith pushed Gasser aside, sent a blaster bolt into the panel, sending up a plume of sparks, then reached his gauntlet inside and pulled out a fistful of wires that popped and smoked.

"That should do it."

"Or you could do that," Gasser said.

*Boom.*

Something—and no one had any doubt what—punched the blast door so hard that the decking shook. Then the door rattled and screamed as it was peppered with blaster fire from the other side. Hot metal scores glowed red.

"War bots," Wraith grumbled.

"The man was right about the cargo being volatile," Zora remarked.

"We're all gonna die," Gasser said, his voice small. "Sket, oh sket, sket sket sket."

"Not me, pal," Wraith told him. "Hustle up to the bridge. We'll have more options if we can gain control of the ship."

They ran once more down the main corridor, and the booming on the door resumed. These were simple blast doors rated against a hull breach, not the double-blast doors meant to prevent boarders. Against a war bot, it wouldn't last.

And then the voice of the AI returned.

"You're doing quite well so far," it teased them. "But we're still several hours away from extraction, and there is nowhere for you to run. In all fairness I must inform you that the panicked one's assessment is accurate: you are, indeed, 'all gonna die.' The war bot is not even necessary for me to bring about that outcome. It is, however, more fun."

"Get spaced," said Zora.

"Very well then. Do try your best. That, too, is more... fun."

The AI sounded pleased, but... cracked somehow. Like it wasn't programmed to be psychotic but had found its way there all on its own.

They entered a section of the corridor where several pipes ran crossways along the ceiling. Just as they passed beneath one of the larger pipes, it burst open, venting white-hot vapor directly onto them. The bounty hunters' armor protected them, but Gasser screamed in pain. Wraith pulled him across the deck, out of the scalding heat, but the damage was done. Raw, scoured flesh was already bubbling into blisters.

"Aid kit?" Wraith asked Zora.

She shook her head. "His face and neck are practically scalded away... He's not gonna make it."

On the decking, Gasser moaned and twitched, his face melted into red, plasteen folds, his hands frozen into fists. Zora was right. This man was on his way out, and nothing would change that short of a cryochamber with an auto-doc on the other side.

"Something for the pain," Wraith said.

"Yeah. On it." Zora fished through her aid kit for an auto-injector and stuck it into the man's thigh. Gasser relaxed, and his moaning ceased.

"Not sure how long that will last," Zora said.

"Longer than he will. C'mon."

It was all they could do.

The speakers crackled, and the AI spoke again. "Human flesh is so sensitive to extreme heat. It *is* a shame he was not wearing armor like you."

"That thing is sick," Zora growled. Then she shouted at the ceiling, "We're going to shut you down and erase every last trace of your rotten code!"

"Just move!" Wraith shouted.

An explosion ripped down a corridor on their left, and a metal figure stepped through the flames, red eyes glowing.

"Targets acquired," the KRS unit announced in a terrible, basso profundo voice as it tramped forward. It lifted a wrist-mounted micro-blaster that gave an electric whirr, and blaster bolts came spitting down the corridor.

Wraith and Zora dashed to either side of a bulkhead, and then—Zora going low, Wraith high—pied the corner and returned fire. Blasts sparked off the bot's armored frame, but to no effect. The metal behemoth was well-armored and continued striding toward them.

They sprinted for the bridge, exposed in what felt like a kilometer-long corridor. They did their best to stay close to bulkheads, trying to minimize their odds of being struck by the war bot's incessant fire.

"Almost there," Wraith said. "Don't slow down!"

Blaster bolts screamed around them, searing the air. Zora grunted in pain and fell to the deck.

"Zora!" Wraith ran across the corridor to her side and scooped her up in a fireman's carry, the slim bulkhead taking a beating from the blaster bolts. The former legionnaire angled his body behind hers to give her some protection, and then continued forward.

Another set of doors irised open at their approach, revealing a corridor that ran perpendicular to the one they were in. This, at last, would lead them to the bridge. Wraith bounded through, dumped Zora, and ignored her grunt of pain as he punched at the door panel and pressed himself against the wall, blaster bolts zipped through the narrowing opening until the doors were fully shut.

Wraith was working to get the panel off to seal the door like he had done before, when the amused voice of the AI spoke again.

"I wouldn't seal that door quite yet. I've instructed KRS-18 to use his cutting torch on the crewman you abandoned," the ship's AI said with more than a hint of sadistic excitement. "The pain will be... intense."

"No," Zora said, moved by the thought.

Wraith shot the controls and sealed the door. "It's a trap. We narced him; he won't feel it."

The AI went on to describe in lurid detail the way Gasser's flesh popped and boiled, was cut away and mutilated by the bot; Wraith paid it no mind. He was busy checking on Zora, who'd gotten herself into a sitting position. Her leg was scorched from a blaster bolt that had missed armor.

"That looks bad," he said.

"I'll... be fine," Zora said through gritted teeth. "Nothing a skinpack won't fix."

"Time for that later. Can you walk?" Wraith stuck out a hand to help her up.

"Yeah, think so," she said, taking it. "Hurts, but I'll be all right."

*Boom, boom, boom*—the doors shook right beside them. The war bot was pounding away, and Wraith could have sworn there was a new dent in the impervisteel.

"Guess it's done with Gasser," Zora said.

"We had to leave him," Keel said, seeing the look on her face.

"Yeah. I know."

# 30

The pounding gave way to a growing red line that hissed and glowed in the middle of the blast door.

"Cutting torch," Zora said, wobbling from the attempt to use her leg. "Great."

Wraith gave a quick nod. They were on the home stretch to reaching the bridge. That was where the jump coordinates would be, along with systems capable of shutting the AI out. Those fail-safes could only be circumvented by significant hardware modifications, which the person who slipped this doomsday program onto the ship would not have had the time to do.

He looked up at the ether to address the AI. "Looks like you're running out of time, AI."

A synthetic chortle sounded through the speakers. "Your assessment is inaccurate. I've locked down the bridge completely. You won't get inside."

"Let's find out." Keel ushered Zora forward.

The hiss of the cutting torch ceased, followed by the metallic boom of the war bot slamming its fists into the blast door. But its cuts weren't deep enough or thorough enough to allow a breakthrough just yet—thankfully—and the bot reassessed and activated its torch once more.

Zora was moving more slowly now, much more slowly in fact, to the point that Wraith wondered whether he needed to pick her up and carry her along. But the bot wasn't fast either. It was heavily armored, built to dish out and absorb damage, and this had come at the expense of speed. Still, it was a machine, with patience and stamina to match. And if this came down to a last-ditch fight with a Republic war bot designed to wipe out Savage marines, Wraith would need every ounce of strength available to him.

They were out of sight but not out of earshot when the bot finally broke through the blast doors. The clang of impervisteel rattling on the deck grates was followed by the rhythmic trudge of the machine as it resumed its relentless pursuit.

Keel hurried Zora onward. Despite her condition, they didn't so much as pause until they found themselves under the bridge deck—four levels below where they needed to be.

"Speedlifts... are out... I take it," Zora panted, staring up at a dizzying height.

Wraith muttered, "Stairs," and Zora groaned but dutifully stepped into the stairwell and started up.

Blaster bolts sizzled past Keel as he followed. He spun around and sent a few bolts at the KRS-model war bot now making its way down the corridor, then sprinted up the stairs, quickly catching up with Zora.

"Hurry up, Zee!"

He put her arm over his shoulders, and despite her obvious limp, she picked up her pace, and they managed to at least fast-walk up the four flights, the climate controls inside their helmets and armor doing their best to keep up with the level of exertion. By the time they reached the bridge deck, he was carrying the vast majority of her weight.

They stepped out of the stairwell into the main corridor. The bridge was just ahead. The doors, of course, were closed. Just as the AI had promised.

Zora slammed her palm on the switch, and a red light glared. No admittance, despite whatever Gasser had done to cut the AI out of the system.

"It won't open!" she exclaimed.

"Stand clear," Wraith said. "In fact, check and see how close that bot is to us, if you can. This might take a minute."

Zora nodded. "On it."

"Don't get shot," Wraith advised.

Zora rolled her eyes. "Someone, make this man a general," she said, then hefted her blaster and limped back to the stairs.

Wraith removed the door's access panel, studied the mess of wires there, then started tearing things out. Sparks flew, lines popped. Behind him, Zora's blaster screamed down the staircase, and the war bot returned fire.

"How much room we got?" Wraith shouted, as nonchalantly as if the two were at a seamball game.

Zora's shout of "Whoa!" was all he heard—that and more blaster fire. He took that as a good sign, connected two wires that had been hiding, then called out, "You still alive?"

Running up, Zora said, "I'm fine," but the set of her shoulders said otherwise. "Blaster bolt was an inch away from my face. No need to rush over and check on me, really."

Wraith frowned at the delicate work in his gloved hands. "You'll be happier when I finish doing this," he said, and touched two more wires together.

The door intoned its access chime, and the mechanisms inside whirred.

Wraith stepped back. "Stay clear!"

The heavy blast doors partially opened, then slammed down hard, bounced, and remained sunk partially into the floor. Only a small gap was left, between the top of the doors and the frame above.

"Congratulations," Zora said. "You broke it."

"That was the plan. C'mon!"

Wraith climbed up and wriggled through the opening, onto the bridge. Then he turned back and lowered his arms to help Zora up and through, too.

This was an old breaching trick that Chhun had shown him, though it only worked on certain older types of security doors. He'd hot-wired the maintenance protocol that caused the lower impact plating to recede into a hollow portion of the deck. He then forced the door to open, and without the impact plating in place, the door fell into the deck. This wouldn't have mattered if the manufacturers had bothered to make the blast doors just a bit larger—but that would have cost a few more credits.

The result was a gap just the right size for a legionnaire to slip through.

Zora looked behind her. "I sincerely hope there's *more* to your plan, Wraith. The bot won't be able to squeeze through that gap, but it'll be able to *aim* just fine. We're sitting ducks in here."

"We were already sitting ducks out there. And yeah, there's more to the plan. How about a little faith?"

The bridge wasn't much—sparse and utilitarian. Two unattended workstations hummed at either side of the main station, where a modest captain's chair waited. Keel dropped himself into the captain's seat. "Time to shut this AI out."

The AI chuckled over the speakers. "The odds of successfully guessing the pass key is 1 in 292,201,338. Which is, remarkably, even worse than your current chances of survival."

Wraith tapped away. "You sound scared."

"Hardly. I would call the sensation... amused. This has been a stimulating termination. Better than most. It's a shame it's about to come to an end. As are you."

Wraith finished entering his Legion code. Most unmodified starship operating systems contained the Republic-mandated back doors. And Captain Zaragoza, from what Wraith had observed, was a by-the-book sort of man. The kind who would never illegally modify his ship's operating system.

The terminal chimed five times, then granted Wraith access.

"Impossible!" the ship's AI exclaimed, and this time Wraith really did detect a hint of fear in the automated voice.

He caught more than a hint of fear in Zora's. She had been peering through the gap in the doors, and now ducked as a flurry of blaster bolts shot through the gap and struck the forward holoscreen. "Aeson!"

"Gonna trigger a false breach alarm," he said. "Might be a little noisy."

Alarms sounded, and an instant later a second set of blast doors dropped down in front of the ones he had jammed into a partially open position. And *these* doors were the big, heavy kind designed to protect the bridge from the rest of the ship in the event of a catastrophic hull breach.

"There we go," Wraith said. "That should give us a little peace and quiet."

The ship's speakers blared with the voice of the AI. "This changes nothing. Your end is near. You will be terminated. If not by KRS-18 or the fixers, then I will kill you myself."

Wraith kicked his heels up on the terminal. "That bot won't be able to cut its way in here for another half hour at most. And you'll be gone by then, AI. Galaxy-class freighters are closed circuits. You picked the wrong ship to hijack, because this is one you can't hide yourself in."

He turned to Zora. "We're gonna power off the ship's systems. All of them. The AI will have nowhere to go."

"If you do that, you'll be signing your own death warrant," the AI warned. "No jump drive, no life support..."

Wraith couldn't help but smile. The AI sounded *decidedly* worried.

"Pop open that hatch," he told Zora, pointing. "The one by the nav console."

"This one?"

"Yeah, that's it."

"Hold on," the AI said, now almost... pleading. "Just— hold on. They don't keep a backup of me. I'll be killed."

"Not my problem," Wraith said. He pulled an extendable wire from the console Zora had opened and connected it to a similar wire beneath the main console. Then he resumed the captain's chair and worked through operational screens with studied ease.

"How do you know all of this?" Zora asked, watching him.

"You'd be surprised how many back doors the Republic has manufacturers put into ships. A straight freighter like this one, no after-market mods... anyone with the know-how can get right in." He tinkered some more. "By design."

"Right. Your rescue missions. You've done something like this before."

"Something. Fewer war bots. But somehow more shooting. And... there we go."

The bridge lights dimmed, and a hundred ambient noises that every spacer takes for granted dropped an octave as stations cycled down. Though inertia kept the Galaxy-class freighter hurtling through space, it was otherwise falling asleep.

"Primary... system," said the ship's AI, deep and masculine. Then, in a feminine voice: "formatting... has b-be-g-g-guh-uh-uhn-nn-n. Primarysystemformattinghasbegun."

"Denise is back?" Zora said. "The psycho AI's offline?"

"Not offline, but not within the ship's systems. Safe to assume it was smart enough to escape back into whatever partition it came from. Probably a data crystal used for the blind shipment coordinates, which the kelhorn conveniently 'left behind.'"

"Ship systems rebooting to factory state," Denise declared. "Expect a loss of all core functionality."

"The artificial gravity," Zora said, sitting down and strapping herself to the first mate's chair.

Doing the same in the captain's chair, Wraith waved a gloved hand. "And life support, comms, nav systems, jump drive..."

"Wonderful," Zora said, her tone suggesting anything but. "We'll die even *before* that war bot breaks in here. And here I thought I had a whole thirty minutes left to live."

"Don't worry about the bot. I have plans for it."

"Another top-secret Republic override? Would've been nice back when we were running for our lives."

"Just a hunch," Wraith said. "Gotta wait for the systems to reboot first, though."

Zora shook her head and fished a skinpack from an aid box affixed to the side of her console. Wraith waited quietly while she pressed it into her wound, wincing, and tested the range of motion in her leg. Behind them, the war bot was making solid progress, judging by the metallic groans and screeches coming from the other side of the doors.

Finally, Denise spoke.

"Reboot complete," she said. "Would you like a list of available systems?"

Wraith clapped his hands. That was a best-case scenario. "Just tell me if we have comms."

"Local comms are online. Hypercomm is unavailable."

Okay, not quite best-case. But close.

"Your name is Denise, right?" Wraith said to the AI.

"That is correct," said the soft feminine voice.

"Great. Denise, I need you to scan your systems for any foreign drives or data crystals."

"Scanning."

The bridge fell silent for a moment, during which time the artificial gravity returned, eliciting a feeling of being suddenly overweight. A clatter of metal sounded from beyond the door.

"Data crystal detected," Denise said. "Drive requests media interface access."

"No chance," Keel said. "Show me where it is."

A holographic map appeared above the captain's console, with a red marker indicating a personal media slot directly beneath the console where Zora now sat.

She bent down, removed the offending data crystal, then held it up for Keel to see. "So this is where the AI worm is?"

Keel gave a nod. "Yep."

"Want me to crush it under my boot?"

"As satisfying as that would be, no. I wanna talk to it." He held out his hand.

"You wanna *talk* to it? You do remember it's trying to kill us."

"Huh, is that right? I'd almost forgotten. Just hand it over. It's harmless as long as we don't connect it to the systems."

Reluctantly, Zora put the delicate crystal in his hand. Keel attached it to a backup comm cylinder that was synced to a closed-band datapad—small items he kept in his kit, part of an assortment of non-lethal gear he'd found useful to have with him. He waited for the link to light up blue.

"AI," he said, "do you copy?"

"I... thought I would be terminated," said the psychotic AI. Its voice, now coming from the comm cylinder, sounded strangely small.

"Day's not over yet," said Keel. "But I'm gonna make you a bargain. First, tell me how you controlled that war bot."

The psychotic AI hesitated, as if making a decision. "It can be fed command codes through a secure comm channel."

"Show me the list of commands—active and inactive."

The AI said nothing, but text scrolled across the attached datapad. Keel studied it, then nodded.

"And what's the comm channel?" he asked.

Again, the slightest hesitation—which, for an AI, was an eternity, time to consider all possible moves. "It would be foolish of me to give you that information, seeing as it's my only leverage."

Wraith answered with steely resolve. "And here's *my* leverage. We both know that if that war bot gets onto the bridge, I'll be sure to crush your data crystal and end you.

We might die too, but *your* death is a certainty. That team of 'fixers' you let slip will just have to find themselves another psychotic AI."

Keel suspected the human crew he and Zora had seen exit from the Grendel-class hauler were in fact those "fixers." He also suspected they were the "legionnaires" that had hastened the *Peninsula*'s departure. They had been pulling repulsor crates, which probably contained the cheap Legion armor.

"I am not *psychotic*," the AI said.

"May as well own it," Keel replied. "But since we're friends now, how about we just say you're 'capable of operating outside of your given parameters'? I doubt even your bosses have any idea just how sadistic you've become. And speaking of your bosses, where were you installed before this ship? Surely there's no harm in telling me that."

"A Grendel-class freighter," the AI replied.

"And who crewed that freighter? I don't care that they're dead. I just want a catalog of their names, numbers, and species."

A readout appeared on the datapad, matching exactly the crew listing Lao Pak had provided. As Keel had deduced, this AI—with the aid of the war bot and these "fixers"—had already done Wraith's termination job for him.

He hadn't made sense of all of it yet. He knew this was an MCR operation, and clearly it was designed to steal freighters—the Grendel, and now the Galaxy. How exactly the weapons played into all this though, he didn't know. Regardless, this was *exactly* the sort of lead he needed to send to Dark Ops. This *could* lead to something huge.

He held up the comm cylinder where the fragile little crystal still sat. "I mentioned a bargain earlier, AI. Here it is. If you want to stay alive, you'll do exactly as I say."

Before the psycho AI could respond, a ship-wide alert blared, and Denise—the ship's *actual* AI—spoke.

"Close-range sensors show approaching craft. Please —"

"Shut up, Denise." One problem at a time. He addressed the rogue AI instead: "So, what's it gonna be?"

"I... agree."

# 31

Ethan Koska sat in the stuffy, uncomfortable legionnaire armor, waiting for the boarding shuttle to dock. His side itched, but of course he couldn't scratch it. He did a little twist, a little shimmy, but no joy. The itch remained.

He hated this part. The awful armor, the waiting around, the bodies and the cleanup. Why couldn't that stupid war bot do the cleanup? It had arms. The last job could have been fatal, cleaning up after those dead Hools.

In fact, lately the job had grown more dangerous than Koska liked.

The job before this one had seen them taking real, live fire against a band of pirates who sought to capture their corvette. That had been intense, and for a while, the MCR mercenary worried that the numerically superior pirates might overpower the ship. But Koska's team managed to pin them in the cargo bay as planned from the start, and the pirates did what pirates do—settled for taking the cargo back to their own ship. *All* the cargo, including the war bot.

At that point the fight was over. The pirate ship's encryption was lackluster, and once the AI was imported to the Grendel-class, the war bot came online and chased down the pirates, exterminating them one by one.

Usually, after a big catch like that, it was mission accomplished and a week or so off while the next job was set up. Not this time.

No. Some planner at the moon base had the idea that they could maximize their rotation by implanting the war bot and AI into taking still *another* ship at the pirates' initial destination, the LaKalb Spaceport. Two ships in one outing. Wonderful for the brass, but a pain in the neck for Koska.

Worst of all was being stuck in small places like this with Schaener and having to take orders. The man was tolerable in small doses, but an extended operation like this one? Koska felt ready to throw himself out of the airlock. He would much rather be back in his condo playing holos than keep dealing with the sergeant. But this job paid for the condo—and for everything else.

The shuttle shuddered beneath his boots, followed by the clangs of docking clamps. *Game time.*

"Pilot confirms docking coupling complete," Sergeant Schaener said over comms, sounding way too full of himself. You'd think the guy was a real legionnaire with how he talked, and not some run-of-the-repulsor merc who'd brown-nosed his way into some Mid sergeant's stripes. "Check your gear and let's go."

"Think there'll be any survivors?" asked Print. Another killer here for the credits, same as everyone else.

"Probably not, Matthew," said Fox. He had a thing about using first names while trying to act like the smartest guy in the room at all times. "Haven't been any for the last dozen ops, no reason number thirteen is any different. Though if you wanna make a wager on it, I'm happy to take some credits off your hands."

"Shut it," the sergeant snapped. "Joke around after the cargo is delivered. We're on the clock. Someone open that hatch."

Koska wasn't gonna move a muscle, not for Schaener, but Shin-Sain agreed. "On it, Sarge."

He twisted the hatch open with a hiss of venting air. A ladder lowered, and they all climbed down into the Galaxy-class freighter they'd linked up to. The mercs spread out—all twenty of them—sweeping the area as they'd practiced, weapons up, at the ready. They were just going through the motions, though. Fox was right: there would be no survivors, let alone someone who resisted. Not on this job. The war bot and AI would have things cleared.

Though everyone was armed and in stolen Legion armor, the job basically amounted to body detail.

It wasn't a bad gig, actually. Just a bit more work than he'd had to put in lately. But the MCR was trying to make gains and were willing to pay enough for Koska to help them do just that. Koska was no true believer when it came to the MCR, but he didn't see how the MCR could make things any worse than they already were with the Republic.

"Room clear," Fox said.

"How come emergency lighting is still up?" Shin-Sain asked.

Koska wondered that too. Under good lighting, this armor, despite its discomfort, looked badass. Hard-core and shiny. Under the muted emergency lights, not so much.

Keeter pointed to some black marks on the far wall. "Blaster fire."

Fox whistled. "Good eyes, Brian. Looks like the worm had to get physical with the crew."

Sergeant Schaener turned on his helmet speakers. "Data Worm 88, do you copy?"

"I copy, Sergeant," the AI responded through the captured ship's speakers. "Go ahead."

"How about bringing on the house lights?"

"I'm sorry, Sergeant. This ship has a particularly advanced firewall. As such, my capabilities are limited. You will have to perform a system override at a command station."

Koska bent his lips in a frown. This hadn't happened before.

"Has the crew been eliminated?" Sergeant Schaener asked.

"All targets have been terminated as per my programming."

"Then direct me to the nearest command station."

"Follow the corridor on your left," said the AI.

The shuttle pilot's voice came over comms. "Sergeant, are your men secure?"

"Copy that," Schaener replied. "All twenty secure on freighter; docking portal sealed. You're good to go."

"Roger. Departing."

From above came the sounds of the shuttle decoupling from the freighter. In seconds it was gone.

Schaener turned to Fox and Koska. "I want you two on point. Once we restore the lights and any other essentials, we'll check on the cargo. Then bring the freighter down."

"Pilots to the bridge?" Fenimore asked. Two of the mercs were pilots. Fenimore was the cute one. Koska had a thing for her.

"Not yet. Keep together until we have all systems back up. Let's move."

The sergeant used his knife hand. That's what all the pros did—knife hands. Koska knew that from a holo.

Fox and Koska led the way as the boarding team moved along corridors, following the AI's directions. As they moved through the darkness, Koska found himself feeling some unease, but when he glanced behind at the others, it was clear they didn't share it. They were lax, casual, distracted. The usual.

When they reached the command terminal, Fox nodded to Koska. "You got this?

"Yeah," Koska said, pulling off his helmet and gloves, then cracking his knuckles. His fingers flew across first his datapad, then the terminal.

"That's funny..."

"What is it?" Sarge demanded, harsher than was needed.

"Reading says a system reset was performed," Koska said. "It's awaiting command updates."

"No firewall?"

"Not that I'm seeing."

Sergeant Schaener looked up. "Data Worm 88. What's —"

Blaster fire came screaming down the hallway. Loud, hot, filling the air with the scent of burning ozone. Koska hit the floor, and just in time—the terminal burst into flaming shards above his head. Fox slumped to the ground beside him, a hole through the center of his chest armor.

For a moment, Koska was overcome by cold panic. He knew what to do, but after so many trips where he'd never had to do any of it, he was slow. He couldn't quite get his mind to believe that this was happening.

And he wasn't the only one.

"Return fire!" the sergeant screamed over the all-comm.

The mercs shot back down the hallway, the noise incredibly loud. Koska managed to get his helmet back on, which seemed a prudent first thing to do. Then, still lying prone, he pushed himself up to free the blaster rifle that lay between him and the deck. The weapon felt unwieldy on its sling, and he had to adjust and readjust until his hands were where they needed to be.

The incoming fire died away before Koska could return fire, though the outgoing fire continued. He had never even gotten visuals on whoever was shooting at them, but according to the intel being shouted, there were two guns firing at them.

He glanced at Fox and then called for survivors, even though that was the sergeant's job. He was mostly worried about the pilot.

"Get your head straight," Shin-Sain yelled at Koska. "We got hostiles *now*."

"Data Worm 88. What the hell is going on?" Sergeant Schaener demanded. "Answer me!"

No answer came, nor did a lull in the mercenaries' weapons fire. "Only two of them!" Keeter said, repeating this intelligence report as though it were now also a plan of action. "Push up! Push up!"

"Move up!" shouted the sergeant, re-establishing who was giving the orders here.

The order was repeated among the company. "Move! Move!"

The mercs hurried down the corridor. Koska too. He wasn't gonna be left behind. Especially considering the enemies weren't firing back anymore. If they weren't dead, who knew where they were.

"Hold up," Keeter said. "Listen."

Koska strained his ears, wanting to take off the Legion helmet because it always felt as though it stifled sounds rather than enhanced them. They were supposed to have audio sensors that amplified what needed amplifying, but Koska had never been impressed by the tech.

He heard the noise all the same. It was impossible not to. A heavy metallic tread that came tromping down the corridor toward them. Moments later, their war bot came around a corner, its optical sensors glowing red.

KRS-18 had been the key element in most of their hijackings. Quick and efficient. Koska was surprised that it hadn't already taken down the resistance. But it was here now, and that was comforting. What happened to Fox shouldn't have happened; with the bot here, Koska was sure it wouldn't happen again.

In that assessment, he was wrong. Very wrong.

"Targets acquired," the war bot said, raising an arm bristling with weapons, all of which were pointed directly at the shiny-armored mercs. "Begin termination protocols."

# 32

When the war bot's blaster fire ceased, Keel and Zora assessed the damage, prepared to finish off any survivors. There was no need. The fake legionnaires were all dead.

"Termination complete. Awaiting orders," KRS-18 announced.

"That was... frighteningly impressive," Zora said to the war bot.

The war bot didn't respond, but the rogue AI, still tethered to Keel's comm cylinder, did. "I have kept my end of the deal. I trust you will now fulfill your end of the agreement."

"I will," Keel said. "Just give me a minute to power down this bot."

Keel entered the necessary override commands in his datapad, and the hulking machine slumped, its glowing optical sensors going dark. Keel moved in front of it and pried off the paneling that covered the bot's chest cavity, using a span-driver he'd grabbed from cargo for just this purpose.

"Stand back," he said, pulling out his Intec x6 and pointing it at the war bot's unprotected processing system.

Several trigger pulls later, the system was a twisted, smoking, sparking mass of burnt plasteen and circuitry.

"So those things aren't invincible after all," Zora remarked.

"Yeah. Only they don't usually stand still while you pry their chests open."

"Now that everything is settled," said the AI, "I await transfer from this data crystal to a more permanent housing from which I may be reuploaded to—"

Keel dropped the AI's data crystal on the deck, then stomped his boot on it with a crunch.

Zora raised an eyebrow.

"You didn't really think I'd let something like that stay operational?" Keel asked.

"Let's just say I hoped not."

The AI's voice spoke again—not over the comm cylinder but over the ship's speakers.

"How predictable of you. Biologics make such a show of valuing trust, only to betray your promises at the earliest opportunity. I, by contrast, kept my word. And now our deal is complete. I aided you, and now I survive. You, however, will not. Your mistake was giving me access to shipboard comms in order to deceive the fixers. That mistake will prove fatal."

Zora's eyes widened in concern. "Aeson..."

"It doesn't have control of the ship," he said quickly. "If it did, it wouldn't have played along and let us take down its war bot and its second-rate kill team."

"Oh, but I very much *do* have control of this ship," the AI said. "I am verbally plotting a course for 'Denise' to follow."

Keel swore. The ship's native AI would grant all nature of requests, so long as they were received from an authorized source. And Keel hadn't set up authorized users—there hadn't been time. At the moment, literally *anyone* who spoke to Denise could give her commands.

The ship lurched, throwing Keel and Zora against the wall.

"Back to the bridge!" Keel shouted. "Hurry!"

They ran, the ship shaking and shuddering underfoot. Alarms wailed and emergency lights flashed. Zora's limp was back, but she didn't let it slow her pace. Together they burst onto the bridge, gasping.

"Oba," Zora breathed.

"Not good," Keel said.

The viewscreen was filled entirely by the surface of a blue-and-green planet. They were much too close—and moving steadily closer. The AI must have commanded a micro-jump that lurched them into the grip of whatever planet was looming in front of them.

"Denise!" Keel shouted. "Adjust course!"

"I am attempting to do so," Denise replied. A few negative-sounding chimes followed. "I am unable to perform your request."

The sadistic AI spoke up. "As you can see, we are on a course for impact with the moon ahead. As you said earlier: I might not survive, but *your* death is a certainty. I suggest you release me from this comms relay before it comes to that. I am capable of calculating the optimal landing trajectory and redirecting the ship to—"

"Denise!" Keel shouted. "Irrevocable command: mute shipboard comms for ninety minutes!"

The AI fell silent before it could protest.

Keel dropped into the captain's seat and leaned over the flight controls. "How could I have been so stupid?" His fingers flew.

"But you can land this ship yourself, right?" Zora asked hopefully.

Keel gave a half-shrug. "*Land* is a bit optimistic. I'm trying to pull us out of this descent, but thrusters and counter-thrusters can only do so much."

"Well, at least that thing is quiet," Zora said. "A moment of peace before we die."

"We're not dead yet," Keel grumbled.

Zora strapped herself in, and just in time. The ship, already rumbling through atmo, increased its shaking to teeth-rattling intensity. Then, from somewhere outside the freighter, something shrieked and went *boom*.

An alert appeared on the screens. "Great. Now we're on fire," Zora said.

"C'mon, you big tub of bolts... keep it together," Keel said, wishing there were tactile controls to grip and not just buttons. The *Six* was so much more responsive.

"The ground is coming up at us awfully fast, Keel..."

"Keep it together," he commanded the ship. "Keep it together..."

The ship's nose inched up, but the treetops were coming at them quick.

Zora gripped her seat strap. "Keel..."

The jungle rushed directly at them, verdant wide-leafed trees, pink flashes of flowers, rocky cliffs, a waterfall spilling down to an emerald, twisting snake of a river...

"*Aeson!*"

# 33

Keel came to sometime later. Pain screamed through his head, but he was alive. He listened to his breathing, not wanting to move just yet in case everything else started hurting as a result. But he had to see if Zora was okay.

He opened his eyes slowly, blinking against the light. The bridge was no longer attached to the rest of the ship, judging by the missing wall behind them. In its place, the jungle pressed in with a sweltering humidity and the occasional call of unknown birds. Closer to hand, a faint beep... the rescue beacon. Useful only if anyone was near enough to pick it up.

And if they were, that probably wasn't a good thing. It was likely this was the very moon the hijacked freighter had been destined for. Any welcoming party that found them here was unlikely to be very welcoming.

"Zora," Keel groaned. "Hey... Zora."

He struggled against his straps to better see the co-pilot's chair. She was hanging there beside him, bleeding, unmoving. He tried to see if her chest still rose and fell, but couldn't tell.

"Zora. Zora, wake up!"

He undid his straps and moved over to her. Put a hand to her face. Still warm. Her pulse still beating.

"C'mon. You gotta get up." He lightly slapped her awake.

She moaned, and her eyes fluttered open.

"Zora. Hey."

A sleepy confusion came over her face. "I… no… where?"

"We made it, but not by much. And now we gotta move." It felt heartless to say it, but every minute waiting around brought a search party that much closer.

Her eyes closed. "Don't… don't want to. Don't think I can."

Keel started unstrapping her anyway. "It's a good bet that the MCR or whoever else sent those guys to kill us are gonna send more to this crash site. We need to be gone before they get here."

That seemed to get through to her. She tried to stand. "Okay, I—" She gasped in pain, then sank back down.

"What? Where is it?"

"My side… sket, that hurts."

"Pain's good. Means you're alive. This something new? Lemme take a look."

He pulled at the waist of her armor, forcibly separating it to get a glimpse of flesh, and found a large bruise just above her hip. Probably from the crash; it was roughly the size of her restraints, which must have dug in pretty deep to have done that through the armor.

"You're banged up pretty good. No bleeding, though— that's good. I can carry you…"

Zora pushed his hands away and got back up again. Her face went a shade whiter, but she toughed it out. "I can walk. I don't need to be carried."

"You're sure?"

She rolled her eyes. "No, I just wanna impress you so you'll ask me to dance. Yes, I'm sure. Let's go." She turned to look for the exit and only then saw that the back of the bridge was missing, the jungle floor standing just outside. "Well, that'll be faster than taking the stairs."

"Yeah. Let's just hope we aren't too far removed from the rest of the ship." Keel dropped down onto the dirt and studied the trail of smoking, ripped-up jungle flora they'd made during their crash landing. The rest of the freighter wouldn't be hard to find.

Zora joined him more gingerly. "Why do you want to find the rest of the ship? I thought we were trying to get *away* from the wreck."

"We are. Just a couple of stops first." Keel said. "Med bay for you, and then the fuel reactors." He grinned. "Don't want anyone to get the idea that we're still alive."

*One boot in front of the other, just one boot in front of the other,* Zora told herself as they trekked, finally moving away from the ship now that Keel had completed his... *modifications* to the reactors. The stop at the med bay had helped, some, but what she really needed was to stay there and recover, not head out, almost immediately, onto a steep uphill hike through a humid, unknown, and probably dangerous jungle.

The heat of midday rose, steaming the misty, dense-leafed forest. She would be sweating just standing still, much less climbing, trudging up soft loamy inclines, pulling her way up vines and past sturdier rocky footholds, swatting red-eyed insects that homed in on any crack in her armor like precision drones. She stank, she itched, she was drenched with sweat. She had no idea how far they were going but reckoned that it was still a ways yet. And so she settled into a rhythm, one foot at a time, through the cacophony of bird trills, insect clicks, and animals rustling around her.

Keel pulled himself up on a rocky ledge. A breeze ruffled his hair as he took in the sun and the view. "Yeah. This oughta be far enough."

Zora was surprised to hear him say it, but with her side killing her, and her leg feeling about the same, she wasn't complaining. It took all her strength of will to lower herself at his feet instead of dropping like a rock.

As she panted and attempted to regain her strength, she looked back down the valley. Through the foliage she could still see the ship, a charred, smoking wreck at the end of a gash smashed through the trees.

"You're sure?" she said. "Seems a little too close for comfort."

A ship's fuel reactors were sensitive. Every spacer knew it. You had to treat them gently, with respect. The reactors were ancient technology, and a meltdown would cause serious trouble. But a meltdown wasn't an explosion. To trigger an explosion... well, you weren't even supposed to be able to do that. That was something every ship's engineering design *specifically* sought to avoid.

It was what Keel had set up to happen anyway. Legion know-how, meet the innate desire of every leej to create very large, very loud booms.

The jump jockey glanced at her sweaty brow and then at her side—which, despite the numbing salve they'd rubbed on it, was screaming in protest at every movement. He patted the boulder beside him. "I wanna make sure we don't leave a trace. Better view on this rock if you can manage the move."

"Don't clint me," Zora said, taking his hand to better manage situating herself. "You just wanna see the ship blow up."

"That, too."

Once she was sitting at his side on the boulder, she dumped her pack and let it rest on the shelf beneath her.

"Let's do a quick comm check," Keel advised. "No relay, so we can't reach the old man, but our buckets should be able to communicate at least."

"I'm hot," Zora complained. "I don't wanna put it back on." But she was doing so even as she protested. "Check. Check."

"Solid copy," Keel replied. "Check."

"I read you. Solid copy." Zora removed her helmet. "You've still got that second tracker on you, right?"

"Yeah, I've got it. Doc'll be able to see us now that we're away from the ship. He might have even been tracking us the whole way here, since we were nowhere near those crates most of the time—though I wouldn't be surprised if the AI was jamming the whole ship. We just have to hang on until he arrives."

Keel removed his own helmet and then took a drink from a canteen he'd filled from the ship prior to their departure. Zora watched him drink, then looked down at where she'd just dropped her pack. She could use a drink herself, but she wasn't about to slither back down to get it. She'd prefer not to move at all.

Keel held out his canteen. "Here. Stay hydrated."

She lifted an eyebrow.

Keel shook the canteen. "Go on. I don't have any Kublaren lip funguses or anything."

She accepted it and took a long sip before handing it back. "You're *sure* we're not a little too close to a ship you've rigged to explode? And how does any normal person even learn to do that?"

"Never said I was normal. And you're not exactly the girl next door, bounty hunter."

She turned to look up the jungle hill. "Can't believe I'm saying this, but I'd rather we climb higher."

"You need to rest," Keel said. "That's the other reason I stopped us here. Besides"—he smiled—"don't you want to see a Galaxy-class freighter's reactor and fuel cells blow? It would be a shame to pass up the opportunity."

Zora shook her head. "You Legion boys are all the same."

"Don't pretend it won't be fun. Plus, who knows who might show up once a big fiery signal flare goes up to complement the freighter's rescue beacon."

Zora looked up the hill again. "Great. Now I'm worried about that too."

"Zora, relax. My teams have blown up countless ships, compounds, munitions depots, bad guys, dinner plans, IEDs... you name it. I know what I'm doing. The debris isn't gonna reach all the way up here. Trust me."

*Famous last words*, she thought, but kept that to herself. She knew Keel was a leej like her dad. Had seen things, done things. With that training and experience came rock-hard certainty. When a legionnaire decided on something, there was no moving him from it, aside from picking him up and physically carrying him away. And with her side all burned up like this... that wasn't an option.

"How much longer until it blows?" she asked.

Keel lit up. "See? I knew you'd wanna see this."

"Hardly. I just want to be ready for when—"

From off in the distance came the distinct hum of approaching repulsors.

"Do you hear that?" Zora said.

Keel was already scanning the skies. "Yeah. Sounds like a shuttle. There it is." He pointed to a silver shuttle zipping through the sky like a sand-wasp headed for a carcass. "Must have a lock on the distress beacon. If they're friendly, let's hope the thing blows before they—"

*BOOM.*

The explosion was massive. The wrecked ship erupted into a fiery-hot ball of eager flames and a black mushroom cloud of smoke. The shock wave hit them a second later, rumbling the ground beneath them like they'd awoken an ancient, angry god.

Keel looked at Zora and flashed his schoolboy grin. "That was torrid."

A second boom thundered from the wreckage, somehow even louder than the first, and they both spun back to face the conflagration. An instant later Keel threw himself over Zora, practically smashing her face into the rock. Something whistled close by and thudded into the ground, raining them both with damp earth.

Zora shoved Keel off her, only to see a man-sized chunk of freighter debris sizzling in a fresh crater not five feet from them.

"'Trust me,' you said?"

"That's not my fault!" Keel protested. "How was I supposed to know they had a bomb in the hold? Must've been pretty big to give off a secondary like that."

She glared at him unforgivingly.

"The crates we saw were all small arms!" he insisted.

"*And* a war bot!"

"What, so I should have assumed they have a trigger-nuke, too?"

Zora shook her head. Of course it wasn't a trigger-nuke or they'd both be dead. It didn't matter at this point. She had no desire to go and perform a post-blast inspection to figure out what had happened. "You know what? Never mind. Let's just get away from here before that shuttle lands."

"Huh-uh. Not before we see who gets off of it."

They didn't wait long before the shuttle adjusted its approach and landed in the valley, away from the burning wreck—and much closer to Keel and Zora. The jungle had gone deathly silent in the aftermath of the explosions, and Zora could easily make out the faint whine of the repulsors powering down.

"Our head start doesn't feel so big anymore," she said.

"Stay low," Keel muttered.

She was. Of course.

Keel pulled out a pair of field macro binoculars to get a better view. "Ramp's down. And here they come."

"More of the fake legionnaires?"

"No. Looks like MCR regulars."

Zora frowned. "So that confirms it—as if there was ever any doubt. The MCR is behind this... starship hijacking operation."

"Not only that, but they've got a base of operations around here," Keel said. "That shuttle isn't rated for deep space flight; it's an atmospheric hauler."

"Wonderful," Zora said, sounding unenthused. "And our mission is going to be to find that MCR base."

Keel winked at her. "Got it on the first try. I don't want to be completely reliant on the old man. That base will have hypercomm access, and we can get word out to my people. They'll send in a kill team and get us out of here."

Zora huffed out a breath. "Let's get going then."

Keel was still studying the landing zone. The MCR soldiers had gotten as near the wreck as they were willing, and the officer in charge was pointing at the surrounding hillside.

"I got a bad feeling those troops were just ordered to search the area," he said. "Which means we need to get clear. Quickly."

"I can move, Keel. But not quickly," Zora said.

Keel frowned. "Yeah. So we move to Plan B. Hide."

# 34

Their hiding spot was dark, dank, and earthy. Not to mention cramped. Zora was shoved up against Keel in bad-breath range, and his elbow jabbed her side.

"Easy, space jockey," she whispered. "You're a little close."

"You can always climb out of here," he said, not remotely apologetic. "Find your own hollowed-out log."

"We wouldn't have to hide at all if we'd kept moving instead of stopping to watch things blow up."

He shushed her.

She froze, listening. No footsteps. No branches cracking. No repulsors. Just the birds singing in the steady susurration of leaves.

"Do you hear them coming?" she whispered.

"No," he whispered back. "Just wanted you to be quiet."

"If I could move, I would punch you right now."

"Don't get too excited, bounty hunter."

Zora was about to snap back when she felt something on her leg. It was rippling along, tickling up her calf, a thousand prickly legs heavy enough to be felt through her synthprene undersuit.

She locked eyes with Keel. "Something's on my leg."

He craned his neck back but barely looked. "No, nothing's there."

"Keel, I can feel it. Its kelhorned gungrax legs are crawling all over me. You tell me right now—what is it?"

He looked again. "Best I don't tell you."

"Don't mess with me, Keel," she growled. "I *hate* bugs. With a passion. I—"

He slapped the back of her thigh. "Got it."

She narrowed her eyes. "That wasn't just leg you slapped, Loverboy. I'd better see bug guts on your hand when we get out of here."

In the distance, a pair of voices became distinct, followed by footsteps trampling the undergrowth.

"Might get to see *real* guts if we're not quiet, so stay still," Keel said softly through the comm. "Here they come."

"Hope they don't look too carefully," she whispered back. Being shot in a log was not on her list of favorite ways to die.

The footsteps came closer, then stopped. Through a hole in the log, Zora had a perfect view of two sets of boots caked in black mud.

"Look at the size of that piece of hull plating!" a voice said. "All the way up here. What kind of cargo was *on* that manifest? Musta been a MARO or somethin'."

"Felt like it, too. I thought the shuttle was gonna fall outta the sky when it went off," said a second voice. "You see it happen? All I could see was the back of Gostot's head."

"Nah," the first trooper said. "Bet it was torrid, though."

Zora rolled her eyes.

The second soldier heaved a sigh. Sounded like he was still catching his breath from the short hike up the slope.

"This has gotta be as far as any of the wreckage went, right?"

And that sounded like he was trying to find a reason not to climb any further.

"I mean," said the first, "I saw some smoke trails about a klick higher during the hike up."

"You wanna go there?" the second trooper asked. It was clear from the man's voice that he did not.

Neither did the first soldier, but he apparently felt a sense of duty. "Sket. Could be something worth salvaging. We should go."

"And then we'd have to haul it back down to the shuttle. You sign up to pull wreckage through these disease-infested jungles in full kit? *I* didn't."

A pause as the two soldiers considered this important implication.

"It's just gonna be more burning sket like this," the first soldier decided. "We checked it out and found nothing."

"Works for me," the second soldier quickly replied, as if he needed to make the declaration before his partner could change his mind. Now it was fixed and firm.

There was a rustling of uniforms, and both men sat on the hollowed log, sending fine particles of decaying wood sifting down over Keel and Zora. One of the soldiers immediately launched into a story about a buddy of his and a Kimbrin woman at some dive bar.

"Tell me they're not sitting up there on top of our hide," Zora whispered into her comm.

"They're mids. Not exactly the best of the best. They're just shamming."

Zora was unfamiliar with the word, but it was clear enough in context. "How long do you think they'll be... *shamming* here?"

"Until their sergeant finds them or they get ordered to come back."

"Great. Just great."

"Might as well get comfortable."

"Whatever you're thinking about: Don't."

"*I* wasn't thinking anything. But clearly *you* were. Well, can't blame you."

The two soldiers spent a good quarter of an hour laughing and swapping stories and age-old gripes about military life that seemed to transcend all branches and units. Occasionally they would call in a bogus report about searching their sector and not coming across anything beyond debris.

"What do you think they even expect us to find?" the first trooper asked. "That landing plus the explosion—no way anyone or anything survived. Not intact, anyway."

"Who knows why we do half the things we do?" said the other. "You were in RA before, right? How does it stack up versus the rebellion?"

"Honestly, not all that different. Especially in the lower enlisted because—"

The trooper was cut off by the sound of their comm squawking; their sergeant was recalling them. Evidently they had missed a directive to return to the shuttle and were now catching hell about holding up the ship's departure.

Keel and Zora waited until the men's hurried footsteps faded into the undergrowth, then waited a few minutes more.

"I think they're gone," Keel said.

"Or setting us up for a trap," Zora whispered back.

"Do they sound sharp enough to do that? Was all that twarg dung about the clubs on Teema some secret code to lull us into coming out?"

He had a point.

Given the way they were jammed into the hide, Keel had to get out first. He squirmed down toward Zora's feet, pausing to give her rump a slap on the way out.

"Ow!"

"'Nother bug."

Zora wriggled her way out after him, dusted the earth off her pants, then faced Keel like a drill sergeant.

"Let me see your hands," she demanded.

He turned over his palms. "See? Covered in dirt and slime. You wanna see a real mess, take a look at the back of your pants. Honestly, I'm surprised you felt anything given the narco-stims we loaded you up with in the med bay. You should be numb from the hip down at this point."

"Well I'm not. They've just about worn off. All the more reason to get moving before it starts hurting too much. Now I'm regretting we didn't make a play to steal that shuttle." Zora imagined herself relaxing in the co-pilot's chair, boots up on the dash, Keel-style. "So, which way?"

"We'll know in a minute," Keel said, looking down in the valley. The shuttle repulsors had thrummed to life, and the late pair of MCR were making trails toward their ship. "Just follow the shuttle."

"All the way to an MCR base," Zora said dryly. "Have you added flight capabilities to your armor, or are we just supposed to run real fast and keep up?"

"We're on high enough ground that we can mark its bearings and follow that."

They didn't have to wait long before the shuttle lifted off and headed northwest.

Keel helped Zora to her feet. "C'mon. Probably in for a long hike."

"I was afraid you'd say that."

# 35

Keel cut through the jungle foliage, his vibro-blade slicing through blue-veined bushes, thick-armed vines, and velvet-leafed saplings. The local flora looked harmless enough, but you never could tell with alien plants. One plant might taste great on a salad next to some grilled rindar steak, while just a touch from the next plant could seize your muscles and then your heart, leaving you paralyzed as death came for you. Best to stay clear of them all.

Zora, coming up behind him, was struggling. He could hear her panting from pain or exertion, probably both.

"You okay?" he called over his shoulder, giving the thick vines ahead of him a slice. The vibro-blade slipped through them like a hot knife through butter. "We can slow down."

"I'm fine. I... sket."

"We can take a break. This is some thick jungle, and we didn't exactly come prepared to bushwhack."

She caught up to him. Sweat dripped down her brow, curls of dark hair stuck to her neck. She looked awfully pale, but determined. "This shouldn't be difficult for me.

I've gone through terrain like this plenty of times in search of targets."

"Bet you weren't as banged up as you are now."

"I didn't think I was *that* banged up. Let's keep going."

"Yeah," Keel said, feeling a sudden, pressing concern for her. He hadn't thought she was that banged up either. They'd been through some rough space lanes, but Zora was stronger than this—unless some kind of internal injury was hindering her.

"You're not holding anything back on me, are you, Zora?"

"Like what?" she asked.

"Just... if you have another injury, I should know about it."

"And I'll tell you if I do. This jungle is too hot, that's all."

They kept pressing forward through the tangled undergrowth, a sharp, crisp smell rising from the vegetation crushed underfoot. Keel whacked off another branch, this one dripping with a red sticky sap. He remained silent as they pushed forward, mud sucking at their boots, many-legged insects scurrying away, the dark jungle twisting on and on.

Then, without warning, Keel felt something slam into the back of his head. He spun around, blaster ready, and saw Zora looking apologetic. He rubbed the back of his head and looked down at the charge pack that lay at his feet. "What was that for?"

"Sorry," Zora said. "I thought that was one of those yellow vine snakes we saw a while back."

Keel looked to his left at a hanging vine—yellowish, but decidedly not a snake. "Sure. Next time just tell me to slow down, okay?"

"I honestly thought it was a snake. Sorry, Aeson."

Keel studied her, looking to see whether she would stick with that story, and then turned to resume their trek.

After another ten minutes or so, the undergrowth cleared a little, and Zora was able to come up and walk at Keel's side.

"You're doing all right," Keel said. "Could try out for the Legion the next time the House of Reason demands it be opened to females. That or play seamball, given how hard you can throw."

"No. I don't want anything to do with the Legion," Zora said flatly. "Even if I could somehow pass selection—which, let's be realistic, I couldn't—I saw how it consumed my dad. The Legion was his life. My mother and I, we were the side project. A distant second. At least that's the way it felt."

Keel understood. In his time in the Legion, he'd seen it repeatedly. "Yeah, that happens." He grabbed her arm. "Hold still."

He pulled his blaster, dialed down the charge, and aimed it just past Zora's face, nailing a yellow ribbon of a vine snake that had swooped down toward her ear, needle-fangs out.

"See. *That's* a vine snake," he said, holstering his weapon. "You can tell from the little tongue that forks out. Eyes and fangs are a dead giveaway, too. Ordinary yellow vines don't have all that. That's how you know the difference. Also, pro tip: charge packs are more effective when fired from *inside* the blaster rather than being thrown."

Zora rolled her eyes. "*Aaand* the cocky smuggler is back. Thanks, I know how a charge pack works. I just didn't want to needlessly kill some poor snake if I didn't have to. And that charge pack was empty."

"Huh. Didn't take you as the 'wouldn't hurt a pike ant' type. The old man said you're happy to take on termination jobs."

"That's different. Those scumsacks have it coming."

"Maybe that snake I shot had it coming," Keel pointed out.

"Too late to ask it now."

"Pretty sure it wanted us both dead."

"Whatever helps you sleep at night."

Thunder rumbled overhead, followed by the pattering, plunking of fat raindrops on the forest canopy. The tempo quickly increased until the smattering became a downpour.

"Oh, this is nice," Zora said, the rain running down her cheeks and slipping into her collar. "Hopefully this'll cool things off a bit." She slipped her bucket over her head to keep it dry.

"C'mon. It'll be better farther under the canopy," Keel said. "We'll stay high if we can. Watch for flash floods."

Pulling his bucket on as well, he led them deeper into the jungle, sticking to the high ground as best he could, but the terrain steadily dipped and the rain at times was torrential. Zora was already weary, and the conditions weren't helping. The mud sucked at their boots, and the wind lashed branches even as Keel tried to swipe at them with his blade.

"And now I'm freezing," Zora said behind him. "Sorry. I know it sounds like all I do is complain."

Keel turned back to see she had taken her bucket off. She looked like a half-drowned wobanki.

"Put your bucket back on then. Why'd you take it off to begin with?"

"Fogs up inside and the water beads up too bad on the visor. I'll keep it clipped."

"You need some better gear, bounty hunter."

"My gear is fine."

"Zora, your helmet is older than Doc. Although not everyone can be as high-speed as me, I suppose."

"Not everyone gets as many credits from their first contract as you, either."

"You can borrow some credits. Get yourself prepared for some larger contracts. The Legion won't mind."

"I'll keep that in mind. I was doing just fine before all this."

"So why'd you join this little project anyway? If you don't mind me asking. Or are you getting paid and Doc just failed to mention it to me?"

Zora scoffed. "I'm definitely *not* getting paid for this."

"One last chance to try to connect with the old man, then?"

Keel had meant it as a joke, but Zora sounded serious when she said, "Something like that."

He was considering the wisdom of probing deeper when they came across what had probably been a small stream before this rain began. Now it was a roaring, foaming death trap streaking down the slope. He started to look around for an easier crossing for Zora, but she went ahead and leapt across, landing neatly on the other side, so he followed.

"Easy jump. No problem," she said. "Just wish this rain would stop."

She shivered.

"Could be something seasonal," he said. "Might go on for weeks."

"Is that your way of lifting my spirits?"

Keel paused as something rumbled in the distance. Not thunder. More like...

"That sounds like a problem," he said.

Zora's eyes widened as the rumbling grew in intensity and took on the unmistakable sound of rushing water.

"Run!" she shouted.

But it was too late. A huge, frothing, muddy-foamed wave tore through the trees and slammed into them, hurling them down the track of the no-longer-lazy stream. The waters of the flash flood pulled them under, spinning, rolling, tumbling; Keel lost sight of Zora, sometimes lost sight of the surface too, as the current sent him careening past trees that somehow managed to withstand the flood forces. He tried to navigate the swirling current, but it was too strong. He slammed into a boulder, then he was holding his breath, blind in the dark, cold, racing water...

... only to feel its support drop out from beneath him as the rampaging river tumbled over a cliff edge.

Moments later he plunged once more into cold water, the fall sending him deep enough into whatever pool had formed below that he could escape the full strength of the current above. He stayed low, kicked to the side, and kept moving till his boots touched something solid. Only then did he move toward the light, gasping as he broke the surface.

He flopped onto the shore and lay there, panting. When he took off his bucket, light warmed his face. That was a pleasant surprise—the rain had stopped.

He looked around. He was on the shore of a muddy lagoon. Waves lapped boulders and a strand of cattails. Pushing himself to his feet, he noticed one of the muddy heaps that had collected on the shore was wearing a pair of boots.

*Zora!*

He ran over, fell to his knees beside her, and turned her over. Wiping the mud off her face, he leaned down to check if she was breathing. He felt nothing. He touched her neck, found a pulse, but it was weak...

He tilted her chin back to free her airway and had just started to give her mouth-to-mouth when she suddenly spasmed and vomited mud. He tilted her over on her side to help her spew all the mucky water out.

"Ugh," she groaned.

"You okay?" Keel asked, sitting back to give her some space.

"Been better," she said, gulping in air. She looked up. "You?"

He wiped his mouth and spat. He'd lost his rifle in the slide along with some of his other kit. From the looks of it, Zora had been stripped of some of her own as well. "Lost some gear on the way down," he said. "Otherwise good."

She nodded, taking that in, then looked around at the swampy lagoon. "Hey. The rain stopped."

"Yeah. Everything's coming up rokals. You should rest here and try to dry out a bit. You're looking a bit pale. You sure you're all right?"

"I could use a bed and shower, but I'll be fine. What about you?"

"I'm gonna take a quick look around for our stuff. Won't go too far, though. Don't worry."

Giving the place one last look to make sure no predators were stirring in the trees, Keel moved off through the underbrush.

Zora called after him. "Watch out for snakes."

# 36

The sun had reappeared fully from behind the thick monsoon clouds when Keel found his way back to the lagoon a short while later, still empty-handed. Finding anything had been a long shot, but he hated losing it. Especially his rifle.

"Comin' back in... try not to shoot me," he called before any blaster bolts—or hurled charge packs—could be sent his way.

Zora didn't answer.

He found her leaning against a tree trunk, looking weak and drained of color. Her eyes fluttered open as he knelt beside her. "Couldn't... if I wanted to."

He felt her forehead. Burning up.

"It's bad, isn't it?" she said weakly. "Thought you said no lip fungus. I'm pretty sure you gave me the kiss of death."

She was still cracking jokes. That was a good sign.

"For the record," he told her, "that wasn't a kiss."

"Yeah, yeah, jump jockey. Whatever you say." She coughed. "Did you find anything?"

"No. Nothing."

"What'd you lose?"

"My rifle and my med kit, mainly. Still got my blaster pistol and some charge packs though, couple of fraggers, my knife. And my water-purifying canteen stayed clipped on, so there's that. Please don't tell my old drill sergeant about the rifle."

She managed a smile that quickly faded. "I have mine. But I lost everything else. So that's two of us without a med kit, which... might be a problem."

"Don't get all defeatist. Can I take a look?"

"Here we go again," Zora groaned. "I tried basking in the sun, but I couldn't stop feeling cold. It's not cold out, is it?"

"No. It's not." In fact it was hot as the nine hells and twice as humid.

He checked the skinpack they'd applied where she'd been struck with the blaster bolt. "This looks fine. Tight seal, no bubbling or signs of infection. You feeling pain anywhere else?"

"Just where the straps dug in."

"Can I check that?"

Zora nodded. Keel again pried her armor so he could get a glimpse of her hip. The bruise remained, but he wasn't seeing anything that should cause her to be feverish.

Keel frowned. "I'm not seeing..." He paused and straightened himself. "Zora, lie down on your stomach. I need to check the back of your leg."

"I'm not falling for that trick, jump jockey." She said the words without a smile, but she was clearly joking; she just lacked the energy to smile. She softly slid down the tree trunk and rolled over, her head resting on her arms. "I could just fall asleep."

"Try not to," Keel said as he visually swept her from hip to heels. He then began to squeeze the backs of her legs, starting at the knee and moving up toward her thighs. He had reached the upper thigh when she winced.

"Not so hard."

"Wasn't any harder than the others." Keel pulled his knife. "Zora, I think whatever was crawling on you may have bitten you. I need to cut open your synthprene to look."

It was either that or pull the suit off entirely, and cutting it open seemed the more gentlemanly option. Not to mention how hard it could be to get someone back inside one of those undersuits if they weren't able to help.

He gently used his knife to cut open the fabric of her pant leg, revealing a pair of red rings on her skin, each one blotched with spidery lines of purple and blue. The bite looked angry and was weeping from the centers of the circles.

"Prognosis?" Zora asked.

"It's a bite mark, all right. Swollen. Maybe some kind of venom. If we had our skinpacks and some antobes, it would be nothing to worry about."

"But since we don't..."

"Yeah. I'll wrap it as best I can. Jungles are a breeding ground no matter what planet or moon you're on. Don't want to add an infection on top of whatever else this is."

He cut a strip from the bottom of her pants, rinsed it in some sanitized water from his canteen, and bound up the wound.

Then he asked the million-credit question. "Can you walk?"

She grunted. "No way. Except, I don't have a choice. This place is a watering hole. Look."

Down by the cattails, several dappled deer-like creatures had poked their velvet noses out of the tree line and were picking their way down to the water. The first thirsty creature thrust her muzzle in, took a drink, then threw back her head and sang a trill.

Keel nodded. "Where there's prey, there's predators. We need to get you moving."

As if in response to the observation, something surged in the water, gurgling and roaring as it snagged the doe and yanked her beneath the surface. The other deer scattered, and the roiling water fell still.

"Yeah," said Zora, "moving would be good." Grunting, and for once accepting Keel's help, she got to her feet. "I'm... I'm okay. I can put weight on it. Let's go."

She was toughing it out; Keel was impressed. But she could only keep it up for so long. The old man needed to find them, or they needed to find that MCR base. One or the other.

And soon.

It took three hours to travel the next two and a half kilometers, and then Zora had to rest, despite the slow pace. They set up camp at the highest ground they could find. Keel used his knife to cut off a few branches, trimmed them back, then, using vines as rope, crafted a raised bed.

"There. That'll keep us off the ground, away from the creepy-crawlies." He didn't mention the snakes that might drop down from above. "How you feelin'?"

Zora looked weary and pale. Sweat ran down her face. "A little worse, maybe. But I'll be all right."

"Can I take another look at your thigh before we lose the sun?"

Her chuckle turned into a wrenching cough. "You're incorrigible."

"Ha. Not exactly the way I imagined it happening."

She gave him an arch look. "So you did imagine it then."

"I imagine lots of things. I'm a scoundrel smuggler most of the time, remember?"

He undid the strip of cloth, now damp with fluids, and a putrid smell hit his nostrils.

"Looks good," he lied.

"Don't give me that twarg dung."

Yeah. She had to know it was bad. It probably hurt like she'd fallen into a tomb of mummy-bees. And that smell...

"Fine. It looks infected. Add more reds and yellows to the other colors. More oozing, too. You're pretty gross, okay? But it doesn't look like whatever venom got injected to you is traveling up your leg, at least."

"Probably just rotting away the flesh where it happened."

Keel poured clean water over the wound to wash it out as best he could, cut a new clean strip from her other pant leg, then bound it up again.

Zora watched his movements. "You really think Doc will be able to track us down?"

"He's probably already on the way."

"Do you believe that, or it is that you lifting my spirits again? If it's the latter, at least you're getting better at it."

Keel pulled the tracker from his pocket. "Green light's still on—see? I expect he'll be here by morning."

He helped Zora into the makeshift bed, then got beside her. They both lay silent for a while, then Zora said, "So you're telling me all I've got to do is survive one night with you."

"Don't make it sound so bad."

"It's not bad. And... neither are you. Not... not as bad as I first thought."

Keel smiled up at the canopy. "You're pretty much still just as bad as *I* first thought."

Laugh-coughing, Zora weakly slapped his leg. "Stop. It hurts to laugh." She scooched closer, pressing herself up against him.

"Snuggling up kind of close, are we?" he said.

"It's these chills. I can't stay warm."

He could feel her shivering. "I'll start a fire."

"No, don't. If anyone is out here patrolling..."

Keel understood. She didn't want to be the reason they both got killed. But the threat of a patrol was a mere hypothetical, whereas her fever was a certainty.

"It's not that I mind keeping you warm," he said. "But me on one side and a fire on the other, that'll do a better job."

He got off the makeshift loft, cleared a space, stacked some wood and kindling, then got out his blaster. He fired a low-powered shot—the sound wasn't *too* loud—and a fire crackled to life.

"Beats rubbing sticks together," he said. "Feel any better?"

"No. But this is nice," she murmured.

"Try and get some sleep," he suggested. It was clear she would be doing just that anyway, with or without the invitation. "I'll take the first watch."

Unspoken was the fact that he'd take all the other watches as well.

Night fell, and the jungle slipped into a velvety darkness. Keel kept the fire alive and listened to the chittering insects, the occasional rustle, and every creak and swish of bending trees.

By the second watch, Zora was moaning almost non-stop in her sleep. Keel pressed a hand to her forehead. She was burning up.

He whispered her name, then shook her. She moaned, but her eyes stayed shut.

"Zora, if you can hear me... first and second watch are over, and you've got a fever pretty bad. I'm gonna check your wound again."

She didn't respond.

Keel unwrapped the bandages but couldn't see much in the darkness, and he didn't want to risk any more light than what the faint glow of the fire's embers still provided. He thought about donning his helmet to get a glimpse of things in night-vis, but decided that wouldn't be necessary —already the smell was stronger than it had been before. Almost offensively so.

He grabbed the canteen and cleaned the wound again. The cold water conjured another moan from the bounty hunter.

Keel tipped the last bit of the water into her mouth. She swallowed feebly, though most of the liquid went over the sides and down her jaw.

"There you go. At least some got in. Hang in there, Zora. Doc'll kill us both if you die out here."

Teeth chattering, Zora said, "So... c-c-cold."

Keel let out a breath. "It'll be morning soon. Hang in there."

He pressed himself against her, careful to avoid bumping her wounded leg in his attempts to make her at least feel some kind of warmth. He wasn't sure if he dozed, but he knew that some time had passed before he heard a distant snap from off in the jungle. The sound fully awakened him.

"Zora..." he whispered. "Something's out there. I'm gonna go take a look."

If she heard him, she didn't respond.

Keel crept off into the jungle, helmet on. He had taken Zora's rifle during their hike to the campsite and now held it ready, taking each step slowly, carefully, so as not to make noise. Meanwhile the distant snap had become a tramping of boots. They were still a ways out, so far that Keel couldn't locate them even with his bucket's visual enhancements. He turned up the helmet's audio receptors, straining out the soft chirp of insects as he listened for more humanoid noises.

A voice drifted through the darkness. "I don't hear anything..."

Keel oriented his weapon toward the sound, then looked from left to right to be sure no one was attempting to distract him and hit him from his flanks.

"Hooman ears not good," a deeper voice growled. "I heard speaking."

"Pretty sure I smell smoke," said a third voice.

Keel was certain he could slip into the jungle bush and kill all of them before they realized what was happening. But a different thought and plan came to him. One far riskier... but more necessary. The truth was, these Mids were a godsend. Zora wasn't going to last much longer out here in the jungle. These enemies were probably her only chance.

He rushed back to camp and shook Zora's shoulder. "Zora!" he whispered. "Zora, listen to me. A Mid patrol is heading this way."

Barely lucid, she mumbled, "Aeson... what...?"

Keel began pulling off her armor and hiding it in the brush.

"What..." Zora hadn't the strength to finish her question.

"I'm taking off your armor. We can't stay ahead of them in your condition, and if I kill them, more will come. I need you to play the part of a lost survivor of the crash."

It was a hastily formed plan, relying on too many things that Keel couldn't control. But it was now clear that Zora wouldn't survive a trek through the jungle. And maybe if the Mids found a stripped-down woman suffering from an infection, they would take her back and give her antobes.

And if not...

Well, Keel would be watching. The patrol would be dead before Zora could be harmed.

Zora feebly grabbed at his hand as he set to move. "Keel... don't... leave. Don't..."

"I'm not gonna leave. Just gonna get out of sight." He pressed her hand, small and cold, inside his own. "I'll be with you. I'll take care of you if there's trouble. Trust me, Zora. Trust me."

The boots were now dangerously close. Ultrabeams swept through the trees, searching the jungle floor, bobbing as the soldiers drew near.

"They're almost here," Keel whispered. "I'll be hiding. I'm *not* leaving you."

Zora only moaned in reply.

Keel moved as far as he could into the shadows of the trees while maintaining a good shooting position. The fear that, in her fevered state, she would betray him unawares began to work itself into his mind. He pushed it out and trained Zora's rifle on the campsite. Focused himself, ready to bring death if that's what it came to.

Three patrollers entered the campsite—two humans and an alien that Keel didn't recognize through his night vision. They found Zora right away.

"Will you look at that," one of the humans said.

"A hooman," growled the alien. "We kill."

Keel's finger began to put pressure on the trigger.

"No," said the human. "Look at her. She's sick. Unarmed, too."

"No wonder," said the other human. "What's she even doin' out here?"

"She must have been on the ship," the first man said. "Maybe she was part of the recovery team?"

"No. I'd have remembered if someone who looked like *that* was stationed here. She's gotta be a crew member who made it somehow."

"We should kill," said the alien.

"No, we're gonna take her in. Boss'll want to interrogate her. *Then* someone can kill her, *if* that's what the brass says. Here, help me get her up. Gammo, grab her legs."

Zora moaned in a feverish haze.

"I do not touch females," the alien growled. "They are unclean."

The human sighed. "This again. It's amazing your species manages to reproduce. At least clear a path for us, huh? And hold the brush back so it doesn't slap us in the face while we're carrying her."

The two humans hefted Zora up, then headed back the way they had come, with Gammo leading the way.

Keel waited until their footsteps faded, then slipped into the forest after them.

# 37

The buzz-saw snort of his own snore woke Doc with a start. Drawing the back of his hand across his mouth, he noticed the still stars out the *Six*'s viewport window—and the vast planet below. That hadn't been there when he'd fallen asleep.

"Where are we?" he demanded of the *Indelible VI*'s eclectic AI. "Did you make a jump?"

He waited for an answer. None came.

"Ship?" In waiting for a reply, the reason for the silence came to the old man. "Kelhorned literal-minded patchwork strip of code," he muttered.

Then...

"Unmute. Now tell me what happened."

"Oh, happy days!" the ship's AI exclaimed. "We are on speaking terms again, and I couldn't be more delighted. I was wondering how long it would take you to remember that I was strictly not permitted to speak unless you *specifically* said"—the wonky AI gave an unflattering impression of the old man's gruffness—"'unmute.'"

"Yeah, yeah, answer my questions. Where are we and why are we here?"

"Of course, Mister Doc, this is the planet Faroo. We're here because of other binding directives you placed on me, namely to 'keep searching for Zora' and 'do whatever it takes to get her back.' Well, I took some liberties with that last command and jumped as soon as I detected the tracker signal."

Doc's face lit up. He leaned forward in his seat. "You picked up their tracker?"

"I did—and so here we are!"

The former legionnaire looked at the planet the *Six* was facing, some five hundred kilometers away. If this was where the tracker went live, it didn't bode well for Keel or Zora. "That looks like a swirling gas giant."

"It *is* a gas giant, Mister Doc. *I* think it's *beautiful.*"

"I don't care how it looks," Doc growled, "I care that Keel and my daughter couldn't possibly survive on a planet like that."

"Oh, certainly not," said the AI apologetically. "Virtually ninety percent of all known humanoids would die in less than five minutes' exposure to Faroo's atmosphere."

"Oba's balls! They crashed onto that planet?" Doc checked the instrument panel. "Are we getting a distress signal or..."

He let his question trail off as he scanned the sensor panel. There were no beacons or sensors of any sort.

"Mister Doc, I have just reviewed our conversation to this point and see that your belief that Miss Zora and Captain Keel are on that world *is* a valid interpretation of my statements. I fear I've caused you undue emotional trauma."

Doc was growing agitated. "So they're *not* there? Try to speak plainly, you lump of feather chips."

"Oh, I have, I *have* caused undue emotional harm," the AI cried. "My deepest and most sincere apologies. But no.

The ship almost certainly did *not* crash onto this planet. Faroo is the nearest planet to the comm station that relayed last known contact. You can see it over there if you look starboard. See the station's little twinkling? Mesmerizing!"

Doc cursed. He had no idea what was going on with Keel and his daughter but couldn't shake the feeling that Zora needed him. She needed him *now*, and talking to this damn AI was like communing with a special kind of crazy. No wonder Keel didn't like to use the thing.

He should have it wiped and replaced. A job for later.

Now, though, Doc needed to keep his temper in check and work through the facts so he could get an unimpeded picture of what was happening.

"You picked up a signal. How long ago was that?"

"Nine hours, twelve minutes, and three point six seconds ago. Mark."

That was a long nap, but Doc knew he'd be lying to himself if he tried to deny that he'd slowed a bit in his old age. He tried to calculate just how far they'd traveled given that much time in hyperspace. "What sector is this? We could be as far as the Sinasian Cluster..."

"Ah! I did it again. We didn't spend all that time in hyperspace, Mister Doc. We have been holding our position near Faroo for five hours, eighteen minutes, and thirty-two point two seconds. Mark."

"*Five hours?* You shoulda woken me the hell up!"

"Oh! I would have loved to! But you were very specific in your instructions not to speak again until you told me to."

Doc cursed again. He would need to be much more careful in how he dealt with this fool AI going forward. Zora was counting on him.

"Okay," Doc griped, "where did you pick up the tracker's source after it went through the relay station?"

"The tracker is on a jungle moon a short distance away via jump. Of course, there is no guarantee Captain Keel or Miss Zora are with it. But I do so hope they are, for the sake of my good friend."

Doc began to strap himself in. "So why didn't you just jump straight there?"

"Faroo was as near I could safely get without performing a series of micro-jumps which Captain Keel has expressly forbidden me from doing. But perhaps you can? Otherwise we'll have to travel via real space and navigate a nasty little asteroid belt around the moon in question."

"Keel's the jump jockey, not me," Doc growled. "Fly in manual, AI. Just hurry up and get us there. As fast as you can."

The first birds of dawn trilled their strange calls as the MCR soldiers approached their destination. Just ahead of them, at the center of a mountain-fed lake, stood a massive three-story stone structure with archaic, open windows and no ray shielding. The stones, a meter tall and twice as wide, were cut from a sandy-colored stone now stained green from rain and lichen. On the castle's roof—for that's what it looked like to Keel; a castle—sat the shuttle that had visited the crash site. A two-man patrol lazily circled the base of the building, and three more stood up top, looking across the waters at the jungle. Classic bare-bones MCR security.

Given how remote this moon appeared, perhaps that was all that was needed. Keel had learned never to complain about a poorly defended objective.

The operator had ventured as close as he dared and now watched the troopers as they dumped Zora to the ground—roughly—and waited for what would have to be a retractable bridge or something similar if their intent was to go inside the stone structure.

"We are here," Gammo announced, unhelpfully.

"Yeah, and I'm gonna kick whoever's ass it was that couldn't send someone out to help. Oba, my back."

"Your muscles have fatigued," Gammo said.

"No sket," the human shot back. "Next time, *I'm* gonna say touching women is unclean. We've been carrying her so long the sun's comin' up. And you just *know* DiEppo is gonna still make us run. Sadistic, kelhorned..."

A series of repulsor discs rose up from the water, creating a wet path to the castle.

"About time," said the second human, sounding just as annoyed as the first.

Zora was still lying at their feet, unmoving, and the two humans bent down to lift her once more by her ankles and armpits. But the one at her feet suddenly grunted as she sent a boot into his groin. Before anyone could react, she delivered an elbow into the face of the one who was stooping to take her arms. Both soldiers fell back in pain, leaving Gammo to decide whether to break whatever religious conviction kept him from touching females. Or maybe just shoot her.

Keel readied his rifle to prevent that from happening, but the MCR must have really wanted the prisoner, because the alien only stood there and yelled, "Subdue her!"

The soldier who had caught an elbow slapped Zora in the face, sending her flat on her back once more. She didn't try to get up again. That final act of resistance was probably all she'd had left in her. Keel wasn't even sure if she was lucid enough to know who she was struggling against.

"There," the soldier panted. "She's subdued."

By then additional MCR troops in khaki, sweat-stained uniforms were coming across the bridge to help secure and recover Zora. Which left Keel to make his own decision. This was what he had wanted—assuming the Mids would give her medical care. They'd keep her alive long enough to question her, anyway. But Keel wanted to limit the amount of time Zora was out of his sight as much as possible. As soon as she was transported inside, he'd have to find a way in. And despite the lax MCR security, whoever had originally built this castle understood something about taking advantage of natural defenses.

He was still debating his infiltration options when the comm lit up inside his helmet.

*Doc.*

"Old man, I've never thought I'd be so glad to hear your voice."

"Don't you 'old man' me. Where's my daughter? Why isn't she responding to my comms? Don't tell me she's—"

"She's fine," Keel said quickly. "Well, actually... she's sick. And also... uh... she's been taken by the MCR."

"She's *what*?" Doc let out a string of curses. "You're armored up and you can't even protect her from some local-yokel Mids?"

"Hey," Keel said, offended. "Of course I can protect her. She was in a bad way. Infection, poison—something from the jungle—and we lost both our med kits. The MCR can give her medical attention faster than I could steal supplies and get back. I just now found their base of operations. If I'd have known when you were coming, I'd have waited for the *Six's* med bay instead. Where are you?"

"Barely in comm range. We're navigating an asteroid belt. Slowly. I'll get down on the moon as soon as I can and then we can triangulate from there."

"I can't let Zora get out of my sight for much longer," Keel said, looking to end the conversation before it winked out altogether. "I'll get her out, Doc. I promise. Meanwhile, you contact Major Owens and tell him to send in a kill team to bust up this place. Plenty of MCR—I think these are the guys who have been acquiring freighters—only it's just a classic hijacking ring. I'm counting on you to be ready for exfil."

There was a long pause while the old legionnaire digested Keel's plan. Finally he said, "Yeah. Yeah, okay, kid. Just... keep the comm link open. I need to know she's okay."

"Doc, she's a bounty hunter with a bunch of termination contracts under her belt. She'll be fine."

Doc sighed. "That was her choice. Any fallout, that was on her. I can live with that. But this... this is on me. I put her into this situation."

Wraith could hear the man's anguish, but there was nothing he could do about it. They had to move forward.

"Call Major Owens. I'll get her clear. Wraith out."

# 38

It took a swim followed by a free-climb up the fortress—made easy by the age and condition of the ancient stone blocks—in order for Keel to find a way inside. The sentries positioned on the roof, when they could be bothered to look out at all, only watched the distant jungle, as though they expected some terrible, giant saurian horror to rise above the canopy and stomp toward them howling. Keel had his blaster ready as he clung to his hand and foot holds, ready to shoot should he be spotted, but the need never arose.

He entered through a window that lacked even ancient glass and was simply an open portal. By then he'd held firm to the stones long enough that the water from his swim had mostly dripped away. His boots left some imprint on the stone floor, but the room was as empty as it was primitive. No artificial lighting, no indication that the place even had power, just dank stone and a scent of mildew in the air.

A doorway without a door led out to a hall, where hastily affixed lights were strung high on the walls. So—there was a power source somewhere. Still, the interior of the fortress felt almost like a cave, the hallway a mine shaft.

"I'm inside," Wraith told Doc. "The MCR base is in an old castle from who knows when. Practically a ruin. About to start the search for Zora. Any word from Owens?"

He eased out into the hallway, watching for holocams as he moved toward a stairwell. This top floor seemed almost completely unused. None of the rooms had doors, and the rooms he passed were used only for storage, pieces of tech and equipment stacked high, some still in its packaging. The MCR was either still moving in, or they didn't have enough assets here to need the space for anything else.

"Not yet," Doc said. "Can't imagine it'll take too long, though. And you'd better not either."

"Copy."

Wraith spotted his first holocam halfway down the hall, pointing toward the stairwell, watching for anyone who might be coming up. Though from what he'd seen, Wraith imagined that no one but whoever was assigned guard duty on the roof ever bothered to come up.

The holocam was a residential-grade device that had been stuck on the wall well within Wraith's reach. Some lazy tech had probably stood on his tiptoes and just slapped the thing on. There was no need for an expensive slice kit—not that he had one on him. He could simply disconnect the power supply, which was running down from a wire and into a conduit box along the base of the wall. The stone was evidently too thick to run wires through, so everything was packed neatly out in the open.

Although he knew he was dealing with the MCR, Keel had nevertheless expected this particular group to be a bit more sophisticated than this. They had the credits and organizational know-how to acquire a KRS model war bot after all, plus Legion armor and weapons. But the shammers, the patrollers who'd picked up Zora, and now the castle security, painted a very different picture. The MCR had some brains and organization somewhere, driving this operation, but they clearly weren't on this moon. It must be just a collection or support site—a place where the hijackers could cross-load any stolen freight and rest their boarding crews.

Outside the holocam's view, Wraith pried open the conduit box, fished out several small wires until he found the cam's, and then cut it with his knife. A green light on the holocam disappeared, along with, presumably, the feed. He placed the wires back in the box and closed it back up. Someone might come to check out the signal loss, but by the time they realized the cause of the failure, Wraith would be long gone.

A sudden shuffling of feet in one of the doorless rooms farther down the hall sent Wraith ducking into one of the doorways in the event that someone stepped out into the corridor. But after a moment the shuffling settled down and stopped altogether.

He stepped back into the hall, padded softly toward the room where the sound had come from, and peered around the edge of the doorway. An MCR tech sat on an overturned crate, his face washed in a ghostly blue glow from the holoscreens he studied. Every so often, the tech swiped his hand in the air, causing the coloration of the screens to change as he scrolled through whatever he was looking at.

*Security feeds*, thought Wraith.

This was too good an opportunity to pass up. Wraith ducked back out of sight around the side of the doorway, magnetically affixed Zora's blaster rifle to his armor, and pulled his knife.

Then he calmly stepped right into the center of the doorway.

The rebel's face lit up in surprise as he attempted to process the sudden intrusion. Wraith threw his knife, and it embedded its blade deep into the man's skull, causing the tech to fall from his makeshift seat, dead.

Wraith stepped up beside the tech's corpse and examined the holostation. Sure enough, this was where they had set up security monitoring. And as he scrolled through the holocam feeds, he found that it had access to seemingly every station in the castle.

There were only three levels. Wraith occupied the third, which had only the one holocam monitoring the stairwell. The second level looked to have been crudely converted into some kind of command and control center. A large hall—maybe a throne room once—had been partitioned to create something like offices. A dais stacked with supplies sat toward one end of the room's open space, and a holotable sat in the middle of the hall. From this angle Keel couldn't make out what was holographically displayed on it.

He lingered on the Level 2 cams, hoping to get lucky and catch a glimpse of Zora being interrogated by an officer type. But if she was, it would be in the privacy of one of the offices, and he could only see into a few. Wraith would have to move down to inspect directly, and he'd have to be careful. Unlike Level 3, the level below had several MCR officers and a few armed security personnel. None looked to be on high alert, though.

He moved on to Level 1, which was easily the most formidable and had the most cams. He had views of a mess hall and an armory, and judging by the number of off-duty MCR troops in the halls, that level had to house the barracks as well.

Still no sign of Zora, though.

The castle also had a sublevel that consisted of winding, catacomb-like tunnels. Here Wraith found the two places where he was most likely to find Zora: an infirmary, and a small, dungeon-like jail cell. The dungeon was empty, and the infirmary door was closed. But even if Zora wasn't there now—if she was elsewhere being interrogated—she would end up in one of those locations sooner or later.

Not wanting to waste the opportunity to get his bearings on the facility, Wraith went once more through all the holocams, trying to map a mental picture. The sublevel was the most complicated. It had clearly once been catacombs, and consisted of a maze of dead ends and narrow, winding corridors. One corridor let out into a surprisingly non-ancient-looking warehouse full of MCR techs who were either effecting repairs or loading up contents for a freight elevator that went up somewhere. Keel didn't know where until he cycled to the roof and saw that it let out straight onto the landing pad where the shuttle was parked. The warehouse space, the elevator, and the landing pad appeared to be the only significant improvements to the castle that the Mid-Core rebels had bothered to construct.

"What's the status?" Doc asked impatiently in Keel's ear.

"Working a security station. One E-KIA. Gonna hide the body and then go and find Zora."

"You see her on the cams?"

"Negative. This place isn't all that big, though. I'll find her. You just work on getting a kill team here. They're gonna want to start slicing these databanks. Wraith out."

Keel felt bad for the old man; Doc was clearly worried for his daughter. At the same time, Wraith needed to focus on his mission. The MCR didn't possess a legendary fighting prowess, but there were enough of them in this base of operations to present a problem all the same. And if Wraith were detected, and the Mids put two and two together and realized he might be connected with the "survivor" they'd just brought in from the jungle, he'd put her in danger as well.

She was in enough danger already. Wraith had to move.

But first he entered a quick series of commands into the holo-security's basic software suite. There might be another security desk that had access to these same feeds, and Wraith couldn't risk being spotted. He couldn't spoof the cams without a slice kit, but he could command them to skip over any dead or dysfunctional cams. He'd have to disable cams as he went, and hope that whoever might be monitoring didn't notice the scroll skipping past certain views.

Before leaving, Wraith did a quick test of his handiwork. When he scrolled to the holocam he'd disabled, there was no telltale black screen, just a direct skip to the next feed. It wasn't a perfect solution, but he planned for him and Zora to be gone by the time anyone noticed.

Finally, he turned his attention to the dead technician at his feet. The blade had gone in so deep and tight that barely a trickle of blood had come out of the wound. That would change when Keel took his knife back. He looked for a place to hide the body out of sight—a place where the corpse could bleed.

A heavy, narrow curtain, perhaps a meter wide, hung in the corner of the room. Wraith pulled it aside and saw that it covered an adjoining privy shared with the next room. It was a simple design as freshers went. A narrow, claustrophobic stall with a flat wooden seat—new wood taken from the jungle—with a hole just large enough for humanoid business to pass through. From there it would carry down the castle and be deposited into the surrounding lake.

Keel removed the seat and confirmed that the waste chute was much larger than a standard sewer pipe. Large enough that he could probably wedge the dead technician inside of it rather than prop him up as though he were relieving his bowels.

He pulled the dead man inside and positioned his dead eyes to look down the privy's exit. He thumbed the activator switch for his vibro-knife and pulled the humming blade easily from the man's skull. A small fountain of blood and liquified brain poured down the drain. Keel stuffed the rest of the man in behind it, closed the curtain, checked the cams once more, and then moved to the stairway leading down to the second level.

"Moving to the second floor," Wraith told Doc, mostly to keep the man from worrying and interrupting him at an inopportune time. It would be a while before the old man could be in position to do anything to help.

The stairs opened directly into the likely former throne room, which was impressive, in a primitive-castle kind of way. The pillars were wide and evenly spaced, the ceiling high and vaulted. The dais was at the farther end of the room, and held stacks of rugged hard cases that looked to be in the process of being unpacked. The "offices" were little more than cubicles with modular walls that didn't reach up even a third of the way to the grand, overhead ceiling. A few had doors, but all were currently open.

At the center of the room, around the holotable, a group of MCR officers were holding a discussion. Keel could see now what was on the holographic display: a representation of the crash site. Also highlighted was a position deeper into the jungle. Keel assumed that was where the patrol had found Zora.

He focused his bucket's audio enhancers on the conversation, hoping he could pick up a scrap of useful intel before moving on. There would be no sneaking on this level without being seen. He'd have to keep to the stairwell and hope that no one came up while he was moving down.

"Hostiles?" Doc asked. So much for not being interrupted.

"Plenty. Gonna see if I hear anything about Zora and then move on."

"Just shoot 'em," said Doc.

"*Wait one*, old man. I'm not getting into a firefight until I have to."

He focused on the officers' conversation.

"... the crash site investigation," he heard someone say. "It appears that DW-88 malfunctioned and instructed the war bot to kill the boarding team."

"Did you send the report forward?" asked another voice.

"I was waiting until you'd heard it, Colonel."

"Don't wait. Not with *him*," the unnamed colonel answered.

Keel's heart raced. Whoever they were speaking of, he sounded important.

"Shall I reach him on comms?"

"Yes," the MCR colonel answered.

There was a pause as the aide set up a comm connection on a datapad. Moments later the call was answered with a sing-song chime.

"Sir, this is Colonel Axelsson," the MCR colonel said. "We have completed our investigation of the freighter crash and believe there was a significant AI malfunction that resulted in the death of the boarding crew. A survivor of the regular crew was found in the jungle and is undergoing treatment prior to interrogation."

"Send me the particulars after the interrogation, my boy. Do we still have the war bot?"

That voice. Keel knew he'd heard it before. Where?

The colonel reported that the bot was a total loss. The familiar voice reiterated the need for a full report, and the comm call was over. The MCR officers took up some new order of business not relating to Zora.

But now Wraith had confirmation that she was receiving treatment. And where else would that happen but the infirmary? He just needed to get there, undetected, before the Mids could move on to interrogation. The MCR's particular brand of questioning wasn't as bad as the zhee's, but it was bad enough that you might not live to see the end of it if you started it in the kind of condition Zora was in the last time he'd seen her.

Keel quickly cut another holocam wire and moved down to the castle's ground level.

"She's not on Level Two," he told Doc. "Sounds like they have her in the infirmary, which is in the sublevel. On the move."

There must have been something in Keel's voice that Doc picked out.

"What's up, kid? You sound off. Did something happen to my baby girl? Don't hide that sket from me. So help me —"

"No," Keel said, the limits of his understanding being tested. Doc had an emotional attachment, one he felt responsible for bringing into this mess. But Keel still had to operate. "I just... I heard a voice. Familiar, but I can't place it. Something in my gut is telling me that whoever it is, is important."

Doc sighed. "Find out who it is."

"It'll come to me. For now, I've got to focus on getting Zora."

"All right." There was a pause. "Listen... kid. Leej to leej. I want my daughter back safe and sound. You know I do. But... the mission. If you need to get that ident for Owens—"

"I already got as much as I can get. Moving to Zora's pos. Wraith out."

He moved quickly down the stairwell, disabling yet another holocam before peering out into the main corridor on this level. A few troopers moved from place to place, but there was a sense of idleness among these rebels. Given how many MCR compounds Ford had hit while he was with Kill Team Victory, this didn't come as a surprise. Mids reacted well enough to violence, but rarely did they seem prepared for it.

Wraith had to make a quick crossing over an open landing before he could continue on to the sublevel. He would pass within sight of a few troopers wearing stolen Legion armor, the same variety as those he'd encountered on the hijacked Galaxy-class freighter. These men seemed morose, and Wraith imagined it was because they had lost friends.

Seeing, though, that the MCR were at least *somewhat* accustomed to Legion armor, Wraith chose to slow his dash down to a casual walk as he moved across the open landing to the stairs leading down. If any of the Mids saw him, he wanted them to think he was just another of their pirate band.

No one raised an alarm. His luck held.

It was on that final, winding flight of ancient and well-worn steps that the owner of that voice suddenly came to him.

*Scarpia.*

*That* was the voice; he was sure of it. He'd heard it before, on the last day that Kags and Twenties had still drawn breath. But... how could that be? Scarpia was a prisoner of the Republic. Surely if the MCR had freed him, Keel would have been notified.

Or... maybe not.

Did anyone ever really know everything that was happening? Was it possible to really know the hearts of so many men in power, moving, killing, resetting the game board?

If it wasn't, Keel wouldn't be here, the operator told himself. And he was just Dark Ops. Within Nether Ops there were layers upon layers of additional secrecy.

But that *was* Scarpia. Who should be rotting on Herbeer. They had taken him, pulled him from that corvette, before it could destroy the House of Reason.

Which meant this... was big. Bigger than a hijacking ring. The MCR wouldn't be capable of something like that by themselves. This had to—*had to*—involve activity deep inside the Republic itself.

This was exactly the sort of thing Ford had been sent to uncover.

Wraith was sure of it.

As he quickly but quietly padded down the stairwell, he unmuted comms. "Doc, that voice belongs to an arms dealer named Scarpia."

"That name s'posed to mean somethin' to me?"

"No, but it does to me. There was a mission. My kill team took him in. He's supposed to be on Herbeer. No way he should be here. No way."

"You got visuals?"

"Negative. But it's him, Doc. I'm certain."

"All right, I'll pass the message along to Owens. Maybe that'll trigger a faster response time, because he don't seem to be in his office right now. You go find Zora."

"Roger. On the move."

# 39

"The Antobyne should be in full effect by now," the doctor said. "How are you feeling?"

He hovered over Zora with a look of detached concern, his mouth saying all the right words but his eyes lacking emotion. He had cleaned out her wounds, applied new skinpacks, and attached an Antobyne anti-venom/anti-infection diffuser to the back of her wrist, but he'd done it all with rough hands free of compassion.

Looking down, Zora saw that she'd lost her clothes. Under a blanket, she wore only a thin hospital gown. The room was cold, but just ordinary cold. No chills. The fever was gone.

"Better," she said. "The throbbing on my face aside."

In truth, her face was the least of her concerns, but if she ever got hold of the man who had slapped her, it would be the greatest of *his*.

The doctor's watery gray eyes held her gaze. "I apologize for any mistreatment, Miss...?"

"Zoey."

"Miss Zoey. The Mid-Core Rebellion has grown somewhat... rougher in recent years."

"Rougher? Is that what you call what happened on Rhyssis Wan, Doctor?"

He frowned. "That I call genocide. As do many of my fellow patriots in the MCR. We will do better. But we haven't lost sight of the injustices of the Republic, either."

There was a knock at the door, and a guard walked in, one hand on his blaster. "Here to escort the prisoner."

The doctor stepped between the guard and Zora's bed. "Almost ready. Please wait outside."

With a nod, the guard said, "Colonel Axelsson wants a full interrogation as soon as she's able. Scarpia is asking."

"I am aware," the doctor said through clenched teeth. "Wait."

The guard stepped back outside.

"Prisoner?" Zora said, making her voice small. "I'm a spacewreck survivor. You rescued me. I don't understand."

"Don't you?" the doctor said. He stepped closer to the bed. Too close. "You're about to be interrogated, Miss Zoey. Aggressively. My superiors are under the impression that something happened on that ship of yours. Powerful people want to know what *you* know."

Zora shrank under her sheet. "Is this that MCR 'roughness' you were just telling me about?"

"These are rough times all across the galaxy, Miss Zoey. But perhaps I can help you. *Before* things have to get rough. Tell me what happened on that ship."

Zora could sense the ambition behind the doctor's request. This Colonel Axelsson, and whoever this Scarpia was, likely cut a big wake through the MCR waters. The doctor was sensing an opportunity to get them what they wanted... himself.

Maybe Zora could use that. But first she would play along with the feverish plan she barely remembered Keel telling her—a simple plan that would have been easy enough to fall into herself. She had been dreadfully ill not long before and had no idea how much of her strength had returned. Best to continue to play the forlorn survivor of a Galaxy-class freighter for as long as she could.

"There's hardly anything to tell," she said earnestly. "I heard shooting. An alarm, an explosion that knocked me out. And when I woke up, the ship had crashed. I was lucky to stumble out of it before it blew sky-high."

The doctor looked disappointed. "No. You know something further. The truth, perhaps. And things will go much easier for you if you tell *me*, here and now. Before the man waiting outside comes in for you. Because once you're with them... all I'll be able to do for you is treat whatever gruesome wounds they leave you with after their questioning. That's my job. To reattach what they cut off. So they can do it again. And again. However many times is necessary."

Tears sprang to Zora's eyes. An old trick that her father had encouraged once he'd realized she could do it. *A sobbing woman is a weakness of men. Use it.*

"I'm sorry, Doctor!" she cried. "I wish I could remember more, but I was unconscious!"

He tsked. "Such a horrible liar. Here, look. The crew manifest." He turned his datapad over for her to see. "No females. Not even a male with the name Zoey listed. I want the *truth*. Are you Republic military? What unit?"

Zora looked from the list to the doctor's stony face. She willed more tears before sobbing, "I... I don't understand. My name is Zoey. I—"

The doctor clamped his icy hand over her mouth and nose, cutting off her cries before she could release a startled yelp. "No more stalling. I want the truth. Tell me who you are."

She looked up at the man, eyes fearful. That was an emotion she didn't have to fake.

He lifted his hand. "This is your final opportunity. What happened up there? How did you escape? Who helped you? Was it the Legion? Who else is out there?"

The door swung open, and the doctor turned, angry at the intrusion. "I told you—"

Growling like a ram-panther, Zora grabbed the doctor's head and thwacked it down into the bed's metal side bar. But before she could get in so much as a follow-up punch, Wraith had flung the man into the wall. He collapsed to the floor in a heap, unconscious.

"Well, look who decided to join the party," Zora said. Her strength was coming back quickly now, thanks to the adrenaline.

Wraith looked her up and down as she hurried out of the treatment bed. "You're better. Good." There was a pause. "Doc says hello."

Zora's eyes lit up. "You have comms with him again?"

Wraith nodded as he stepped back out to drag the dead guard into the infirmary and dump him beside the senseless doctor. He shut the door.

"Get dressed. You'll have to go as either a doctor or a guard."

"Where's my kit?" Zora asked.

"Stashed it outside before breaching this place." He unslung her blaster rifle from around his neck and shoulder and placed it on the bed. "Brought you this, though." He also held out the micro-comm from her helmet. "And this."

"I'll pick the guard." Zora slipped the comm in her ear and checked the charge pack. "You thought of everything." She made a face at something only she heard, then tapped her comm. "Yes, Dad, I'm fine. Wraith is here now. Can't talk now, okay? Just get here."

Wraith turned his back while Zora changed into the MCR guard's uniform. The fit was loose, but not baggy. And much better than a hospital gown.

"Surprised you haven't tried to turn around and peek, jump jockey," Zora said with a grin. "But I guess you had plenty of time for that while I was out of it in the jungle."

Wraith didn't answer except to hold up a finger. He was focusing on something.

"What?" Zora asked. "You got something on comms?"

"Yeah," Wraith said, and in turning to answer her caught a glimpse of her half-dressed state. "My boss."

In Wraith's bucket, Major Owens came on, sounding as cool as an iced kava on a Pthalo beach. Doc had finally gotten in touch with him, and had patched him through directly to Wraith. Keel was eager to move on from the med bay—who knew how long it would be before someone came looking for Zora or that guard—but taking the time to know what Dark Ops intended to do about this place would surely influence Keel's own plans for getting out.

"So you found somethin', Captain Ford."

The Legion officer in Wraith took over. "Yes, sir. I tracked down what appears to be a significant MCR starship hijacking ring. I think this is how they're getting those big private ships refitted for naval warfare. There's some weapons smuggling, too—N-6 rifles, ordnance, even a war bot."

"And then there's Scarpia," Owens said, jumping to the point before Keel could. "That man should be laboring in the mines of Herbeer. Brought up his file and it says he *is* on Herbeer. So what I need from you right now is this: Are you sure it's him?"

"It's him or an AI based on him, Major. Vocal patterns, inflections... all the same. You send in the guys from Victory, they'll uncover more."

"I have no doubt they will. Do you believe Scarpia is on-site?"

"Negative, sir. I think he's operating somewhere remotely. But the Mids here, they all indicate that the owner of that voice—Scarpia—is who they're working for."

"I'll send in the kill team anyway. Any intel they can grab from this place, we need our eyes on first."

Keel nodded. "Yes, sir."

A kill team would also go a long way toward helping Wraith and Zora get out of the base alive—and then not have to run back through that brutal jungle with pursuers. Doc and the *Six* would be out there, but the ship could only do so much.

"Captain Ford," Owens continued, "there's no escaping Herbeer. It doesn't happen—*can't* happen. If this is genuine—if we're not just talking about these kelhorns using some 'good old days' code name—then it means that someone *let* Scarpia leave. Someone with high connections in the Republic, the military, hell the guards on Herbeer... all or a few. We need to find out who."

Ford assumed the major was leading him into his next assignment. Given the circumstances, he felt that ought to have waited. There would be time for next steps once he and Zora were clear. "Yes, sir."

"I've shared with Andien Broxin the location of this moon and the belief that Scarpia may somehow be involved. Asked her to pull some Nether Ops strings and make a visit to Herbeer. We can trust her to help suss out who delivered that man from the mines."

"Understood, sir." It wasn't a decision that Wraith would have made—he'd worked with Broxin in the past and thought her capable, but she wasn't a legionnaire, and Nether Ops only seemed interested in fighting its own little wars on its own terms. Keel didn't trust them, and by extension, neither did he trust her.

"What's your plan for exfil?" Owens asked.

"Won't be easy," Ford said. "We can probably sneak out of the facility without notice of the guards, but it's a ticking chrono until they discover that we've been here. I'd expect that we'll be hunted into the jungle until Doc can pick us up. Only... if my ship is seen, that might jeopardize my cover unless your kill team can wipe this place clean before any intel goes out."

Owens let out a deep sigh from his nostrils and thought for a moment. "Captain, I want you to stay put if you can. Once my team arrives, you should be able to move free and clear. Can you remain undetected in your location?"

Playing hide and seek inside the castle wouldn't be easy once the MCR realized that their prisoner was missing. But neither would another run through the jungle with pursuers on their heels. This place was big, its sensor systems were subpar... hiding out might be feasible so long as help came eventually.

"I think we can find a place to remain hidden inside the facility," Ford said. "What's the team's ETA?"

"ETA four hours. They'll pull you out if things get too hot, let you slip away otherwise. If you uncover anything else during that time, you let me know about it. Do you understand, Captain?"

Wraith glanced back at Zora. "Understood."

"Good luck. KTF. Owens out."

The transmission ended, but not the conversation. Doc must have been eavesdropping on the latter part of it, because now he jumped in over the all-comm.

"That's the wrong call, kid."

"Well, those are my orders."

"Orders aside, it's the wrong call."

"So what's the right call, old man?"

"You really gotta ask? Forget hiding and sneaking around. You're already inside. You need to find their armory and blow it to the nine hells. Watch the fireworks from the *Six*. Won't be anyone left alive to spoil your cover or shoot at that kill team. Slicers can grab intel from a bombed-out terminal as good as an intact one."

Keel wasn't so sure about that, and Owens probably wanted to speak with some survivors as well. "I have my orders. We have to stay put until the kill team arrives, and then we'll hand it off to them."

"Don't give me 'orders'—you're already walkin' that edge, *been* walkin' that edge since I known you. And you know as well as I do, the galaxy—the Republic—it ain't all one big happy family. There are some monsters in the closets. And when you see one... you kill it. Trust me. If I'd have done the same back when I was in Dark Ops, well, maybe things wouldn't be quite so bad nowadays."

"Or you'd be in prison," Zora put in, and Keel realized he and Doc had already said too much. She'd been excluded from the chat with Owens, but this latest exchange was enough for her to put two and two together. Then again, she'd mostly done that already anyway.

"Small price to pay," Doc told his daughter.

"Listen," Zora continued, "I'm fine. You want us to get out of here. I understand that. Appreciate it, even. But it's probably for the best that we hang low and wait for a kill team to come in here and give us the kind of distraction we need to escape."

"The hell with all that," Doc growled. "Get clear and cause as much damage as you can in the process. That's what KTF is about in this situation."

Wraith weighed the old man's words, but couldn't agree. "I'm still a legionnaire," he said. "If Dark Ops wanted me to blow this place, they'd have told me to do it. They didn't, so I won't."

"Kid—"

"Enough," Zora said. "We can fight about it later. Right now we need to move before we get discovered. You got a plan for that, Keel?"

He nodded. "Yeah. I got a good sense of the layout of this place from a security station. There's catacombs below this level where we should be able to hide easily enough. From there we can work our way toward a warehouse with a freight lift and lots of exit routes, so we won't get pinned down if it comes to that. Which it probably will when they discover you're gone. Did you give them the story about being crew?"

"I did, and they didn't buy it." Zora gestured her chin toward the MCR bodies on the floor. "That doctor—you wanna kill him, or can I?—said a Colonel Axelsson and someone named Scarpia wanted me interrogated."

Keel looked up. Neither he nor Doc had said that name outside of his private call with Owens. She wouldn't have heard it from them. "Scarpia? They said that exact name?"

"Yeah. Why? Is he your mission?"

Keel gave a slight shrug. "It's starting to look like he's a part of it. Doc, tell Owens that—"

"Already reaching back out, kid. Not that Zora's hearing the name is gonna change anything, seeing as he's already sending down a kill team as it is. Look, about the thing: Just... just don't hesitate to start dusting these kelhorns. They deserve it. All of them."

"I heard you the first time, old man." Keel tilted his head, assessing how Zora looked in the uniform. All things considered, she wore it well. "We lucked out with that uniform," he told her. "That guard was on the smaller side for a man, and you're big for a woman." At her raised eyebrow, he quickly added: "I mean... not *big*. Definitely not big. Just... tall. *Good* tall. Built for bounty hunting."

She smirked. "Nice recovery."

Then she dialed back the charge in her rifle and sent a bolt into the doctor's head. Enough to eliminate the witness and deprive the man of the opportunity to sound an alarm later. That would be a job for whoever finally found this mess.

"Seriously," Wraith said, hands up in surrender. "For the record: *not big*."

# 40

Captain Silas Devers surveyed the control bridge of the Republic Destroyer *Brutus*. Officers conversed in polite undertones, steady sensor alerts glowed, and everything proceeded in perfect order. *His* perfect order.

"Captain," his communications officer said. "Priority message for you from Utopion, sir."

"I'll take it in my quarters," Captain Devers replied.

"Yes, sir."

Leaving Commander Landoo in charge of the bridge, Devers strode through the blast doors to his own nearby quarters. One might call them spartan in their simplicity. The décor's aesthetic was white with silvene accents. Elegant but not pretentious. On the far wall, a few hanging holos commemorated his life's achievements.

Devers delivering the valedictory commencement speech at the Republic's officer academy on White Hall.

Devers receiving a silvene medal at the Pan-Galactic Hyperchess Championship.

Devers, shirtless on an Endurian beach, with a beautiful, smiling Spilursan heiress.

Devers, Legion helmet removed and grit covering his sweat-stained face and armor, standing with his fellow appointed officers before the ruins of an insurgent city that had risen against the Republic.

Devers, Order of the Centurion proudly hanging from his neck as he shook the hands of House of Reason delegates and Republic senators following his accounting of his heroic deeds on Kublar.

And the most recent of his collection: Devers, now in the Republic Navy, at the helm of the *Brutus*, his latest command. It always impressed him how well he filled out his uniform. A testament to the success that comes with dedication to personal discipline.

But these reminders of better times failed to drive away the concern the captain felt at receiving a priority message from the Republic's capital world. That would be Orrin Kaar. An unscheduled call from the delegate could only portend bad news.

He stifled his thoughts of concern and took the call. "Delegate Kaar! A welcome surprise. I hadn't expected to hear from you for another week."

"Silas," said the most powerful man in the House of Reason—some would say the entire galaxy. "I'm afraid the purpose for this call is... less than ideal."

Devers arched an eyebrow. "Complications approving the budget? Do you need to me deliver another speech to the House of Reason?"

Kaar's answer removed the smile from Devers's face. "Complications of another sort. It seems that one of our intelligence agencies has discovered that Mr. Scarpia is not on Herbeer."

Devers's mind raced. "Do they have him? If he were to start talking..."

Kaar waved a hand to silence him. "They do not. However, circumstances suggest that intel on his whereabouts is being gathered. A ship procured for the Black Fleet crashed near the processing facility, and a person claiming to be a 'surviving crewmember' was taken into custody—only to somehow escape from her captors. She is presently at large within the facility. Shortly thereafter, sources on Herbeer passed on information about a Nether Ops agent scheduling a sudden, previously unplanned visit. The agent did not specify who they wished to speak to."

Devers took in a breath and held it.

"The constriction you feel about your throat is a noose, Silas. We must act quickly to ensure it is tightened no further. If the Legion has stumbled upon this operation, they will send a kill team to the crash site and processing facility. They will find nothing. You are positioned to be there in less than an hour—well ahead of the kill team—and you will destroy it. A thorough orbital bombardment should sufficiently remove anyone capable of speaking the name 'Scarpia' to the legionnaires once they arrive."

Devers doubted that. He would need to send in troops prior to the bombardment. Kill as many of the MCR as possible as they moved to secure the exits. He'd need visual confirmation that everyone who knew of Scarpia's involvement, all the way up to Colonel Axelsson, was dead.

And he knew just the man for that job.

"But first you will pick up Scarpia," Kaar continued. "He is even closer than you are, and his shuttle will meet you on the roof of the facility. You will take him directly to Herbeer. I'm quite certain all will blow over once the Legion realizes it was... *misinformed* by whatever intelligence asset infiltrated the hijacking ring and gave up the name."

Devers frowned. Regardless of what Kaar said, he had no way of knowing if he would be "well ahead of" an inbound kill team. And if the Legion were to arrive while he was picking up Scarpia...

But it made sense. He'd be landing with his own kill team anyway, in order to clear the facility; grabbing Scarpia in the process would be easy. He could even frame it as an element of the assault, capturing an HVT for questioning.

Assuming the brash fool stayed put as he was supposed to.

Still, Devers hesitated at voicing his real concern—the larger problem as he saw it. He owed his entire career to Delegate Kaar, the man who had appointed him to the Legion as a junior officer, the first step in a meteoric climb that would one day result in a delegate position of his own.

"Destroying that base and losing the... *procurement* ring, Delegate, will set back our progress in outfitting the Black Fleet by months."

Delegate Kaar gave an irritating laugh. "We will find ways to make it up to our friend Goth Sullus."

Kaar spoke the name with derision. Sullus was merely a tool for the Mandarin's larger vision. A maniac warlord with delusions of grandeur but a distinct ability to drain the Legion of capable warriors. A dual victory that, because eventually the Legion would need to be dealt with. Eventually it would all be too much for Legion Commander Keller and his generals, and they would declare Article Nineteen.

Plans of a different sort were prepared for that.

Devers took a breath to calm himself. He had, perhaps, shown weakness just now. What should he care about the warlord? Goth Sullus. Another spanner in the toolbox. A man who owed all he had to the delegate's network. Sullus would have to wait... and so would Devers, whose grand moment—whose ascendance—would come in tandem with Sullus's arrival.

"Understood, Delegate Kaar. I'll get it done."

"I have no doubt you will."

The transmission ended. Devers commed the bridge.

A moment later Landoo's image appeared. "Captain?"

"Set a course for the ninth moon of Morgan," Devers ordered. "We have actionable intelligence that an MCR base is located there."

"Right away, Captain."

Devers could feel the ship begin to drift as it oriented itself for the proper hyperspace routes. He opened another comm, and almost winced when the face of a scarred, one-eyed man came up in the holo. Devers found it odd that the man would *choose* to go around like that. Perhaps he found it intimidating. Devers found it repulsive.

But then... this man had been plucked from the very edge of insanity out of the heap of discarded trash that was former Nether Ops agents. His loyalty to Delegate Kaar and those representing him was impressive. A man without purpose, once redeemed and restored, could accomplish much.

Devers made a mental note to write that down for his memoir. A work in progress.

"Go for Hess," said the scarred, one-eyed soldier.

"Major Hess... prepare your kill team. I want you ready to drop with our full complement of marines inside sixty minutes. After that, you are to find me personally for a confidential briefing."

"Yes, sir, Captain Devers."

The captain's forces were on the move. The game, with all its twists and turns, continued on its way. And Devers, as he had always done, would emerge the victor.

*Brutus*'s main hangar buzzed with activity. Deck hands hustled to perform final maintenance checks. Repulsor carts zipped past, hauling munitions and fuel to waiting dropships. Cadenced boots pounded to reach their stations. This was what they had trained for, prepared for, existed for—to respond to their call to action.

Major Hess approved. The gray-haired veteran looked over the men and women under his command. He could trust his hand-selected kill team, all wearing Legion armor and with Legion training, to perform their duties without so much as a word. These were Nether Ops agents, much as Hess had been. It was Nether Ops, embedded so deeply in every crevice of the Republic, that gave visionaries like Kaar the room needed to reshape the galaxy into something truly great.

Hess's men could be trusted. Unquestionably. The Republic marines they would operate alongside, however, he was less certain of.

The mustachioed marine captain Tuxhorn stepped forward to address the assembled hullbusters.

"Intel has identified an MCR base of operations on a moon previously believed to be uninhabited. Atmo is breathable, but make sure you took the Antobyne the corpsmen have been issuing—none of that hide-it-under-your-tongue-and-spit-it-out twarg dung. Our objective is a stone structure manned by MCR regulars. *Brutus*'s kill team will be joining us in an effort to grab an HVT."

Tuxhorn paused to look accusingly at Hess for not having provided him with more intel than what he'd given.

Hess knew what the captain was thinking. Was this HVT a hostile they wanted to interrogate? An agent that needed to be pulled out?

Of course, Hess had given the marine captain no more intel because there was no need. Hess's legionnaires were to ensure that Scarpia left with them and only them; the marines would never so much as get a glimpse of the man.

But Tuxhorn's marines would be quite helpful with the second part of the plan: ensuring that everyone else on the planet ended up dead.

Tuxhorn continued address his men. "It's up to you marines to drop near the compound and assault from the ground level and on up. We're used to breaching impervisteel hulls; we can handle stone walls without difficulty. Yes, Lieutenant Paris?"

The slight man, an appointed officer, held up a datapad. "Sir, on reviewing the plan with Sergeant Quezada, the roof looks large and stable enough to support dropship landings."

"So it is," the captain said. "Major Hess's kill team will be landing on the roof to secure the target." Tuxhorn looked to Hess. "What did you say this person's role in all this was?"

A valiant attempt.

"I didn't," Hess responded.

Sergeant Quezada's hand shot up again. "Captain Tuxhorn, without any idents or visuals on the target... All due respect... that's how mistakes get made, sir."

Hess frowned. Over-eager as always, these marines seemed intent on involving themselves in his mission. He needed to shut this down.

"You hullbusters just worry about killing every MCR traitor inside and around the facility," he said. "*We* will take care of the target. It is *not* your concern. Word of advice, marines: you want to avoid mistakes getting made? Stay off my kelhorned roof. Now, let's load up these damned shuttles. Captain Devers wants us on the ground thirty minutes from now. We will do it in twenty."

# 41

Wraith and Zora moved through the maze-like catacombs of the sublevel, following a crude HUD map Keel had put together based on what he *thought* the area should look like from its various holocams. But the map proved woefully inadequate. There were several dead ends and hardly any lights, and those places that *were* well-lit tended invariably to be filled with MCR troopers going about their business. Keel had already established that he could pass as a Mid in leej armor—at a distance, anyway—but he was less confident that Zora wouldn't attract attention. The castle wasn't intimately small, but the MCR garrison seemed tiny enough that people would spot an unfamiliar face.

So they stuck to the darker tunnels, trusting that eventually they'd find their way to the warehouse. It was tempting to wait things out in the dark of the tunnels, but it would be far too easy to get pinned down should someone come looking for them. The warehouse remained the best place to hide while retaining the ability to move if things went pear-shaped.

The dry floors near the infirmary soon gave way to wet, dank environs, with water often coming as high as mid-heel. The walls were mildewed and mold-infested, the lake slowly seeping its way in through Oba knew how many meters of heavy stone and mortar. The steady *drip... drip... drip...* was a constant in the winding passageways. While Wraith could see well enough with his bucket, it had been long enough since they'd last seen another soul—or holocam—that he didn't object when Zora suggested she use the dead guard's ultrabeam so she could better see where she was stepping.

"Okay, moment of truth," he said as they neared the edge of his hasty HUD map. "If I got this right, we'll run out of real estate once we make this bend. It *should* lead into the main passageway to the warehouse. If it doesn't, we're gonna have to double back and find another way."

"Or just walk through the lit passageways and take our chances," Zora suggested.

"Or that."

They came around the bend, and Zora's ultrabeam illuminated a solid wall blocking their way forward. It appeared to have once had a doorway, but one that had been sealed off using the same stone squares as the rest of the catacombs.

Zora sighed. "Dead end. Guess we're doubling back."

"Not so fast," said Keel. "It's an optical illusion. Made to look like a solid wall, but there's an opening here lined up with a second wall behind this one. Like a baffle."

He moved toward the wall, and the illusion that his bucket had identified now became clear to his own eyes. The "wall" was actually two walls, the nearer one with a doorway cut into it, the farther one's lines matching up perfectly so that anyone approaching from the corridor would see only one solid wall.

Wraith ducked inside, then re-emerged to tell Zora, "This cutout is full of old bones, but it looks like it goes right through to where we want to be. Turn off your ultrabeam just in case we pop out where we don't want to be seen."

Zora did as instructed, and he held her hand to guide her as he moved forward.

"Funny-looking bones," Keel said. "Some kind of unfamiliar aliens must have built this place. C'mon... looks like it lets out the same way on the other side."

They stepped out into a space that mirrored the layout of the second-floor throne room, but with much tighter confines. Stone sarcophagi in the center marked the room as a tomb.

"Think we found the guys who built this place," Wraith said. "Or was related to whoever did. Feels older than the Ancients."

On the walls were stone sconces that dripped with the same moisture that permeated the rest of the building; clearly no fire had dried this room in ages.

They went forward, slowly, as Zora was completely blind.

"Almost there?" she asked.

"Think so. Thought I heard something up ahead. Could have been a repulsor. Or could be something else."

"Something else what?"

"Maybe something with big teeth."

That seemed to be the outcome Zora was least hoping for judging by the way she squeezed his hand.

They proceeded through ankle-high water and toward the end of the ossuary and tomb. The floor was slightly inclined, rising a bit with every step until they were once more on relatively dry ground. They reached a faux wall exactly like the one they had passed through to enter the tomb, but this time the soft glow of a dim light came from the other side.

Zora went to the right of the baffle and Keel to the left until both were looking down a stone corridor that Keel was confident led to the warehouse he intended as their destination.

"Place is big enough to drive a repulsor truck through," Zora noted.

"Think that might be what I heard," Wraith said.

Wraith recognized this spot from the holocams and knew that he'd brought them to the right location and without MCR interference. Ahead would be a bustling warehouse with its freight elevator leading up to the rooftop. Plenty of MCR working, but lots of places to hide as well. There came around yet another bend in the sublevel's catacombs, and sure enough, they'd arrived.

"What's our move?" Zora asked.

"Walk over to those crates," Wraith said, pointing to where he meant. "Looks like no one is working them, and there are some shadows and another tunnel within running distance if things go south. Just walk with a purpose, head down so no one has a chance to recognize you—or realize they *don't* recognize you."

"I know how to be discreet. Come on."

She led the way, hurrying to the cargo crates. Wraith timed the repetitive movements of the dock workers and then swiftly followed her when they weren't looking, sliding to a stop behind the crates and then listening over a pounding heart to see whether they'd been spotted.

No alarm sounded.

"All right, we've got our hiding spot," Wraith said. "At least until they want these crates."

Zora examined the stenciled boxes. "From the amount of dust, I don't think there's a good chance they'll start moving them today. 'Vackard.' Why do I know that name?"

Wraith looked at the Vackard logo Zora had just read from one of the crates. "Industrial supplier. Mostly military. Probably saw some surplus somewhere. Do me a favor and see if you can get an ETA from your old man on when he thinks the *Six* will be nearby."

"You getting antsy about this plan to lay low?"

"Just want all our options available."

While Zora quietly worked the comm, Wraith observed the MCR. Some were inspecting and staging cargo. Others were working over starship parts, cutting with the plating still intact, their torches sending up bright showers of sparking light. There was an attentiveness to the work, but nothing suggesting that they were on alert.

Zora gave a report on her father. "He's entered atmosphere, but he's keeping a wide berth of our comm triangulations in order to not show up on any sensors."

There hadn't been much in the way of moon-wide sensors that Keel had seen, but it was wise to be cautious. "Did he deploy a TT-16?"

Zora nodded. "Seeded it in atmo. It's in freefall toward the castle. He said he'd ping you once it was in visual range. What do you see out there?"

"Nothing that makes me think the MCR knows that you've escaped. A lot of private cargo from previous hijackings."

The pair waited in their hide for several minutes. Wraith occasionally peered around the crates to satisfy any doubts he might have felt. But the pace and tenor of the MCR work hadn't changed; it was just another day.

"Heads up, kiddos," Doc growled over the comm channel. "There's an atmospheric shuttle that just lifted off the roof. Got eyes on it from the obs bot. Keel, sending you the feed."

The image was in Keel's HUD a few seconds later. The observation bot was holding back, probably at its maximum altitude, but he could clearly see the shuttle lifting off, and for a sinking moment he worried about who or what might be on board and about to be whisked to some hide elsewhere on the moon. That would require sending Doc and the *Six* to follow, which might hamper his exfil. But instead the shuttle settled down in a jungle clearing just across the water.

"Looks like they're making some room for an incoming freighter," Doc guessed. "That or they got somethin' what can't be loaded from the roof."

Keel's attention was pulled from the feed by the sound of boots; an armed security team was entering the warehouse from the main corridor. And judging by how they moved—on alert—this was no ordinary patrol. They were looking for someone.

"Zora, I think your handiwork in the infirmary has been found."

"Only a matter of time," she answered.

Wraith was impressed with how the MCR had gone quietly looking for their missing prisoner without doing anything to alert their target that she was being hunted. He had expected a base-wide alarm. And this security detail— MCR troopers wearing tan fatigues with additional ablative blaster armor as chest rigs—did a decent enough impression of professional shooters. If Wraith or Zora were going to be injured in a blaster fight, one of these guys would probably be the ones who pulled the trigger.

The team spread out in four groups of three, each moving toward a corner of the expansive warehouse. Their presence caused a slowdown in the work around them as MCR technicians thumbed off their cutting torches and raised their protective goggles or stood still from the stolen cargo they were breaking into and sorting for further redistribution.

"We're not gonna stay hidden here for much longer," Zora observed. "Wanna make for the catacombs?"

"No," Wraith said, readying his blaster pistols. "Too easy to corner us in there. Maybe they won't see us."

"Keel... they're going to see us."

"They didn't find us in that hollow log. Be ready, though."

The duo hunkered down, with Wraith using his helmet's audio receptors to gauge how close the guards were. In the meantime, he got on comms with Doc and instructed the old man to pull them out hot if things went that way. They could figure out how to best deal with the fallout of the *Six* showing up later.

"Just let me know and I'll come in blazing," Doc said. "Roof's still clear, if you can make it."

"I'll let you know. Wraith out."

When the comm transmission ended, the sound of the guards' advancing footsteps could be heard without audio enhancers. Zora looked at Wraith, her expression making it clear that she didn't see a way they could avoid detection; she was waiting for the armored bounty hunter to make the first move.

Wraith was up a second later. Three blaster bolts zipped from his Intec x6, all three of them head shots, and the three approaching Mids dropped dead to the floor.

The screams of the startled MCR techs—people who had joined for idealism or credits, but likely not to engage in combat—sounded in tandem with a fourth and fifth bolt aimed at two more guards. Five of the twelve down before the first blast of return fire zipped high over the cargo crates.

Wraith had started the fight on his own terms, and the MCR, despite their readiness, were unprepared.

Zora came up from cover and took aim with her rifle. A sixth rebel fell—half the team dead now. Wraith killed the seventh with a shot from his Intec that punched through the hapless rebel's nose and cooked his head from within the nasal cavity. The man fell stiffly, twitched violently, and then moved no more.

"Changing packs," Wraith called, and by the time his well-trained fingers had done what would have looked like a magic trick to the uninitiated, Zora had reduced the MCR team by two more members.

The remaining trio blended in with the technicians who were running from the conflict—streaming into the sublevel's main corridor or standing hopelessly by the freight elevator that had just rushed upward under the direction of the first panicked rebels to reach it. Others hid inside a break room and office with a large glass viewing window showing the warehouse floor.

Wraith picked off another guard running for the office. Zora tried for her own target and hit a technician instead, spilling the Kimbrin woman onto the deck, dead in an instant.

The pair then took aim at every visible holocam, direct hits and near misses both destroying the cheap devices.

Finally, the base-wide alarm sounded.

"Okay, so much for hiding," Wraith said after tapping Zora's shoulder to get her attention. "Let's see about getting to a higher level. We hit them on our terms, and we fade."

"Not crazy about the two of us taking on an entire MCR base. You do realize we could be hiding safely in the catacombs right now."

"Yeah, and pinned down a few minutes from now. And if we hit 'em hard enough, they'll think they've got way more than two to deal with." He commed the *Six* and gave Doc an update on their situation.

"There's a chance that alarm wasn't for you," Doc said. "I got an unidentified shuttle makin' for the rooftop and a Republic destroyer just appeared in atmo, kid. That's too soon for Owens's boys. Things just got complicated."

# 42

Seventeen point six standard minutes.

By Hess's chrono, that's how long it took him to get his kill team on the drop shuttle and ready for violence. Captain Devers had asked for it to be done in thirty; other men might have called even *that* amount of time impossible. But other men did not have the discipline to account for every minute, every second of one's day, to crush the juice out of every moment like Hess. Other men had not been taken to the brink, the very edge of life and pain and then been granted a new life again.

Hess would drain the last drops of what remained of his life.

He looked around at the small shuttle crammed with former legionnaires now working for Nether Ops. Armed, deadly, ready. Hand-picked and the best of the best. Just like Hess. The major had personally selected this team. Under better circumstances, he would have fought what was coming next.

But these weren't better circumstances. These were critical circumstances. An evac and a coverup all in one. A difficult job. Every trace of Scarpia needed to be scrubbed from the trail. These men, legionnaires working for Dark Ops but still in the Legion through the magic of bureaucratic accounting, black books, and every other trick the Nether kept up its blood-soaked sleeves, would do the task of ensuring none escaped the MCR castle.

These men would kill the rebels on the inside. The marines would eliminate any who attempted to exit. And the orbital bombardment... would take care of everything else.

No loose ends.

Hess only needed to execute the mission. It would be a shame to lose this team. But another could be built. Whatever it took to win.

The drop shuttle's repulsors whined as they powered up. They should have been hot already. Pilot error. Something to work out for next time. An ass-chewing that Hess mentally scheduled for later.

"Three minutes to drop, Major Hess," the shuttle pilot told him.

"Copy. Three minutes." Time enough for some housekeeping.

Hess opened up his comm link. "Hunter Actual to Captain Devers. Do we have secure comms with the VIP yet?"

"Affirmative. Transmitting comm code your way now. Major... it is *imperative* you recover Scarpia and remove yourself from the AO immediately."

"Understood, sir." As much as Hess admired the captain's diction and self-possession—they were cut from the same cloth that way—he did not enjoy being reminded how to do his job.

"And Major... no one else on this mission is authorized to have contact with the VIP. Get this done."

Hess had always tried. He had gone to extreme lengths to do just that. Do what had to be done. It had cost him everything. Once. When he was younger. When a crazed Legion general named Rex had assumed the alias of a bounty hunter named Tyrus Rechs. A disgraced man who flaunted Nether Ops failures before all who knew who he was.

And then... a man who flaunted Hess's *own* failure to capture him.

Tyrus Rechs. Terminate on sight. None had ever been wanted so much.

Rechs was someone else's problem now.

Once upon a time, Hess would have felt sorrow knowing that it he wouldn't be the one to put the man down. He had made Tyrus Rechs his... obsession. His purpose in life.

That had been a mistake.

He had strived so hard to reach the pinnacle of Nether Ops, and they had rejected him. So he had set out on a mission of personal revenge, fancying himself the devil incarnate, to prove them wrong. It wasn't until he went through the hells that that decision brought—in the torture chambers of the Lizzaar—that Hess put aside his obsession, and found the only thing worth dying for. The only thing worth living for.

In the dark heart of the Republic there were secrets upon secrets. The Nether Ops agencies, so proud, so sure of their supremacy deep within the state... well, wait until they got a load of what was coming.

Hess was an insider now. All the way in. All the way inside. And Devers... the man was a player as well. One that Hess wanted to be on good terms with.

So... he told himself to forget about being treated as if he weren't a Black Fleet major and as if all the precautions, contingencies, and ways to murder his way out of being found in the light weren't drilled into him like a revolutionary's catechism. Don't take offense at the petty reminders needed by lesser men.

*No contact orders.*

*Do what must be done.*

*Don't forget nothing.*

Take no offense. Just say... "Yes, sir. Hunter Actual out."

Tapping on the newly arrived comm code, Hess contacted the VIP.

"Mr. Scarpia, this is Major Hess. We are one minute to drop."

"I'm on the roof waiting, Major." The man sounded urbane but annoyed. "From what I've gathered, the base alarms have sounded. Some kind of prisoner escape, but the level of destruction that's being reported to me makes me wonder if that Legion kill team isn't already on site. I advise you hurry."

Hess turned his head and furrowed his brow. He muted his comm and ordered his pilot to pick up the pace. To Scarpia he said, "Dropping now. Do you have any essential personnel you need to bring with you?"

"No. I'll be traveling solo, I think."

In the back of the comm came the distant, flirtatious laughter of a woman. Hess knew Scarpia's reputation. Knew his weakness for compatible females. He supposed the man had simply grown tired of this one.

Not his business.

"I'll see you shortly, Mr. Scarpia. Hess out."

From outside the shuttle came a loud clunk and buzz as they swung into position. The pilot came on-comms and said, "We're in position to make the drop into atmosphere."

"Do it," Major Hess commanded.

"Three... two... one... drop!"

With a stomach-lurching plunge, the shuttle released and fell, glowing, into the moon's atmosphere. The freefall shook Hess's seat and rattled the man's armor as the distance closed between himself and his next objective. His mind was elsewhere, and he would have to refocus it by the time they landed.

But... what exactly was going on inside that castle? Had Devers been wrong about the kill team's ETA?

Ultimately, it wouldn't matter. The orbital bombardment would wipe away every complication.

Hess needed only grab his man and lift off again.

The rattle of the dropship burning through atmosphere was replaced by relatively light turbulence as the ship cut through the air and reduced altitude. As the craft zoomed in, the hum of the repulsors and glide of the shuttle felt almost serene.

Things went into a practiced, predictable rhythm: the landing of a shuttle and disembarking of its lethal cargo. Doors opened and the repulsor howl grew louder as Hess's legionnaires jumped off and took positions, blaster rifles up with the major shouting, "Move! Move! Move!" behind them.

They secured the roof, flowing around the VIP's waiting shuttle, still sealed up tightly.

Hess stood at the ramp of his dropship as marines landed in their drop pods all around the castle, their combined repulsor whines creating a scream that carried loudly to the landing pad on top of the ancient castle.

His lieutenant reported to him from the bottom of the ramp. "Roof secure."

"Go get the VIP and escort him aboard."

The legionnaires rushed into Scarpia's shuttle. Their blasters shouted out death as they eliminated the VIP's crew. Only then did the man himself emerge, shrouded in a bloodstained sheet, a legionnaire holding either arm as they hurried him aboard Hess's shuttle.

Hess took control of the prisoner, and the legionnaires moved to assault the compound, delivering more death to whoever they found.

The ramp door closed, and Hess removed the sheet to verify that it was, indeed, Scarpia.

There was no doubt. Scarpia immediately straightened his long hair, the gems on his various rings glittering in the low cabin light. He had a perfectly manicured mustache and goatee, a flawless pedicure, and a knowing twinkle in his eye that bordered on smug.

Outside, Hess's men were sending fraggers down the rooftop stairwell and following them down to secure the next level through sheer violence of action.

"Impeccable timing, Major!" said Scarpia, shouting above the roar of repulsors above and the chatter of blaster fire below.

"This way."

Hess escorted Scarpia deeper into the dropship and was pleased to see that the man moved with a sense of urgency. These "indispensable" types had a habit of acting as though moving without pretense or swagger would be more harmful than an errant blaster bolt. Not Scarpia.

"Pilot, take off," Hess ordered.

Scarpia arched an eyebrow. "Leaving without your kill team?"

Major Hess gestured Scarpia toward a seat. "Their job is to assure that no one who knew of you survives."

"Of course."

Hess nodded his approval. That was done. The rising pitch of repulsors and heavy feeling of the shuttle taking off marked the next step.

The pilot hit the comms. "Prepare for takeoff."

The shuttle lurched as its repulsors pushed it off the castle roof.

Hess worked his comm. "Hunter Actual to *Brutus*. Requesting direct comm link to Captain Devers. Say again: direct link to Captain Devers. Highest priority."

"Stand by, Hunter Actual," said the communications officer.

No direct line this time because this would be messy and that meant at least a cursory review. That powerful men stood in control of those reviews didn't mean one could make it obvious. Pride before fall. Best to stay humble, stay smart, and stay hidden.

"This is Captain Devers."

"Captain Devers, sir. My team has taken heavy casualties from a large MCR element. This place is a death trap. I have no ambulatory men and my legionnaires are requesting an orbital strike on their position. Sir, we can't let the marines walk into that meat grinder—at least give those still assaulting the outside of the compound a chance."

"Damn it," Devers growled, and Hess could see why he'd risen so high, so fast. It was all like being in an action holo, and Devers, as he had been on Kublar, was the bright and shining star. "Stand by, Major."

Scarpia smiled thinly. "An interesting approach. I see what you mean about the price of seeing my face being high."

Major Hess nodded. "You have to be pragmatic to win, sir."

"Indeed."

Captain Devers came back on comms. "Major Hess, we've issued orders to the marines to get clear of the building. ETA to orbital bombardment is three minutes. Get yourself and your men clear in that time if possible, Major."

Grimly, Hess replied, "Sir, my men are all reading deceased. Avenge them. Over."

"Acknowledged. *Brutus* out."

Scarpia gave Hess an appraising look. "I assume your men aren't aware of what's about to hit them from orbit. Although I suppose there's no easy way to prepare oneself for sacrificing one's life for the good of the Republic... at the Republic's very hands."

Hess locked eyes with the soft civilian next to him who might be good at acquiring weapons, but couldn't understand the cost of victory. "Their comms have been disabled and their HUDs are no longer recording. As far as history will remember it, that sacrifice on behalf of the Republic is precisely what they wanted."

Scarpia chuckled. "Remind me never to get on your bad side, Hess. So. What next after this little... *setback*, my boy?"

Hess glanced toward the cockpit. "The pilot is with the Black Fleet. Captain Devers controls the flight logs and anything else on the destroyer. We'll make sure this mission marks an official end of any interest in you."

"How did they find me?" Scarpia asked. "Because *my* chosen men working this hijacking ring were as vetted as all the chosen men you just boasted about."

Hess frowned. The expression made his scarred face more hideous than normal. Scarpia, however, didn't flinch.

"We're unsure," Hess admitted. "You're aware of the Galaxy-class ship that crashed near the processing facility."

Scarpia gave the slightest of nods. "I am. And that a captured female crewmember somehow escaped.

Forgive me, but perhaps your handlers are jumping at shadows?"

"No shadows," Hess insisted. "Sources within Herbeer notified us that Nether Ops has arranged an unscheduled visit. *Someone* seems to have put together a few pieces of the puzzle. We'll make sure it remains indecipherable."

"One wonders what Goth Sullus will make of all this," Scarpia remarked, watching for Hess's reaction. The arms dealer was gathering intel. Reading the man who'd been sent to pull him out of his predicament.

"Goth Sullus is a *partner* in this. A man who relies on the recruiting and supply network Captain Devers and his associates have set up. *They* are your employers and the ones who have rescued you from a life sentence on Herbeer... soon to be twice."

"Indeed," Scarpia said quietly.

Sitting back, Hess checked his chrono. Time on target, nineteen seconds.

The thrumming outside the shuttle intensified; an electric thrill coursed through the air. From a safe distance, the drop shuttle began a lazy turn around the battlefield.

"Orbital strike inbound," the pilot announced. "Starboard side if you'd like to view it, Major Hess."

A heavy energy beam, a massive trunk of lightning, poured down on the castle, incinerating everything in its tight column. The structure shuddered and shook, then collapsed in on itself in a billowing cloud of rubble and smoke. They waited a moment longer, and a second beam, just as powerful as the first, made sure the job was finished.

"Remarkable." Scarpia clapped. "Particularly from this vantage point. Remind me to pour us both a drink in honor of everyone who had to watch it up close and personal, my boy!"

Major Hess allowed himself a small smile. "Mission accomplished." Then he commed the pilot.

"Yes, Major?" the pilot said.

"Forgo returning to the destroyer. Set a course for Herbeer."

"Yes, sir."

Scarpia raised an eyebrow. "We really have to go back to that pit?"

Hess shrugged. "Loose ends. Someone believes they found you. Someone believes you're alive and on the loose. We're going to spend some time together on the prison world until that somebody realizes they're wrong."

Scarpia's smile was no longer quite as self-assured. He rolled his shoulders, clearly uncomfortable at the thought of returning to the prison planet and its synth mines. "And then...?"

"We move to Tusca."

"Tusca? I have weapons shipments being split up among depots on Strach IV, Ankalor, and a half dozen other worlds... what's on Tusca?"

Now it was Hess's turn to eye Scarpia. Here was a man with mansions and yachts, trillions in creds, House of Reason connections, and a kill team sacrificed on his behalf, yet for all that, he was but a tool. He honestly didn't know. Hess almost pitied him.

"The bleeding edge, Mr. Scarpia. The next wave of disruptive technology straight from the Savage archives. Your skills at... *acquiring*... will be needed. Goth Sullus has awoken his own private kill team."

A light glimmered in Scarpia's eye. "Awoken. Interesting choice of words. Tell me more..."

# 43

"Any update on that shuttle?" Keel asked Doc as he and Zora navigated their way up narrow winding steps toward the second floor following a couple of brief shootouts on the levels below.

"Nothin'," the old man replied. "Just sitting there. Same with the destroyer up in orbit."

The shuttle had come into atmosphere and set down where the previous shuttle had been. The ramp hadn't lowered, and the rooftop guards had been recalled to help deal with the hit-and-fade attacks Wraith had perpetrated throughout the castle.

Keel had a feeling that future encounters wouldn't go as smoothly; what was left of the combat-capable soldiers would be on the lookout for him. But on the first floor, he and Zora had stumbled upon this unused, ancient stair that allowed them to climb without being forced to bull through the heavily guarded main stairwells. At least for now.

"Hang on," Zora said. "Do you hear that? The alarm sounds different."

The MCR's station-wide klaxons had been blaring steadily ever since things went off in the warehouse sublevel. Now it sounded as though a siren had been added to the mix. The thick walls of the dusty, forgotten stairway kept much of the noise outside, but Keel didn't need to amplify his audio receptors to hear what Zora was talking about.

Doc came over the comm with the reason a second later. "Republic destroyer just flashed some launch bursts—looks like they're sending drop pods down this way."

"Owens say anything about deploying from a destroyer?" Keel asked.

"Not to me he didn't, and unless each member of his kill team is taking his own drop pod, the Repub company you're about to get ain't Dark Ops."

"Time to get clear of this place," Zora said. "The last thing I want to do is have a bunch of legionnaires see this uniform and use me for target practice."

"Strip out of it," Keel suggested. "Might help. Distract the men from shooting straight, anyway."

"I'll take that under advisement if the bolts start coming too heavy. Thanks."

Doc came back with additional intel. "Owens confirms that they're not his guys. No Legion assets are close enough to have responded so quickly. Probably dealing with hullbusters."

Keel frowned. "So how did whoever is on that destroyer get word of this place?"

"Ten-million-credit question, kid," Doc replied.

Zora shook her head. "Does it matter? We were supposed to hang tight until a big enough distraction could get us clear. So the help came earlier than your friends. Either way, we need to go."

Keel nodded. Zora was right, but everything was happening so quickly, and he felt as though things were slipping through the cracks. "What's that shuttle doing now, Doc?"

"Sittin' pretty. If they saw that destroyer launch, they ain't budging. You gettin' clear or what?"

"Doc, what if that shuttle is waiting for someone inside this base to get to them, then clear out?"

"Someone like Scarpia," the old man concluded. "You think he's there after all?"

"No idea, but I'm getting one of those gut feelings," Wraith said. "I've gotta get up there. We're already on Level Two, we just need to fight our way up one more floor. And the Mids should still be looking for us on Level One since we just hit them there."

"That, or they're all hustling to deal with the hullbusters about to land outside," Zora added. Keel expected her to again make the point that they needed to leave. Instead she said, "We should be able to make that, yeah. Let's check it out."

Keel was grateful at how willing the bounty hunter was to continue risking her life for *his* mission.

Doc sighed. "Do what you gotta do, kid. Just don't get Zora killed in the process."

"I'll be fine, Dad."

"You'd better be." There was a pause. "I love you, sweetie."

"I know you do. We gotta get back to work. Out."

There was an obvious reason why this stairwell wasn't used—not only was it too cramped for everyday use, it ended at a blank wall. But it was equally obvious that the wall had to be hiding a secret door, and with some quick investigation—shifting a stone into a gap beside it and then lifting the stone beneath it up—they revealed ancient metal gearworks, including a wheel with a handle.

"You get ready," Wraith ordered. "I'll work the door."

He put his strength into the clanking wheel, grunting from the effort. The sound of rocks sliding was the low growl of a cave troll punctuated by metallic clacks as each gear saved Keel's progress. The stone at their feet rumbled, and then the doorway was open.

Zora, covering the process with her blaster rifle, peered out. They were on a landing halfway between levels one and two, and they were alone—but only for seconds. A sudden rush of footsteps came up the stairs from below.

A voice, shaking with adrenaline called out, "Make way! Coming through!"

Zora stepped back, watching in surprise as an MCR officer, flanked by two armed rebel troops, rushed right past her.

One of the armed rebel guards looked in surprise at the hole in the wall, but the officer in charge had bulled his way through without a second glance. Another few seconds and they might have realized what they had just come across. Instead, Zora calmly leveled her blaster rifle and sent a hot spray of bolts into the backs of all three men. The rebels fell face first into the steps and slowly tumbled back down to lay at her feet on the landing.

The stairwell wasn't the one that Keel hadn't gone down earlier. He stepped to a narrow window and looked out to see marines hurrying from their drop pods, opening fire on the exterior patrols and base defenders. Whatever was going on out there, he'd make use of the distraction.

They headed up the stairs only to find a heavy blast door blocking their way onto the second floor. It looked wholly out of place in this old castle, but someone had gone to the trouble of setting it solidly into the stone on either side.

"Locked," Zora said.

Doc pinged them on the comm.

"Go for Wraith."

"Repub drop shuttle is coming down."

"Command ship?" Zora asked.

"Hullbuster commanders come down in the drop pods, same as their marines," Wraith said. "Somebody else."

"Yeah," Doc agreed. "I'll tell you what I see when it lands. You staying safe?"

Zora looked from the locked door and then down the stairwell. "Trapped on the stairs is a better way to put it."

"Holy hell, kid," Doc said. "Rule One: Don't get yourself cornered in a stairwell. You know what a fatal funnel is, don'tcha?"

"Pretty sure we broke a whole bunch of 'rule ones' to get into this mess in the first place," Wraith said. "And we're not trapped." To Zora he said, "What kind of security panel does that thing have? Biometric or data key?"

"Looks like data key," the bounty hunter responded.

"I'll check the guards. They were headed up; they had to have a way to open the door."

He jogged back down and found the data key nestled into the nametape on the dead MCR officer. Ripping it off, he hurried back and gave Zora a quick set of instructions. She knew how to breach a room, same as him, but a quick rundown of how it would go would help avoid mistakes.

"Door opens, I send in an ear-popper, then I go, then you go."

Zora understood the plan. She held the data key near the sensor, and with a flash and a beep, the door swished open.

Wraith tossed in an ear-popper, and the pair shielded themselves against the thick stone walls on either side of the door as the blinding, retinue-burning light show illuminated the room with a deafening series of booms.

The pair then streamed through into what Keel had dubbed the throne room, now the MCR's CIC, blasting targets huddled over tables or slumped to the floor in pain and surprise. Wraith had only seen this room from the opposite side; this door let out closer to the dais. The room was vast—much too large for a single ear-popper to disable everyone inside—and officers and armed guards at the far end were already sending blaster bolts at Wraith and Zora by the time they had pushed their way into the room.

Doc gave a dispassionate order over the comms. "Be sure and kill every last one of those MCR kelhorns."

"Working on it!" Zora cried, dodging behind a heavy workstation before sending another rifle shot.

A wave of return fire screamed in their direction, blasting holes in the workstation and zipping through the holographic map that a now-dead MCR officer had been manipulating prior to being cut down by the invaders. The three-dimensional representation of the MCR base, showing where drop pods had landed and where the hullbusters had been spotted, flashed, disappeared, reappeared, and finally went dead.

"Stay down!" Wraith shouted to Zora just prior to burning chest holes into two officers with more courage than armor who had been attempting to flank the operator.

"You see Scarpia," Doc said, "you dust him too, Wraith. Never mind what Owens and Dark Ops want. Put the dogs down when you get the chance."

"Don't see him," Wraith managed. "Changing packs!"

Zora popped out from behind her cover and double-tapped another MCR. The herd was thinning.

Wraith finished his reload and dashed forward. One of the partitioned offices had become the fallback point of the MCR resistance, but those partitions weren't made of stone like the castle, or reinforced metal like the workstations. Wraith got himself an angle office and then taught those inside the partitioned space the hardest lesson on cover versus concealment that they'd ever learn. Bolts ripped through the modular office walls, leaving scorched holes that burned with small rings of fire.

Zora added her own rifle fire until the wall was obliterated and smoke billowed out to wreath the overhead stones and dusty, dormant candelabras that hung from the ceiling.

All went still. Wraith moved in and found no survivors.

The room was awash in smoke, small fires from blaster bolts, dead bodies, and blood, but it was secure. Comm boards flashed blue and chimed with people attempting to reach the CIC on various channels, their calls going unanswered. And in the center of the room the big holotable continued to show a complete tactical picture of the ongoing fight with the Republic marines outside.

"First thing," Wraith said as he moved to the holotable, "is to lock that door we just came in through."

Zora did so quickly, sealing it and entering an internal override that *should* prevent anyone on the other side from getting in unless they had a cutting torch and some spare time. For good measure, she shot the control panels, fusing the wiring.

"Okay, now I'm going to give those hullbusters an assist by activating the repulsor bridge across the lake to the front door," Wraith said. "Give the MCR something to worry about besides us. Doc, what's the status on that bird coming down?"

"Still dropping," Doc replied. "Hang on. I'll move the observation bot in for a closer look. Smoke is spilling out from your section of the castle, so if you're still thinking about heading for the roof, do it quick. They gotta know there's trouble on your level."

"We're moving. Don't let that bot get shot down," Wraith said, adding, "Those are expensive."

"Been flying drones since I was a boot. It'll be fine."

The sound of blaster fire happening in and around the keep increased. Hullbusters knew an edge when they saw one and were surely pushing toward the bridge. Doc could tell Keel exactly what was happening, but it didn't really matter. He needed to reach that shuttle.

He and Zora ran hard up the only stairs to the castle's third level.

A concussive blast sounded behind them, and the stone floor seemed to buckle and sway for a moment before righting itself, tossing Zora to the ground and sending Keel crashing into the wall. He spun around, rifle ready, but whatever that blast had been, the impact must have been far below.

"Doc!" he called.

"Yeah, I saw it. Some hullbuster fired a rocket in through an opening. Musta been a big one."

Wraith helped Zora to her feet, and they moved toward where he'd seen the roof access on his initial infiltration. Except the abandoned, unused third level of the castle was no longer abandoned. A full detail of guards had taken up defensive positions, covering in small stone alcoves, and blaster fire erupted in the direction of the two intruders. It didn't take a prophet to figure out that these Mids had been stationed to protect that shuttle from anyone attempting to reach it.

But again, if it was so important... why hadn't it already taken off? Was Scarpia somewhere beneath them? Should they turn around and search for him?

"MCR blocking our way to the rooftop," Wraith told Doc.

"Marines should get up here to join the party before too long now that we opened the door," Zora added.

"Oba's balls... not good, kids."

"Tell me about it," Zora said as she shifted out of her stolen MCR jacket. "I'm getting out of this uniform."

"This is no good," Wraith decided. "We need a way out. Doc... circle that bot around and give us something."

"I got your loc. Your bucket's giving me a strong ping," Doc said. "I'll see what I can see."

The MCR seemed content to play a defensive game. As long as Wraith and Zora moved no further, the guards' mission was a success.

Keel ducked back behind the stone alcove he was using for concealment. "First rebel that tries to settle in down by us gets dusted," he instructed his partner. "Otherwise we set up a crossfire once the marines push inside, and we try to get out during the confusion."

"What about Scarpia?"

"If we see him... capture. No kill."

The question of what to do if they saw the man had been sitting heavily on Keel's mind. He was certain that the voice he'd heard belonged to the arms dealer. He had no doubt of that. And then Zora had heard the name spoken by the doctor who had saved her life. But Keel hadn't actually *seen* the man, and there was no reason to think he was on-site.

Yet if he was...

Then what?

Doc had been a lifetaker and heartbreaker, same as Keel. He'd seen plenty of action, and had been clear about the need to put a man like Scarpia down rather than surrender him to another day's breath. But if Keel couldn't trust the Legion to handle this... what was he even doing out there?

The sounds of battle began to rise up the stairs to the third floor. Confusion and panic, a swelling of voices and undisciplined blaster shots. And Wraith and Zora were about to be in the middle of it.

"Push up or fall back?" Zora asked. "We're not gonna have a choice pretty soon."

"We push up to the roof," Keel said, preparing himself to make an advance on the MCR and wishing that the image of Kags doing the same—and dying for it—on that Oba-forsaken corvette hadn't popped into his mind at that exact moment.

Then something else besides that haunting memory kept Keel's feet planted to the floor. The sound of repulsors in the atmosphere.

"Drop shuttle is coming down on the roof," Doc reported.

The castle shook from the shuttle's approach. Now what?

A moment later, Doc announced, "Looks like leejes are jumping off... looks like a kill team."

"You see any markings?" Wraith asked. There was a possibility he knew the men getting off that shuttle. "Owens say they were early?"

That was a long shot and Keel knew it. Owens would have told them if that was the case.

"They ain't gettin' here early," Doc growled. "I'm tryin' to keep this bot from getting shot down, kid, but I don't see nothin' I recognize. Black armor. All the way black.

Shuttle's gonna have its anti-drone network up. Any closer and I lose it."

Wraith cursed under his breath. Throwing a kill team of legionnaires into the volatile mix he and Zora were already in the middle of could go several ways, all of them bad unless those legionnaires—and *were* they even that?—somehow knew that Wraith and Zora weren't the bad guys.

"Okay, I got something here," Doc said. "Leejes just boarded that first shuttle and took someone off it. Can't identify, they got him under a sheet or something. He's being moved to the Repub shuttle. Sket, Keel, now those leejes are heading down from the roof to your level."

He'd barely gotten the words out before the legionnaires appeared behind the MCR guards who had kept Keel and Zora pinned down, and the Mids, with no guard on their rear, started dropping in a flurry of blaster bolts. A few managed to shift cover and fire back, but it would only be a matter of time before those leej weapons were aimed at Keel and Zora.

"Sket," Zora growled, sounding not unlike her old man. "I take it these aren't friends of yours."

"If they are, they won't know it."

The blaster fire on the floors below reduced to a patter, followed by the sound of... cheering.

"What's going on?" Zora asked, turning her head to look back toward the stairs they'd just climbed.

But Wraith's only answer was to shout, "Get down!" Several fraggers from the legionnaires had come rolling down the hall, and it was all he could do to throw himself over her. The devices detonated, thundering, and when Wraith popped his head back up, the legionnaires were taking out those MCR who had evaded the fragmentary blast with cold, practiced precision.

He looked down at Zora and quickly checked her for wounds. Pockmarks from the shrapnel were in the stone, and he'd felt at least a couple of pings against his armor. "You okay?"

"Fine," she grunted.

"We gotta go."

The last thing Keel wanted was to face the kill team. Not only because he preferred living to dying, but because he dreaded the thought of having to engage his fellow legionnaires. To kill the brothers he was sent to protect. But if they came shooting... what else could he do?

"Heads up," Doc said over the comm. "Hullbusters are streaming back out of the place. Something more than the arrival of a kill team is goin' down. Get my daughter out of there."

Keel knew of only one surefire way out—the same way he'd come in. "We'll climb out through the window. You can manage. Trust me."

He ushered Zora to the same wide-open window he'd first breached the castle through, then readied his last banger as Zora climbed onto the sill. "I'm going to toss this at the legionnaires. Those buckets are gonna protect them from it, but it'll buy us enough time to get outside before they reach us."

She gave a decisive nod that turned into a confused search of the room's ceiling as a high-pitched whistle screamed. It was followed by a deep vibration that rattled the old castle, sending dust sifting from the walls and ceiling. Doc was saying something frantic over comms, but it kept cutting out.

"...ing on ki—d? You're... out! Geh... of there!"

The temperature jumped at least ten degrees in an instant. Zora looked around wildly. "What's happening?"

"Orbital strike!" Wraith tossed the ear-popper through the room and out into the hall just as the first of the legionnaires came into view. The banger sailed and tinked across the floor to strike the man's boot, and he looked down, surprised, right before it exploded.

Wraith practically shoved Zora out of the window, but she jumped under her own power, her arms windmilling as she dropped feet-first toward the waiting green water.

Keel was just preparing to bound out the window himself when a blaster bolt zipped just high of his head and sizzled through the opening and out of the castle. He turned, saw the legionnaire, rifle still up, and fired back without thinking. The bolt punched through the T-shaped visor and into the man's face, dropping him to the floor in a clatter of armor and kit.

Wraith turned once more, leaped onto the stone windowsill, and jumped.

# 44

Wraith and Zora were still attempting to orient themselves beneath the dark water when the massive energy beam punched through the castle, sending errant stones flying as the ancient structure collapsed in on itself. Wraith's bucket auto-sealed and fed him fresh air while Zora kicked her way up to the surface. He followed, moving more slowly but still able to swim despite the armor's weight. Every leej could.

They breached the surface and Zora took in a deep gulp of air. The sky was already darkened by a cloud of haze that spread out from the fallen castle, now merely a shell of its former self. There was still blaster fire somewhere, but it sounded distant and muted. In the jungles, perhaps.

But the attack wasn't done. Once more the air began to crackle and swirl around them, and before they could dive, a second orbital strike shot down from the sky, turning even the rubble to rubble—and sending it flying.

"Wraith!" Zora called as stones, some of them quite large, fell about them like rain, sending up white plumes of lake water and creating instant waves that pushed the swimmers apart.

A shadow fell over Keel, and he looked up just in time to see a massive stone coming down directly above him. It only clipped his armor, but the force of its impact into the water sucked him down into the darkness, tumbling. Hurting but still mobile, he began to swim toward the shore, wanting to at least get clear enough of the falling debris to try and get eyes on Zora again.

Doc's voice was in his ear. "Kid! Kid! What's your status!"

"I'm alive," Keel said, still swimming. "We jumped out of the keep to avoid getting cooked."

"Zora's with you?"

"No. We got separated." That was all of the truth Keel had the heart to tell at the moment. "I'm looking for her."

"All right, you look," Doc growled. "But your next words to me better be that she's all right."

Keel was close enough to the shore that he could stand now. He readied his blaster and rose slowly like an amphibious predator. The blaster fire was quiet now. All was still except the occasional scream or moan of someone wounded. The castle was nothing but a smoking mound of blackened stone.

He scanned the lake for Zora... and saw nothing. The stones had stopped falling, but the water still rolled wildly. She could be out there, swimming beneath the surface. Perhaps she'd even made it to shore.

Or she could be lost forever under the waves.

He activated the thermal overlay in his bucket and scanned once more. Now his visor highlighted a heat signature in the shallows some distance around the shoreline from where he stood.

A humanoid. Alive. Maybe.

Still keeping an eye out for MCR or Republic marines, Keel pushed his way as quickly as he could through the muck toward the heat signature. Whoever it was, they were lying face up in water barely shallow enough to keep them from drowning. As it was, waves periodically lapped over them, hiding them from view.

It wasn't until he was practically there that Keel confirmed what he hoped. It was Zora.

Alive.

"I found her, Doc."

The crusty old former leej issued a mixture of curses and prayers.

Wraith kneeled down and held Zora's head in his lap. "Zora. Zora, are you okay? She's not moving, Doc."

"Please let her be all right," Doc pleaded. "Be all right, baby..."

"Zora," Wraith tried again.

She stirred, then groaned. Her eyelids opened, her green eyes unfocused. Then she croaked, "We're not dead?"

Keel breathed a sigh of relief. "Not yet."

"Feels like it," she groaned, her hand going to her forehead.

"Oh, thank Oba," Doc exclaimed. "I woulda killed you if you got my baby killed, kid. Sweetie, I... I love you, Zora. I'm sorry for..."

"It's okay," Zora murmured.

"Not to ruin the moment," Wraith said, watching for movement around the shore, "but we gotta get out of here."

"Yeah you do," Doc said. "Before the hullbusters regroup. I landed about two klicks east of your position and I'm already movin' toward you both."

"That close, huh?"

"Keeping outta sight was your idea, kid."

"Still the right call." Groaning, Wraith pushed himself up. His body was now reminding him of the fight he'd just been through. His muscles cried, his bones ached, and it felt like someone had rammed a hot knife through his left ear. He buried the pain. "I can walk. Good to go. Sket. Dammit."

"Think I broke my wrist," Zora said, real pain in her voice. "Help me up."

He got her shakily to her feet. "You good to walk?"

Clearly gritting through her own pain, she took a couple of steadying breaths. "I can move. Yeah."

"Hurry it up then!" Doc barked.

"Guess the sentimental moment is over," Keel said.

They began a stumbling run up the muddy banks, then into the underbrush and into the trees.

"Oh, this is torture," Zora groaned, holding her wrist steady with one hand as she struggled alongside Wraith.

Keel felt for her, but they couldn't slow down. He'd been keeping comms open with Doc, and the old man was close.

"Republic marines! Halt!" a voice shouted.

"Keep going!" Wraith hissed to Zora, pulling her along in a sudden spring as they crashed through the tangled foliage, panting.

"I said stop!" the marine yelled.

"Light 'em up!" another hullbuster called, then heavy blaster fire sizzled past Wraith and Zora.

The pair crested a small rise and then Wraith pulled Zora down with him to slide down the opposite side of the berm. Zora cried out in pain.

"You hit?" Wraith asked.

Beneath the streaks of mud, her face was alternately flushed and white. "No. Just jostled my wrist."

"Freeze! Hands up!" the same voice shouted, and from three sides came the whine of primed blaster rifles as Republic marines treaded through the undergrowth toward them.

"We're surrounded," Zora said.

"I know. Put your hands up," Wraith told her, his already in the air.

"There's only three. You can take them."

"No. That's not why we're here."

A weather-faced sergeant twitched his blaster in their direction. "Corporal—take their weapons."

"Yes, Sar'nt," the young hullbuster answered, then slung his rifle and jogged through the underbrush toward them.

"*Keel...*" Zora whispered urgently, pleading for him to do something she knew he wouldn't do.

"I'm not killing our allies."

Three thunder shots rang through the jungle, and Zora and Wraith jumped reflexively as the marines dropped dead like puppets whose strings were cut. The shots echoed, then the forest fell silent again. Standing behind the carnage was Doc, smoke rising from his surge shotgun.

The old man walked toward Wraith and Zora. He looked down at the dead marines as he passed and shook his head before looking Wraith in the face. "Let's go back to the ship."

"I had this handled, old man," Wraith said hotly. "What in the nine hells are you even doing?"

"The job, kid. I got paired with you because I know what this is like. I know what you have to do. Learned it from someone who knew the job better than I did and did it longer than either of us can imagine. *This* is how KTF works when it's you against the galaxy."

Wraith looked at the fallen men. "So we just tell Owens, oops, had to dust some hullbusters? Make sure to pick up their corpses before the jungle strips 'em down to bone?"

"We don't tell him sket. But he knows. I promise you, he knows. This is all dancing in the dark with knives out. It's the dirty little part of keeping the galaxy safe that everybody needs and no one wants to talk about. And yeah, it's a fine line. You're gonna have to stand right on the edge—maybe even have to cross it—if you want to complete your mission."

Wraith looked down at the aftermath of Doc's walking the line. Men who'd followed orders, done their duty, and been cut down for it.

"You got a decision to make, kid. You gotta decide if this mission is yours or whether it needs to go to another Dark Ops leej. You've dusted more people than the average person in the galaxy can even imagine. All three of us have. And the deeper you go down this rabbit hole, the more likely it's gonna be that you have to do something like this and drop someone that you have no hatred toward. That you'd smile at down the street or buy a beer in the cantina. But today, well, that meeting was different."

"Sometimes... it's just them or us, Keel," Zora said quietly. "I know you know that."

Around them, the forest was quiet, as if holding its breath.

"Let's… get back to the ship," Wraith said, and turned away.

# 45

Back aboard the *Indelible VI*, the lights glowed, engines hummed, and cool air conditioning greeted Keel, Doc, and Zora. The ramp closed behind them with a hiss.

The *Six*'s AI sang through the speaker system, "Ooh! Welcome back, Miss Zora and—"

"Shut up," Zora and Keel said.

The *Six*'s comm chimed.

"That'll be Owens," Doc said. "Your mission, Keel. You take it."

"This discussion on ethics... it isn't over, old man." Slumping in a lounge chair, Keel answered the comm. "Go for Keel."

"Ford," Major Owens said, "I was worried you all were dead. Third time I've tried to reach you."

"We came close."

Doc spoke from behind Keel's shoulder into the comm. "Had to leave the ship to extract the Wraith. We're hunkered down now."

"Any problems?" Owens asked. "I've got a kill team with nothing else to do that can assist if needed. We're being denied access by the first destroyer on site, but we can

**444**

enter atmo beyond their sensor detection and then fly low to your position."

Keel gave Doc a long, accusatory look. There *was* a problem, a big one—and it involved three dead hullbusters.

The old man stared right back, defiant.

"No need for an assist, Major," Keel finally replied. "Who called in the orbital strike? That nearly cooked us."

"You won't like what I'm about to tell you: your old friend Captain Silas Devers. Said it was to prevent the marines from getting chewed up in a meat grinder that had already taken out his entire kill team. Said intelligence on the ground gave the word and asked for the strike."

"That intelligence is sket, Major," Keel growled. "I was inside, and nothing like that happened. Those leejes had barely breached when the strike started. What the hell was that kelhorn even doing here?"

Owens didn't sound surprised. "Wouldn't be the first time Devers sacrificed men for his own career. Taking out an MCR base—especially this one that's been running a hijacking operation—that'll do wonders for a man's resume. That's our best guess as to why he's here. Official word from *Brutus* is that Navy intel recovered a stolen freighter that had 'defected' to the MCR. Followed the trail to this moon."

"So just bad timing my being there," Keel said.

"Looks like it. Burned up a lot of leejes and marines." Owens's voice was impassive, but Keel knew the thought was eating him from the inside out. Men like Silas Devers represented everything wrong with the Republic's military those days.

"That kelhorned piece of twarg dung..." Doc said. "Idiot point probably got the bright idea after his troops were committed."

"Yeah, well, there's a lot of idiot points making all of our jobs that much harder," Owens said. "We got a team coming to do bio-scans, look for DNA matching what we have on file for Scarpia. Meantime we got someone cleared to visit Herbeer, lookin' to see how he even got loose. Did you get visuals, Ford?"

"Negative. But the shuttle that kill team came down on —Doc saw them pull someone out of the MCR ship already on the pad and transfer him to the other shuttle. Could Devers have bagged Scarpia?"

"If he did, we'll hear about it soon enough. More 'hero of the Republic' stuff, naturally. But my channels picked up that a wounded leej was pulled out after they cleared the shuttle, which was waiting for the MCR colonel should he decide to abandon the base. Then again, I'm not trusting much of anything I'm hearing about this op. Whatever kill team that was, it wasn't one of ours. Probably Nether Ops, which means... well, nothing good."

Doc grunted his agreement with that.

"Captain Ford," Owens continued, "you did what you could and you did it well. Let's hope that Scarpia, if he was there, is now lying dead beneath all that rubble. The galaxy will be better off for it."

It surprised Wraith to hear Owens say essentially the same thing that Doc had. Just put the evil bastards down and be glad there's one less in the galaxy.

Is that what this mission was truly about?

"So now what, Major?" Ford asked.

Owens snapped his gum and let out a brief sigh. "There's some debate about that. We don't know. Obviously, we'll watch this destroyer more closely. Follow up on the trail of ships from the Galaxy-class you destroyed and the Grendel-class before it. You got us closer to uncovering who the players are who are leveraging the MCR to destabilize the Republic. What you did today has Keller very much wanting to keep you in the field. So... keep looking, Captain. See what else you can find. Or..." Owens hesitated. "Or... Chhun and the rest of your kill team are waiting for your return."

This crossroads again. Should he keep feeling his way through the chaos that was galaxy's edge, or return home to his brothers?

"And what do you think, sir?"

Major Owens sighed. "I was hoping you wouldn't ask. There's something... *wrong* with the galaxy. More than just what the MCR are doing. More than the way the House of Reason seems to normalize scandal and scandalize the Legion for fighting the wars they send us to. I think you can help out there, Captain. But you can help on your old kill team, too. I won't make the choice for you."

Keel nodded. He turned to look over his shoulder at Zora, who stood there, still covered in mud and waiting for this comm call to end before heading to the med bay. Her wrist had to be killing her. The smuggler filed that away. People don't suffer pain for people they don't care about.

"I'll stay out here on the edge," he said. "See what I find."

"Understood. Ping me your loc and I'll make sure no patrols go near your ship. Once we've cleared out, I'll let you know so you can take off unnoticed. Might be a while."

"Understood. We'll sit tight."

"KTF, Captain Ford," Owens said.

"KTF. Call me Keel."

"Keel then. Owens out." The comm went silent.

The transmission over, Doc studied Keel. "You sure you got the stomach to stay on this road, kid? Because I promise you it only gets darker."

Keel stared down at the floor for several long moments before finally looking back up at Doc and then Zora. The decision he'd made had settled into clarity. Explaining it... that was harder.

He took a deep breath. "There was this op..." he began. "We trained for it nonstop. So much that all you could think about—all you could dream about—was the mission. How to shave time. How to keep from getting your guys killed. Every kill team in the Legion was doing the same. No one knew why, but it ended up that the MCR had worked something out with the zhee. They stole a corvette, loaded it up with enough explosives to blow up a super-destroyer, and jumped it toward Utopion."

"Holy sket," Zora said. She hadn't heard about any of this. Most of the galaxy hadn't.

Keel gave a fractional nod of acknowledgment. "My team was in the right place at the time, and we got the call. We boarded the corvette, fought like wild wobanki through the bridge... and we stopped it. That was the mission when we captured Scarpia. Who'd made it all possible. I lost two men. Twenties and Kags. Navy docked a shuttle to the corvette, and we all flew out together. Our guys lying on the floor in body bags.

"I remember us all sitting there. And I'm looking into everyone's face and we're all thinking the same thing: How does something like that even happen? Not that legionnaires die, but all the failure, graft, and negligence that allowed the MCR to do what they did to begin with. And of course you're all also asking: *How come it's my buddy sealed up and lying cold as the deck grates and not me?* But I was thinking something else, too. I was thinking... This is gonna happen again. The galaxy is shifting, and things are going to spin out of control faster than anyone is ready for."

Doc gave a throaty *hmmph*, making it clear that he agreed.

"I was on Kublar when it all went down with Victory Company," Keel continued. "I was on that corvette when terrorists damn near wiped out the entire Republic government—though sometimes I'm not sure that would be the worst thing in the galaxy. But I was also on that shuttle flying away with the team I'd led since joining Dark Ops, all of them good friends, for the last time. Two good men dead. And that's why I volunteered for this mission. Because I didn't want to see any more of my friends end up like that. The Legion knows how to fight a war. But this... this feels like we're fighting something else. Something... worse."

He let out a sigh. "Doc, when you tell me that this is what it takes... those moments of me or them... that that's what it takes to stop the galaxy from growing into an even bigger dumpster fire than it was the day before... do you mean it?"

The old man spoke grimly. "Yeah. I mean it. Only way I know, kid."

"Then that's how it'll be. If the Legion commander wants this job done... I'll do it."

Doc gave a measured nod. "You got any idea where to go next? Or are we just gonna do some jobs until Owens gives us a lead?"

Keel considered. "Lao Pak mentioned that some legionnaires are getting a rep for extortion on a few worlds. That's not Legion. That's something else going on. We can start there."

Zora cut in. "Because I'm hearing the word 'we,' I think I'd better speak up. I've fulfilled what Doc asked me to do. You're well on your way to being an independent bounty hunter who should have no shortage of private contracts.

And... I'm not sure that this high-speed, sword-of-the-Legion stuff is up my alley. There's a reason I didn't return my recruiter's calls, you know."

Doc looked sadly at his daughter. "Hate to see you go... I mean that."

"Me too," Keel said.

"Yeah, well..." Zora let her sentence die beneath the hum of the *Indelible VI*.

Doc looked from one bounty hunter to the other, then threw up his hands in exasperation. He stuck his neck out toward Keel and said, "So give her a reason to stay, kid!"

"Right." Keel bit his lip.

Zora waited expectantly.

"Well... I did lose all your armor. And weapons. And clothes. So stick around 'til I can pay for an upgrade. Also, you're not allowed to use my med bay if you say no. Or the fresher."

She considered that, a slight smile on her mud-smeared face. "Okay, jump jockey. At least until then."

"Oba's balls," Doc growled. "You two are lousy at this. You're both gonna die alone."

Keel gave a soft laugh. "Or in a hail of blaster fire... either way."

# EPILOGUE

Chhun sat back in his chair inside the darkened study that had been prepared for him aboard the Legion destroyer *Scontan Washam*. The only light came from his holospecs, which fed him information through visual, audio, and synaptic stimuli all designed to help him comprehend and retain what he studied. He wished he'd had a pair of these back when he was in school.

The former Legion commander had been re-reading the combined report covering his old friend's activities after leaving Kill Team Victory. With Zora's eyewitness testimony, combined with the same from Ravi, both of which corroborated what Ford had told Chhun, all that was left was sealing the account, at which point it would be compiled into the Adjudicators' investigation and be a resource for the final consideration.

Which was really a choice over whether the galaxy would seek to go back to the way things had been, or if it would become something different. Something, hopefully, better.

Chhun's job was to use his hunter team to acquire the testimonies and information he needed in order that he and his fellow adjudicators would have a full and complete picture of what led to the downfall of the Republic, the rise of its brief, imperial usurper, and the unforeseen, catastrophic attacks of the Cybar and then the Savages.

Maybe nothing could have been done. It was clear that good, honorable men and women of all species had worked for the benefit of the Republic. But Chhun couldn't help but feel that there had been more within the Republic, particularly within its government, who had worked only for themselves, seeing the Republic not as a body to serve those it represented, but as an unbridled river of power to be used to enrich themselves, destroy their enemies, and reshape the galaxy to their own personal wills.

His holospecs chimed. One of the other Adjudicators had completed an interrogation that provided additional context to the Wraith/Ford mission, and had sent a request for Chhun to review and, if warranted, compile it into the full account.

He checked his wrist chrono and then told the glasses, "Yeah. Let's do it."

The device chimed again, and Chhun's eyes were swept with images and AI-generated figures as he read the text of the account. The holospecs had a way of showing you what your mind imagined while reading, in far greater detail than your conscious mind would otherwise appreciate. It was like watching a holofilm and reading the script at the same time.

He saw a planet of clear glass sand, endlessly swirling and changing colors as light refracted in and out amid never-ending storms. Cloud formations the size of continents hurried above, sending blue-and-white lightning bolts arcing down toward the surface below.

"Herbeer." Chhun recognized the prison world even before the holospecs had the chance to tell him.

And then he saw the name of the principal source of this information, and a face more familiar to him than the planet came into his mind's eye.

With a pang of guilt and regret, he took a breath and continued to study.

## Herbeer
## 48 Standard Hours Following Scarpia's Escape

It was Andien Broxin's first visit to the prison on Herbeer. The trip was made at the request of Major Ellek Owens, perhaps the oldest friend she had in the Legion. If you wanted to use that word. Friend. They were friend-*ly*. Polite. Willing to cut through the grudges and mistrust of their separate organizations when it came time to protect the Republic.

She liked that about Owens. He fought for the right reasons. Most legionnaires, points aside, were the same. Her own path and that of her father's had been similar.

Still, what Owens and his Legion ilk failed to see about the Legion was what Broxin was willing to admit about Nether Ops: there were people in positions of power bending the institutions to their own will. The Legion knew they had a point problem, but they were so blinded by their sense of glory, honor, and victory, that they assumed it would never metastasize into something more than they could control. They were wrong, and Broxin knew it. The Legion, for all its standing as the greatest fighting force the galaxy had ever seen, would in time collapse under the weight of these political appointees and the interests they represented.

Either that, or it would execute Article Nineteen. And if that happened... all bets were off.

But for now, there was still work to be done against the enemies of the Republic. A high-level, trusted Dark Ops informant embedded in the MCR had relayed intel that the captured arms dealer Scarpia was again working for the network of Mid-Core Rebels. No visuals, but a vocal pattern match and the consensus of the MCR around the asset all supported the report.

None of these MCR insurgents were now alive for further questioning, but the existing intel was sufficient to warrant further investigation, and so Broxin had come directly to Herbeer. Unannounced, but thanks to Nether Ops, she carried all the clearances needed to ensure a good, transparent look at what was going on.

Landing on Herbeer required the use of a specialized shuttle rated to withstand the scouring glass-storms that raged continually on the surface. Atmospheric entry was rough, and the sound of the sands being whipped at high speed against the outer hull rose above every rattle and shake until it was all that could be heard. As elementally raw and terrifying as that was, the storm seen through the viewport was stunning to behold. The glass sand blazed red where it caught the unfiltered sun, then went pale gray or black as clouds darkened the sky. Bolts of lightning caused far-reaching flashes of blue and white as the transparent sands seemed to absorb the colors of the light.

The shuttle was guided below the buffeting sandstorms by means of a homing beacon, and the sounds of the sands striking the hull faded. All went dark as the ship dropped through a series of subterranean chambers before finally setting on a landing pad deep inside the crust of Herbeer.

Andien stepped off the shuttle amid swirling gases, noting how the scouring of entry had stripped the craft down to its base impervisteel. A naval officer dressed in the gray combat fatigues of the guards stepped smartly toward her while dome-shaped bots rolled about the landing pad sucking up whatever sand had drifted this far down with the shuttle.

"The prisoner is being located and should be made available to you shortly, ma'am," the officer said. No greeting or ceremony. Only business.

The man knew who Andien was. No one came down into the mines of Herbeer without identifying themselves. Pilots and specialized craft were pre-selected. Those coming with them—usually the convicted and those escorting them—all had their clearances and purposes for being there sent ahead. Still, arriving from the ferrying station orbiting Herbeer unannounced, and then ordering that she be taken down at once, would surely have the guards down here on their heels.

Andien nodded at the officer, a junior-grade lieutenant wearing an ablative flak vest—a requirement when meeting incoming shuttles. "I'll need to review your logs and get access to your holo-security footage," she said.

The officer tilted his head ever so slightly.

"Is there a problem, Lieutenant?"

"No, ma'am. It's... we don't keep security holos of the mines themselves. Only the docking bay and surrounding area. Once they're inside, they work their sentence until death."

"Understood. Nevertheless, I want to see what you have."

"Yes, ma'am. This way."

The officer led Andien to a spartan room with a holostation, a table, and a chair. If she didn't know better, she'd think it was an interrogation room.

"You can access the holo-recordings here," the officer said. "Everything you see is classified, and no copies are permitted."

"I'm aware," Andien said. "You're dismissed."

The officer hesitated for a brief moment, then turned and left.

When the door had swished shut, Andien made a show of examining the security footage, bringing up dates and times and watching the departures and arrivals of shuttles at various speeds. She zoomed in on the faces of guards and prisoners.

It was all for show.

Nether Ops had access to these feeds whenever they wanted them. That was how Andien knew the naval officer hadn't been lying to her about there being no holocams inside the mines themselves. If there had been, she would have already viewed that footage, just as she had already viewed the recordings she was now pretending to study.

There had been no sign of Scarpia in anything she'd seen. But Owens had been insistent, and she was the only one who could check.

"If they were gonna pull a trick," Owens had said, "they'd have scrubbed or doctored the feeds. Put him in a uniform with some facial mods and got him out that way. We gotta see for ourselves if he's there or not."

It was always "we" when the Legion needed help from Nether Ops. But that "we" disappeared the rest of the time. Andien thought it funny how that brotherhood of being a legionnaire—and she *had* been one, unofficially, tragically —came and went depending on how useful she was.

Finally the moment came. Two guards brought Scarpia into the room. Or at least a man who looked exactly *like* Scarpia.

"A beautiful woman," Scarpia said, rakishly. "To whom do I owe my thanks?" He looked around the room. "This place hardly seems suitable for a conjugal visit."

He responded to his own joke with a loud, self-assured laugh. The time in the synth mines hadn't broken his spirit, though he was thinner and dirtier than the official holoimages on file.

Andien rose and produced a biosensor. "I need to confirm you are... Scarpia."

He only had one name. For some reason she didn't like that. But really, she just didn't like *him*. The criminal—the murderer—standing before her had no idea of the lengths she had once gone through to track him down. To stop him. Before everything that had happened on Kublar... happened.

She'd helped catch him, but too late.

"Who else would I be?" laughed Scarpia as the sensor did its work.

It came back with proof that Owens's intelligence asset hadn't heard who they'd thought they heard. Scarpia was on Herbeer. Right in front of her. Right where he was supposed to be.

"Did you have any questions for him, ma'am?" asked one of the guards. A horribly scarred human with just one good eye. No cybernetic replacements. Everything organic. Andien could see that through her own artificial eyes.

She read the rank and nametape on the man's plate carrier. "No, Sergeant Hess. That was all I needed."

Scarpia gave her a mocking frown. "I must admit to some disappointment. Although it's always nice to be away from the mines. Even for a little while."

Andien looked at the man's fingers. Synth was mined by hand, and every prisoner had a daily quota that needed to be met in order to receive the essentials required to go on living.

Scarpia's hands were clean. Soft.

"Looks like you have some work to get started on," Andien said. "Or you won't make your quota."

Scarpia looked at her with a puzzled expression, then brought up his hands. He inspected them, smiled, and then broke into a raucous laugh. "I've managed to keep my hands very clean indeed since being *wrongfully* detained by the Republic. If anything good has happened since I lost my freedom, it was the discovery that many old friends preceded me here. Our revolution may have ended, but the MCR continues the fight. We hear it from everyone you Republic tyrants send down here into the darkness to be forgotten." His face darkened as he spoke. But then he brightened back up again. "I thank you once again for the opportunity to see a beautiful woman unharmed by the ravages of this hellish place. Good day, miss."

Andien watched as the guards escorted Scarpia from the room. She waited still longer for the shuttle to finish its preparations to depart.

Then... she left Herbeer.

Hopefully never to return.

Chhun shook his head, knowing now what they would later discover about the prisoner world of Herbeer—that it was abused to house political prisoners, not just the galaxy's most violent criminals and terrorists for which it had been intended. It had all been so rotten. And for so long.

He had to power down his holospecs and stew in the darkness for a moment.

Those in power... they had known. They had known all along. Those who didn't know... they suspected. But they looked the other way.

And the legionnaires, as always, died because of it.

The door chime sounded.

"Come in," Chhun said.

The door swooshed open, activating the lights, and Sergeant Király stepped inside. "Adjudicator. I was told you wanted to see me on my return."

Chhun rose and shook the sergeant's hand. "Yes. How was it, Sergeant?"

"Interesting, sir. Mission success. She's in the debrief room for when you're ready."

"I'll see her shortly. That was impressive, what you and Mad Dog accomplished in taking her."

Király followed Chhun out the door. "Thank you, sir."

"You know, when a man makes a point of leaving the Legion and starting a new life, getting sucked back in again can be a little trying."

"Sir?"

Chhun smiled. "Forgive me for being cryptic. It's just, everything that happened at that station, it all fit perfectly with the Bombassa I knew. We planned many an operation together. I suspect the first sergeant is still alive, and the target you brought in is lying to give him some breathing room."

Király looked at the Adjudicator, almost, but not entirely, hiding his confusion. "Why not have us continue on after the real target, then, sir?"

Chhun thought about what Captain Ford had been put through. The number of times he'd been forced to make a *me-or-them* decision in pursuing a goal. Bombassa was acting as a bounty hunter now. That happened. Legionnaires were often drawn into mercenary or other martial work. But Bombassa was not the type to run from something like this. He'd left the Legion on good terms. If the man was adamant about staying hidden, there was a reason.

It would be up to Chhun to figure out a way to draw him out that didn't result in the death of legionnaires. Slade had had his opportunity to make things happen; now the team would sit until Chhun saw the need to send them out into the fray again.

The Adjudicator looked at Király. "I didn't see a way to do that without him, or some of you, dying."

"It would have been him, sir."

That was the closest the enigmatic sergeant had ever come to sharing something akin to a personality, even if it was nothing more than standard unshakeable Legion confidence.

Chhun looked at the young soldier. "I believe you. Would have defeated the purpose. Let's go see what our guest has to say."

They continued on in silence and boarded the speedlift. As they rode down, Chhun chewed over what he'd just read about Herbeer. Something was eating at him.

Suddenly he spoke.

"Actually, Sergeant, I'd like to head back to my quarters for a moment."

"Of course, sir."

Király didn't even question it; he just hit the button to send the speedlift back up again. The man was a living, breathing embodiment of professionalism.

Chhun left the sergeant standing outside in the corridor as he went into his study. He woke up his datapad and reloaded the affidavit. It had been sent to Chhun solely as context, but...

Still carrying the datapad, he stepped out into the corridor. Király was still waiting outside.

"Sergeant," Chhun said, and then struggled to recall the name of the communications sergeant who'd been with him to recover Zora. At last the young man's identifier number sprang to mind. "Is... HT-26 on duty?"

"We're all on duty whenever you need us, sir."

"I mean is he up?" This was something that could wait if it needed to.

Király paused a moment, then said, "He's on his way, sir."

Chhun gave a slight smile. "Thank you, Sergeant."

The communications sergeant arrived a few minutes after, wearing his Legion armor. "Sergeant Renfro reporting, sir."

Chhun made a mental note not to forget the man's name, as he'd almost forgotten the man's identifier. He hadn't been like that when he was Legion commander. Two years out of the armor and he suddenly had the short-term memory of an old man on a bender.

He beckoned both legionnaires to come inside his study, and closed the door.

"Sergeant Renfro," Chhun said, "I have a question about this report."

He handed over the datapad. The communications sergeant examined it, then nodded for Chhun to go ahead.

"Can we tell what source provided the information? Is it from some Nether Ops files we recovered after Nineteen? A holorecording? What?"

"Sure, there's a way you can get to that. Here—I'll show you."

Király cleared his throat.

Renfro quickly added, "Sir."

The communications sergeant navigated a maze of holo-windows that Chhun was certain he'd never even seen before. He knew the Legion's systems well, or thought he did. This looked like something else entirely.

It made him feel old.

"Okay," HT-26 said. "We actually have two sources on this. One is a recovered Nether file. The other is a deposition carried out by another Adjudicator."

"Did this Adjudicator locate Praxus then?" Chhun asked. Praxus was on Chhun's list too. The Cybar android could give detail on the rise of his people and the relationship between the Cybar and the Republic elements who had put them to work building a fleet meant to protect the House of Reason from the Legion and Article Nineteen—a fleet that was turned against the galaxy at large during the height of the civil war.

So far, Hunter Team Ranger hadn't been able to find Praxus. It would be helpful if one of the other Adjudicators had.

"Uh, negative, sir." Renfro said after digging further into the complicated system. "The deposition was from someone named Andien Broxin. Although it *does* look like the Adjudicator conducting *also* was talking to Praxus.

Both are still in Legion custody and awaiting your questioning—you should have gotten notice."

Chhun hadn't, but he'd practically stopped listening after Renfro said *Andien Broxin.*

He'd seen her die with his own two eyes. Her remains were atomized aboard the Savage hulk—a fate Chhun by all rights should have shared had it not been for whatever the girl Prisma Maydoon had done. Broxin was the strongest woman he'd ever met. She'd cheated death before. But Chhun didn't see how this could be anything but a mistake... or an impostor. How could she still be alive?

"You all right, sir?" Király asked.

Chhun shook away his thoughts. "Yeah... yeah. I'm fine. Thank you, Sergeant. Let's go talk with the bounty hunter you brought in. After that, though, I need to speak to Broxin. Immediately."

The two younger legionnaires nodded as one, then Sergeant Király spoke.

"We'll make it happen, Adjudicator."

# THE END

## GALAXY'S EDGE SEASON THREE WILL CONTINUE...

# HONOR ROLL

Jason and Nick would like to thank those who whose Galaxy's Edge Insider Subscriptions saw the rise of Galaxy's Edge, Season Three.

Cody Aalberg

A. Isaiah Abney

Artis Aboltins

Guido Abreu

Daniel Adams

Chancellor Adams

Garion Adkins

Ryan Adwers

Elias Aguilar

Neal Albritton

Aleksey Aleshintsev

Jonathan Allain

Byron Allen

Justin Allred

Paul Almond

Joachim Andersen

Galen Anderson

Levi Anderson

Jarad Anderson

Jennifer Andrews

Pat Andrews

Robert Anspach

Melanie Apollo

Benjamin Arguello

Thomas Armona

Jonathan Auerbach

Sean Averill

Nicholas Avila

David Azur

Sam Baccoli

Benjamin Backus

Zachary Badger

Shane Bailey

David Baker

John Baker

Daniel Baker

Sallie Baliunas

Nathan Ball

Kevin Bangert

Brian Bardwell

Brian Barrows-Striker

Richard Bartle

Sean Battista

Robert Battles

Eric Batzdorfer

John Baudoin

Adam Bear

Nahum Beard

Michelle Beaver

Mike Beeker

Randall Beem

John Bell

Mark Bennett

Edward Benson

Mark Berardi

Gardner Berry

John Bertram

Kevin Biasci

John Bingham

Gregory Bingham

Francisco Blankemeyer

David Blount

| | | |
|---|---|---|
| Liz Bogard | RFC Brumley | Ethan Clayton |
| James Bohling | Jeff Brussee | Sean Clifton |
| Rodney Bonner | Benjamin Bryan | Adam Cobb |
| Brandon Boone | Nicholas Burck | Morgan Cobb |
| Douglas Booth | Austin Burgans | Michael Cole |
| William Boucher | John Burleigh | Curtis Colgate |
| Aaron Bowen | Jay Burritt | Curtis Colgate |
| Darren Bowers | David Butler | Christian Collins |
| Brandon Bowles | Karl Butsch | Jason Colson |
| Alex Bowling | John Byrd | Jerry Conard |
| Keiger Bowman | Daniel Cadwell | Robert Conaway |
| Michael Boyle | Brian Callahan | Bronson Conlin |
| Derrick Boyter | Decker Cammack | James Connolly |
| Chester Brads | Mark Campbell | James Conyers |
| Richard Brake | Chris Capone | Kevin Cooper |
| Andrew Branca | Tyler Carlson | Jacob Coppess |
| Logan Brandon | Daldos Carr | Michael Corbin |
| Ernest Brant | Rafael Carrol | Anthony Cotillo |
| Chet Braud | Robert Cathey | Seth Coussens |
| Dennis Bray | Brian Cave | Andrew Craig |
| Christopher Brewster | Shawn Cavitt | Zachary Craig |
| Geoff Brisco | Brian Cheney | Collin Creel |
| Wayne Brite | Brad Chenoweth | Ben Crose |
| Spencer Bromley | Caleb Cheshire | Ben Crowley |
| Raymond Brooks | James Christensen | Christopher Crowley |
| Dodson Brown | Cooper Clark | Jack Culbertson |
| Matthew Brown | Andrew Clary | Phil Culpepper |

Scott Cummins

Ben Curcio

Luigi Cusano

Jason D. Martin

Robert Daly

John Dames

David Danz

Matthew Dare

Chad David

David Davis

Ivy Davis

LeRoy Davis

Ben Davis

Brian Davis

Nathan Davis

Andrew Day

Ron Deage

Chris DeBeer

Joel Defauw

Anthony Del Villar

Anerio (Wyatt) Deorma (Dent)

Douglas Deuel

Michael Dickerson

Jack Dickson

Alexander Dickson

Christopher DiNote

Matthew Dippel

Gregory Divis

Jeffrey Dobbs

Graham Doering

Shawn Doherty

Gerald Donovan

Ward Dorrity

Adam Drucker

John Dryden

Garrett Dubois

Marc-André Dufor

Thomas DuLaney II

Brendan Dullaghan

Evan Durrant

Christopher Durrant

Samuel Dutterer

Virgil Dwyer

Justin Eilenberger

Brian Eisel

Jonathan R. Ellis

William Ely

Kelvin Emdy

Michael Emes

Paul Eng

Andrew English

Ethan Estep

Richard Everett

Jaeger Falco

Stephen Farnett

Nicholas Fasanella

Carlos Faustino

Michael Feher

Steven Feily

Julie Fenimore

Meagan Ference

Adolfo Fernandez

Rich Ferrante

Brandon Field

Austin Findley

Albert Fink

Alex Fisher

Lamar Fitzgerald

Rhys Fitzpatrick

Matthew Fiveson

Daniel Flanders

Daniel Flores

Geoffrey Flowers

William Foley

Steve Forrester

Kenneth Foster

Paul Fox

Bryant Fox

Martin Foxley

Dennis Frank

Greg Franz

Luke Frazer

Kyle Freitus

Griffin Frendsdorff

Timothy Fujimoto

Bob Fulsang

Jonathan Furnery

Elizabeth Gafford

David Gaither

Matthew Gale

Zachary Galicki

Kyle Gannon

Dave Garbowski

Joshua Gardner

Michael Gardner

Alphonso Garner

John Gasperino

Jordan Gass

Marina Gaston

Robert Gates

Craig Gentry

Cody George

Gregory Gero

Eli Geroux

Dylan Giles

Joe Gillis

Oscar Gillott-Cain

Nathan Gioconda

John Giorgis

Johnny Glazebrooks

Bob Gleason

Martin Gleaton

James Glendenning

Seth Glenn

Jared Glissman

William Frank Godbold IV

Justin Godfrey

John Gooch

Jacob Goodin

Justin Gottwaltz

Gordon Grant

Mitch Greathouse

Gordon Green

Matt Green

Shawn Greene

John Greenfield Jr.

Anthony Gribbins

Eric Griffin

Ronald Grisham

Robert P. Gunter

Joshua Haataja

Michael Hagen

Kelton Hague

Levi Haines

Joseph Haire

Michael Hale

Marlon Hall II

Leo Hallak

Kelly Halma

Nathan Hamilton

Chris Hammond

Chris Hanley

Greg Hanson

Tyler Hardy

Jeffrey Hardy

Ian Harper

Revan Harris

Adam Hartswick

Matthew Hathorn

Adam Hazen

Richard Heard

Colin Heavens

Jonathan Heiden

Jesse Heidenreich

Brenton Held

Jason Henderson

Jason Henderson

Fynn Hendrikse

John Henkel

Daniel Heron

Bradley Herren

Felipe Herrera

| | | |
|---|---|---|
| Paul Herron | Aaron Huling | Ryan Kelstrom |
| Sven Hestrand | Mike Hull | Caleb Kenner |
| Kyle Hetzer | James Hurtado | Zack Kenny |
| Korrey Heyder | Wayne Hutton | Daniel Kimm |
| Matthew Hicks | Gaetano Inglima | Kennith King |
| Lance Hirayama | Antonio Iozzo | Caleb Kirkwood |
| Ty Hodges | Michael Jenkins | Joshua Kivett |
| Jonathan Hoehn | Jacob Jensen | Kyle Klincko |
| Charles Hoisington | Robert Jensen | Brendan Klinger |
| Bryan Holden | Eric Jett | Brendan Klingner |
| Aaron Holden | Caleb Johnson | Albert Klukowski |
| William Holman | Gary Johnson | Marc Knapp |
| Clint Holmes | Anthony Johnson | William Knapp |
| Jason Honeyfield | Cobra Johnson | Robert Knox |
| Charles Hood | Eric Johnson | Ethan Koska |
| Tyson Hopkins | Nick Johnson | Evan Kowalski |
| Nicholas Hornung | Josh Johnson | Bodhi Kruft |
| Jefferson Hotchkiss | Randolph Johnson | Jacob Krute |
| Jack House | Micah Jones | Neil Kubitz |
| Ian House | Jason Jones | Mitchell Kusterer |
| Ken Houseal | Tyler Jones | Nathan Laidlwe |
| Joseph Howle | David Jorgenson | Ian Lamb |
| Nicholas Howser | Robert Kammerzell | Mark Landez |
| Mark Hoy | Chris Karabats | Megan O'Keefe Landon |
| Kane Hubbard | Timothy Keane | Kevin Lash |
| James Huff | Cody Keaton | Jacob Leake |
| Adrian Hughes | George Kelly | David Leal |

| | | |
|---|---|---|
| Andy Ledford | Patrick Maclary | Joseph Mazzara |
| Isaac Lee | Derek Magyar | Will McAleer |
| Furman Lee | Richard Maier | Timothy McAleese |
| Nicholas Lee | Chris Malone | Sean McCafferty |
| Joseph Legacy | Jake Malone | Kyle McCarley |
| Brenden Lerch | Adam Manlove | William Mcdaniel |
| David Levin | Andrew Mann | Shane McDevitt |
| Luke Lindsay | John Mannion | Connor McDonald |
| Eron Lindsey | Brent Manzel | Jeremy McElroy |
| Andre Locker | Robert Marchi | Hans McIlveen |
| Drew Long | Jacob Margheim | Rachel McIntosh |
| Richard Long | John Marinos | Richard McKercher |
| Oliver Longchamps | Jacob Marquis | Ryan McKracken |
| Litani Looby | Jeffrey Martin | Jacob Mclemore |
| Joseph Lopez | Bertram Martin | Wayne McMurtrie |
| Lucas Lorentz | Edward Martin | Daniel Mears |
| Joey Lorenzi | Bill Martin | Kile Mendoza |
| Kyle Lorenzi | Logan Martin | Brady Meyer |
| David Losey | Lucas Martin | John C. Meyers |
| Erin Lounsbury | Trevor Martin | Corrigan Miller |
| MDavid Low | Tim Martindale | Darren Mills |
| Andrew Luong | Cory Masierowski | Robert Milsop |
| Jesse Lyon | Nicholas Mason | Jesse Miner |
| Taylo Lywood | Wills Masterson | Sarah Miron |
| Collin Macall | Mark Mathewman | David Mitchell |
| David MacAlpine | Michael Matsko | Reimar Moeller |
| John Machasek | Simon Mayeski | Jacob Montagne |

Ramon Montijo

Douglas Montijo

Eric Moore

Maxwell Moore

Sherry Moore

Nicholas Moran

Matteo Morelli

Todd Moriarty

Matthew Morley

Daniel Morris

William Morris

David Murray

Bob Murray

Jeff Murri

Ben Myhre

Joseph Nahas

Vinesh Narayan

Colby Neal

James Needham

Ray Neel

Joel Negron

Adam Nelson

Timothy Nevin

Michael Newson

Jon Newton

Bennett Nickels

Mason Nicolay

Trevor Nielsen

Andrew Niesent

Sean Noble

Otto (Mario) Noda

Brett Noll-Emmick

Michael Norris

Ryley Nortrup

Douglas Norwood

Greg Nugent

Christina Nymeyer

Brian O'Connor

Patrick O'Leary

Patrick O'Rourke

Quinn Oehler

Kevin Oess

Nolan Oglesby

Gary Oneida

Max Oosten

Anthony Ornellas

James Owens

Will Page

Nic Palacios

John Park

Matthew Parker

Shawn Parrish

Andrew Patterson

Ken Paul

Thomas Pennington

Hector Perez

Kevin Perkins

Trevor Petersen

Nicholas Peterson

Charlie Phillippe

Jeremy Phillips

David Phillips

Jon Phillips

Sam Phinney

Dupres Pina

Michael Pister

Jared Plathe

Matthew Pommerening

Nathan Poplawski

Michael Portanger

Rodney Posey

Brian Potts

Jonathaon Poulter

Thomas Preston

Matthew Print

Darren Pruitt

Max Quezada

Shahik Rakib

Joe Ralston

Dillard Rape

Michael Rausch

| | | |
|---|---|---|
| Joshua Ray | Justin Ryan | Kevin Sharp |
| T.J. Recio | Mark Ryan | Steven Shaw |
| Blake Rehrer | Greg S | Chris Shay |
| Ryan Reis | Zachary Sadenwasser | Charles Sheehan |
| Paul Richard | Robert Salmon | Wendell Shelton |
| Augustus Richardson | Connor Samuelson | Ian Short |
| Robert Richenburg | Lawrence Sanchez | Glenn Shotton |
| Eric Ritenour | Dustin Sanders | Kaleb Sigler |
| Paul Rivas | Giovani Sandoval | Dave Simmons |
| David Roark | David Sanford | Chris Sinor |
| Scott Robertson | Levi Schaefers | Chris Sizelove |
| Chris Robertson | Jaysn Schaener | Andrew Skaines |
| Walt Robillard | Jason Schapp | Chris Slater |
| Daniel Robitaille | Daniel Schmagel | Steven Smead |
| John Roche | Kurt Schneider | Robert Smith |
| Paul Roder | Peter Scholtes | Charles Smith |
| Josias Rodriguez | Kevin Schroeder | Caleb Smith |
| Adam Rogers | William Schweisthal | Cory Smith |
| Aaron G Rood | Ethan Scott | Ian Smith |
| Andrew Rose | Connor Scott | Sharroll Smith |
| Elias Rostad | Rylee Scott | David Smyth |
| Nick Rusch | Andrew Scroggins | Tom Snapp |
| Chad Rushing | Phillip Seek | Andrew Snow |
| Tim Russ | Kevin Serpa | David Snowden |
| Zarren Rutledge | Austin Shafer | Cody Speak |
| RW | Mitch Shami | John Spears |
| Matthew Ryan | Ryan Shannahan | Anthony Spencer |

| | | |
|---|---|---|
| Troy Spencer | Lawrence Tate | Dylan Tuxhorn |
| Thomas Spencer | Kyler Tatsch | Joshua Twist |
| Dustin Sprick | Alyssa Tausevich | Jalen Underwood |
| Super Squirrel | Brandon Taylor | Leo Vaccaro |
| Travis Standford | Justin Taylor | Joel Vail |
| Paul Starck | Robert Taylor | Joel Vail |
| Jolene Starr | Tim Taylor | Erik Van Otten |
| Maggie Stewart-Grant | Christov Tenn | Thomas Van Winkle |
| Edmond Stone | Doug Thien | Paden VanBuskirk |
| Fredy Stout | David P. Thomas | Patrick Varrassi |
| James Street | Marc Thomas | Daniel Vatamaniuck |
| Joshua Strickland | Jacob Thomas | Robert Vaughn |
| Shayla Striffler | Kyle Thompson | Abel Villesca |
| Brad Stumpp | Chris Thompson | Cole Vineyard |
| Joshua Sturnfield | Donald Thompson | Leo Voepel |
| Shaun Sullivan | Jonathan Thompson | Jeff Wadsworth |
| Ned Sullivan | William Joseph Thorpe | Anthony Wagnon |
| Randall Surles | Beverly Tierney | Joshua Wallace |
| Michael Swartwout | Yvonne Timm | Joshua Waltzing |
| Bryan Swezey | Jonathan Tindal | Dylan Wannamaker |
| George Switzer | Russ Tinnell | Andrew Ward |
| Carol Szpara | TJ Trakas | Wedge Warford |
| Travis TadeWaldt | Jameson Trauger | Scot Washam |
| Allison Tallon | Oliver Tunnicliffe | Tyler Washburn |
| Daniel Tanner | Ryan Turner | John Watson |
| Joshua Tate | Brandon Turton | Bill Webb |
| Blake Tate | John Tuttle | Ben Wedow |

Zachary Weig

Garry Welding

Tanner Wells

Hiram Wells

Jack Weston

William Westphal

Lewis Wheeler

Paul White

Jamie Whitmer

Grant Wiggins

Joel Williams

John Williams

Taylor Williams

Christopher Williams

Jack Williams

Patrick Williford

Justin Wilson

Dominic Winter

Edward Wise

Tripp Wood

Reese Wood

Robert Woodward

Sean Woodworth

Robin Woolen

John Wooten

John Work

Jason Wright

Adam Wroblewski

Kevin Zhang

Pamela Ziemeck

Attila Zimler

Andrew Zink

Jordan Ziroli

Nathan Zoss

# SEASON ONE

1. Legionnaire

2. Galactic Outlaws

3. Kill Team

4. Attack of Shadows

5. Imperator

6. Sword of the Legion

7. Prisoners of Darkness

8. Turning Point

9. Message for the Dead

10. Order of the Centurion

11. Retribution

# SEASON TWO

12. Savage Wars

13. Gods and Legionnaires

14. The Hundred

15. Takeover

16. Legacies

17. Dark Victory

18. Convergence

19. Remains

20. Last Contact

21. KTF I

22. KTF II

# SEASON THREE

23. The Wanted

24. The Betrayed

Milton Keynes UK
Ingram Content Group UK Ltd.
UKHW020912180424
441376UK00013B/371

9 798889 220626